ON THE WRONG TRACK

ON THE WRONG TRACK. Copyright © 2007 by Steve Hockensmith. All rights reserved. Printed in the United States of America. No part of this book may be used or reproduced in any manner whatsoever without written permission except in the case of brief quotations embodied in critical articles or reviews. For information, address St. Martin's Press, 175 Fifth Avenue, New York, N.Y. 10010.

www.minotaurbooks.com

ISBN-13: 978-0-312-34781-9
ISBN-10: 0-312-34781-2

First Edition: March 2007

10 9 8 7 6 5 4 3 2 1

Also by Steve Hockensmith

Holmes on the Range

On the Wrong Track

STEVE HOCKENSMITH

ST. MARTIN'S MINOTAUR

NEW YORK

FOR MAR, AS ALWAYS

ON THE WRONG TRACK

PRELUDE

Or, Headed for Trouble

ew things dampen a man's appreciation for natural splendor more quickly than the sound of another man retching. It's just not possible to revel in the magnificence of creation when the fellow next to you sounds like a cat hacking up a hair ball.

So as much as I might have enjoyed basking in the visual poetry all around me—the last rays of the late-evening sun streaming through distant mountains to paint the harsh alkali plains of the desert as wispy pink as cotton candy, etc.—I instead resigned myself to an utterly unpoetic task: patting my brother's back as he bent over a railing and painted the tracks whipping by beneath us an array of far less pleasing colors.

I've never been afloat long enough to see anybody seasick, but I reckon I know what it looks like. Old Red had been *rail*sick before the conductor even called out, "All aboard!"

"Feel better?" I asked when my brother stopped heaving.

He nodded—then immediately leaned back over the railing and picked up where he'd left off. I sighed and patted his back again and hoped no one stepped out of the train's observation car and observed *us*.

Eventually, Old Red utterly emptied himself, and his retching subsided. He stayed hunched over the rail, though, staring miserably at the tracks that shot straight as an arrow into the heart of the darkening east.

"We could get off at the next stop," I suggested.

"No need for that," Old Red replied—as I'd assumed he would.

While sensible men set out to become bankers or lawyers, business tycoons or president of the United States, my brother had what was, in his mind, a far loftier goal. He wanted to be a detective. More specifically, he wanted to be *the* detective: the late, great Sherlock Holmes. While no one was going to mistake a couple of dollar-a-day cowhands like ourselves for gentlemen deducifiers, through a combination of tenacity (mostly my brother's) and luck (mostly bad) we did manage to get ourselves hired on as detectives . . . of a sort.

We were aboard the train as confidential agents traveling *incognito*, as the magazine sleuths call it when they slap on some greasepaint and a wig and pretend they're an Italian fishmonger or some such. Our disguises were pretty plain by comparison, consisting entirely of fake names and clean clothes, yet I still felt embarrassed by it all, like a boy talked into playing dress-up with his sisters.

"Well, I'm sorry you feel poorly," I said. "But maybe now you know how *I* feel. I've been queasy about this whole thing from the get-go."

Old Red looked up at me, his glare doing all the talking. *There's a cure for that,* it said. *Quit.*

I replied with a cocked eyebrow that shot back, *Maybe I will.*

Old Red shrugged and looked away, the gesture saying, *No, you won't.*

I conceded with a curse and a kick to the rail.

As debates go, it was hardly Lincoln versus Douglas, but then again it didn't have to be. When you've been on the trail together as long as me and my brother, you stop needing words to argue—one all-too-familiar look can say as much as ten minutes of talk.

Not that I'd ever deprived my brother of the sweet music of my voice. A look might be all that's necessary, but a good harangue's a lot more satisfying.

"Alright, go on—leave a trail of upchuck from here to Oakland. There's nothin' I can do if you won't listen to good sense or your own pukey stomach. I'll just sit on my ass and enjoy the ride."

"Works out fine, then," Old Red grumbled. "Ass-sittin's what you do best, ain't it? Me, I'm tryin' to land a chance to do some doin'."

"Oh, yeah?" I growled, about to tell him the only *doing* coming his way would be done by me—in the form of a swift kick to the seat of his pants.

A muffled thud cut me off. The sound came from beneath us, and I leaned over the rail next to Old Red just in time to catch sight of a large, dark, oval object bouncing out from under the train. It was spinning as it went, and for the briefest of moments I wasn't just staring at *it*. *It* was staring at me.

The *it*, you see, had eyes. And a nose, a mouth, ears, and a mustache, as well.

It was a man's head.

Suddenly, *I* was the one with the knot in his belly. My brother, on the other hand, was getting just what he'd been angling for—or so he thought.

3

One

SADDLE BUMS

Or, Two Cowboys Cross Three States and Find No Jobs

Having spent the last year studying detective yarns, I know how one's supposed to start. Somebody walks into the hero's office (or sitting room, if the hero happens to be Mr. Sherlock Holmes) and spills out a tear squeezer. There's a little gore in it, maybe, as well as a few details that make about as much sense as trying to saddle smoke. A girl finds her father dead in his bed, for instance, and he's got a big grin on his face, a solid-gold dagger in his chest, and a bowl of bloody walnuts balanced on his head. The sleuth nods, sends the girl on her way, then turns to his pal (there's always a pal) and says something like "By thunder, Dickie, this is the most mystifying case I've ever encountered!" Then they're off to the walnut farm and *bang*—the detectiving kicks right in.

So I've got a little problem explaining how I came to be face-to-face with a flying head. Yes, it's a detective story, but I can't start it the proper way at all. There's no office, no sitting room, no bloody nuts. There's not even a proper detective. All I've got's an illiterate cowboy who fancies himself the Holmes of the Range and his not-quite-so-ambitious pal.

I'm the pal, by the way—Otto "Big Red" Amlingmeyer. The fellow with the grand ideas about himself is my elder brother, Gustav, better known along the cow trails as "Old Red." Not that he's some white-bearded coot babbling about his rheumatism and the War Between the States. Gustav's old in spirit, not age. He's only got twenty-seven years on him, yet he tends to droop around like each and every one was a loaded pack strapped upon his back.

He's been a little less droopy of late, though, if only because he finally found something in this sad old world of ours about which he could actually become enthused. It happened about a year back, in the summer of 1892. One night by a cattle-drive campfire, the trail boss whipped out a magazine story called "The Red-Headed League," and Gustav acted like the man it was about—Sherlock Holmes—was Moses, Abe Lincoln, and Santa Claus rolled up in one. Not only did he make me read that story to him over and over (his own knowledge of the alphabet petering out somewhere in the vicinity of *g*), he went digging for more detective tales. We got to know Nick Carter, King Brady, "Old Sleuth," and the rest of the dime-novel crowd pretty well. But Holmes was the only one of the bunch my brother respected. Even the so-called range detectives—cowboy Pinkertons like Charlie Siringo and Burl Lockhart—didn't impress Old Red.

"Stringin' up rustlers and horse thieves ain't so tough. Most of them poor bastards ain't got enough brain between their ears to fill a thimble," he said. "Now Mr. Holmes, he goes up against fellers packin' some smarts . . . only he packs more."

Before long, my brother wasn't just eager to hear and talk about Holmes, he was trying to *act* like him. He detected. He deduced.

He got us in a hell of a lot of trouble.

Nevertheless, when Gustav decided to take a stab at professional detecting, I didn't buck. I'd seen him test his deducifying on some bona fide mysteries, and by jingo if he hadn't cracked those puzzles open like peanuts. On top of that, I owed him—for a lot. If he wanted to play detective, the least I could do was play the pal.

Unfortunately, I was the only one willing to play along. Old Red and I spent this May and June ricocheting around Montana, Wyoming, and Idaho paying calls on each and every detective agency office we could find. Openings were scarce. Contempt for jobless drovers, on the other hand, was in ample supply. In fact, the closest we ever got to an offer of employment came after we crossed into Utah Territory, when the head Pinkerton agent in Ogden snickered that he was always looking for "no-account saddle bums" like ourselves . . . because they had a price on their heads.

"How far we gonna take this, Gustav?" I asked as we stewed in nickel beer over this latest humiliation. "We've got enough cash to get us to a few more towns, but if this detectivin' job you're after is in New York or London or the Belgian Congo . . . well, I'm sorry. We ain't gonna make it."

"No need to go that far yet," Old Red said. "We're only a hop and a skip from Salt Lake City. May as well head there next."

"And after that?"

My brother shrugged. "After that we'll try again somewhere else. And somewhere else after that and somewhere else after that, if we have to. No matter how many bad turns we take, we'll find the right trail sooner or later . . . long as we don't stop lookin' for it."

I could've pointed out the irony of Gustav Amlingmeyer, the man who looks for the dark cloud around every silver lining, sermonizing on the importance of hope. But my brother got in his own jab first—and it caught me right in the gut.

"There's only one thing worse than givin' up, Otto, and that's not havin' the balls to try to begin with."

"I've got balls," I protested. "I just ain't anxious to have 'em stomped on."

Old Red gave me his *excuses, excuses* look, which combined a frown, a roll of the eyes, and a shake of the head in one quick, well-practiced movement. Perhaps because he was so doggedly chasing his dream, he found it galling that I should be so sluggish in pursuit of my own.

If Gustav was to become a homegrown Sherlock Holmes, I'd once figured, it was only natural that I should assume the role of his biographer, Dr. Watson. Yarnspinning has long been a specialty of mine, and I found it remarkably easy to put pen to paper and chronicle my brother's amateur sleuthing in a book.

What hadn't been so easy, however, was working up the nerve to do something with the damned thing once it was finished.

"You can't haul that big ol' bundle of paper around forever—it ain't fair to your horse, let alone yourself," Old Red said. "What're you waitin' for? *Harper's* to send you a letter askin' for it?"

I lifted my glass and took a long, slow pull, hiding behind a wall of suds. As I drank, I prayed in vain for some disruption—a brawl, a stampede through the streets, the tooting of Gabriel's trumpet, *anything*. I got nothing, though, and eventually I had to either face my brother or drown in beer.

"Well?" Gustav prodded the second my glass left my lips.

"I just need a little more time to think on it, that's all."

"What's left to think? It's *done*."

"Yeah, but I might wanna whittle it down some. When I read it to you, you yourself said it's long-winded."

"Well, so are you, but I don't keep you tied up in my war bag on account of it."

I took another drink, but there was little more than foam left, and I didn't get much of a respite.

"Look," I said, "we been over this. I'm just . . . bidin' my time."

"Pissin' it away, more like."

I sighed. There were days my brother hardly spoke at all, except to say "Mind that gopher hole" or "We'll camp here" or (when our unvarying trail diet of pemmican and beans had its inevitable consequences) "Whew! *Damn!*" Yet when it came to my failure of nerve as a would-be writer, I could not get the man to shut up.

"Speakin' of pissin' . . . ," I began, intending to escape the subject of my cowardice by (appropriately enough) running away.

But before I could beat a retreat toward the privy, the distraction I'd hoped for finally arrived. It came in the form of a thin, gnarled jerky-stick of a man staggering toward us from the bar. I would say he was three sheets to the wind, only I think he had a good many more sheets a-flapping than that. I was almost surprised when he managed to come to a swaying stop in front of our table instead of collapsing across the top of it.

"Hey," he said, and even as simple a sound as that came off his whiskey-numbed lips quivery and slurred. "I remember you."

"And I remember you," I said, not bothering to sound like I treasured the memory.

He'd been in the Pinkerton office that morning—a sixtyish, sour-faced fellow hunched over at a desk toward the back of the room. I'd once worked in an office of sorts myself, clerking in a Kansas granary, and I pegged him as a type I knew well: the sullen sluggard. I'd met plenty such men in the drovering profession, too, but they seem to particularly flourish in the shadowy corners of dimly lit offices.

The old man hadn't said a word as his boss belittled us. His only contribution to the conversation had been a sour chuckle when I'd pointed out that famous lawmen like Charlie Siringo and Burl Lockhart had been no more than "no-account saddle bums" themselves before the Pinkerton National Detective Agency hired them on. Another laugh at our expense was all I expected now, and I waited for him to fire some quip at us he'd been too slow on the draw to pop off earlier.

My low expectations must have been obvious, for the man tried to put on a reassuring smile. Such displays of good humor didn't appear natural to him—his face was so leathery I could practically hear the skin creaking as his lips curled into a grin.

"I might be able to help you," he said, his words still coming out as gloppy thick as oatmeal. "You see . . . I'm Burl Lockhart."

"*The* Burl Lockhart?" Gustav asked, looking him up and down.

What my brother beheld before him was hardly fodder for a dime novel—unless it concerned itself with the adventures of a palsied clerk or boozy newspaperman. That's what the fellow resembled more than anything else, what with his shabby trousers, ink-splattered shirt, poorly knotted tie, and crinkled and discolored collar. Only one thing about him suggested derring-do on the open range: the .44 with a mother-of-pearl grip that was slung at his hip. It looked as out of place on him as bloomers on a bull.

"At your service," the man said, his grin going lopsided as it spread itself wider.

"Mighty pleased to make your acquaintance, Burl." I stretched out my hand. "It's about time we bumped into each other. You see, I'm Buffalo Bill Cody, and this here's Annie Oakley."

My words turned the man to stone. His swaying and blinking and even *breathing* stopped, and only two parts of him still seemed alive at all—his lips, which flattened into a straight line that cut across his face like barbed wire pulled tight, and his right hand, which didn't reach out to take mine but instead started moving toward the grip of his gun.

Suddenly, I was looking at a different man—one who wasn't so much gaunt as he was pure, having shed everything soft about himself until all that remained was gristle and bone and bitterness. And this new, infinitely more daunting fellow did indeed seem strangely familiar. I thought back on the newspaper and magazine illustrations I'd seen of Burl Lockhart. If I added wrinkles and whiskers and subtracted meat and muscle . . .

Sweet Jesus, it really was him!

We were face-to-face with a man who'd traded potshots with the James brothers, befriended (and betrayed) Billy the Kid, and tucked more rustlers, robbers, and renegades under dirt blankets than any other lawman in the West.

He was more than a man, really. He was a legend . . . and I'd practically spat in his face.

And now he was getting set to spit lead in mine.

Two

LOCKHART

Or, A Close Shave Leads to a Hairy Predicament

I hadn't just put my foot in my mouth—I'd dipped it in arsenic first. Burl Lockhart was famous for his quick temper and even quicker draw, and it looked like I was about to be on the receiving end of both.

"Oop," I croaked, so discombobulated by my blunder my usually velvet tongue was choking me like a mouthful of sawdust. "Uhhhh."

Fortunately, my tight-lipped brother was able to loosen those lips of his quick.

"I'm sorry, Mr. Lockhart—Otto here don't mean no offense. It's just that his brain and his mouth ain't always on speakin' terms, if you know what I mean. We'd be mighty pleased if you'd sit and let us buy you a drink."

"That's right, sir," I managed to throw in. My hand was still held out to Lockhart, offering a shake he didn't take, so I flipped the palm up and offered the man a chair instead. "It'd truly be an honor to wet your whistle."

Whether a simple apology would have done the trick, I don't know. But an apology marinated in alcohol Lockhart was happy to accept.

"Well . . . no harm done," he said, dropping into the empty chair beside me. His smile returned, though it was smaller and more rueful now. "Who'd expect to see ol' Burl Lockhart kitted out like this?"

Indeed, with his rumpled dress clothes (not to mention his stubble-covered face and bleary eyes), Lockhart looked nothing like the gallant cowboy detective the newspapers and magazines made him out to be. But seeing as dime-novel sleuths are ever passing themselves off as salty peg-legged sea dogs or blind beggars or what have you, I figured he might be in the midst of some such masquerade himself.

"Say, Mr. Lockhart." I leaned close and dropped my voice down low. "Are you in disguise?"

Lockhart cocked a wispy, salt-and-peppered eyebrow at me, apparently searching for any sign I was guying him again.

"I suppose you could say I am," he conceded with a bitter chuckle when he saw I was sincere. "We're in a new age, boys. Gunpowder and nerve just ain't enough anymore—not with all this pansy talk of 'clues' and 'dee-deductions' and what all. Nowadays, a proper dee-tective's gotta have more tricks up his sleeve than a goddamn sideshow magician. Disguises, magnifilizin' glasses, beakers and burners and all that Tom Edison crap. Ya gotta be 'modern.' Ya gotta be *scientific.*'"

Lockhart showed us what he thought of "modern," "scientific" detectives by spitting on the floor.

"Lavender-ass bullshit," he said, just in case we needed a translation. "Now . . . where's that drink?"

Though I could practically see the steam from my brother's boiling blood puffing out his ears, Old Red let the insult to Mr. Holmes slide by without a reply in kind.

"What'll you have?" he said.

"Whiskey. With a whiskey chaser."

Gustav turned to me and nodded at the bar. "You heard the man."

Under normal circumstances, I might've leaned back, planted my heels on the table, and said, "I surely did . . . and I'll have the same." But seeing as the circumstances were neither normal nor particularly comfortable, I chose not to fan the flames with any sass.

"Two whiskeys, comin' up," I announced cheerfully, hopping up and heading for the bar.

The saloon's sweaty, tub-gutted bartender was gawking at our table as I walked up, so after putting in my order I asked if I really was fetching drinks for the great Burl Lockhart.

"That's Lockhart, alright—though I can't vouch for the 'great.'" The bartender produced two dirty glasses and filled them with the peppery, brownish liquid he so shamelessly sold as "whiskey." "First came in yesterday afternoon with two other Pinks. Local fellers. He would've spent the night here, too—on the floor—if they hadn't dragged him out."

"He say what he was in town for?"

The bartender shook his head. "Just said he's working on something secret—though he don't make no secret of who he is. At first, I figured he was sniffing around after Mike Barson and Augie Welsh, seeing as the bounty on 'em's up to ten thousand a head now. They've hit four trains outta Ogden the last six months, so some folks think this'd be the place to start hunting."

"Some folks" included about every newspaper in the country. Barson and Welsh's gang, the Give-'em-Hell Boys, had stopped so many Southern Pacific trains that spring they could probably join the conductors' union, and already Old Red and I had run across dime novels like *Barson and Welsh: Robin Hoods of the Rails* when hunting for new Holmes tales. Coming from farming folk, we had no fondness for the railroads ourselves, so it hadn't bothered us in the least that the Southern Pacific couldn't pluck this particular thorn from its side. A part of me was rooting for the thorn.

"Well, I don't reckon the Give-'em-Hell Boys have much to worry about from Lockhart even if he *does* chase 'em down," I said to the bartender.

"Yeah. Just look at him."

We stole a peek at the pickled Pinkerton, who was jabbering away at my brother without bothering to look at him. Lockhart's attention was focused entirely on the drinks resting on the countertop before me. The man was practically licking his lips.

"Only chasin' he's interested in is the kind you do with a shot glass," the bartender said.

"I suppose I best let him get to it, too." I slapped down a couple coins, swept up the glasses, and headed back to the table.

As I walked up, Lockhart was rambling on about the Cross J, a Texas outfit Gustav and I worked a few years back. Apparently, Lockhart put in a season there himself before turning Pinkerton. While this shared history disposed him toward us warmly, it didn't stop him from describing in excruciating detail elements of the ranch's operations and geography we knew just as well as he, if not better. I put down his whiskeys, took a seat, and did my best to disguise the glazing over of my eyes.

"Those were the days, boys," Lockhart said after wrapping up a painfully thorough account of a cattle drive of the very type Old Red and I have worked over and over ourselves. "Before barbed wire. Before the railroads. It's all changed now . . . and the changin' just don't stop."

Lockhart looked like he was about to spit again, but instead he chose to wash the bad taste out of his mouth by sucking down the last drops of his whiskey.

"Christ," he sighed, "even the goddamn changes keep changin' on me."

"People gotta change, too," Old Red said.

"What's that supposed to mean?" Lockhart shot back, his booze-fuzzed voice suddenly utterly clear.

I jumped in to explain Gustav's remark before my brother could do any damage by explaining it (truthfully) himself.

"That's what we keep tellin' ourselves, Mr. Lockhart. *We* gotta change. Like you did all those years ago. The big cattle drives are dryin' up. Drovers on the drift like us—we ain't got nowhere to drift *to* anymore. That's why we thought we'd give the Pinkertons a try. If a top-rail cowhand like Burl Lockhart could make the switch, well, we kinda hoped we could, too."

Of course, Burl Lockhart had about as much to do with Old Red's interest in detecting as the hairs on my ass had to do with Sherman's March. And it would've been easy for Lockhart to deduce as much if he'd noticed how my brother was glowering at me just then.

Fortunately, the old Pinkerton had something else to look at—a slick-dressed fellow in a bowler hat who came toddling up to our table.

"It's time, Lockhart," he said. "He's here."

"Oh, he is, is he?" Lockhart snarled back. "Well, he can just wait a damn minute while I conclude my business with the boys here." He began rummaging through his pockets, his face growing redder with each fistful of lint and crumbs he produced. "Somebody give me something to write with, damn it."

The dude in the bowler produced a scrap of paper and a stubby pencil from his vest pocket. Lockhart snatched them away with a muttered curse.

"Yessir . . . ol' Burl Lockhart's still got himself a friend or two . . . ," he mumbled as he wrote.

He finished with a flourish—a series of hard, stabbing dots that jabbed at the table like knives. Then he thrust the paper at me and lurched to his feet.

"There! Sorry I can't help you with the Pinks. An old-fashioned, guts-and-guns lawman like myself don't have no pull with the muckety-mucks no more. But believe you me—you don't wanna sign on with them limp wrists anyhow." He turned a glare on the fellow who'd come to fetch him, then pocketed the man's pencil and stomped away.

"Thanks, Mr. Lockhart!" I called after him, though as yet I had no idea what I was thanking him for.

The dude lingered behind with me and my brother, pushing up the brim of his bowler and regarding us coolly. "You two wanna be Pinkertons?"

"That's right," Old Red said.

The dude shook his head and snorted. "Stick to 'dogies,' cowboy." Then he followed Lockhart toward the door.

I was about to tell the man what *he* could stick to—or, more precisely, what he could stick where—but Gustav cut me off with an elbow to the ribs.

"Well?" he grunted, pointing at Lockhart's note.

The old Pinkerton had folded the slip of paper, and I read out what he'd written on the front:

Col. C. Kermit Crowe

S.P.R.R.

Union Station

When I unfolded the paper, there was even less to see on the other side. Lockhart's message consisted of just four letters.

O.K.

B.L.

"Well, ain't that just the way," I sighed. "We finally get ourselves a lucky break . . . and it's broke."

I was a half second from balling up Lockhart's note and tossing it over my shoulder when my brother reached out and plucked it from my fingers.

"Hold on there."

He stared down at the paper, even though Lockhart's wobbly scrawling couldn't have meant less to him if it'd been written in Chinese.

"It's obvious, ain't it?" I said. "That's the shortest letter of recommendation a man could write. And it's to a railroad—the Southern Pacific to be specific. We wouldn't have anything to do with them sons of bitches." After a moment went by without a reply, I added, "Would we?"

Old Red kept staring at the note. He was chewing something over, and he obviously didn't like the taste of it. In the end, though, he didn't spit it out.

"I reckon we'll cross that trestle when we come to it," he said, and he stood and headed for the door.

Three

267 AND 268

Or, We Learn We're Just What the S.P. *Isn't* Looking For

My brothers and sisters and I didn't hear much cussing when we were growing up. *Mutter* wouldn't tolerate it, and even so mild a word as "heck" would get your tongue slathered with soap.

Yet when our *Vater* or Uncle Franz cut loose on the railroads, a ton of lye wouldn't have been enough to wash away all the obscenities. Even sweet old *Mutter* would join in from time to time (albeit *auf Deutsch,* thinking we wouldn't understand). If that revealed a little streak of hypocrisy in a woman we all worshipped, it was easily overlooked. Farming's a tough enough life without Eastern fat cats charging more to ship your crops than folks could ever pay to eat them.

It had been nearly a decade since Gustav had spent any time behind a plow, yet when it came to the railroads, he apparently remained as bitter as any Granger. For proof, one need look no further than my butt—and the unheavenly host of saddle sores it sported. Old Red insisted that we do by horse and trail what anyone else would do by rail, and through all our wanderings he hadn't allowed us to subsidize the railroads' monopolizing, rate-gouging, land-stealing ways with the purchase of a single ticket.

Which explains why the first words out of my mouth when I caught up to Gustav outside that saloon in Ogden would have had *Mutter* reaching for her soap.

"Now, now—no need to get your bristles up," my brother replied, leaning casually—almost *too* casually—against the post our horses were hitched to. "We gotta at least see what that note means, don't we?"

"And what if it means what it seems to mean?" I shot back. "Jobs."

"Then we think it over."

"You who'd steer us a thousand miles out of our way so as not to put a single penny in a robber baron's pocket? *You* would think about workin' for the Southern Pacific?"

"I'm always willin' to think . . . unlike some people," Old Red replied—though there was something strangely halfhearted about his gibe.

"If you're so eager to think, why ain't you thinkin' about what *Mutter* and *Vater* used to rant about? Jacked-up freight rates keepin' farmers poor, people dyin' cuz the tycoons was too cheap to put proper brakes on their cars. You forget all that?"

My brother gave me a slow, chagrined nod, the way a man does when he recognizes the wisdom of a friend's advice while reserving the right to ignore it.

"That was years ago," he said.

"Try tellin' that to the Give-'em-Hell Boys—you know they're all sodbusters just like our people was. The papers say they never would've turned outlaw if the Southern Pacific hadn't grabbed their land for a new line last year."

"Well . . . it ain't like we never worked for assholes before," Old Red said limply. "They just owned cattle 'stead of cattle cars."

"Yeah, but when we work for an asshole cattleman, we're cowboys. What the hell's a railroad man gonna hire us to do? Yard bulls, that's what they'd peg us for. Thugs to kick the shit out of hoboes."

Gustav shook his head. "I don't think so. I reckon there's a reason the S.P. would be on the lookout for fellers like us—and you said it yourself."

My brother's usually not keen on "theorizing" without all the facts, as Mr. Holmes looked down his long nose on idle guesswork. But Gustav was willing to make an exception now to sway me—and perhaps himself.

"The Give-'em-Hell Boys," he said.

"You think the railroad's puttin' together a special posse?"

"They'd have to be, the way Barson and Welsh have been robbin' 'em blind."

I thought it over a moment. It made sense—and it didn't make a lick of difference.

"The Give-'em-Hell gang's a hole the S.P. dug for itself," I said with a shrug. "I don't see why we should hop down into the pit with it."

"It'd establish our bona fides as law enforcers," Old Red said.

"Enforcers, anyway," I scoffed.

"It wouldn't be forever. We'd make the jump to *real* detectin' sooner or later."

I let a raised eyebrow do all my scoffing this time.

"Just look at it like this," Gustav persisted. "The point of ridin' on a train ain't the train. It's where the train takes you. Understand?"

"What if you get on the wrong damn train?"

I thought this was a pretty clever retort, actually, but Old Red had an even better one.

"You get off."

He didn't say it like a platitude. He said it like a promise.

"Really? It's that simple?"

Gustav nodded. "It's that simple."

"We don't like the setup, we just walk away?" I said—not realizing the mistake I was making using the word *we*.

My brother nodded again.

"Alright," I sighed. "You win. For now."

Old Red didn't look much cheered by his victory, though. In fact, he almost seemed disappointed that I hadn't managed to change his mind for him.

It was easy enough to find our way to the local S.P. office, for it's at the center of the colossal web of wood and steel that stretches out from Ogden to cover half the nation. The Southern Pacific, the Union Pacific, and a slew of local lines all join up just west of town, their tracks tangling together at the foot of the massive brick mountain called Union Station. We'd skirted the snarl on our way into Ogden the day before, but now we were riding right into the heart of it.

As we drew close enough to hear the whistling, clanging, and chugging of the trains, the horses grew jittery . . . and so did my brother. He had a twitchy look about him—a jumpiness he tried to wipe away with his handkerchief as we entered the station.

"Change your mind?" I asked him.

"Just feelin' a touch poorly, that's all." He dabbed at his face a second time, for it was already slick with sweat again. "Maybe you oughta do the talkin' when we find this 'Col. Crowe' feller. I wouldn't be at my best, augerin'-wise. And my best ain't half as good as yours anyhow."

"Oh, I don't know—that was some pretty good blarney you laid out just now." (When my brother comments on my flair for balderdash, it's usually not to offer his appreciation.) "Anyway, I'd hardly be at *my* best tryin' to wrangle a job I don't even want."

"Still . . . you're the talker, Otto. I need you to handle this."

I looked over at Old Red and found him gazing back at me, his eyes saying the word he couldn't quite bring himself to put on his lips.

Please.

My brother was placing his dream in my hands. I couldn't very well drop it, no matter how peeved I might be.

"Alright," I grumbled. "Gimme Lockhart's note."

Gustav clapped me on the back, something he feels moved to do not once in a blue moon but more like once in plaid one. There's another word he and I rarely use with each other, and he used it then.

"Thanks."

When we found the Southern Pacific office tucked away in a quiet wing of the station, I asked to see Colonel Crowe with all the breezy confidence of an old pal.

"Got a message for him from Burl," I told the pimply young clerk who'd greeted us with a quizzical stare. *"Lockhart."*

The clerk loped off down a hallway, and I took the opportunity to shoot another peek at my brother. He seemed less fidgety now that we were away from the smoke and bustle of the depot, yet so much color had drained from his face he looked like a pillar of salt with a red mustache. He'd taken a nasty wound a couple months before—a gunshot courtesy of someone his deducifying had displeased—and I started thinking he might not be as healed up as I'd assumed.

"Down the hall, last door on the right," the clerk told us when he returned, flashing a smile that didn't offer friendliness so much as advertise his amusement at some private joke. "He's waiting for you."

I'd pictured Colonel Crowe as a stout, barrel-chested Ambrose Burnside type. But the puny fellow we found awaiting us hardly had the chest for a mug of beer, let alone a barrel. Whichever regiment the colonel had served with, I could only assume his commanding officer had been General Tom Thumb.

Runty as he might have been, Crowe didn't lack for lung power. When he snapped out "Close that door behind you," the words cracked at us like a whip.

"Now," he said with only slightly less snip once I'd complied, "who are you and what do you want?"

"Otto Amlingmeyer's the name," I replied with (what I hoped was) imperturbable smoothness. "This here's my brother Gustav. Burl Lockhart sent us to you with this."

I pulled out the note and placed it on the desk before Crowe. He flipped it open, grunted, then crumpled the paper into a ball and jammed it into a pocket of his dark suit coat.

"Either of you have experience as lawmen? Guards? Gunmen? Anything like that?"

I put on a cocky grin and patted my holstered Colt, thinking I'd concoct some suitable flummery about our careers as pistoleros. But I could see in the squinty pucker of Crowe's face that he was on guard for the slightest whiff of bullshit, so I stuck to the truth.

"'Fraid not, sir. We're just a couple drovers. Seen our fair share of trouble, that's for sure, but never from behind a badge."

I half-expected Crowe to offer the same advice as the Pinkerton who'd collected Lockhart from the saloon: *Get your ass back to cattle, cowboy.* But instead his head snapped down and up in a brusque nod.

"Good. Do you know who I am?"

As honesty about our inexperience had seemingly served us well, I came clean on our ignorance, too.

"I haven't the foggiest notion, sir."

That got me another nod.

"I believe you. Excellent. You're just the sort of men I'd be looking for if I could be looking for men like you."

"Come again?" I said.

"Spies!" Crowe spat the word out like it was a bee that had buzzed into his mouth.

"Now, hold on. You think we're—?" I began.

Crowe dismissed the question with a flutter of his stubby fingers. "No, no. Not you. That's why you're here. Because of them. The spies."

"I hope you'll pardon my askin', sir," Gustav said, "but . . . spies for who?"

"Who do you think?" the colonel snapped. "Those dirty, thieving clodhoppers! Barson and Welsh! They've hit our big runs time and time again! The ones carrying payrolls and"—he dropped his voice to a hoarse, angry whisper—"*gold.*" Then he thumped his desk with a tiny, clenched fist, so bubbling over with rage I began to think he'd blow apart like an overstoked boiler. "There's only one explanation! Spies inside the Southern Pacific! Informers! Goddamned *traitors!*"

The colonel's face grew redder and redder as he raved, but he managed to catch a deep, calming breath before he self-induced a stroke.

"We're doing what we can to root out such vermin, but it's not easy," he said as the angry blush faded from his face. "We've got all our best men hunting for the Give-'em-Hell gang, and I can't just open up my doors and recruit more—not when anyone who comes to the S.P.

21

looking for work could be another spy. So I've instituted a new policy: I only hire people I'd have no reason to hire, and they, in turn, must have no intention of being hired by me."

"Which is why Burl Lockhart sent us here," Old Red said. "Instead of hirin' for yourself, you've got friends—folks you trust—pickin' fellers out and herdin' 'em your way."

The colonel gave the deduction an approving nod. "That's right. I see Lockhart chose well. He's not what he used to be, but he's still got an eye for judging men. Except . . . he wasn't *drunk* when he gave you that note, was he?"

"No, sir," I said, sensing that honesty was no longer our best policy—it was time to lie like a sonofabitch. "He seemed a touch hung-over maybe, but he was sober as a judge."

"Alright, then." The colonel leapt up to his full height (which wasn't much higher than he'd been in his chair) and put his right hand in the air. "Repeat after me: I do solemnly swear . . ."

Old Red raised his hand. After a moment's hesitation, I did like-wise.

"I do solemnly swear," we said in unison.

"That I am not a dirty damned spying bastard . . ."

My brother and I gaped at the colonel.

"Swear it!" he barked.

We swore it.

"And that I will do my utmost to protect the property and passengers of the Southern Pacific Railroad."

We swore this, too.

"So help me, God."

Again, we repeated the words—though I meant them more as a plea than a pledge.

Crowe pulled one of his desk drawers open and fished out a couple of silver-gray doodads. One he handed to me, the other to my brother.

They were stars—badges. For Old Red's benefit, I read out what was engraved on mine:

POLICE SERVICE

267

S.P.R.R. CO.

My brother stared down at his star, numbered 268. He rubbed it with his thumb as if he needed the feel of the cool metal to convince himself it was real.

"So," he said, "we're off after Barson and Welsh, then."

Crowe scowled. "Certainly not. As I said, that's for my best men. I want you on the next express over the Sierras—you'll get your training in San Francisco. Oh, by the way . . ." The colonel pulled a pencil and a ledger from the same drawer that had held the badges. "What were your names again?"

I answered for both myself and Old Red, as my brother had such a look of shock upon his face I was afraid for him to open his mouth lest a scream escape. His dream was finally coming true—but you'd have thought he was faced instead with his greatest nightmare.

Four

TERRA INCOGNITA

Or, Colonel Crowe Gives His New Recruits Their Marching Orders

I t fell to me to offer the necessary head nods and yessirs as Crowe ran through the particulars of our employment, since my brother remained so thunderstruck I could've stuffed stogies in his hand and sold him as a cigar-store Indian.

We'd be paid ten dollars a week, the colonel told us, and we'd report to a fellow named Jefferson Powless at S.P. H.Q. in San Francisco. We were to make our way there on a joint Union Pacific–Southern Pacific Chicago-to-Oakland special called the Pacific Express, which had arrived in Ogden that morning and would carry on shortly. While aboard the train, we were to keep our connection with the railroad under our hats, as we were "terra incognita" (in Crowe's words) to the "turncoat sons of bitches" infesting the S.P.

Old Red remained so catatonic through it all he didn't even raise an eyebrow when the colonel concluded by throwing open his window and directing us to climb through.

"It would be best if you weren't seen leaving my office," he said.

Of course, two men climbing out a window in broad daylight might attract more attention than the same fellows strolling out by way of the door. But I thought it best not to argue, as Colonel Crowe struck me as the kind of military mind that could make Custer look like a model of common sense and coolheadedness.

"Pick up your tickets at the Southern Pacific desk downstairs—they'll be waiting for you under the name Dissimulo," the colonel said as I maneuvered my substantial bulk none too gracefully through the window. (While my by-no-means-elderly elder brother is "Old Red," I've been branded "Big Red" with no irony whatso-ever.) "I'll send a coded wire to Powless with word that you're coming."

Once Gustav had followed stiffly after me, Crowe leaned out the window and crooked his stubby little arm into a salute.

"Good luck, men."

"So . . . that's it?" I asked, offering a limp salute in return. "There's nothin' you want us to do till we get to San Francisco?"

"Of course, there is," Crowe snapped. "I should've thought it went without saying."

Old Red and I merely stared back at him, making it clear that *saying* was indeed needed.

"If anyone tries to rob the Pacific Express," the colonel said, "kill them."

He ducked inside and slammed the window shut.

"You know . . . I'd have liked it better if that *had* gone without sayin'," I said.

A lone locomotive was puffing its way toward a roundhouse not far off, and my brother turned to watch its approach with an expression that was equal parts wistful and queasy.

"I wasn't expectin' things to move so fast," he said.

"That don't mean we gotta keep movin' with 'em."

"We took the badges," Old Red said, sounding curiously resigned. "We took the jobs."

"Jobs with the Southern goddamn Pacific," I pointed out. "Come on, Brother . . . we got more in common with Mike Barson and Augie Welsh than with that little lunatic in there."

Gustav shook his head, shaking himself from his dreamy stupor in the process. "Barson and Welsh are outlaws," he said firmly. "We're detectives."

"*Railroad* detectives," I corrected him.

"*Detectives.*"

"Well, if it's really as simple as that, why'd you go all ghostly a minute ago? When Crowe said he was sendin' us out on the next train, your face turned so pale it practically bleached your mustache."

"Like I said—things are movin' fast, that's all." Old Red turned and headed away down the side of the building. "And we gotta move fast, too, if we're gonna make that train."

I cursed, I grumbled, I dragged my heels—and I followed.

After we'd collected our gear, changed into our nicest clothes (which is to say our clothes with the least number of stains and rips), and settled up at our boardinghouse, my brother took a mighty big step—a giant *jump* for the likes of us. He sold our horses. There was a practical reason, since it was unlikely we'd be allowed to stow our ponies under our seats on the train. But I figured there was a personal reason, too: Gustav was making it that much harder to back out.

When we set off for Union Station again, we went via mule-drawn streetcar, an experience I enjoyed heartily as it offered seemingly endless opportunities to tip one's hat to pretty shopgirls. Such charms were lost on Old Red, though—and not just because my bashful brother practically swoons at the sight of a skirt. Though our speed never topped a lazy amble, he stared wide-eyed at the tracks before us as if the streetcar line terminated not at Union Station but *into* the Grand Canyon. When I asked if he was alright, he just grunted out, "Fine," and tightened his white-knuckled grip on the nearest pole.

Once we reached the station, I took on more than my fair share of our gear, yet Old Red still lagged behind as we went inside. To say that he walked toward the ticket desk like a man headed to the gallows doesn't do it justice. He walked like a man headed to the gallows with blocks of granite tied to his feet.

"Oh, for Christ's sake," I said, dropping my load and waiting for my brother to catch up. "If you're sick, just say so."

"I . . . ain't . . . sick," Old Red wheezed unconvincingly as he trudged past me into the station.

Our tickets were waiting for us under "Dissimulo" like Colonel Crowe said, though the clerk behind the counter gave me the evil eye when I had trouble pronouncing what was supposedly my own last name.

"Dissimulo—what kinda handle is that, anyway?" I asked Gustav as we went looking for a porter to take our things.

"Sounds I-talian," my brother muttered.

"I guess I oughta start callin' you Giuseppe then. You can call me Leonardo."

"How 'bout I just call you Chucklehead?" Old Red said wearily, as if making digs at me was an obligation he could barely muster the strength to meet. "If we're gonna take on another name, it may as well be something that fits us."

That actually seemed sensible to me—which is why, soon afterward, I checked in our saddles and war bags under the name Gustav Holmes.

"You've always wanted to be another Holmes. Well, now I went and made you one," I told my brother, who'd plopped himself on one of the long benches stretching like cornrows through the huge station.

Old Red nodded, his eyes on the pile of trunks, crates, and bags our gear had been tossed onto. "I hope you didn't give that porter anything you wouldn't wanna lose."

"Don't worry. I got all the essentials right here." I patted the worn carpetbag we'd purchased at a pawnshop before boarding the trolley. In it was everything I thought we'd need in the days ahead (extra clothes, toothbrushes, a shaving kit, Gustav's Holmes yarns) and a few items I hoped we wouldn't (our holsters and guns). But none of this was the irreplaceable "anything" my brother was referring to.

"Otto," Old Red said, "get over there and dig that book outta your war bag. We got us a few minutes yet. There's still time to mail it." He dabbed his sweat-beaded face with his handkerchief. "I admit it. I feel like shit. But if I can drag my achin' carcass onto a train, you can walk your book a block to a damn post office."

"So what exactly's ailin' you, Brother? A bruised conscience, maybe?"

I was just trying to change the subject, of course. And Old Red returned the favor, though he went about it with less finesse. He simply shook his head, got to his feet, and walked off toward the doors along the western wall of the station.

The Pacific Express was just outside.

Low as my opinion of the railroads was, that didn't prevent me from appreciating the *train*. Looking at it for the first time, I understood what it must be like to step inside a grand opera house. When so much is sumptuous and shining, the gaudy spectacle of it is enough to make you forget, just for a moment, the ramshackle shoddiness of your everyday world.

And that was the locomotive alone. It was dark green with red trim and gold leaf on top of that, all of it polished to such a gleam the huge headlamp mounted above the cowcatcher seemed unnecessary: Surely the engine was so well varnished it would glow in the moonlight as brilliantly as the brightest star. Yet I spotted a pudgy, fussy man in overalls—the engineer, no doubt—working a rag over the knobs and levers in the cab like a fellow giving a spit shine to a diamond.

Behind the locomotive was a matching, equally ornate coal tender, which was followed by a Wells Fargo express car and a baggage car that were about as dazzling as a couple crates of cabbage. But then it was on to three Pullmans, a dining car, and finally an observation car, all of them done up in green, red, and gold so vivid you'd think the paint was still dripping wet.

My wonder must have showed on my face, for someone called out, "A beautiful sight, isn't she?"

I turned to find a squat, curly-haired man looking down at me from the open side door of the baggage car. His lips were curved in a grin so gigantic the ends of his waxed mustache practically pointed straight up.

"That she is," I said.

"Well, enjoy it now. By the time we're twenty feet down the track, she'll have so much dust on her you won't remember if she's green, purple, or pink."

I shared a chuckle with the man, then he wished us a pleasant journey and got back to his work, checking baggage tags and jotting down notes on a piece of paper attached to a clipboard.

My brother didn't seem to hear a word he'd said. He was gaping at two long wooden boxes resting side by side near the baggageman's feet—a pair of coffins.

"Don't worry," I said. "I'm sure they ain't bringin' those along for *us*."

"Come on," Old Red growled, heading toward a burly, fifty-or-so fellow who was either a conductor or a steamboat captain, judging by his flat-topped cap and frock coat.

"Howdy, Admiral!" I said, offering him my ticket. "Could you tell us where our seats might be?"

The conductor glared at me with such undisguised disgust you'd have thought I was handing him a fresh cow pie. It was only then that I remembered something that hadn't meant much to me before, given that I'd only been on a train once, and that as a lad: Railroad men *hate* cowboys.

I suppose it's because our profession attracts a boisterous breed that doesn't make for the most mannerly of passenger. And the fact that drovers resent the railroads for a multitude of sins, not least of which is the withering away of the old cattle trails. And I'm sure it doesn't help that many a waddy thinks it great sport to shoot out the headlamps of night-traveling trains.

Although Gustav and I had given ourselves new names, we hadn't acquired new duds, and it was plain to see that we weren't doctors, lawyers, or Indian chiefs—all of whom would've been more welcome aboard the train than us.

"Ask a porter," a voice snapped at me. I could only assume the voice belonged to the conductor, as I couldn't see his lips move—they were hidden beneath a thick mustache-goatee that flowed over his mouth and down his chin in a bushy, black-gray stripe.

"Whadaya say—should I kick his ass?" I said to Old Red as the conductor moved off to harangue the baggageman about something or other. "I mean, what's the good of havin' a badge if you can't abuse your authority, right?"

Gustav didn't reply. He was staring pensively at the steps up into the car.

"Second thoughts?" I asked.

It was as if that was just the prod he needed.

"Nope. Still stuck to my first." And he grabbed the handrail and hauled himself up. Then he turned and stretched a hand down to me like *I* was the one who needed help. "You comin'?"

It wasn't a question I heard from him often, since my brother tends to march around as if I'm little more than an extra spur attached to him at the heel. It rarely seems to occur to him that I might roll free one of these days. But it had occurred to him now—as it had occurred to *me*.

"Occurred to" doesn't always amount to much, though. Especially not when it's stacked up against a "got to."

I took my brother's hand and let him pull me up into the Pacific Express.

"Welcome aboard," he said once I had my feet planted inside.

"Why, thank you, Mr. Holmes."

He let go of my hand and flashed me a thin grin.

It was the last smile I'd see on his face from that day to this.

Five

THE PACIFIC EXPRESS

Or, We Settle In on the Train—and Spot an Unsettling Sight

My one and only previous trip by rail had been on a rundown line of the Atchison, Topeka & Santa Fe. The cars were packed with just the sort of high-class passengers you'd expect on a two-dollar run from Peabody, Kansas, to Dodge City: farmers, soldiers, cowpokes, pickpockets, and snake-oil peddlers, all of them squeezed in wall to wall and practically floor to ceiling. Yet I'd never felt more alone in my life.

Just a few weeks before, a flood had swept away Amlingmeyer farm and family both, and I was on my way to meet the only blood relation I had left west of the Mississippi. I hadn't seen him in four years, not since he'd taken to drovering, and I feared I wouldn't recognize him . . . or he wouldn't show up to be recognized. The only guarantee he'd come was a promise on a piece of paper, a telegram he couldn't even have written out himself.

Gustav came, of course. I spotted him the second I stepped off the train. He'd changed, but only by becoming more of everything he'd seemingly always been: weathered, tetchy, morose.

But *there,* that was the important thing. He was there—with me.

And he'd stayed there ever since, no matter where *there* happened to be. So if he decided it was on the Pacific Express, well, that meant I'd be there, too.

As *there*s go, this one was a hell of a lot nicer than the last one I'd seen aboard a train. The car I rode in from Peabody had all the lavish amenities of a chicken coop. The paint was chipped, the air reeked of sweat and smoke, and the splintery seats were so hard on your hindquarters they made church pews seem like feather beds.

The Pacific Express was something else entirely. The Pullman car Old Red and I stepped into could have been a fancy hotel lobby squeezed up concertina-style. Rows of what appeared to be divans ran down each side, their invitingly plump curves draped in red crushed velvet. Above them were handsomely carved panels of dark wood, like a series of doors turned sideways and laid end to end. Behind them (I knew from the travel articles in *Harper's*) were the sleeping berths the porters would pull down at night. When the time came, climbing into an upper berth hardly seemed necessary, as the carpeting was so thick and springy you could probably *bounce* up with but the slightest bend of the knee.

I would have been happy just to stand there soaking up the splendor of it all (and blotting out my lingering misgivings about being aboard in the first place) had there not been passengers anxious to use the aisle for walking rather than gawking. In fact, the hustle-bustle was growing more hectic by the second, and each "Excuse me" we got as we were bumped and elbowed sounded less sincere than the one preceding it. If we didn't find our seats soon, it seemed like we'd simply be shoved out the nearest window.

Fortunately, it was easy to spot help. One and all, our fellow passengers were white folks in dark dress clothes. So the Negro porter in a crisp white jacket stood out like a snowball in a bucket of coal.

It's entirely possible the porter—a lanky, middle-aged fellow who told us to call him Samuel—was no more fond of cowboys than the conductor. Yet he chattered away amiably as he snatched our bag from my hands and led us through the train's narrow aisles and vestibules.

"You gents are up this way. The back two sleepers are all through passengers—forty-seven Presbyterians from San Rafael, California. We'll be hearin' hymns from here to Oakland! They're comin' back from . . . pardon me, ma'am . . . the Columbian Exposition in Chicago. We been runnin' people out to the fair and back for months. Now, mind . . . yes, sir, I'll fetch you one directly . . . this line strung up along here. That's the bell cord. For the brakes. Runs all the way up to the engineer. Don't tug on it 'less you want the passenger across from you in your lap. We've got those . . . sir, you'll find a spittoon in the corner, if you please . . . new air brakes on this run. You'll be thankful for that when we're swoopin' into the Sacramento Valley at sixty-five miles an hour! And here we are: your seat. Just make yourselves comfortable. If you need anything . . . you look a little peaked, sir, if I may say so . . . just call for Samuel!"

Though he was obviously a busy man, Samuel lingered, grinning, even after Gustav and I settled ourselves onto the snug little settee we'd be sharing.

"Thank you, Samuel," I said. "You've been mighty hospitable."

Samuel nodded, his smile beginning to look unnaturally stiff.

"Yeah, thanks," Old Red mumbled as he squirmed around, trying to find a comfortable position. He looked sweaty and tense, and having Samuel hovering over him like a vulture obviously wasn't helping his nerves.

Someone cleared his throat, and I glanced across the aisle to find a fortyish sport in a checked suit giving me the eye in a friendly, amused sort of way. He had a face as flat and pink as a slice of ham, and atop his head was a pompadour of such impressive proportions I wouldn't have been surprised had I spotted the great explorer Sigerson attempting to climb it with a team of native guides.

The man brought up his hand and rubbed his index and middle fingers over his thumb.

"Oh!" I stuck my hand in my pocket and pulled out a penny. "There you go."

That coin looked awful small in the palm of Samuel's long hand, so much so that it seemed to take a moment of searching for the porter to even see it was there.

"Thank you, sir," he finally said rather glumly. Then he hurried away to help a black-draped widow herd her boys—a pair of cackling, curly-haired twins—up the aisle to their seats.

I looked over at my etiquette instructor and knew immediately that I'd failed his first exam. He was shaking his head and snickering at my notion of a gratuity.

"A good porter's the best friend you'll ever have on a long train trip," he said. "You want him to *stay* your friend, you better dig out a dime from time to time."

"You gotta bribe a man to do his job?" Old Red griped, his eyes on the widow. She was in full mourning, veil and all, and the black crepe trimming her long skirts shushed like sorrowful whispers as she moved.

"It's not a bribe. It's *appreciation*," our neighbor replied jovially—after a respectful pause to let the widow pass us by. "I'm a drummer by trade, so you'll see no moss on me. And when you spend as much time cooped up in train cars as I do, you're grateful for anyone who brings a little comfort into your life. Why, I bet you couldn't find a traveling salesman on the whole of the Southern Pacific who'd tip a porter anything less than a nickel just for saying hello."

The drummer continued in this vein (and on into several others) over the next few minutes. Chester Q. Horner was his name, and he'd just spent the last month at the Columbian Exposition promoting "the wonder food of the future," a supposedly miraculous "health paste" made from boiled peanuts. This "nut butter" concoction sounded anything but miraculous—or edible—to me, but Horner preached its virtues with such evangelical zeal I soon agreed to try a spoonful of it with my dinner.

It was one of the few times I was allowed to speak: Horner worked up such a wind, it nearly blew me out of the conversation entirely. I didn't mind, though. I've been known to spread the gab on thick myself, so I could appreciate the man as a master of the art. To Old Red, however, he was merely an annoyance, and it wasn't long before my brother wasn't even pretending to listen.

Instead, he was practicing his own art—Holmesifying—by staring at the passengers taking their seats. He was looking for a limp, a stain on a sleeve, a threadbare valise, anything that might give him a glimpse into a stranger's circumstances or soul. After a while, though, I felt him stiffen up beside me, and I knew he'd gotten a peek at something he *didn't* want to see.

We were seated facing the back of the train, and up till then the seat directly across from us had been empty. But now someone arrived to claim it, and Gustav was terror-stricken for the same reason I was delighted: That someone was a pretty young lady.

Of course, an unescorted female of a certain age traveling in close proximity to two unrelated males of a certain class would strike your more prudish, old-fashioned folks as not altogether proper. And I feared (and Old Red probably *hoped*) that the lady was just such a folk herself, for she hesitated, looking first at her seat, then at us.

"Good afternoon, ma'am," I said, leaping to my feet. "If it would make you more comfortable, my brother and I would be happy to have the porter move us elsewhere."

I was going for broke, hoping that by offering to do the courteous thing I might relieve us of the burden of actually having to do it.

"Thank you, but your company won't compromise *my* comfort in the least," the young lady replied, grinning in a way that seemed to say she welcomed any opportunity to scandalize the scandalizable.

As she settled in across from us, Old Red muttered a greeting that lacked even the warmth necessary to be labeled halfhearted—perhaps "eighth-hearted" would be closer to the mark. Then he made his escape by turning his attention to the final flurry of late-arriving passengers outside.

"I'm afraid my brother won't be much company, miss—he's feelin' poorly," I said. "Fortunately, I talk enough for two, so things should balance out alright."

I was being forward, I know, but the smile had lingered on her face, seemingly inviting conversation. And she was just so darned *cute* I probably would've tried chatting her up even if she'd been frowning or foaming at the mouth. She had wide brown eyes and a fleshy, slightly upturned nose and an impish tilt to her full lips that suggested youthful mischief even though she was undoubtedly older than me. (I pegged her at twenty-five, closer to Gustav's age than mine.) Her dark hair was pulled up in a bun, revealing . . . well, if I get to writing about her long, slender neck, this could turn downright lewd, and I'll just conclude by saying her appearance was powerfully pleasing to the eye.

So you can imagine my gratification when she greeted my sally with a chuckle.

"Somehow, I get the feeling you're not exaggerating, Mr. . . . ?"

"Amli-*ow*-olmes."

"Excuse me?"

"Holmes," I said, sliding my toe from beneath Old Red's bootheel. "Otto Holmes. My brother here's Gustav. And whose acquaintance do we have the pleasure of makin'?"

"Diana Caveo."

I was about to reply with "Charmed, I'm sure"—a half-assed stab at cosmopolitanism cribbed from some magazine story about the upper crust. Fortunately, a commotion drew our attention to the back of the car before I could make a complete boob of myself.

A man was making his way up the aisle, and a low rumble of unhappy murmurs grew louder with each step he took. He was a small, mild-looking, bespectacled fellow wearing the impeccably tailored suit of a successful businessman. He wasn't carrying a gun or an open whiskey bottle, nor did he smell of dung or upchuck or smoldering brimstone.

Nevertheless, his presence was clearly repugnant to many on the train. The man, you see, had committed an unforgivable social blunder: He'd been born Oriental.

"The Chinaman's back," I heard one affronted gentleman grumble. "And he brought a new friend with him."

"Honestly," the lady with him harrumphed. "Two hundred dollars for these tickets, and the railroad coops us up with one of *them.*"

If the Oriental got tongues wagging, the "friend" who followed stilled them. He was a gaunt, sloppy-dressed fellow with a glare that shot like lightning at anyone whose carping grew too loud.

"Hel-lo," Gustav whispered when he caught sight of him.

I said more than that, for I quickly recognized the Chinaman's companion—despite his having somehow grown a dark, droopy mustache in the span of four hours.

"Well, I'll be! It's good to see you again, Mr. Lockhart!"

The Chinaman slid into one of the empty seats just down from Miss Caveo, and Burl Lockhart paused next to the seat across from him. He stared at me a moment, either trying to remember me or decide if he *should.*

"You got me confused with somebody else," he finally said. "The name's Custos."

And he turned his back and took his seat.

"All aboard!" the conductor roared.

A whistle screamed. The car lurched.

The Pacific Express was under way.

Six

THE COLLYWOBBLES

Or, Our Journey Begins, and So Do Our Troubles

I turned to get my brother's reaction to "Custos," but he was no longer paying the man any mind. Gustav had his hands pressed against the window, and he was huffing out short, shallow breaths as the platform fell away and we moved into the train yard.

"You alright?" I asked.

"Sure," he rasped without taking his eyes off the switches, sidetracks, and freight cars we were passing. "It's just . . ." He swallowed hard, managing to stifle his panting. "I'll be fine."

"Well, if you ain't, let's do something about it—like get off the train."

Old Red's only reply this time was a growl. My gaze darted toward Miss Caveo—and found hers already fixed on *us*.

"Like I said, my brother's not feelin' well," I explained, "and the two of us don't ride trains much."

"So I gathered," she replied, a touch more cool than she'd been a minute before. "If I may ask, what brings you aboard the Pacific Express?"

I opened my mouth before giving any thought to what said mouth might say, and my jaw just dangled there when I realized I had no ready answer.

"Uhhh . . ."

"Business," my brother cut in, turning to face Miss Caveo. He couldn't quite manage to look her in the eye, so he addressed himself instead to the handbag in her lap. "Nothin' you'd find interestin', miss."

"Don't be so certain, Mr. Holmes. My interests are quite wide-ranging."

Hearing the lady address him directly—and as "Mr. Holmes" no less—magnified my brother's bashfulness, and his gaze dropped so low it now appeared that he was deep in conversation with her shoes. As Gustav was unable to focus on anything above ankle level, Miss Caveo turned her attention back to me.

"What sort of business is it that takes you to California?"

I still had no answer. Fortunately, I didn't need one—a gangly kid at the far end of the car interrupted with a sudden, booming "Evenin', folks!"

He was wearing a blue uniform with buttons polished to a blinding shine, and set atop his head was a cap with the words NEWS AGENT engraved on a brass plate. He came bounding up the aisle as if his skinny legs were made of rubber, and I could hear whatever was in the shallow tray he carried rattling like rocks in a tin can.

"Your news butcher has arrived!" he announced. "Ice water, ice cream, hard candies, toiletries, every quality magazine known to man and a select few that aren't! If you need it, he's got it! Just call for Kip and quick as a whip he'll have you equipped! No lip, no gyps, so bring on the tips!"

Kip stopped beside our seats and turned to us with a friendly grin. His smile grew even wider when he got a good look at me and my brother, and I had a notion as to why. The news butch was perhaps fourteen or fifteen, not quite old enough to have abandoned the romantic notion that cowboys are carefree paladins of the range living lives of derring-do and high adventure. In actuality, of course, cowboys are careworn drifters living lives of backbreaking labor and low pay, but just try telling that to a kid once he's read an issue of *Deadwood Dick Library*.

"Samuel tells me one of you gents has a sour stomach," Kip said. "Anything I can do?"

I shrugged. "Not unless you got something to cure pigheadedness. Cuz that's the real problem, if you ask me."

"I'll be *fine*," Old Red grumbled.

"Don't worry, friend—nothin' to be ashamed of. Plenty of passengers get the collywobbles." Kip took a small paper bag out of his box and offered it to Gustav. "These might help. Peppermints. Folks swear by 'em. On the house."

My brother took the bag and muttered his thanks, though he made no move to dig out one of the candies.

"You wouldn't happen to have the new *Harper's*, would you?" he asked.

"What kind of news butch would I be if I didn't?" Kip shuffled through his wares and quickly produced a magazine. "Twenty cents, please."

"*Twenty cents?*"

"You should've asked before the train left the station," Kip said. "Back then it was only twelve."

"What'll it be when we're up in the Sierras?" I asked. "A buck?"

"Oh, I don't bother sellin' magazines past Reno," the kid told me. "Unless there's a Rockefeller aboard, nobody can afford 'em."

While Kip and I bantered, Old Red dug out a couple dimes and slapped them onto the news butch's outstretched palm.

"I'll drop by later to see how those peppermints are workin' out," the kid said with a no-hard-feelings, business-is-business wink. He handed the magazine over and off he went, hollering enticements for rock candy, peanuts, and "edifyin' literature that just melts the miles away."

Doing some literary mile-melting was exactly what Gustav had in mind. He flipped through the magazine eagerly, then stabbed at a page with a pointed finger.

"There!"

My brother might be illiterate, but he isn't blind: He'd found a drawing of Sherlock Holmes alongside a new story by the great detective's amigo, Dr. Watson.

Miss Caveo leaned forward just enough to see what Old Red was pointing at.

"Sherlock Holmes?" She looked back up at my brother with obvious surprise—and not some little amusement. "You're an admirer?"

Gustav's face went as red as his hair.

"Yeah, I am," he mumbled.

Behind the lady, Burl Lockhart groaned out a sound halfway between a horse's whinny and the bleating of an angry goat. He was well within eavesdropping range, and I heard him murmur something about "that damned English nance."

"There ain't a detective alive who could hold a candle to Mr. Holmes," Old Red said, his voice kicking up a couple notches. For the first time, he managed to look the lady in the eye, but clearly he was really speaking to someone else. *"Not one."*

With another exasperated grunt, Lockhart threw himself to his feet and marched away up the aisle, leaving the Chinaman to turn and peer after him nervously.

"I admired Holmes, as well," Miss Caveo said to Gustav, ignoring Lockhart's grousing. "I doubt if we'll ever see his like again."

"Oh, I wouldn't be so sure about that," Old Red replied. Whether he was referring to his own deducifying or his hero's imminent return, I don't know. (Like a twelve-year-old who still refuses to accept there's no St. Nick, my brother pathetically clings to the notion that Holmes might not be dead, no matter what the rest of the world knows to be true.)

"He wasn't a relation of yours, was he?" a wide-eyed Miss Caveo asked, mock-shocked.

"A distant cousin," I joshed back. "Though I expect everyone in the world named Holmes makes the same claim."

The lady chuckled, then pointed at the magazine in Gustav's hands.

"So what's this new story about your cousin called?"

My brother didn't just blush this time—his face flushed so dark it seemed to bruise. He's touchy about his lack of letters, and admitting it in mixed company would surely shame him into silence for the next eight hundred miles.

I took a quick peek at the *Harper's*.

"'The Crooked Man.'" I shook my head at Old Red. "I can't believe you left your readin' specs back at the boardin'house. That's the third pair you lost this year."

It was a lie so lame there was nothing to do but put it out of its misery—which Gustav did by utterly ignoring it.

"Stow this away, would you?" he said feebly, closing the magazine and handing it to me. "I ain't up for it just now."

He slumped back into our seat, his face pointed at the window. There wasn't much to see out thataway—just scrubby desert flatland stretching off toward gray mountains. The windows across the aisle from us were where the real scenery would soon be seen. A distant blue shimmering had steadily been growing there, off to the southwest: the Great Salt Lake.

If Old Red had no interest in his magazine or what beauty there was to find outside, that was fine by me just then. It allowed me to focus all my attention on the beauty *inside*.

"Looks like we got us a mighty pretty view comin' up," I said to Miss Caveo.

"By the time we're through the Sierra Nevadas, Mr. Holmes, you'll be sick to death of pretty views," she replied pleasantly. If she'd been put off by my brother's moodiness, she didn't show it.

"So this ain't your first trip to California?"

"Hardly. I'm going home, actually."

"From Chicago?"

She nodded. "I went for the World's Congress of Representative

Women and then stayed on as a volunteer in the Women's Building at the Exposition. I stopped for a short visit in Salt Lake City on my way back—I just *had* to see the Tabernacle—and now—"

"Please pardon my intrusion, but I couldn't help overhearing," Horner said, and he leaned across the aisle and wedged himself into our conversation like a salesman's foot jammed into a closing door. "Do I take it, miss, that you're a suffragette?"

"You could call me that," Miss Caveo answered drily.

"Well, I have to admit I'm rather surprised," Horner said. "From what you see in the newspapers, you'd think all suffragettes were hatchet-faced man-haters. But you hardly seem to qualify on either count."

He grinned wolfishly.

Though I'd been happy to help the lady flaunt convention before, now I felt like a champion of propriety—whose duty it was to wipe the dirty smile off Horner's face. But the fair damsel didn't need me to strap on any shining armor.

"I don't hate men," Miss Caveo said. "Though I do find some extremely irritating. The presumptuous ones, in particular."

Horner laughed as if she'd just passed some private test of his.

"You lost that round, Mr. Horner," chuckled the middle-aged matron who'd taken the seat across from him. With her conservative, billowy black dress, high collar, and neatly pinned blond-gray hair, she was too old and obviously respectable for any snipings about unseemliness when she'd been seated alone with a man.

"Bravo," she said, turning her plump, pleasant face toward Miss Caveo. "I've rarely seen a fly shooed away with such grace. You might not believe it, but they used to buzz around *me* in great swarms. And if any of them proved as pesky as this rascal here, why, I just swatted them flat!"

She illustrated her point by giving the drummer's knee a playful smack with her black lace fan. Horner and Miss Caveo laughed, and that was that. The cozy duo I'd been hoping for was now a lively foursome. The lady (she introduced herself as Mrs. Ida Kier of San Francisco) proved to be every bit as gabby as Horner, and though the train made the occasional stop to take on coal and water as it rounded the Great Lake, the chatter never slowed.

Talk returned briefly to the suffragettes (Mrs. Kier being of the opinion that women had already proved their superiority to men by staying *out* of politics) before moving on to the Women's Building at the Exposition and finally the fair itself. Most of which left me in the dust, since I wasn't as well-read or worldly as my companions, nor had I visited the "White City" in Chicago. Thus I was relegated to the occasional folksy observation or attempted witticism, as when Horner brought up a speech that had apparently caused quite the stir at the Exposition the week before—some high-minded university type's declaration that the frontier was "closed" and the country's pioneer days behind it.

"If he wants to see some frontier, he should tag along with me and my brother sometime," I said. "The trails we ride sure as heck ain't paved with brick."

"I think the professor's remarks were more of an esoteric, metaphorical nature—as professors' remarks tend to be," Mrs. Kier replied, eyes twinkling. "He was talking about our spirit as a people. We're not just a nation of farmers and cattlemen anymore. We have great industries, great cities. We're changing."

"But not everyone welcomes change, Mrs. Kier." Miss Caveo cocked an eyebrow at Horner. "That's why suffragettes are made out to be 'hatchet-faced man-haters.'"

"Well, I'm with Otto," Horner said, dodging the lady's barb. "It's too early to talk about 'the frontier' like it's in a museum someplace." He pointed at the window on my side of the car—and the desolate expanse of sand beyond it. "That's wild out there, with wild people. It's not 'the Be-Polite Boys' we're all worried about, am I right? Barson and Welsh hit this very run two months ago—the Pacific Express!—and they're still on the loose. Until we reach Oakland, anything could happen. A barricade on the tracks, a loosened rail, dynamite. God forbid they should mess with a trestle. The way those crazy hayseeds hate the

S.P., I wouldn't put it past them to send an entire train crashing into—"

"Je-*zus* Key-*rist*!"

We'd all been paying Old Red about as much mind as the pile of coats in the corner at a Christmas barn dance, so his sudden—and ear-piercingly profane—entry into the conversation got a jump out of all of us. Without another word, he staggered to his feet and started stumbling down the aisle toward the back of the train.

I sat there a moment, stunned, before tossing out apologies and setting off after my brother. Curiously, I wasn't the only one on his trail: The Chinaman hopped up and got to hustling after him first.

The screaming started before either one of us could catch him.

Seven

CHAN

Or, A Doctor Offers a Helping Hand, but Lockhart Gives Him the Boot

ustav had veered left at the end of the aisle, just before the passageway to the next Pullman. We'd passed a lavatory there as Samuel showed us to our seats a couple hours before, and I'd noted something about it that my brother couldn't—the word written on the door.

LADIES.

So the first shrieks after Old Red went barging into the john (or should that be the "jane"?) were, as one would expect, distinctly feminine. They were quickly joined by a male counterpart, though: For once, my brother's fear of females was completely justified, and he screamed the scream of the freshly damned finding themselves in hell.

"Can't you read?" a woman shrieked as Old Red staggered out of the privy. A hand shot out after him, bringing a drawstring purse down over his head three times before he could back out of range. Then the hand disappeared, the door slammed shut, and my brother bolted from the car.

I followed him through the vestibule into the next sleeper—as did the Chinaman.

"Gustav!" I called after him.

He kept going.

"Mr. Holmes, wait, please," the Chinaman said.

Old Red stopped. And it wasn't just because the Chinaman had said "please." Gustav was still white-faced and wild-eyed when he turned around, but his curiosity was apparently enough to overcome his nausea and embarrassment.

"Yeah?"

"If I might have a word," the Chinaman said, stepping closer to my brother. "In private, perhaps?"

His gaze darted past Old Red, down the aisle—at the churchload of curious Presbyterians who were now gawking at us.

"Alright," Gustav said. "Over there."

He shuffled into a small, recessed nook next to another washroom nearby. This privy had a sign, too—GENTLEMEN. Old Red stopped just outside the door.

"What you got to say?"

"I couldn't help but notice your . . . discomfort, and I think I can be of assistance." The Chinaman's accent swallowed up a word here and there, but overall I understood him better than some Southerners and New England Yankees I've met. "Ginger can be quite effective in relieving motion sickness, and it just so happens that I—"

"I ain't in the market for no patent medicine," Gustav cut in brusquely. His urge to upchuck might have passed for the moment, but he looked sickened again in a wholly different way. "You can go peddle your tonics elsewhere."

"I'm not trying to sell you anything, Mr. Holmes," the Chinaman replied, slipping a hand into one of his coat pockets. "I'm a physician. Dr. Gee Woo Chan."

He spoke gently and moved slowly, the way a cowboy approaches an unbroken horse. When he pulled out his hand again, it was clutching a small, brown paper bag.

"I brought some ginger tea along. For myself. And I'd be happy to give you—"

"That's enough of that," a raspy voice snapped.

Burl Lockhart stepped from the washroom behind us. Rather than lightening his bladder's load while inside, however, he'd clearly been adding to it: When he spoke again, the nostril-singeing scent of cheap whiskey blasted into our faces like the heat from a blacksmith's forge. It's a wonder the man's floppy false mustache didn't burst into flame.

"Get back to your seat."

"But Mr. Holmes here is—," Chan began.

"Back to your seat."

Chan eyed the old Pinkerton a moment, then turned back to my brother and held out the bag of tea. "You really should try it."

"Thanks, Doc—maybe I will," Gustav said, sounding decidedly more friendly than before. But even as he took the bag from the Chinaman, his eyes were locked on Lockhart.

"Good day, gentlemen," Chan said, and he headed back toward our car, his back so straight he could've been a soldier on review. He might've been the uncivilized foreigner, as some folks reckon it, but to judge by manners, dress, and dignity of bearing, it was Lockhart, Old Red, and me who were the savages.

"Hey, 'Custos,'" Gustav said. "What gives you the right to boss the little feller around?"

"Hey, 'Holmes,'" Lockhart replied. "Mind your own goddamn business."

And with that, he left, too. Except he didn't follow Chan toward our sleeper. He spun on his heel and returned to the gent's. Before he got through the door, I saw him fishing something out of his pocket. I had the sneaking suspicion it *wasn't* ginger tea.

"Whadaya think that was all about?" I asked my brother.

He shook his head and sighed. "That's just the thing—I *can't* think right now. I gotta find somethin' that ain't"—he waved a hand at the dark wood that boxed us in—"*this.* Come on."

He turned and hustled away, heading down the aisle toward the back of the train.

On our way through the next Pullman, we discovered that Samuel had predicted correctly: An impromptu Presbyterian choir was indeed singing hymns. We escaped the sickly sweet strains of "Nearer, My God, to Thee" by hurrying into the dining car. Though the inviting aromas drifting from the kitchen reminded me that I hadn't eaten since breakfast, they seemed to remind Old Red that he was sick to his stomach. He picked up his pace, rushing on to the last car of the train: the observation lounge.

There wasn't much to observe there, at the moment. We'd left the Great Salt Lake behind, and the Great Salt Desert is hardly a feast for the eyes—it's more like an empty plate. Yet still the lounge was a popular place. There were passengers standing in nattering knots, bent over foldout tables absorbed in games of euchre and whist, and arrayed around the brightly upholstered, circular couch that dominated the center of the compartment.

Even on Gustav's most sociable days, this would have been more enclosed humanity than he'd happily subject himself to, and it didn't surprise me when he weaved his way through the throng to the very back of the car. There was a final door there—one that didn't lead to more train. Instead, it opened onto a small, brass-gated observation platform. Beyond that was nothing but track.

Old Red stepped out onto the platform, and I followed, closing the door behind me. Evening was coming on by then, and the rapidly cooling desert air rushed past so fast it felt like blustery October instead of the stagnant, stifling July it was.

We were alone.

"Yeah . . . this ain't so bad," Gustav said as he took in the view— dingy alkali sand, scruffy scrub brush, and distant peaks just starting to glow orange-pink with the last rays of the day. He didn't so much lean on the railing as prop himself up against it. "Maybe out here I can catch my breath."

"How'd it get away from you in the first place, that's what I wanna know."

My brother swatted at the air dismissively. "Oh, that mouthy drummer was just gettin' on my nerves with his blab about the Give-'em-Hell Boys and wreckin' trains and all."

"You were ailin' a long time before Horner opened his big yap."

"Yeah, I suppose. But it ain't nothing to worry about. I'm just—"

" 'Feelin' a touch poorly'? Let me tell ya, that's startin' to wear mighty thin . . . and it wasn't exactly thick to begin with."

"I said don't worry. I'm alright."

"Oh, sure. You're the very picture of health."

Color was returning to Old Red's pallid face, but it was the wrong kind. He wasn't going rosy-cheeked. He was turning green.

"Look, Brother," I said, "I know how you feel about detectivin' and all, but something's wrong here. Maybe that bullet you took's messin' with your innards again, I don't know. Whatever it is, you need to stop and take stock of yourself. You're sick as a dog with a damn Southern Pacific badge in your pocket. That can't sit right."

Gustav straightened up and looked me in the eye.

"It sits just *fine*."

At that exact moment, the train gave a powerful jerk, and the landscape around us tilted. We were moving down now, into the Humboldt Valley and Nevada, and the patchy sagebrush and grass of the desert were soon whipping by at a noticeably quicker clip.

The train's jostling pressed my brother back up against the rail—and squeezed a heave from his gut.

I offered Old Red a few pats on the back and soothing words as he spewed out onto the tracks. As soon as he could talk, though, we could squabble, and my tone quickly turned less than soothing. But just as we picked up our bickering again, a thumping clatter rose up underneath us, and something about the size and shape of a watermelon came caroming out from beneath the car.

Which brings us, dear reader, back to the door you stepped in through: Old Red and I were face-to-face with a man's head.

Having as I do a basic grasp of human physiology, what came next wasn't nearly so surprising. Heads, after all, are generally attached to bodies—and even when they're not, it's a safe bet you'll find a torso and limbs and such nearby.

The carcass Gustav and I spotted was rolling to a stop by the side of the tracks as we sped past.

"Sweet Jesus," I croaked. "You reckon we oughta—?"

But my brother had already done his reckoning: He was rushing into the observation car.

I'd only managed a couple steps after him when someone inside cried out, "Wait! That's the bell cord! What are you—?" And then I was hurtling through space and slamming into the doorway as the brakes clutched hold and the Pacific Express came screeching to a stop.

Eight

HEAD HUNTING

Or, We Go Looking for the Head and Almost Get Ours Shot Off

I checked my face for splinters as I got to my feet, but all I'd picked up from the doorway was a fat lip. A chorus of groans—like a barbershop quartet with a toothache—rose up from inside, and when I stepped into the observation car, I found most of its occupants piled atop each other on the floor.

"I'm terribly sorry, ma'am," my brother was murmuring as he hauled himself off Mrs. Kier, of all people. With her billowy skirts and matronly girth, she'd undoubtedly made a fine cushion when the brakes kicked in.

"No harm done," the lady replied, still clutching a fan of cards even though her companions, the folding table they'd been playing on, and the rest of the deck were now scattered willy-nilly around the car. "This isn't the first time a man's thrown himself at me. It's just never been so *literal* before."

Old Red helped her to her feet, then backed away quickly.

"Best fetch the conductor," he said to no one in particular. "We got a body on the tracks."

He hustled past me out the door—which was probably wise given the murderous glares being directed his way by our fellow passengers.

"I hope you won't mind my asking, Mr. Holmes—," someone said, and I spotted Miss Caveo crawling out from under a mortified porter, "but is your brother entirely *sane?*"

"Miss, if he's nuts, then it's contagious—cuz I saw that body, too." And I hurried off after Old Red.

He was already marching down the tracks, having opened a side gate in the railing and dropped to the ground. By the time I caught up to him, we were halfway to the body.

It was full-on dusk now, and the shadows around us seemed to grow longer with each step we took, swallowing up the smears of blood splattered on the rails and ties and sand. Dr. Watson himself had written of this place once, in *A Study in Scarlet,* and I couldn't take issue with his description of "the Great Alkali Plain": It was "an arid and repulsive desert," a "region of desolation and silence." Indeed, there wasn't a sound to be heard beyond that of our own footfalls, and I could easily have believed we were the only living creatures within a hundred miles.

There was certainly no life left in the man we soon came upon.

"Looks like he was a short feller, even with a head on his shoulders," Old Red said as we stopped by the body. "Powerful, though. Them muscles practically pop out of his shirt. And that's denim he's wearin'. He was a workin' man . . . but not a cowpoke or a farmer. Got store-bought lace-ups on his feet, not boots. Scuffed, but not muddy."

We'd practically sprinted to the corpse, but my brother seemed in no way winded as he rattled off his deductions. It was as if the chance to detectify was some kind of miracle cure—Holmes's Genuine All-Natural Anti-Collywobble Elixir—and to look at my brother you'd never have guessed this was a man with puke still on his breath.

He turned and gazed off to the east. The sky there was a purple-black wall, featureless save for a few dim pinpricks—the first stars of a nightfall rushing to overtake us.

The head was nowhere in sight.

When my brother turned around again, he locked eyes on something behind me.

"Bring lanterns!" he called to a small party approaching us from the Pacific Express. "We got some huntin' to do!"

After a brief consultation, one of the men—even from a distance I could see it was a tallish porter, probably Samuel—ran back toward the train. His three companions continued toward us. As they drew closer, I could make out who they were: the conductor, the engineer, and Burl Lockhart.

"Any of your bunch makes a move for the train, you'll have holes in your heads quick as lightnin'!" Lockhart shouted, bringing up his .44 and thumbing back the hammer.

"Ain't no 'bunch' here, Mr. Custos!" I yelled back. "Just two fellers with heads and one without—and not a one of us is packin' iron!"

The conductor was a big man who pumped his arms fast as he walked, and he looked for all the world like a locomotive chugging down the tracks, indifferent to what or who might be run over.

"Which one of you pulled the bell cord?" he barked at us.

"That'd be me," Gustav answered coolly. "Saw a body"—he nodded at the corpse—"*this* body—by the tracks. Saw the head, too. Came out from under the train and went bouncin' Lord knows where."

"Oh," Lockhart mumbled, chagrined, as he and his companions came to a stop a few yards away. He lowered his gun. "It's *you*."

In addition to possessing the world's worst false mustache, the old Pinkerton apparently had him some pretty crappy eyes, too.

"You know these men, Lockhart?" the conductor asked.

Old Red and I exchanged a quick glance: So Lockhart wasn't "incognito" anymore.

"Couple of drovers," Lockhart said. "Wanna be lawmen."

"What we *are*," Gustav said, addressing himself to the conductor as he fished out his badge, "is agents of the Southern Pacific Railroad Police."

My brother clearly imagined this revelation would buy him some respect. What he got instead was a roll of the eyes.

"Crowe's Folly blesses us again," the conductor groaned. "I wondered how trail trash like you could afford the Pacific Express."

The engineer was equally unimpressed. "Shit," he said, and he leaned over and spat in the dirt just as Samuel came hurrying up with two lit lanterns.

"Pussyfooters," the conductor explained, jerking his head at us.

"Well, well" was all Samuel said. Whatever his opinion of railroad police, he was keeping it to himself.

Gustav took one of the lanterns, and I helped him eyeball the scrub and sand on the north side of the tracks while Lockhart, Samuel, and the conductor moved down the south side. The engineer stayed rooted in place on the roadbed, muttering bitterly as the rest of us walked away slowly, heads down.

"Didn't see a thing from the cab. Must've been lying on the tracks. If he was alive when we hit him, well"—the engineer spat again, having to lean quite a ways forward to get the tobacco juice beyond the round curve of his boulderlike belly—"screw him. Man wants to die, he oughta just throw himself off a cliff and spare other folks a lot of bother. Could have been a hobo riding the blinds or the rods, I suppose. Slipped, fell. If so"—once again he spat—"serves the dumb bastard right."

All this callous grousing within literal spitting distance of a man's carcass got under my skin, and I was about to turn around and question just who the dumb bastard was around here when Gustav pointed at a low patch of brush to our left.

"There."

He lifted his lantern high, and the shadows around us shifted and shrank, revealing something round and moist up ahead.

"We found him!" I called out.

Samuel, Lockhart, and the conductor crossed the roadbed and joined us just as Old Red went down on his haunches and brought his lantern in close. The head was facedown in the sand, and all I could see of it was curly, black hair ripped away here and there to offer glimpses of glistening bone and brain. My brother stretched out his hand and rolled the head over, and we found ourselves looking into a young man's face, his eyes wide, his mouth open.

Which was exactly how I looked, for I'd seen this face before—and not just when it was bouncing from beneath the train. It belonged to the railroader I'd chatted with briefly back at Union Station, the one who'd told me to appreciate the magnificence of the Pacific Express before it was buried under dust and soot.

"Christ Almighty!" Samuel gasped. "Joe!"

"Joe?" Lockhart said.

The conductor turned his back on the gruesome sight and hunched over, clutching his knees.

"Pe-zul-lo," he panted, obviously struggling to keep his last meal from joining Gustav's in the sands of the Great Salt Desert. "Our baggageman."

The engineer finally unstuck himself and took a few uncertain steps toward us. "Wiltrout . . . did you just say that's . . . ?" He stopped next to the body. "*This* is Joe Pezullo?"

The conductor nodded weakly.

"So he wasn't lyin' on the rails," my brother said. "He was on the train."

The conductor—"Wiltrout," apparently—nodded again. "Riding in the baggage car."

What little light there was dimmed by half—Old Red had spun around and started back toward the Express, taking his lantern with him. Lockhart and I lit out after him, leaving Wiltrout, Samuel, and the engineer to reunite their compadre's head with his body.

When we reached the tail end of the train, we had to zigzag our way through a throng: Twenty or thirty male passengers had come outside to gawk. They pelted us with questions as we passed—"What's happening?" and "Is that really a body?" and "Are you robbing us?"—but we answered only with shouts of "Make way!" and "Comin' through!" There was no escaping the crowd, though, and a string of men trailed us like baby ducks waddling after their momma.

"Get back inside, you damned idjits!" Lockhart shouted over his shoulder. But everybody seemed to assume the "damned idjits" referred to everyone else, and no one broke off the chase.

When we finally reached the baggage car, we found the side door pushed all the way back, leaving an opening at least six feet across and seven feet high—more than enough space for a man to tumble through.

"Now how'd the engineer miss that when he walked to the back of the train?" Lockhart asked.

"Must've come down the other side," I suggested. I turned toward Gustav, assuming he'd want to weigh in, but my brother had already moved on to other questions.

"Kip," he said, and only then did I realize our young news butcher was amongst the mob behind us. "You know Joe Pezullo? The baggage-man?"

"Sure. He's a friend of mine." Kip started to move closer to the baggage car—and froze midstep. "Oh, jeez. That's Joe back there on the tracks, ain't it?"

Old Red stuck his lantern up into the car and moved it this way and that, its light playing over stacks of boxes, trunks, and bags—and a bottle sitting upright on the floor, uncorked and half-filled with amber liquid.

"Pezullo a drinkin' man?" my brother asked.

"I . . . I don't know," the news butch stammered, his voice quiet and quivery.

Gustav was staring at the bottle, Lockhart was using his .44 to menace shadows inside the car, and the passengers present simply stood around gawping like they were watching a sideshow geek tear into a chicken. Which left it to me to walk over and place a comforting hand on Kip's slender shoulder. He looked into my eyes, his own glistening in the dim light of the lantern, and nodded silent thanks.

"Hey!" a muffled voice cried out from somewhere nearby. "What's going on out there?"

"Now who in the hell is that?" Old Red asked, swinging his lantern around.

Lockhart pointed at the next car up. "It's comin' from the express car. Must be the Wells Fargo man."

"I think his name's Morrison," Kip said with a hint of a sniffle.

"Is there a door between the baggage car and the express car?" Gustav asked him.

"No, they ain't—," the kid began.

"Talk to me!" Morrison called to us again. "Who's out there?"

The panic in the fellow's voice was plain to hear—and easy to understand, given how many express messengers have been blown straight through the pearly gates by bandito dynamite the past few years. Unfortunately, a card in the crowd decided it was time to lighten the mood, and he called out a reply before a straight-thinking man could.

"It's me—Jesse James, back from the dead! And I'm here with my pals the Give-'em-Hell Boys!"

"Who said that?" Lockhart bellowed, turning on our audience and waving his gun. "So help me, I'll blow the fool's goddamn head off!"

Not wishing to see mortal harm done to even so irritating an acquaintance as Chester Q. Horner—for it had been the drummer's voice that had answered Morrison—I started to move between Lockhart and the crowd. But I'd barely taken two steps when there was a blast behind me, and my hat whipped off my head and sailed into the darkness. Within seconds, every man there had a face full of sand as we all went diving for cover.

"Don't come any closer!" Morrison hollered. "I'm armed!"

"We know!" I shouted back. I was sprawled on my belly, and I peeked up to see where the gunfire had come from.

There were two barred openings, too small to be called windows, beside the express car's side door. Pointing out of one was the barrel of a rifle.

"Don't shoot, Morrison!" Lockhart shouted. "We ain't outlaws! That was just some asshole's idea of a joke!"

"Why should I believe you?"

58

"It's me, Mr. Morrison! Kip Hickey!" the kid called out. "Trust me! We ain't bein' robbed!"

"They might have a gun to your head! They might be *making* you say that!"

"But they're not!" Kip yelled back.

"But they might be!"

"But they're *not!*"

"But they *might be!*"

As the debate raged on, I peeked around to see what had become of my brother. He'd found the safest spot of all: underneath the train, directly below the baggage car door. He still had the lantern with him, and its light created eerie, oily shadows amongst the bars and boards beneath the Pacific Express.

A long, lumpy silhouette stood out from all the rest. It was stretched out on some of the rods under the car, behind Old Red. I blinked my eyes, hoping they'd come to their senses, but they insisted on seeing what they saw: the outline of a man.

"Holy shit, Gustav . . . I think there's another body stuck up under there."

But I was wrong. It wasn't a corpse. It was a living, breathing man, and he dropped down onto the tracks before my brother could turn around.

Nine

EL NUMERO UNO

Or, A Crowned Sovereign Lands in a Royal Mess

There was a thud, and Gustav came flying out from under the train. His lantern spun from his grip, throwing wild flashes of light into the night before cracking Lockhart full on in the face. It was only by a miracle the lamp didn't bust open and cover the Pinkerton in burning oil, lighting up his head like the tip of a six-foot match.

"Ow!" howled Lockhart.

"What was that?" yelled Morrison.

"Somebody *kicked* me," grumbled Old Red.

"There's a man under the train!" hollered I.

Bang! said Morrison's rifle.

"Eyaaah!" screamed just about everybody else.

The only person who *didn't* have anything to say was whoever'd put the boot to my brother. With the lantern doused, all I could see of him was a hunched, shuffling shape, but it was clear where that shape was headed—over to the other side of the train. Once he got out from beneath the car, he'd have no trouble losing himself in the desert's black expanse.

"There he goes!" I shouted. "Stop him!"

Nobody near me was in any position to give chase, however, as a fellow's hardly at his speediest when he's flat on his stomach with his hands over his head. So Lockhart opted to do his chasing with a bullet, raising his .44 and pointing it at the underside of the car—and more or less at *me*.

Not only was I uncomfortably close to the line of fire, I wouldn't have trusted the old Pinkerton's aim at high noon, let alone in the dark of night. And even if he did manage to miss me, there was plenty of metal nearby—wheels, rails, rods—that could easily ricochet his shot through the wrong skull.

"Uhhh, Mr. Lockhart—," I began.

But there was no time for talk. Gustav was closer to him, and he simply reached out and twisted the gun from the man's grip.

Lockhart gaped at him a moment before his shock gave way to fury.

"You stupid son of a—"

He was interrupted by an *oof* and a heavy thump from the other side of the train.

"Hey!" I called into the blackness. "Is somebody over there? Did you catch him?"

"I got him," a deep voice replied. "What's goin' on over *there*?"

"The express messenger's takin' potshots at us!"

"Oh, for Christ's sake. *Morrison!* It's Bedford! The fireman! Get your finger off the trigger 'fore you hurt somebody!"

"But we're being robbed!" Morrison yelled back. "Aren't we?"

"This ain't no robbery! A circus is what it is! Now just get ahold of yourself, would you?"

"Well . . . alright," Morrison said weakly. "But I'm still not opening the door."

The rifle slowly slid back into its slot and disappeared.

As the men scattered around outside began pushing themselves to their feet, an unexpected sound arose with them: laughter. The passengers were just gray outlines there in the gloom, but I'd seen them well enough on the train. They were tradesmen and merchants, comfortable men headed home to comfortable lives. No wonder they were chuckling and chattering like it was intermission at a Wild West show. This *was* a show to them. They hadn't seen enough death to know better.

I suppose a gunfight would've been the perfect capper to the evening as far as they were concerned, and Burl Lockhart seemed ready to oblige. He snatched his gun back from my brother as the both of them stood up.

"Don't you *ever* get in my way again."

He stepped even closer to Gustav, literally going toe-to-toe with him. The blow he'd taken from the lantern had knocked his mustache so askew, one end was practically poking him in the eye, yet there was nothing even remotely funny about it—not if you could see the bitter scowl on his bony face.

"Fine," Old Red said. "Next time you wanna do a damn fool thing, I'll just stand aside and let you."

"Why, you cocky little—"

"Say, fellers," I said, somehow managing to squeeze my not insubstantial bulk between them, "let's go see who that was under the train, huh?"

I turned to drag Gustav away, but there was no need. A party with another lantern was rounding the locomotive, and both Lockhart and Old Red hurried toward the light, moving side by side like a couple thoroughbreds in a dead heat.

It was Wiltrout, the conductor, with the lantern. Behind him was the engineer and a muscle-bound Negro in soot-stained overalls—the train's fireman, by the look of him. But it wasn't a coal shovel the Negro was hefting now. He was dragging along a heavily bearded fellow in clothes so tattered it looked like he'd dressed himself in old mops. The tramp tried to dig in his heels, yet that didn't slow the Negro one jot, and the man's flap-soled shoes merely plowed up twin furrows in the sand.

"Unhand me, you great brute!" the hobo commanded, his voice surprisingly deep, his diction highfalutin. He even rolled his *r*'s. "Have you no respect for royalty?"

"Anybody hurt here?" Wiltrout asked us, ignoring the tramp's protests.

After a moment of head shakings and mumbled noes, the conductor turned toward the express car.

"I'll have a word with you later, Morrison," he said sternly.

I couldn't be sure, but I thought I heard a whimper rise up from inside the car.

"Now." Wiltrout faced us again and jerked his head at the Negro. "Bedford here says this little yegg crawled out from under one of the cars. Anybody see where he came from?"

"I did." I pointed at the baggage car. "He was tucked away under there."

While Wiltrout walked to the baggage car and shined his lantern underneath, Bedford and the engineer turned suspicious glares on their prisoner, the both of them practically growling and baring their teeth.

"He was riding the rods, alright," the conductor announced, leaning in to inspect the undercarriage. "His bindle's still here. When'd you get on, 'bo? When we took on water at Wells? Or was it Promontory?"

With a sudden twist of his shoulders, the tramp freed himself from Bedford's clutches. But rather than flee, he began brushing off his ragged clothes with leisurely, exaggerated dignity. The dust flew from him in great billowing clouds that swirled like smoke in the lamplight, and he ended by giving his beard a shake that turned it from ash white to coal black.

"I embark and disembark where I please," he said when he was through preening. "The particulars are no concern of yours."

"Is that a fact?" Wiltrout said coldly. He turned to the crowd with a stuffed and mounted smile on his face. "Alright, folks. Everything's under control. Return to your seats. We'll be under way shortly."

"Oh, no, you don't—I know what you're up to!" the tramp jeered at him. "Hustling away the witnesses so you can beat the helpless 'bo into a false confession. Well, it won't work." He took a step forward and spread his arms wide. "Ladies and gentlemen! Hear my words! I am

El Numero Uno, King of the Hoboes—and I had nothing to do with that man's death!"

This pronouncement landed amidst the passengers like an anvil in a pond, and a wave of excited jabber rose up and swept across the crowd.

"There won't be no beatin's," my brother assured the hobo. "Just a proper investigation."

Lockhart coughed out a mocking guffaw.

"All anyone needs to 'investigate' are the stains on this filthy yegg's clothes," Wiltrout said, moving his lantern closer to El Numero Uno. "Fresh blood."

The passengers' babblings turned to gasps. Forget Buffalo Bill—old Will Shakespeare himself couldn't have put on a better show.

"Of course, I was splattered with some blood!" the King of the Hoboes protested. "The man got caught in the gears not four feet from me. Why, I saw his head plucked from his neck like a grape off the vine. But that's all I did. *See.* He fell off the train with no help from me."

"You expect us to believe you? A dirty bum?" Kip wailed, his eyes wide and wet. He aimed a finger at the hobo like the barrel of a gun. "You killed Joe! You killed my *friend*!"

"I'm sorry, kid," Old Red said, giving his head a slow, sorrowful shake. "But the data don't back that up."

" 'Data'?" Lockhart sneered.

"Facts." Gustav pointed at the baggage car. "This El Numero Uno feller was tucked away under there, right? So tell me how he could swing up to the side of the car, open the door from the outside, kill the baggageman, and swing back down again without gettin' chopped to mincemeat himself? And if you can give me all that *how,* then I'll just ask you for a single good *why.*"

What Lockhart gave him instead was a tremendous raspberry. (It's entirely possible the Pinkerton produced the sound via another method—it was so dark out there I couldn't say for certain. Nevertheless, I'm giving him the benefit of the doubt in this account.)

"The how *and* the why of it are plain as day," he said. "The King of the Riffraff there didn't start out ridin' the rods. He sneaked inside with the baggage before we left the station. The baggageman found him and got knifed for his trouble, and the tramp pushed him out the side door. When the train stopped, El Assholio Grande knew someone had spotted the body, and he needed a new place to hide. So he ducked up under the car."

There was a flurry of motion through our audience—two dozen satisfied nods. The crowd hadn't gotten a gunfight, but it was seeing a duel, and just then Lockhart looked to be the winner.

"Poppycock!" El Numero Uno blurted out. "I never stepped foot inside that—"

Bedford clapped one of his big hands on the tramp's arm and gave him a jerk that sent a puff of dust into the air.

"Shut up, you," the Negro snapped.

"Hel-lo," Old Red mumbled, his spine snapping up straight. Then, louder: "Hey, Bedford—do that again."

"Do what again?"

"Give him a good shake."

Bedford looked bewildered, but he wasn't going to pass up another chance to beat out the hobo like a dirty rug. He yanked the man left and right, and so much dust went billowing off him that Wiltrout and the engineer started coughing. Seeing as a fireman like Bedford needs the muscle to shovel a ton of coal a day into a white-hot furnace, El Numero Uno was lucky his arms and legs didn't go flying off, too. Not that he looked particularly grateful.

"*Stop* this *at* once, *you* black *devil!*" he protested, his words fading in and out as Bedford snapped him like a bullwhip.

"Thank you, that'll do," my brother said.

The fireman let El Numero Uno go.

"Barbarians," the tramp spat as he set about straightening his rags again.

"Tell me, Bedford," Old Red said, "did you bread El Numero Uno after you caught him?"

"*Bread?*"

65

"You know—roll him in flour for fryin'. Cuz if you didn't, I'd have to say that's *dust* the man's coated in head to foot. And if it is dust, well . . . where did it come from?"

Bedford and his fellow railroaders responded with mere glares, leaving it to their prisoner to offer the answer.

"From riding under the train!" El Numero Uno shouted out like a "Hallelujah!" He laughed and ran his fingers roughly through his hair, sending out yet another cloud of dust. "Yes, indeed! Ride the rods through the Great Salt Desert and you'll look like you've been bathing in talcum. You'll end up looking like *me*!"

"Please," Lockhart snorted. "So he's dirty. So what? The man's a goddamn bum."

"It *had* to be him," Kip blurted out, practically sobbing. "There's no other—"

"Enough!" Wiltrout roared. He hoisted his lantern high over his conductor's cap, and suddenly he seemed a foot taller. "The Southern Pacific has a schedule to maintain, and we're late enough as it is. Everyone—back aboard!"

"Hold on," Gustav said. "I need to do some more clue-huntin' before—"

"*Now!*" Wiltrout bellowed. When he spoke again, he wasn't talking *to* my brother so much as *through* him. "We're less than ninety minutes from Carlin, Nevada. It'll be up to the law there to sort all this out."

"What about him?" Bedford asked, jerking a thumb at El Numero Uno.

"We'll keep him in the baggage car till we reach town." Wiltrout shifted his gaze back to my brother and me. "I suppose I'd be hoping for too much if I were to ask if you brought handcuffs with you?"

"You most certainly would," I said.

The conductor looked disgusted but unsurprised. "How about you Lockhart?"

The name sent yet more murmurs through the crowd.

"I told you it was him," a fellow nearby said.

"I didn't think he'd look so *old,*" his friend replied.

66

If Lockhart heard them—and he'd have to have been deaf not to—he didn't let on.

"Just get me some rope, and I'll take care of the son of a bitch."

El Numero Uno shuffle-stepped backward until he was stopped by Bedford's brick wall of a chest.

"Keep him away from me!"

Lockhart grinned. "What I meant to say is, 'I can tie him up for you.'"

The King of the Hoboes wasn't put at ease by this rephrasing, yet it hardly mattered. Bedford clamped down on him, dragged him to the baggage car, and tossed him inside like he was little more than a carpetbag stuffed with feathers. Then the brawny fireman hopped up into the car and reached down for Lockhart. After he'd hauled the old Pinkerton up next to him, he shut the side door with a thunderous slam.

"Anyone who doesn't wish to be left here should return to his seat at once," Wiltrout announced in a tone of voice that suggested he not only wasn't joking, he'd enjoy the chance to prove it.

As everyone else scurried toward the Pullmans, my brother headed in the opposite direction, toward Wiltrout.

"Listen, all I need's two minutes to look for—"

"*All aboard!*" Wiltrout bellowed straight into Old Red's face.

Gustav stood there, wiping spittle from his cheeks, as the conductor stomped away.

"I think that meant no," I said.

"Undoubtedly," said someone behind us—someone who shouldn't have been anywhere near us, given that mingling with a mob's not the sort of thing a lady does, no matter how "modern" her sensibilities might be.

"I'm afraid it also means our conductor isn't very fond of you, Mr. Holmes," Miss Caveo said as I spun around to face her. She was drifting back toward the Pullman with Chester Q. Horner at her side.

"Well," Old Red said, his gaze suddenly so downcast it almost looked like his eyes were closed, "it ain't my job to be liked."

"You can thank God for that," I said to him.

"Now, Otto—show some respect," Miss Caveo scolded. "That was quite a display of ratiocination your brother put on. I daresay your late 'cousin' would've been proud."

"That's right," Horner threw in. Then he leaned in closer to the lady and added, "It's just too bad the man can't *deduce* the difference between the ladies' room and the gents'."

He was snickering at his own funny as he helped Miss Caveo up the steps into the car.

"Why a gal like that would be within a mile of a jackass like him . . ." I grumbled, shaking my head.

"Women," Old Red said, as if this one word solved a multitude of mysteries. "The real question is what the hell was she doin' out here in the first place?"

I shrugged. "She's adventurous."

My brother sighed in a sad, long-suffering sort of way, though I couldn't tell if it was my thickheadedness causing the suffering or something else entirely. The last of the passengers had just reboarded the train, and the time had come either to hop back on ourselves or spend a very long, very cold, very dry night in the desert.

Gustav almost seemed to be thinking it over. He closed his eyes and took in a deep breath, holding the cool night air in his lungs for a moment before letting it go.

Then his eyes popped wide, and he marched back to the Pacific Express on legs that looked about as steady as jelly.

Ten

BLACK CURTAINS

Or, The Passengers Get Ready for Bed As Gustav Goes to Work

he train's porters hadn't been lollygagging while the rest of us worked our jawbones outside. In our absence, the sleeper cars had been transformed. Where once had been rows of well-cushioned settees was now a narrow passage hemmed in on either side by dark, velvet draperies. Behind these curtains were our beds—pulled down from ceiling cabinets in the case of the upper berths, folded together from our seats for the lower.

It was a jarring sight to return to. What had seemed like a long sitting room when we'd left now had the cramped, clammy feel of a mausoleum.

But the real tomb was up ahead of our Pullman, in the baggage car. Word quickly spread that porters had deposited the baggageman's body there . . . stuffed in a stewpot from the dining-car kitchen.

Oh, that's bunk, I almost replied upon hearing this from Horner, who relayed it with the eyebrow-waggling leer men usually reserve for off-color jokes. *The body was banged up, sure, but you couldn't squeeze it into no pot. You'd need at least a washtub.*

I held my tongue out of deference to the ladies milling about nearby. The Pacific Express was under way again, and our fellow passengers were preparing for bed. As a result, a steady stream of females pressed past us, either going to or coming from the women's washroom Gustav had so briefly toured earlier that day.

Pullman travel, it turned out, had a side benefit of which I hadn't been aware—a relaxation of the normal rules of decorum. Most of the ladies were attired only in their nightgowns and perhaps a flimsy robe or wrap, and I had to be careful to conceal the degree to which I found such sights distracting.

My brother was unable to pull off such a masquerade himself. In fact, he was quite obviously mortified, and he shuffled up the aisle sideways, his face pressed into the drapes and his hands plastered to his sides lest they accidentally brush against female flesh.

He was headed for the privy at the front end of the car—the *men's* privy, he was careful to confirm—and I'd been instructed to follow once I'd recovered our carpetbag from our berth. It was hard to escape from Horner once he got his lips up to a gallop, though.

"I'll bet this is it for the Pacific Express," the drummer was saying. "It's supposed to keep on through October, when the Exposition ends, but I don't see that happening. The Give-'em-Hell Boys hit the very first run back in May, and now a drifter murders one of the crew? When word gets out, you won't be able to *pay* people to take the Express."

"I wouldn't be so sure," Mrs. Kier said. She was still in her day clothes, having been roped into conversation with Horner before she could flee to the WC. "After all, what some consider 'danger,' others consider 'excitement.' I don't think one robbery and one unfortunate death are going to scare many customers away. Just look at me. I was on that first run to Chicago myself—I saw Barson and Welsh with my own eyes. And I came back."

I didn't think Horner's mouth could open any wider, but his jaw dropped so low I could've rolled a doughnut down his throat.

"*You* were on the Express when . . . oh, pardon us, Miss Caveo. Do you have room to get through?"

I had to fight to keep my gaze at eye level as the lady joined us. I could see enough of her shoulders to know she was in sleeping attire of a frilly, lacy design, and the urge to peek lower was difficult indeed to resist.

The three of us stepped back to let her maneuver into her bed (though I couldn't help noticing that Horner didn't give her quite the leeway Mrs. Kier and I did). But rather than retreat behind the curtains of her berth, Miss Caveo lingered in the passageway.

"Reviewing the day's excitement, are we?"

"That's right, miss," I said. "We ain't covered much you don't know, though, seein' as you were outside for a lot of it yourself."

"I hope you're not about to tell me that was no place for a lady." She was smiling as she spoke, but it was the kind of smile a man learns not to trifle with if he wants to stay in a woman's good graces.

"Oh, no. I'm simply relieved you didn't come to any harm, what with all those bullets whizzin' about."

"Mr. Horner here was concerned, as well. When the gunfire started, he threw himself right on top of me. Shielded me with his own body."

Horner pressed his hands to his heart and offered a bow as deep as the crowded corridor would permit. "Any gentleman would have done the same."

"Truly, chivalry is not dead," Miss Caveo said drily.

"Truly," Mrs. Kier agreed, and the two women shared a little smirk.

"You and your brother were in the thick of things yourselves," Miss Caveo said, turning to me.

"Gustav likes it thick, alright."

"In an occupational capacity?" Mrs. Kier asked. "Or more as a hobby?"

"Yeah, what's the story with you two?" Horner threw in.

I found myself surrounded by quizzical stares. I was still hunting for an escape (which is to say, a decent lie) when a familiar voice barked out, "Otto!"

I turned to see Old Red up at the far end of the car, looking peeved.

"You'll have to excuse me, folks—I hear my mother callin' me."

I pulled back the curtain to our berth, snatched our carpetbag off the bunk, and hustled away up the aisle. Before I got out of earshot, I heard Horner steer the conversation back to Mrs. Kier's encounter with the Give-'em-Hell Boys. He seemed quite insistent that Miss Caveo stay to hear the tale with him—most likely to keep the scantily clad young lady from disappearing into her berth.

As I neared the end of the corridor, I was stopped by a waist-high roadblock in matching nightshirts: the twin boys I'd seen boarding the train with a widow woman that afternoon. They were cute enough as kids go—perhaps six years old, chipmunk-cheeked and wide-eyed, with such voluminous golden curls they could have been hiding slingshots and frogs in their hair with their mother none the wiser.

"What's your name?" one of them asked me.

"Otto. But my friends call me Big Red. What are your names?"

"Oh," said one twin.

"Oh," said the other.

The boys glanced at each other, looking disappointed.

"I'm Marlin. He's Harlan," said the one who'd spoken first.

"We heard Burl Lockhart was on the train," his brother added. "We thought it might be you."

"Thanks, boys. That's quite an honor. But I ain't no Pinkerton." I brought up a thumb and waggled it at the corridor behind me. "You heard right about Lockhart, though. He's right back there—the feller with a checked suit and a head of hair that looks like a coonskin cap." I leaned down and dropped my voice to a whisper. "He's in disguise, you understand. Calls himself Chester Q. Horner. But I bet you could get him to bring out his six-guns if you asked him enough times."

"Oh, boy!" said Marlin.

"Come on!" said Harlan.

They squirmed around me and darted off down the aisle.

"I was startin' to think you'd fallen through the floorboards," Gustav said as I walked up. He was at the end of the line for the washroom, but he would've surely been excused had he cut to the front, so pale and wet with sweat was he. The collywobbles were back.

When he saw how I was eyeing him, he quickly turned toward the next fellow in line—the Chinaman.

"You two weren't really introduced properlike before, were you? Dr. Chan, this here's my brother Otto."

"Howdy, Doc."

I was expecting a bow, which I would return, giving us the opportunity to knock heads as the minstrel-type Chinamen in music-hall revues invariably do. But instead Dr. Chan held out his hand, and we shook. He wore no pigtail (or queue, as the Chinese call it), and from what he did wear—dark suit, wire-rimmed spectacles, shoes polished to a diamond shine—it would have been easy to mistake him for an upper-crust plutocrat with a lineage traceable to the *Mayflower* itself, as long as you weren't looking him in the eye.

"Pleased to meet you," Chan said, and it sounded like he meant it. When you're the only Oriental amidst a trainload of white folks, you probably appreciate anyone with the courtesy to speak to you, let alone shake your hand. "I was just telling your brother about some other remedies I know of for—"

"Yeah, yeah—thanks, Doc," Gustav cut in. He nodded at a doorway just a few feet off. Beyond it was the forward vestibule and, beyond that, the baggage car. "So . . . I ain't seen your pal Lockhart come outta there yet."

Chan stiffened. "That's right. He's still in there," he said reluctantly, as if my brother had brought up a topic decorum would have us ignore. "And how is it *you* know Mr. Lockhart?"

"Oh, I suppose you might call him a colleague," Old Red replied, brushing the question off as easily as lint from his sleeve. "You comin' from Chicago?"

73

"Yes," Chan said, still wary. "I spent the spring there preparing for the Columbian Exposition. Perhaps you've heard of 'the Joss House'? The Chinese exhibit?"

Gustav and I nodded. I'd been reading out newspaper and magazine accounts of the Exposition for months, and both Horner and Mrs. Kier had mentioned visiting the fair's magnificent Chinese temple.

"I'm one of the organizers," Chan said, pride seeping through his caution. "I had planned to spend the summer overseeing the exhibit's operations. Unfortunately, a private matter of some urgency has called me back to San Francisco."

"But you didn't meet up with Lockhart till Ogden."

"That's true," Chan said slowly, looking unsettled to find my brother so well acquainted with his travel plans. "Another *colleague* of his accompanied me there from Chicago. Mr. Lockhart is my companion for the rest of the journey."

"I see," Old Red said.

And I thought I saw, too. The railroads may have been built largely upon the back of the Chinaman, yet for a Chinaman to ride upon the railroads was another matter entirely. In fact, the Express would be passing through many a town where the killing of an uppity "yellow devil" would be viewed as an altogether laudable public service.

Gustav and I hadn't been raised to harbor such hatreds ourselves, as our parents came from fiery abolitionist stock and wouldn't brook any talk of the supposed superiority or inferiority of this, that, or the other bloodline. (Though, for reasons we never learned, our dear old *Mutter* did possess a powerful prejudice against the race of men known as "Texans.")

Still, you don't have to feel something in your heart to understand it in your head, and I knew a Chinaman with a need for haste and a pocketful of cash would have but one way to go: Hire the Pinkertons to smooth the way and keep it smooth.

"Well, best of luck to you with that 'urgent matter,'" Gustav said. "I just got one more question for you before we go."

" 'Go'?" I said, unaware that my brother and I were going anywhere other than the privy and, from there, directly to bed.

"Did you happen to see anyone come through that door right before the brakes kicked in?" Old Red asked Chan, nodding at the passageway to the baggage compartment again. "Or right after, maybe?"

Chan shrugged. "No—I wasn't looking this way. Before we stopped, I was reading. Afterwards, I was looking out the window for bandits like everyone else."

"How 'bout Lockhart? Was he back in his seat when the train stopped?"

Chan frowned, and for a second I thought he'd finally lost his patience with my brother's prying. But when he spoke, I realized it wasn't Gustav he was pissed at.

"No. Mr. Lockhart was still gone."

"You don't say," Old Red said . . . and said no more himself. He just stared at Chan, glassy-eyed, as if the Chinaman had hypnotized him.

" 'Go'?" I said.

That broke the spell.

"Thank you, Doc," Gustav said. "Good night."

"Mr. Holmes . . . may I ask *you* something?" Chan didn't wait for permission—he fired off his question, quick and nervous. "What is your interest in the matter?"

"Well . . . I guess that bush has been beat around enough, ain't it?"

Old Red had pocketed his badge after flashing it out on the tracks a while before, and now he took it out again—and pinned it to his vest. He gave me a nod that said I should do likewise.

"We're railroad detectives," he said with a touch too much self-satisfaction for my taste.

I set down our carpetbag and pulled out my own badge, coughing gently as I affixed the copper star to my shirt.

"Upside down," I whispered.

Scowling, Old Red looked at his chest and began fumbling with his badge.

75

"Alright," he growled once he had it right-side up, "let's go."

"Go?" I asked yet again.

"To work," Old Red finally answered.

He snatched up our bag and stomped off. I gave a rather stunned-looking Chan a hurried good-night, then followed my brother.

"Close that door behind you," Gustav said as we stepped into the vestibule leading to the baggage car. He put our carpetbag on the floor, crouched down over it, and started rummaging through our things.

When he stood up again, he was holding his gun.

Eleven

MESSAGE IN A BOTTLE

Or, My Theory About Pezullo Just Doesn't Stand Up

Did you spot a bear back here or somethin'?" I asked as my brother strapped on his holster. "Cuz I have no idea why you'd need to be packin' iron just now."

"You wanna be treated like a lawman, you gotta look like a lawman. Get yourself heeled."

Gustav nudged our carpetbag toward me with his toe.

I nudged it back. "Who says I wanna be treated like a lawman?"

"Fine." Old Red waved a hand at me as if he was excusing an unruly child from the dinner table. "You just go to bed or smooth-talk the ladies or whatever it is you think's more important than *a goddamn murder*. I'll handle this by myself."

"Brother, from the looks of you, you can hardly *handle* standin' up just now. For Christ's sake, get some rest."

"I'll rest when it's time to rest—not when we got us a killer to catch."

I sighed. "Do you know how much I hate it when you start talkin' like a dime novel?"

"Not half as much as *I* hate it when *you* won't get off your big butt and—"

"Alright, alright," I said, throwing up my hands to call for a truce. "Enough bickerin'. Let's just stop for a second and talk this out Holmes-style. I ain't had much time to think on it, but it don't take much thinkin', as I see it: Your 'killer' ain't nothin' but a bottle of whiskey."

My brother greeted this (to my mind) dramatic pronouncement with nothing more than slightly raised eyebrows and a look of strained forbearance.

"There was a bottle in the baggage car, remember?" I forged on. "Right by the side door. Well, that deducifies up pretty plain. Half-empty bottle, completely drunk baggageman. That Pezullo feller probably opened the side door to take a piss or get some fresh air or make like you and do some pukin', and—*whoopee!* The train does a shimmy and he goes flyin'. Ain't no mystery to it, really. So what does that leave for us to do? Hang the bottle?"

Old Red shook his head. Not to answer my question, mind you—more to register his weary disappointment with everything I'd just said.

" 'Whoopee,' huh?"

I shrugged. "Why not?"

"Because that bottle was upright when we found it, that's why not."

Gustav stared at me a moment, waiting to hear something I didn't know to say.

"How is it," he finally said when it was clear he'd get nothing from me but a blank look, "that this train could brake so hard the passengers end up on their asses, yet a half-empty bottle sittin' by an open side door not only doesn't roll out, it doesn't even fall over?"

"Oh," I said. "Damn."

Someone had put the bottle there *after* the train stopped. And the only reason they'd have for doing that was to lead lunkheads like me to a false assumption.

Without another word, I squatted down and fished my Colt from our bag.

" 'Ain't no mystery to it,' " my brother grumbled as I hitched up my holster. "Feh."

When I was ready, he turned and gave the door handle a twist. Or tried to, I should say. The door to the baggage car was locked.

"Shit . . . and I ain't got any pickin' wire on me," Gustav said.

"We can't just knock?"

"Best we don't announce ourselves."

Old Red tried the handle again, as if it might have taken a shine to us in the last few seconds and unlocked itself. It hadn't.

"Trouble, gents?"

We turned to find Kip joining us in the vestibule. At the sight of our badges and guns, he let loose a low whistle.

"So . . . you really are railroad dicks."

He looked impressed—and I felt embarrassed. The badge on my chest seemed silly, childish, like a costume party getup. Wearing it would take some getting used to.

"You tryin' to get into the baggage car?" the news butch asked.

"Yup. O-fficial business," Old Red answered. He wasn't embarrassed in the slightest.

"I can let you in." Kip put down his box of gimcracks and started fishing around in his pockets. "I keep all my merchandise in the baggage car, so I've got a passkey."

Gustav's eyes took on such a shine they practically glowed like hot coals. "A passkey? Like a skeleton key?"

"Yessir. Everyone in the crew gets one. It'll open any door on the train."

"Everyone in the crew, huh?" Old Red mumbled, the fire in his eyes dimming to a smolder as he drifted off into one of his dreamy trances.

"Don't worry," I said to Kip. "He'll snap out of it in a minute or two. If he don't, we can just throw a blanket over his head and come back for him in the mornin'."

Kip gave me a small smile, but it wilted quick. He'd gone through every one of his pockets, and now he was starting over again.

"Where'd that little bugger go?"

"You can't find your key?" my brother asked, blinking his way from his stupor.

The butch gave his trouser pockets one last, irritated smack. "It's gone."

"When'd you last use it?"

Kip shrugged. "A while ago. I came up to get a special package for that drummer—the one seated across from you two. He asked for something I don't carry around with me when I'm workin' the aisles. A Parisian novelty. For discreet gentlemen only." He clucked his tongue and gave us a wink. The kid was sixteen at most, but he already fancied himself a worldly sport.

"This was before the train stopped," Old Red said.

"Yeah."

"Is there any chance he might've—?"

Suddenly, all the talk about a key seemed beside the point, for the door to the baggage car came swinging open.

"Alright, then. I'll—," Wiltrout was saying over his shoulder as he stepped into the vestibule.

The conductor's words turned into a grunt as he collided with my brother.

"What do you want, 'Holmes'?" he sneered when he saw who'd just bumped off his belly. He drizzled so much acid over the "Holmes" his tongue should've sizzled and melted.

"To do our jobs," Old Red snapped back, pressing past him through the door. I was on his heels, and Kip was on mine.

"Ahhh, my champion—come to rescue me at last!" El Numero Uno called to Gustav merrily, sounding darned chipper for a man with enough rope wrapped around him to hog-tie a dozen calves. "Well, don't you worry. Aside from being lashed to my throne here, I haven't been mistreated—yet."

He was hitched to a chair on the right-hand side of the car, near a small desk upon which sat, among other things, the whiskey bottle—which was now empty. An unused stove lurked in a corner, its pipe running out through the ceiling. The rest of the compartment was crammed with boxes and bags in a maze of tall stacks. The only freight in the car that wasn't buried under yet more freight was on the left-hand side, opposite El Numero Uno: two coffins and something long and bulky wrapped in red-stained sheets.

Sitting next to the beshrouded body was a large, lidded cooking pot.

Lockhart was nearby, hunkered atop one of the caskets. He'd finally discarded the collection of barbershop sweepings he'd tried to pass off as a mustache, and without the distraction of it hanging from his nose as long and limp as a bat from the rafters, I noticed again how truly worn and hollow the man looked.

At the sight of us, however, that hollowness was quickly filled— with rage. The Pinkerton came unsteadily to his feet, his hand hovering over the glossy pearl grip of his gun.

"Just the man we came to see!" I said, stepping in front of my brother. "We're here to relieve you, Mr. Lockhart. Figured you were up here on guard duty and thought that was rightly our chore, us bein' on the S.P. payroll and all—thanks to you, I might add. The train'll be in Carlin in . . . what would you say, Mr. Wiltrout? Another hour? There's really no more to do here in the meantime but sit on your duff. And believe you me, that's the one and only thing my brother and I could do just as well as you! So you might as well turn in. I reckon you've done enough on-the-house law work for one day."

The more I talked, the more Lockhart cooled, and by the time I finished, the fire in his eyes had almost entirely flickered out.

"I don't know why a feller like you'd wanna be a detective," he croaked, his voice husky, his words slurred. There was so much booze on his breath you could get drunk off the fumes, and the Mystery of the Empty Whiskey Bottle was quickly solved. "You got enough mouth on you to be a politician."

He started to stumble away, moving with such a decided leftward tilt he could almost have stretched out his long, thin arm and touched the floor.

"Yeah," he said, coming to a stop beside me. "*You* I like." Then he moved on, "accidentally" bumping Gustav as he headed for the door.

"Well, we will be in Carlin soon," Wiltrout said as Lockhart staggered past him. "I suppose I can trust you two to guard a man tied to a chair . . . for fifty minutes, anyhow. I've got rounds to make. Try not to wreck the train before I come back."

And then he was gone, too.

El Numero Uno shook his head in wonderment. "My, my, my—you two are almost as popular as *me*."

"Good looks and charm just rub some folks the wrong way," I said.

"At least *they* didn't kill anybody," Kip spat at the tramp.

"Nor did I, my boy," El Numero Uno said. "In addition to being an accomplished ne'er-do-well and a dedicated inebriate, I am a committed coward . . . I mean, pacifist."

"You sure talk fancy for a damned dirty hobo," Kip shot back.

"Well, I am *king* of the hoboes, remember," El Numero Uno replied with an air of indulgent benevolence.

"You'll have to excuse my impertinence, Your Grace," I said, "but I've heard of other fellers who claim the same title."

"I've heard of twenty or thirty," Kip threw in.

The King of the Hoboes smiled broadly. "So why not one more?"

I chuckled, but Kip shook his head, looking disgusted. His gaze drifted to the big, white-draped bundle on the floor and the pot sitting next to it.

"You really think this tramp didn't kill Joe?" he said, aiming the question at my brother.

"Yup," said Old Red, who'd squatted down to examine the floor near the desk.

"So what happened, then?"

"That I can't say." He stood and pointed at the bottle. "Was that Pezullo's?"

Kip nodded reluctantly. "He always had some squirreled away somewhere. I didn't want to say anything before, but I guess it can't hurt Joe now. He looked at Rule G as sort of . . . voluntary."

"Rule G?" Old Red asked.

It was El Numero Uno who offered the answer.

"The railroad's regulation against drinking on the job. Get caught breaking it, and you're blacklisted for life." The tramp lowered his head, as if contemplating the tragedy that is man. "Barbaric. Fortunately, in my line of 'work,' drinking on the job is practically mandatory."

My brother cocked an eyebrow at him. "*Were* you drunk when Pezullo went through the door?"

"Sadly, no. I was sober for every ghastly second of it."

"So did you see anything that might tell us what happened to the man?"

"No. Suddenly, he was just . . . there. Or at least part of him was." It was hard to tell, what with the rocking of the train and the ropes wrapped around El Numero Uno, but it looked like a shudder passed through the 'bo's body. "There was no warning. Not even a scream."

" 'Not even a scream' . . . ," Old Red repeated slowly, as if trying to wrap his tongue around some strange foreign lingo.

"Joe was probably too pie-eyed to know what was happenin' to him," Kip said, carrying his tray of merchandise to a large strongbox next to the desk. He unlocked the chest and stashed his wares inside. "Well . . . I'd better turn in. I have to be up early to start hawkin' the mornin' papers." He tipped his cap to me and Old Red as he headed for the door. "Night, gents."

We offered our own good-nights—even El Numero Uno—as Kip left the car.

"Tough on the kid, losin' a pal like that," I said.

Gustav walked over to the coffins.

"Death's always tough on somebody." He knelt and stroked the top of one casket, then the other. "Funny . . . it's 'the great equalizer,' the preachers say. Yet even now I can tell rich from poor." He gave the darker of the two coffins a rap with his knuckles. "Brass fittin's on mahogany for the gentleman." He tapped the other coffin, and the wood gave off a surprisingly low *thunk*. "Rope handles on pine for the pauper."

He eased himself onto the sturdier of the two coffins, using it like a bench just as Lockhart had. Any other time, I might've reminded him to show respect for the dead. But my brother was so pale gray and hollow-eyed, a casket actually seemed like a pretty natural place for him to rest himself.

"You know, it's a wonder *you* ain't ended up like our friends here," he said to our prisoner. "I mean, good God—ridin' under train cars. That ain't something a 'committed coward' is gonna try."

"One doesn't become King of the Hoboes without some capacity for daring," El Numero Uno said grandly, doing his best to puff out his chest. Then he deflated, chuckling at himself. "Of course, I prefer to ride the blinds. Any sane man does."

" 'The blinds'?" I asked.

The hobo nodded, looking pleased to be passing on the lore of his realm. "A section between cars where there's no door. Between the express car and the tender, say, or the baggage car and the express car. There's no way anyone on the train can spot you. But you're totally exposed to anyone who's *not* on the train. Fall asleep, and you'll wake up at the next station with a bull's billy club breaking over your head."

"Do bums ever try to sneak *inside* trains?"

Gustav's question hit El Numero Uno like a slap to the face.

"Well, I can't speak for bums," he huffed. "Or boomers or yeggs, for that matter. I, sir, am a hobo."

"I apologize for my brother's ignorance," I said, trying to look appalled even though I had no idea what elevated the noble hobo above any other vagrant. "What he should have said was, 'Do your subjects— or any of the lesser men of the road—ever avail themselves of unofficial berths in the interior of a train car? Your Majesty.'"

El Numero Uno nodded and smiled, appeased. "That's a very good question. Boxcars are fair game, but you'll never hear of a 'bo trying to sneak inside a car on a passenger train. Yeggs and bandits have been known to attempt it, though. There was even some buffoon a few years back who smuggled himself onto a train in one of those." He nodded at the coffins. "The baggageman heard him and got a gun, and when the dolt tried to hop out and rob the train, he got a bullet in the gut before he could say, 'Stick 'em up!' Then the baggageman just loaded him right back in his coffin, and they buried him in it at the end of the line."

As El Numero Uno wound down his little tale, Gustav jumped up and stared at the box that had been beneath him like it had bitten him on the butt.

"What?" I said.

Old Red stooped over and started running his fingers over the coffin again, this time taking special care to pick at the edges and fittings. He even did what I was dreading—grabbed the lid and tried to lift it—but the top of the casket didn't budge. When he was through with the showy mahogany coffin, he turned his attention to its humble pine neighbor.

"Sealed up tight—both of 'em," he finally announced. "He wasn't hidin' in either of these."

"He?" El Numero Uno asked.

"The killer." Gustav's gaze moved from the caskets to the gently swaying towers of crates, boxes, and bags filling the rest of the car. "There's tags on these coffins. Give 'em a read for me, would you, Otto?"

My brother and I crisscrossed in the middle of the compartment as I headed for the coffins and he walked back toward the mounds of cargo. When he reached the first stack of baggage, Old Red went down on his hands and knees and brought his face in so close to the floorboards he could've used his mustache as a mop.

"Are you huntin' for clues or passin' out?" I asked him.

"Clues," he sighed without looking back at me.

"Just checkin'."

"You know, I've got to hand it to you two," El Numero Uno said, a big grin peeking out from beneath his dark beard. "I've met plenty of cinder dicks in my day, but you're the first I've come across with *personality.*"

"Oh, we got plenty of that—it's good sense we're short on." I crouched by a small, yellowed card attached to the mahogany casket with twine. The pencil markings on it were sloppy but legible. "The tag on the fancy box says, 'Mrs. C. J. Foreman—San Jose.'"

"The widow lady with the kids, I betcha," Gustav said as he crawled off into the labyrinth of luggage. "That'd be *Mr.* Foreman crated up there."

I waddled over and snagged the tag on the other coffin.

"The pine box belongs to . . . I'll be damned."

Old Red peeked around the side of a battered steamer trunk. "And why is that?"

"Because this coffin's registered to Dr. Gee Woo Chan of San Francisco."

"Well . . . I'll be damned, too."

Gustav disappeared again.

"What exactly is he looking for?" El Numero Uno asked me. "You don't really think there's a murderer aboard, do you?"

"That's two different questions," I said. "The answer to the first is, 'I don't know.' And the answer to the second is . . . 'I don't know.'"

"Well, if there is a killer creeping around, I'm actually glad to be tied up in here with my own personal guards," the hobo said. "All of a sudden, I feel like the safest person on this train."

It was at that exact moment that someone cut loose with a blood-curdling shriek.

Twelve

STRANGE CARGO

Or, We Find More Than One Snake in the Grass

In my mad dash into the stacks of baggage, I managed to clip a particularly wobbly heap with my broad shoulders, and I was quickly letting out a pretty good yelp of my own as an avalanche of leather, cloth, and wood sent me sprawling to the floorboards.

"What happened?" El Numero Uno shouted.

"Nothin' I'd care to admit to," I groaned from beneath a layer of luggage.

A moment later, I was helped to my feet by the very man I'd intended to rescue.

"Next time," Old Red panted, winded from digging me out, "just ask if I'm alright."

I rubbed the back of my head where a satchel apparently stuffed with hammers had left a sizable lump. When I glanced down to see which bit of baggage to blame, I found myself looking at a very familiar war bag.

I'd been knocked senseless by my own book.

I used to think a man's dreams carried no weight for him, but rather lifted him up like heated air lifts a balloon. I now knew better. A dream can weigh upward of ten pounds, and when it falls on your head, it *smarts*.

"You know," Gustav said, "that wouldn't have been there to brain you if you'd—"

"Yeah, I *do* know, alright? So there's no use pointin' it out."

"There is if it'll get you to send the damn thing to *Harper's* like you oughta."

"Can't we talk about this later?" I peered over my brother's shoulder. "I could've sworn I heard a little girl screamin' somewhere back here. Did you happen to see her?"

"Come on," Old Red grumbled. "Let's find out what *you* sound like when you see it."

He led me toward a shadowy corner of the car.

"I spotted somethin'"—Gustav grimaced and glanced back at the heaps of debris we'd just picked our way through—"which is pretty much buried now, thank you very much. It trailed off thisaway . . . and I noticed *that*."

He pointed at a peculiar crate at about waist height in the nearest stack of freight. Built into its side was a small, latched door covered with chicken wire. There wasn't enough light to see anything inside it other than some sawdust and a coil of black rope or rawhide.

I bent over and brought my face even with the crate, determined not to make the slightest peep when I laid eyes on whatever had spooked Gustav.

"Go on. That's it," my brother said. "You're just where I was when—"

The rope launched itself at me, its gaping mouth flying into the chicken wire and chewing at it furiously.

I didn't scream like a little girl, as Old Red had. I screamed like a big girl with substantially more powerful lungs.

"For God's sake, someone tell me what's going on back there!" El Numero Uno called out.

"We found a snake!" I'd jolted backward onto my butt, and I

pushed myself up and began dusting the seat of my pants. "Don't worry, though—he ain't loose!"

"Why all the shrieking, then?"

"You want me to haul him up there and show you?"

The hobo shut up.

"What the hell kind of snake is that?" I asked Old Red.

My brother shrugged. "Too dark to tell. And I sure ain't gonna take him out of his cage for a better look."

The snake retreated out of the light, then turned, pointing its arrowhead skull at us again. Its crate had a different kind of tag than the coffins. Instead of a slip of paper, a small, brass disk was attached to it. Stamped into the metal was a number.

I was carrying four such disks in my own pocket just then, the numbers on them matching four more tied to our war bags and saddles. It was an efficient enough method for claiming luggage, but for one drawback: It gave you no way to identify anyone's baggage but your own.

Well, *almost* no way.

"Hel-lo," Gustav murmured, staring first at the box atop the snake crate, then at the one below it. Each was emblazoned with the same emblem: the words PROFESSOR PERTWEE'S HEALTH MIRACLE NUT BUTTER above two peanuts radiating wavy lines as if glowing like gold.

"That say what I think it says?" Old Red asked.

I read out the words, then checked the numbers on the claim tags. The nut butter boxes were 144 and 146. The snake's box was 145.

"So all three of these was turned over to a porter at the same time by the same person," my brother said. "That loudmouth drummer."

"Why would a feller like Chester Horner be haulin' around a *snake*?"

"Let's jar that up and set it aside for now." Gustav turned and began gathering up the valises and hatboxes and whatnot that cluttered the narrow aisles between piles of baggage. "We got somethin' to attend to first."

"And what 'somethin' would that be?" I asked as I pitched in to clear off the floor.

"A trail," Gustav said. "Of blood."

"Did he say *blood*?" El Numero Uno spluttered.

"The subject did arise," I replied.

"Well, cut me loose, then! You can't leave me alone back here trussed up like a Christmas turkey!"

"You ain't alone, Your Grace," I said. "You can't see us, but we ain't more than thirty feet away. If a madman rises up out of one of them coffins and comes at you with a meat cleaver, just do what comes natural: scream. We'll be there in two shakes."

"Oh, *thank you*," the 'bo said. "I feel *so* much better."

We were almost through reheaping the upturned luggage by then, and I noticed that my brother had set two bags aside from the rest.

"You got special plans for our war bags?"

"Just wanna make sure everything ends up in the right place," Old Red said. "Alright, that's enough housecleanin'. I can pick up the trail again now."

He went into a squat and pointed at a small, dark smear on the floor. He waddled over to it, and his finger jabbed at another blotch a few feet away. And then another and another.

"Those ain't drops," I said. "They're streaks. Pezullo was *dragged* to the side door."

"That's the way I got it 'duced," Gustav mumbled, duckwalking along the blood trail. "Towed him from somewhere . . . back . . . *here*."

My brother—and the trail—came to a stop before an exceptionally large crate pushed up against the back wall of the car.

"What's that say?"

Old Red pointed at a message scrawled in blue chalk on the side of the box—three words accompanied by an arrow pointed skyward.

I was tempted to reply with something like CAUTION: POINTY STICKS or HEY, NICE HAT or simply "What the hell do you think it says?" But it's my policy never to make light of Gustav's lack of letters, as *I* only learned to read and write because my brother and the rest of our brood took up the slack around the farm while yours truly was granted the privilege of pursuing an education past grade two.

" 'This end up,' " I said. I rapped my knuckles on the top of the crate. The resulting knock was loud and high-pitched—the sound of cheap wood and loose packing. "What do you think's in here, anyway? Must be enough space inside for a piano and the feller to play it."

Old Red flinched like I'd just told him Barson and Welsh were perched atop the box, guns drawn.

"Oh, I bet it's a rolltop desk from Monkey Ward, somethin' like that," he said, his voice casual, his expression dead serious.

He brought a finger to his lips, then leaned in close to the crate, inspecting each board and edge. He took special care going over several gouges in the wood along the left-hand corner. When he was done with the scratches, he went up on tiptoe to get a look at the top of the box. Soon his finger was on the move again, stabbing at three identical holes, all of them perfectly round.

I held up my hands and made a cranking motion.

"Drilled?" I was asking.

Gustav nodded, and I could see from the wide, wary set of his eyes that he was thinking back on the same thing as me—that story El Numero Uno had told about the stowaway bandit.

Those weren't knotholes we were looking at. They were *air*holes.

Without any signal from either of us, we prepared to do some drilling of our own, drawing our .45s and aiming them at the crate.

"If there's somebody in there, who's to say he ain't got a six-shooter, too?" I whispered.

"Them holes ain't from bullets," Old Red pointed out, his voice so quiet I could barely hear it. "And Pezullo didn't have any bullet holes in him, neither. If he was killed cuz he opened up this crate . . . well, at least we know he wasn't shot for it."

"That ain't much comfort."

"It ain't. But there's no way around it. We gotta open that son of a bitch. Stay here."

Gustav headed back toward the other end of the car, leaving me alone with the box. While I stood there, the grip of my Colt growing slick with sweat, I listened for telltale noises from the other side of the wood: voices, the cocking of a hog leg, the growl of a tiger, *anything*. But all I heard was my own breathing and the humming and clacking of the train.

When Old Red returned, he was clutching a crowbar.

"Alright," he whispered, "you cover me while I—"

I shook my head, holstered my Peacemaker, and plucked the crowbar from his hand.

"We both know who'll get this thing open quicker."

Gustav nodded brusquely, then stepped to the side and drew his .45 again. I found a good spot—the same side of the crate that had been pried at before, to judge by the scratches—and slid in the crowbar's claw. It didn't take much muscle to work the side panel free, for the nails were small and already loose in the wood.

"Don't make a fuss, now—there's a gun pointin' your way!" Old Red barked as I pried the panel off. "Put your hands up and . . . ! Oh. Well. Hel-lo."

"What's going on? Is someone in there?" yelled El Numero Uno, who'd apparently been apprised of the situation when my brother went off to fetch the crowbar.

"Not a some*one*," I called back to him. "A some*thing*. A bunch of 'em."

"Well? What?"

"Bricks," Gustav answered, staring in puzzled wonderment at the orange-red blocks spread neatly across the bottom of the box.

"Did you say 'bricks'?"

"Yeah, yeah—*bricks*!" my brother hollered. "Now would you shut up for a second?"

Old Red stooped down to get a better look at the crate's cargo. There were forty-nine bricks in all—a single layer laid out in seven rows of seven.

"Whoever was in there, we know this much about him," I said. "He's got one hell of a tough rump. Personally, I would've packed myself in with *pillows* to sit on, but maybe I'm just soft."

"Only from the neck up," Old Red murmured as he picked up one of the bricks from the outermost row. It was different from its neighbors, flecked with small, dark dots. Gustav flipped it over to look at the side that had been facedown to the floor.

It was coated with dark blood and curly, black hairs.

"Well, that settles it. This is it," my brother said, and then he used a phrase he'd picked up from the Holmes case Doc Watson had labeled "Silver Blaze": "The scene of the crime."

"So Pezullo got his head stoved in by a stowaway?"

Old Red slid the brick back into its slot and stood up slowly—so slowly I wasn't entirely sure he was going to make it.

"Sure looks that way," he said, slumping against the crate. "So now the question is, where'd the bastard get to?"

"Probably jumped out when we stopped for the body and snuck off into the desert," I suggested. "Which means you can get yourself some rest. Whoever it was killed Pezullo, he'll get what's due him tomorrow with no help from you. The sun'll have him charred to a crisp before he even gets to hell."

Old Red mused a moment, looking like he found my logic tempting in more ways than one. But then he sighed and gave his head a weary shake.

"It don't wash. El Numero Uno would've seen him."

Then he straightened up and strode away, starting out sluggish but picking up steam with each step.

"We gotta turn this train inside out," he said. "We'll find Wiltrout—get him and the porters to help."

"May as well bring Lockhart in on it, too," I said, hustling after him.

My brother made the kind of noise you'd expect to hear from a rabid dog.

"Hey, what about me?" El Numero Uno asked as we came out of the baggage stacks and walked past him. "You can't leave me here all by myself!"

"Not only can we, we got to," I told him. "But don't worry, Your Majesty. We done searched this car, remember? Ain't nothin' gonna happen to you he-*arrrr-ooph*!"

If the word *he-arrrr-ooph* is unfamiliar to you, no doubt you've never seen a man fly off his feet, tangle midair with his brother, and slam down so hard on his side his guts practically pop out like candy from a piñata.

Which was exactly what was happening to me.

The Pacific Express was braking—hard—and Gustav and I weren't the only ones thrown to the floorboards. El Numero Uno's chair toppled over, as did the tower of luggage my brother and I had rebuilt just a few minutes before. There was an ear-piercing squeal of metal on metal, and when the train finally came to a stop, the unnerving din was replaced by an equally unnerving silence.

"Sweet Jesus," I said, shoving Old Red's boot from my face. "If the engineer'd hit the brakes any harder, we'd be plastered against the end of the car like wallpaper."

El Numero Uno cleared his throat. "If you please . . . ?"

I crawled over and righted him and his throne.

"We sure made good time to Carlin," my brother muttered, pushing himself to his feet and shambling toward the car's side door. As he reached for the handle, the door to the Pullman opened.

There was Kip, gaping at us from the vestibule with such bug-eyed terror I almost glanced over my shoulder to make sure Death himself wasn't sneaking up on me, scythe at the ready. But then the news butch took a wobbly step into the car, and I could see that he wasn't stupefied with fright by something behind *me*. The something was behind *him*.

"Alright, you two," croaked the masked man at Kip's back. "Unbuckle your gunbelts and let 'em drop."

He brought up a Colt and rested it on Kip's shoulder. The barrel nuzzled the butch's ear, and the kid let out a mewling little moan.

"If you ain't unheeled yourselves by the time I count three, this boy's gonna have a bullet where his brains oughta be."

I shot a quick look at my brother. He was just standing there, sizing the bandit up, neither challenging him nor yielding to him.

"One," the man growled. "Two."

Thirteen

MYTHS AND LEGENDS

Or, A Dime Novel Come to Life Is Nearly the Death of Us

"Alright, alright," I said, reaching for my buckle just as Gustav got to loosening his. "We know what comes after two—you don't have to say it."

"Just take it easy," my brother added as we eased our holsters to the floor. "No need to hurt the kid."

"I'll be the judge of that," the bandit sneered.

It seemed hard to believe, such ominous words coming from so unimpressive a physical specimen, like thunder booming out of a licorice whip. The man was reed thin, with the squinty, close-set eyes one usually encounters in farm families who don't know the dangers of inbreeding their stock, animal or otherwise. He was dressed like a sharecropper, in frayed denim and sweat-soaked flannel, the duds so dirty they gave off a little puff of dust when he tugged Kip backward into the passage to the Pullmans.

"Come with me," the man said.

"Good luck," El Numero Uno whispered as Old Red and I headed for the door.

"Thanks, Your Worship," I said. "We'll be alright. You just sit tight."

"Do I have any choice?"

We followed the bandit through the vestibule. His gun never left Kip's ear, and the kid's terror-stricken gaze never left *us*. As we stepped through into the sleeper, I heard muted murmuring and weeping up ahead—the sound of dozens of passengers cowering behind the curtains of their berths.

"Ahhh, the guests of honor!" a cheerful voice called out. "Welcome, gentlemen, welcome!"

The scrawny gunman pulled Kip into the nook outside the men's washroom, giving us a clear view of the corridor. About two-thirds of the way down the car stood two armed men, both dusty and dressed for rough riding. Neither wore a mask. One was lean, close-shaven, blond, handsome, smiling. The other was the flip side of the coin: lumpy, hairy, dark, brutish, scowling.

A stooped figure in a blood-dappled nightshirt was hunched at their feet.

"Get up front with the others, Gunnar," said the good-looking one. "See if you can't convince the express messenger to join the festivities." He waved a shiny, long-barreled .44 at Kip. "Take the kid with you. If there's any sign of trouble back here, dust him."

"With pleasure."

The grimy little fellow grabbed Kip by the collar and dragged the whimpering news butch back toward the baggage car.

"That boy comes to any harm, you're gonna regret it, *Gunnar*," I said.

The threat sounded empty even to my own ears, and the bandit's eyes crinkled before he disappeared through the door. Behind his mask, he'd been smiling.

"So," Old Red said coolly to the fellow giving orders, "you'd be Mike Barson, then. The papers all say you're the pretty one." He turned his attention to the man's companion, who scowled back at Gustav like he was snot in his soup. "Which makes you Augie Welsh."

"The Give-'em-Hell Boys, at your service," Barson said, offering us a bow.

"Long as we're makin' introductions, let's do it proper," Welsh said. He pointed his gun squarely at Old Red's head. "Come here. Let's shake."

Only two passengers dared peeks out at us as we moved down the aisle: little Harlan and Marlin, the twins, who gaped at us so wide-eyed you'd think we were ghosts (already). As we drew closer to Barson and Welsh, the man at their feet turned to look at us, too, revealing the bloody, bruised face of Burl Lockhart. It was a face racked by pain—but not the kind that comes from a wound of the flesh. There was fear there, and despair.

"What a couple of darin' desperadoes you are," I spat before I could stop myself. "Beatin' an unarmed old man. What're you gonna do next? Pistol-whip a baby?"

My little outburst actually seemed to cut Barson to the quick. His smile faded, replaced by an expression I can only describe as rueful.

Welsh had a very different reaction.

"Pistol-whip a baby?" he said as Gustav and I finally came up close. "Alright . . . why not?"

He stepped around Lockhart, spun his gun, and drove it butt-first into my brother's stomach. Old Red wheezed and crumpled to the floor.

"Why, you godda—"

Welsh cut short my blasphemy by bringing his gun up sideways and ramming it into my face like a bulky set of knuckle dusters. I only retained my teeth because my nose took the brunt of the blow, and I staggered back with blood spurting from my nostrils. I managed to remain upright, though, and I stepped toward an extremely surprised Welsh intending to top with bare fists what he'd just done with cold steel.

"*Don't,*" Welsh growled, whipping the business end of his artillery so close to my blood-gushing nose I had to go cross-eyed to look at it.

"Let me give you some advice, friend," Barson said amiably. "Fall down this time."

He said this as if I had a choice. But I assure you, when Welsh walloped me upside the head, there was nothing voluntary about my quick trip to the carpet.

In the hazy, topsy-turvy moments that followed, I was dimly aware of curses, grunts, and thuds. As my brain dragged itself out of the fog, I realized that some of these noises were even emanating from *me*. Old Red and I were having the metaphorical shit kicked out of us, and it might've turned literal if someone hadn't yelled, "That's enough!"

To my surprise—and everyone else's, I imagine—these words were not spoken by Mike Barson.

It was Diana Caveo. And just in case Welsh chose not to listen to her, she sprang from her bunk and threw herself on her knees between his boot and my belly.

"You've made your point! There's no need to kill them!"

Welsh froze—though he didn't seem to be considering mercy so much as mulling over who to kick next. Barson appeared beside him, more amused than ever.

"Leave it to a lady to tell us when we've overdone it," he said. "Miss, you are entirely correct. Augie—keep 'em covered."

But Welsh had one last lick for us: He hacked and spat on each of us in turn. Miss Caveo was the only one he spared.

"Ladies and gentlemen—may I have your undivided attention?" Barson boomed. He noticed me groggily staring up at him, and I swear he actually *winked*. "Though I suspect I have it already." He reached into a pocket and extracted a folded piece of paper, which he shook out with one crisp snap. "We have a statement to make!"

He cleared his throat, took a deep breath, and clutched the lapel of his coat with his free hand just like a politician on the stump.

"Two months ago, the 'outlaw' band known as 'the Give-'em-Hell Boys'—aka, us—detained a Southern Pacific special—aka, the Pacific Express—outside Carlin, Nevada—aka, *right here*. Through the use of friendly persuasion, the 'gang' gained access to the train's Wells Fargo car and the special freight therein. Wells Fargo and the Southern Pacific have subsequently reported their losses in this instance at forty-four hundred dollars in cash. We would like to set the record straight. In actuality, our profit from this enterprise is beyond our ability to assess. Suffice it to say, we are now the proud owners of one hundred bars of U.S. Treasury gold. Since personal enrichment has never been our primary motivation, we are prepared to part with said gold in the service of a greater good. As robbers—and we don't deny that the label fits us—our crimes pale in comparison to those of a far more ruthless gang: the directors of the Southern Pacific Railroad. These unrepentant thugs have seen fit to offer bounties for our killing or capture, so we think it only fair that we be allowed to do the same to them. We are therefore placing a price of eight gold bars on the head of each and every member of the S.P.'s executive committee, as well as two bars each on their villainous henchmen Jefferson Powless and Colonel C. Kermit Crowe. We will deliver rewards in secret, pending proof that justice has been meted out. In the meantime, we will retire to our sovereign kingdom, the Humboldt Mountains, extending an invitation to all railroad dicks, Pinkertons, Wells Fargo agents, and freelance bounty hunters to join us at their convenience. We promise them a warm welcome."

Barson glanced up from the paper, his pale blue eyes twinkling in the dim light. He almost looked like he was waiting for applause.

"That's it," he said. "This has been purely a social call, and I'm pleased to inform you that the passengers of this train will not be molested in any way. Our complaint is not with you. It's with the Southern Pacific Railroad and its lackeys."

At the mention of "lackeys," he looked down at Miss Caveo and shook his head with an almost wistful sadness.

"Miss, may I suggest that you immediately apply for employment with the Southern Pacific Railroad Police? You make a much more impressive guard than these two."

Barson's gaze flicked over me and my brother quickly, as if we were some nauseating sight he couldn't quite stomach.

"As for you, Mr. Lockhart . . . this might sound crazy, but I'm actually disappointed you didn't turn out to be a real threat. I mean, here we are—the West's greatest lawman and the world's greatest robbers. Living legends, face-to-face. And you turn out to be more of a *myth*."

He sighed and shrugged. "Well, I suppose those dime-novel scribblers will make the most of it. Obviously, they have a way of making things seem grander than they truly are."

He held out the paper on which his speech had been written and let it go. It floated down toward us in the zigzag swoops of a falling leaf.

"For the newspapers."

"Don't leave this car till we're gone," Welsh snarled as the paper settled with a gentle rustle on Old Red's lap. "If we see anyone so much as poke a nose out a window, I will personally slash that news butcher's throat."

He stretched a leg over us, spinning around once his feet were planted to keep us covered as he backed away up the aisle.

Barson tipped his hat to Miss Caveo. "I hope you and I might meet again under more pleasant circumstances."

"If you and I meet again, I assure you there will be nothing pleasant about it," she shot back.

Barson grinned. "Miss, if every man with a badge had half your grit, I'd take up knitting and never leave the house again. Enjoy the rest of your trip."

Then he followed Welsh, picking his way gingerly past Lockhart, Gustav, and me much as a man in new shoes might navigate the steaming piles in a cow pen. Unlike Welsh, he didn't bother keeping a watch on us as he headed to the other end of the car. Somehow, the sight of his back was more disheartening than the sight of Welsh's gun.

The moment the door to the forward vestibule slammed shut behind Barson, we were joined by another passenger: Dr. Chan.

"Oh, Mr. Holmes—your face!" he said when he saw me.

"Jeez, Doc," I groaned. "Now you got me worried."

I touched my jaw: still attached. My cheeks: no holes. My nose. "*Shit!*"

I was jolted by a bolt of pain so intense I swooned, and the already dimly lit hallway around me spiraled into blackness like dirty water going down a drain. The spell passed as quick as it came, though, and when the world was fully in view again, it had brightened considerably, for Miss Caveo was peering down into my face, looking concerned.

"Pardon me for the language," I said. "And thank you for what you done. That was mighty brave."

"Mighty foolish is what it was," Old Red groused feebly. "Miss, you coulda got yourself killed."

"Fortunately, I didn't stop to consider that." Her gaze darted down the aisle, to the door to the baggage car. "And no need to apologize for cursing, Otto. I wouldn't mind doing some swearing myself just now."

My nose was still stinging something fierce, but hearing the lady call me Otto provided considerable balm.

"There could be internal injuries," Chan said. "All three of you need to remain as still as possible until I can—"

"Thanks, Doc," Gustav said, struggling to push himself upright. "But I don't think so."

He faltered, sinking back toward the carpet, until a hand stabbed out of the nearest berth to catch him by the arm.

"Listen to the man, Mr. Holmes," Mrs. Kier said, steadying Old Red with what seemed to be a surprisingly strong grip. "You looked dreadful even before that beating you just took. Now you *really* need a rest."

"Yeah, take it easy, pal," Chester Q. Horner threw in from the berth above her, his tremendous brown pompadour so thoroughly pillow-mussed it looked like his whole scalp had been twisted around sideways and stood on end. "There's nothing you can do, anyway."

Lockhart came lurching to his feet.

"I'll tell ya what *I'm* gonna do. I'm gonna get out there and *kill* those sons of bitches!"

"Mr. Lockhart, no," Chan said. "The boy. Your injuries. Let me—"

"Keep your filthy monkey-paws off me! I don't need your help!"

Indeed, now that the old Pinkerton was standing, I could see that he was right: He really didn't need a doctor. His nose, like mine, had been bloodied, and there were scuffs on his face and hands, yet other than that he'd come through the whupping remarkably unscathed.

"Somebody get me a gun!" he roared. "They took Aunt Virgie!"

Old Red and I glanced at each other uneasily. Had the old man taken a boot toe to the *head*?

"Aunt Virgie?" Miss Caveo asked.

"My gun! *Burl Lockhart's* pearl-handled Smith and Wesson .44! They took it from me!"

"I know how you feel, Mr. Lockhart," I said soothingly. "They got our guns, too. I don't like it one bit, but we can't—"

"Somebody in this damn car must have a gun, and *I want it!*" Lockhart hollered, spraying whiskey-scented spittle over everyone around. "I'm not just gonna stand here while those bastards get away!"

"Calm down," Old Red snapped. "Long as they've got Kip, we ain't gonna go rushin' out there like—"

Lockhart responded with a blunt two-word expression that is widely considered the very acme of obscenity. So foul is this phrase held to be, it actually elicited a collective gasp from some of the female passengers who were beginning to emerge from their berths.

But rather than go all faint and fluttery over a little vulgarity, Miss Caveo seemed to steel herself. She moved closer to me, turning to face Lockhart fully, as if the man would have to go through not only my brother and me but *her* if he intended to run outside waving a six-shooter.

The tense silence that followed was shattered by a pair of thunderclaps in quick succession—gunshots from up ahead, in the baggage car.

"Sweet Jesus!" I blurted out, but no one bothered with a gasp this time. There was more to worry about than propriety now. "Kip!"

There were other sounds outside the Pullman—shouts, horses whinnying, the thump of hooves.

Horner rolled back into his bunk and pressed his nose to the window. "They're leaving!"

Gustav and I dashed up the aisle, pushing our way past dazed passengers with Miss Caveo and Lockhart and Chan on our heels. The door at the end of the vestibule was still locked, but Samuel appeared from the men's washroom and produced his passkey, and soon we were rushing into the baggage compartment.

We found the body flat on its back, lifeless eyes staring up at the gunsmoke that roiled above it like a sky full of dark clouds.

Fourteen

SUSIE CREEK

Or, The Pacific Express Returns to the Scene of the Crime

Chan rushed in and knelt down beside the body, but it was clear there was nothing any doctor on earth could do: The king was dead.

El Numero Uno had two bullets in him—one in his gut, one in his heart. He was still tied to the chair, which had pitched over backward when the slugs struck.

Chan stretched out his fingers and gently closed the hobo's eyes.

"Damn it," I said. "Why'd they have to go and do a thing like that?"

"You think those sons of bitches *need* a reason to kill?" Lockhart snapped.

"They had 'em a reason," Gustav said, his gaze sweeping over the floor, the walls, the luggage, everything. "We just don't know it yet."

"Maybe he overheard something about the gang's plans," Miss Caveo suggested. "Or the location of their hideout."

I moved to block her view of the body. I'd come to admire her backbone, but that didn't mean I was the kind of lout who'd let her get an eyeful of a murdered man.

"I don't think this is a fittin' place for a lady just now."

"And *I* don't think this is the time to worry about what's 'fitting,'" Miss Caveo replied.

She had a point—which did nothing to change anyone's mind.

"Samuel," my brother said, "could you help the passengers settle down *in the Pullman*."

"You, too. Out," Lockhart said, pulling the Chinaman up by the arm. "Anything happens to you, it'll be my hide."

Both Chan and Miss Caveo started to protest, but Samuel got to work quick, stretching out his long arms and steering them toward the door as skillfully as a top hand working a herd.

"Ladies and gentlemen!" the porter bellowed over their heads at the leering passengers crowded into the vestibule. "On behalf of the Southern Pacific Railroad, I would like to offer every one of you a complimentary restorative from the dinin' car. I can take your orders as soon as you return to your berths. We have brandy, whiskey, beer, wine, port, sherry . . ."

The gaggle of gawkers began drifting away, and with a minimum of shooing Samuel was able to clear off the last reluctant stragglers—a frustrated Chan and a fuming Miss Caveo—and get the door shut.

When I turned around again, Lockhart was scooping something bulky up off the floor: my gunbelt. The side door was open wide, and the old Pinkerton strapped my holster around his nightshirt as he headed toward it.

"Pardon me, Mr. Lockhart, but that's *my*—"

"Quiet!" Lockhart barked, not bothering to follow his own order. "Someone's movin' around out there!" He drew my Colt and pointed it out at the darkness, the barrel bobbing and weaving in his quivery grip.

Old Red grabbed his own gunbelt and took up a position across from Lockhart.

"There's somebody there, alright," he said, squinting out at what was, to my eyes, a wall of solid black.

"Easy, fellers," I said. "Best keep your trigger fingers loose till we know what's become of Kip."

If anything, Lockhart's finger curled tighter.

"You don't have to tell ol' Burl Lockhart how to handle this kinda thing! I know what I'm doin'!"

He thumbed back the hammer.

"Give us a holler if you're out there, Kip!" I yelled, stepping up beside Lockhart—the better to make a grab for my gun should it become necessary.

My eyes slowly adjusted to the dark outside, and I could make out the lay of the land—mostly brush and rocky bluffs sweeping upward to distant mountains. Off to the left things swept downward, though, into a creekbed, and it was there that I caught sight of someone creeping closer to the train.

"It's me!" Kip called out. "I'm alright!"

Lockhart sagged, weighed down by what seemed like disappointment. He'd been more anxious to see Barson and Welsh dead than our news butch alive.

"Come on back to the train!" I shouted. "We'll keep you covered!"

As Kip made a dash for the baggage car, another voice called out, this one from the car ahead of us.

"Don't worry—they're all gone! I held them off!"

It was Morrison, the jumpy Wells Fargo messenger who'd nearly blown out our candles the last time the train had stopped.

"Good work, Morrison!" a gruff voice replied from the opposite direction, down toward the Pullman cars. "It's a relief to know that rifle of yours is good for something other than shooting the hats off passengers."

"Sounds like Wiltrout," I said.

"Where the hell has *he* been?" Lockhart grumbled.

Kip and the conductor appeared at the side door from opposite directions, and a moment later the engineer and the fireman showed up, as well. Gustav, Lockhart, and I hopped down to the ground to join them.

"Why'd we stop?" Wiltrout asked. "A barricade?"

"That's right," said Bedford, the Negro fireman. "Not much of one, though—just a few boards propped up with rocks. Won't take us long to clear off."

"Recognize where we are?" the engineer asked Wiltrout, nodding at the gully nearby. "Susie Creek. That's right where they stopped you last time, ain't it?" He leaned forward and spat out a viscous brown-black stream of tobacco juice. "It's a wonder Barson and Welsh don't just build a station here for you, Captain."

"Clear the tracks," the conductor snapped back, his glare and voluminous chin whiskers giving him the appearance of a billy goat about to butt. "I want this train highballing to Carlin within ten minutes."

"Hold on," Gustav said as the engineer and fireman walked away. They didn't even slow down. "We got questions to chew over 'fore we go into town."

"Such as what, for instance?" Lockhart asked.

Old Red described the crate we'd found with the loosened side panel—and the bloodied brick.

"So what are you saying?" Wiltrout asked when he was done. "You think one of the robbers was loaded on the train in a *box*?"

He couldn't have looked less convinced if Gustav had told him there'd been a stowaway in the conductor's own underpants.

"I don't see how else it makes sense," my brother said. "That's why Pezullo's dead. He found one of the gang crated up."

"Look," Lockhart cut in, using the word the way men do when they're about to explain something they think shouldn't need explaining. "Before they got on the train, Welsh and Barson had been on horseback. That was plain from the trail dust on 'em. Same goes for that grubby little prick who put a gun on the butch here. None of 'em came out of any crate."

Gustav nodded slowly, looking at Lockhart for the first time with something approaching respect. But he'd staked out a theory, and he wasn't going to give it up so easy.

He turned to Kip. "How many men did you see out there?"

The kid had returned from the shadows tousled and tense, and I'd watched him struggle to smooth his features into a mask of cool, grim

purpose such as the men around him wore. He hadn't entirely suc-
ceeded, and Old Red's question rekindled a flicker of panic in his eyes.

"I . . . I don't know. I didn't get a good look. The one who took me
off the train . . . he threw me down and told me to keep my eyes shut."
The news butch gave an apologetic—and humiliated—shrug. "So . . .
that's what I did."

"Them fellers weren't foolin' around, Kip," I assured him. "You
did right."

Both Lockhart and my brother looked like they begged to differ,
but they had the decency not to do so out loud.

"Here's the thing," Gustav pressed on. "If that stowaway found
himself another hidin' place after Pezullo opened his crate, who's to say
he's not still aboard? And once we go on into town, it'll be easy as pie
for him to slip off and—"

Wiltrout stopped my brother with a raised hand and an exasperated
shake of the head. "Before I listen to anything more you have to say, I
want to see this mystery box of yours."

"Fine."

Old Red hoisted himself back into the baggage car. He headed off
into the piles of luggage looking steadier than he had in quite some
time, the rubber in his legs hardened back into bone.

"Here," he said once we'd all followed him to the gloomy corner
with the crate.

The panel he and I had pulled out earlier was leaning so snug
against the side of the box you couldn't even tell we'd ever touched it.
Gustav reached out for it.

"The brick with the blood on it's in—"

Old Red sputtered into silence, a calliope running out of steam
midtune. His fingers had come flying off the crate when he'd given it a
tug. The front panel hadn't budged.

He tried again, grabbing the edge and pulling on it hard.

Nothing happened. The crate was sealed up tight.

Fifteen

THE SCOUT

Or, We Get off the Train Again—and Almost End Up Beneath It

Which are you, 'Holmes'—a fraud or a fruitcake?" Lockhart asked my brother.

Before Gustav could answer, the Pinkerton swiped a gnarled hand at him like he was swatting at a fly.

"Aw, forget it. I don't even give a shit."

The lanky old lawman whirled around so fast the bottom of his nightshirt flew up to an almost indecent height, and he trudged off muttering about "goddamned muddleheaded amateurs."

Wiltrout didn't look any happier.

"I've got an express to get to station and sixty-six passengers on the verge of hysteria—I don't have time for this bullshit." He grabbed Kip by the shoulder and spun him around roughly. "Gather up your gewgaws and come with me. Half price on everything till the last passenger's asleep, understand?"

"They must've sealed the box up again!" Old Red shouted as the conductor herded Kip away. "You can't wait two minutes while we open it?"

"For you, I wouldn't wait another second," Wiltrout said without looking back or slowing down. "I don't know what you two are up to, but you're *through*!"

A door squeaked open and banged shut. Lockhart, Wiltrout, and Kip were gone.

"We ain't through," Gustav growled.

"Really? That looked kinda 'through' to me," I said. "I mean, Jesus, Brother—they didn't even believe us."

"We'll *make* 'em believe."

Old Red turned and glared hatefully at the crate as if he expected it to apologize. After looking it up and down a moment, he rolled his eyes and moaned like a constipated mule.

"Ohhhh, for Christ's sake! Would you look at that?"

I peered at the box and saw . . . a box.

"I don't see nothin'."

"Exactly," Gustav said. "It's kinda like that 'dog in the nighttime' from the 'Silver Blaze' case. Sometimes it ain't what's there. It's what ain't there."

Only then did I see the same nothing Old Red saw.

The writing on the crate—THIS END UP—was gone. The scratches along the edges, too.

"Surely, that ain't a new box," I said.

"Surely."

Old Red pointed down. There were scratches aplenty on the floor—among them an arc of deep, fresh gouges that hadn't been there an hour before.

Someone had simply swiveled the crate around so the front panel faced the wall.

"Here we go again," I sighed.

Gustav stepped back and drew his Peacemaker. "Alright in there! We got guns and they're pointed right at you! Don't try anything stupid, now!"

He gave me a nod, and I grabbed the box and slowly spun it around. The panel we'd loosened earlier had been reattached, but the job had been done with such sloppy haste I didn't even need the crow-bar to pry it off this time.

Once again, the only stowaways we found were of the baked-red-clay variety. But something *was* different this time: The brick with the blood on it was gone.

"So," I said, "the Give-'em-Hell Boys stopped the train so they could sneak back here, spin around a box, and borrow a brick?"

Old Red did a spin of his own, whirling on his heel and darting off.

"Somebody's been coverin' his tracks," he said, his voice fading fast as he wound his way through the baggage. "That brick was the only proof we had that Pezullo was murdered."

"Well, there ain't nothin' we can do about it now," I said as I ambled after him. "It'd be mighty easy to just toss that brick out into the desert, and we don't have time to—"

I heard a dull thud from up ahead.

"Gustav?"

There was no answer.

I spurred myself to a sprint. When I reached the front of the compartment, I was alone (if standing over a dead hobo tied to a chair can be said to be "alone"). My brother was gone.

"Gustav?"

"Out here!"

I moved to the side door and spotted a dark shape scurrying around low to the ground about fifty feet from the train. It was either the world's biggest coyote or Old Red zigzagging through the darkness bent over at the waist.

"What do you think you're doin'? The train's gonna leave any second!" My nose was still tender and swollen from the pasting it had taken earlier, and with each hollered word I could feel it pumping up bigger, like the rubber wheel on a velocipede. Yet I couldn't resist adding, "Have you lost your goddamn mind?"

"Gotta do a scout while I can," Old Red answered, staring straight down. "Might come across that brick or some other—"

He'd been making quick, jagged turns every few steps, but suddenly he came to a dead stop and picked something off a clump of sagebrush.

"Hel-lo!"

"It's gonna be 'good-bye' if you don't get your ass over here!"

"He's right—you need to get back aboard fast!" added Morrison, the Wells Fargo man. Apparently, he'd been watching my brother's weaving, lurching search from his perch inside the express car. "Once we're moving this time, the engineer won't even stop for the bell cord!"

"Listen to the man, Brother! *Come on!*"

"Oh, hold your water," Gustav said. "I still gotta check that creekbed yonder for—"

The rest of his words were swallowed by a tremendous, chuffing grunt from the engine. The train heaved forward—and I spilled outward, tumbling through the door into the desert.

There are worse ways to break a fall than landing in sand. Unfortunately, one of them is landing on an engorged, blood-clotted nose. Which is exactly what I did.

I let out a screech that made the blast of the engine whistle seem as soothing as the cooing of a dove. And when my watering eyes regained their focus, I had even more to howl about: the huge steel wheels rolling past just inches from my face. I spun away and staggered to my feet, ignoring as best I could the pain exploding in my brain like fireworks. I had a train to catch.

It took me just a dozen wobbly strides to draw even with the baggage car. But "even" and "inside" are two very different things. The side door was a good three feet off the ground, and it was moving faster by the second while I was already slowing down.

I had to jump for it—quick. So I did.

I landed half-in, half-off the train. If I fell now, I'd be ground into two hundred pounds of chuck before I could so much as scream. I flailed about desperately for purchase, and my fingers caught hold of something moist but firm. I pulled hard.

When I finally managed to clamber up into the car, I found myself eyeball to vacant, staring eyeball with El Numero Uno: I'd hauled myself inside by grabbing hold of the rough, bloody fabric of his coat.

"Ooooottoooo!"

I whirled around and spotted a pair of hands clamped to the lowest edge of the door—Gustav was being towed beside the train, his feet dragging so close to the wheels they could be plucked off clean any second. I bent out as far as I dared, took hold of his wrists, and pulled with all I had.

Fortunately, I've had plenty, and I was able to swing my brother up and in like I was tossing a bale of hay. He landed a few feet away, rolling to a stop against the coffins.

"You alright?" I asked him.

He sat up and panted a few words I couldn't make out, so I pushed the side door closed, muffling the clacking of the train and the howling of the wind. "Come again?"

"I said 'dandy.' And '*thanks.*'"

"My pleasure . . . though not really. You just about gave me a coronary."

Old Red nodded, chagrined. "I just about gave myself one."

I started looking for something to cover up El Numero Uno. It didn't seem right, us chatting away with his glassy eyes on us.

"Well, I sure hope it was worth it," I said as I shrouded the King of the Hoboes under a newspaper I found in Pezullo's desk.

"Oh, it was worth it, alright. If I hadn't gone out there, I wouldn't have found this."

Gustav stuffed a hand into one of his pockets and tugged out what seemed to be a tiny porcelain bowl. It looked more like a dainty teacup than anything you'd dump a ladleful of oatmeal into, only it had no handle. What it did have, I noticed after reaching down to take it, was a ring of dense indigo patterns, almost like checkerboard, running along the inner lip. A thin branch with delicate leaves was painted on the side.

"Pretty," I said, handing the bowl back to my brother. "And pretty peculiar."

"Oh, you ain't even *seen* peculiar yet."

Old Red reached into another pocket and produced what looked like a small patch of sheepskin, the wool still attached. It was golden yellow, though—far brighter than any fleece I'd ever seen.

"What is that? Some kinda pelt?"

"Ain't no pelt. See for yourself."

My brother tossed me the round clump of hair. The moment my fingers wrapped around it, I noticed that its thick curls were smoother and silkier than anything I'd handled off an animal. When I got a better look at it, I understood why.

Old Red was right—it wasn't fur or wool. The hair was most definitely human.

Sixteen

MANIFEST DESTINY

Or, Gustav and I Round Up Our Clues—and Find One's Gone Astray

Sweet Jesus . . . a *scalp*?" I said.

My brother nodded, looking both puzzled and pleased, like a fellow who drops a bucket down a well and hauls up a twenty-pound catfish.

"You don't think Barson and Welsh are ridin' with Indians, do you?" I asked him.

Old Red shook his head. "Indians ain't the only ones known to bark folks. That scalp there ain't fresh-cut, so for all we know some asshole bought it in a saloon for two bits."

"How does it help us, then?"

Gustav gave me that droopy-eyed "Some folks never learn" look he often puts on before bludgeoning me with a quote from Mr. Holmes.

"Too much data's like too much money," he said. "Ain't no such thing."

This was, for once, not a quote but an attempt by my brother to craft a Holmes-style homily all his own. While it was pithy enough, I found it lacking in another, more important regard: truth.

"I don't know, Brother," I said. "The way I hear it, 'it is of the highest importance in the art of detection to be able to recognize, out of a number of facts, which are incidental and which vital. Otherwise, your energy and attention must be dissipated instead of concentrated.'"

Old Red's expression went from smug to smoldering, for he knew whose words I'd turned against him: It was Holmes himself, sermonizing to poor, patient Watson in "The Reigate Puzzle."

"Yeah, I can quote the man, too," I said. "It's a wonder I can say anything that *don't* come outta one of them stories, the number of times you've had me read 'em out."

"You might've done you some memorizin', but you ain't *learned* squat," Gustav grumbled. "A goddamn scalp lyin' around ain't 'incidental.'"

"Alright, alright. Don't get your bloomers in a bunch, granny."

I looked down at the tuft of hair again. The locks on top were blond and curly and silky to the touch. But the bottom, I noticed now, rubbed coarsely against my fingertips, almost like burlap. When I flipped it over, I saw a pattern woven into the underside—a dense tapestry of tiny loops.

I poked my tongue up against my cheek, the better to bite it should the urge to laugh become overpowering.

"You know, there's something mighty strange about this here scalp." I offered it back to Old Red. "You didn't have no light to go by outside. Maybe you oughta look at it again."

Gustav snatched the scalp out of my hand and turned it over—and realized instantly it was no scalp at all. He looked up at me, scowling, and waited for me to crack a funny.

I bit my tongue.

"It's a wig," he finally mumbled.

"A wig? No!" I leaned closer and pretended to give the hairpiece another going over. "Well, I'll be . . . you're right! Looks like the kind they make for bald fellers. I believe they call 'em toupees."

"For Christ's sake, you don't have to humor me," Old Red said glumly. "I was wrong, that's all. I ain't gone feebleminded."

"Now that's a debate I wouldn't mind havin'. Cuz if today's any indication—"

"Otto?"

"Yeah?"

"Shut up."

"Well . . . since you asked so nicely."

For the next minute, Gustav just sat there cogitating, and I just stood there watching him do it. Oftentimes, my brother comes out of these little quiet spells with some new deduction to show for it. This time, however, all he came out with was a curse.

"Aw, shit," he moaned, hunching over and putting his hands up against his face.

He'd hardly broken a sweat during his dash to catch the train, but now his skin glistened with fresh beads of perspiration.

"I'm all tangled up," he said miserably. "At first, I was sittin' here thinkin', 'It was the feller from the crate a-wearin' that wig. That's how he disappeared after tossin' Pezullo's body off the train. He costumed himself and mixed in with the passengers.' But then I got to thinkin', 'If it's so damn easy for him to sneak around in the Pullmans, why was he hidin' in the baggage car in the first place? Why not just buy a *ticket*?' And then I think, 'Hold on—if he didn't buy a ticket, how'd he get his crate on the train?' And then out of nowhere I start thinkin', 'A little bowl? A dinky little goddamn fancy-ass *bowl*? What the hell's that all about?'"

"Sounds like you're thinkin' too much."

"I ain't thinkin' *enough*—not straight, anyway."

I couldn't have asked for a better setup for another easy gibe at my brother, but I let it slide past.

"Look," I said, "I don't know about the wig or the stowaway or the bowl. But I got an idea about that box. If we wanna know who had it put on the train, all we need do is find the manifest. Pezullo had to have one. Ain't no way he kept track of all the crap back here off the top of his head."

Old Red nodded with a weariness that bordered on despair. "That's a good thought, Brother. But didn't you notice? The crate didn't have no tag."

"Torn off, most likely," I said. "Still, with a box that big? Wouldn't surprise me if Pezullo made some kinda special note on it in the manifest. You know, 'heavy load' or 'overweight—extra charge' or 'pain in the ass—bang this bastard up.' Something like that."

"What would a manifest look like?" Gustav asked, brightening up a bit.

I pointed at a clipboard loaded with crinkled papers hanging just above Pezullo's desk. I'd noticed it up there earlier, when I'd fished El Numero Uno's newsprint shroud from the drawers.

"Like that, I reckon." I pulled the clipboard down and gave the papers a look—and glanced over my shoulder to flash my brother a grin. "We got us a trail."

As a granary clerk once upon a time, I'd become accustomed to poring over ledgers crammed edge to edge with numbers and names scribbled so teeny it's a wonder I didn't need one of Mr. Holmes's "magnifying glasses" to read them. In comparison, Pezullo's manifest was as clean, clear, and easy to read as the sign above a saloon.

There were four columns: passenger names, boarding stations, destinations, and baggage. All I had to do was scan the fourth column for some mention of a box big enough to hold a buffalo, then pop over to the first column to see who it belonged to.

Or so I thought. I quickly noticed that something about those middle columns was very wrong. Instead of saying "Ogden" and "Oakland," they said "Oakland" and "Ogden."

I looked at the upper-right corner of the first page, reading a group of numbers I'd originally skimmed over: "7/14/93."

The date was July 16. Which meant the manifest wasn't for the run to Oakland—it was for the last run *from* Oakland.

I went back to Pezullo's desk and rifled through the drawers, finding more old manifests there. But there was no manifest for an Ogden–Oakland trip departing on the 16th of July.

"Well, hell," I said. "I guess they got rid of the real manifest same time they got rid of that bloody brick. If that pigheaded conductor had just given us five minutes for a good look with lanterns, maybe we . . ."

I turned to find my brother staring at the floor, slouch-backed and glassy-eyed. He was off in another of his trances.

This one he snapped out of quicker, though—and without any cussing.

"Why tear the tag off the crate? Why get rid of the manifest?" he asked in a way that called for no answers—because he already had the answers himself. "Why cover your trail unless it leads somewhere?"

"Like where?"

"Like to somebody you're tryin' to protect, of course," Old Red said. "Somebody who's still on this train."

Seventeen

CARLIN

Or, The Express Stops Again but the Peculiarities Don't

The train gave a little jerk, and the pulsing rhythm that throbbed through the floorboards began to slow.

"Let's have a look," Gustav said, hobbling toward the side door.

I slid the door open, and together we watched large, boxy shapes glide past us in the gloom outside. The distance between them shrank even as the boxes themselves grew—scattered shacks and farmhouses were giving way to clustered stores and warehouses.

We'd finally reached Carlin, Nevada.

"Supposin' whoever killed Pezullo really is still aboard," I said. "This'll be his chance to slip away, won't it?"

"Depends."

"On what?"

"On whether he *wants* to slip away."

Old Red sucked in a chestful of cool night air. He blew it out slowly, as if reluctant to let go of something precious.

"Who'd even *think* to get rid of a baggage tag and a manifest?" he said. "Not a hobo. And not a farmer turned long rider, neither. It had to be someone who knows a thing or two about how railroads run things."

"Like an S.P. employee, you mean." I snorted out a mirthless chuckle. "Maybe Colonel Crowe ain't so crazy after all."

"Whoa, there—wouldn't have to be a railroader we're talkin' about," Gustav chided me gently. "A passenger could learn plenty about how baggage is handled on trains . . . provided he'd been ridin' the things enough."

The Pacific Express was moving so slowly by now a man could out-race it at a brisk walk. We'd be stopping any second.

"Well . . . you may as well get to the gents' and clean yourself up," my brother said. "We're gonna be talkin' to the law soon, and I don't want you smellin' like a bull's balls when we do it."

"Gee, thanks, Brother—it's so sweet the way you look out for me the way you do."

I started for the door to the Pullmans. Old Red didn't.

"You ain't comin' with?" I asked him.

He gave his head a weary shake. "I wanna do some more pokin' around in here."

"Oh, come on. Haven't you poked enough for now? You're baked. Give yourself a rest." ·

Gustav had been slumping next to the side door, but now he straightened up and folded his arms across his chest. "I'm gettin' my second wind."

I licked my index finger and pointed it straight up, as if testing the air. "That's funny. I ain't gettin' so much as a breeze offa you, let alone a wind."

"How could you even tell, with all the hot air *you're* always blowin'?"

"Alright, suit yourself—just be careful," I said. "I am retiring to the washroom to complete my evening toilette."

I stepped into the vestibule—then spun and poked my head back in before the door could close behind me.

"But just so you know . . . you ain't exactly smellin' of lilacs and lavender yourself."

"Dammit, would you get already?"

I got.

When I reached the WC, the first thing I did was take a look at myself in the mirror. It's a wonder the glass didn't crack. Dried blood speckled with sand ran in a stripe over my lips and chin, and my swollen nose was as bulbous and purple as an oversized radish. All I had to work with there in the privy was a sink basin the size of a smallish spittoon, but I made the most of it, scrubbing up as quickly (and, when washing anywhere in the vicinity of my nose, as gently) as possible.

Just as I got myself looking more or less human, the train stopped. After a few last splashes over my face and under my arms, I went back to the baggage car and gave the door a few quiet little raps. (Despite the night's excitement, most of our fellow passengers had somehow managed to fall asleep, if the snores from their berths were any indication.) Gustav didn't answer, though I tried some not-so-little raps, too, so I headed outside to hunt him down.

I hopped off the train onto the darkened platform of a small station. The brick ticket office nearby was lit up, and I could hear men inside talking excitedly—or perhaps angrily.

"Better get in there," Kip said.

I whipped around to find the news butch stepping from the shadows near the Wells Fargo car.

"Lockhart's liquored-up somethin' fierce," he said. "And the things he's been sayin' to your brother shouldn't oughta be said man-to-man unless—"

He said more, I guess, but I wasn't listening. I was running.

Even before I made it inside, I heard the words "goddamned shpinelessh coward" bellowed at such a volume I would've recognized the voice had I been all the way back in Ogden. It was Lockhart, and I had no doubt who the old Pinkerton was hollering at—though I knew all too well he was the furthest thing from "shpinelessh."

"For the last time, we ain't goin' with you," my brother was saying as I came rushing in. "But we ain't stoppin' you, neither. If you wanna go off and get yourself killed, you're more than welcome to do it."

"Well, that'sh jusht what I'll do if I have to!"

Lockhart was dressed now—after a fashion. He'd pulled on trousers, but fastening any but the topmost button was beyond him in his current state, and the nightshirt he'd tucked into his pants flopped lewdly out through the fly. He'd thrown on a suit coat, as well, but it was too thin for a long ride through a chilly desert night. Not that he hadn't given some thought to keeping himself warm: A bulge in his right coat pocket exactly matched the size and shape of a flask.

Lockhart pivoted slowly on his heel, his stare piercing each man in the room in turn. There were five of us: Gustav, me, Wiltrout, and two fellows I didn't recognize.

"Not a one of you ish willin' to posshe up with ol' Burl Lockhart?" He stopped his spin with me, and when he spoke again, he sounded less badgering than beseeching. "Not a one?"

"I'm sorry, Mr. Lockhart . . . I gotta stick with my brother," I said. "And anyway, if you're talkin' about settin' out after the Give-'em-Hell Boys, hadn't you oughta wait till—?"

"Shpinelessh *cowardsh*!" Lockhart roared, and he went staggering out into the night.

A moment of awkward, sheepish silence followed. After all, what does one say after being berated by a national hero, even if he is a drunk, deranged one?

It was one of the men I didn't recognize who spoke first—a stoop-shouldered fellow with the tousled hair and sleepy, disappointed demeanor of someone who's recently been roused from a comfortable bed.

"Well," he said, shambling through a low gate into what looked like a small corral of worktables and filing cabinets, "I guess I'll go check with Ogden again."

He took a seat in front of a telegraph key and got to clacking away on it.

"So what'd I miss?" I asked my brother. "Other than more abuse from ol' Burl, I mean?"

"The stationmaster there sent word to Ogden and San Francisco about the holdup," Old Red said, nodding at the fellow working the telegraph. "I gave him that speech of Barson's to tap out, too. We ain't heard nothing back yet, but Lockhart was anxious to head off after the Give-'em-Hell Boys. I told him we still got business on the train."

Wiltrout snorted at my brother like an old hog nosing up to a trough full of slop. "'Business on the train'? What would that be? It was your 'business' to protect us from Barson and Welsh, and you sure as hell didn't do that. It's a miracle they didn't make off with another fortune."

He was standing next to the other fellow there I didn't recognize, a middle-aged gent with slicked-back silver hair and a mustache so neatly trimmed it looked like a single gray pigeon feather balanced atop his lip. The conductor clapped him on the back.

"Thank God Morrison here kept his head."

So I *had* seen this man before—or at least the barrel of his rifle. He was the itchy-fingered messenger from the Wells Fargo car.

"Just doing my duty." He flashed a nervous, here-and-gone smile, his mustache feather fluttering up and down on twitchy lips.

"So what happened, exactly?" Gustav asked him.

"They told me to open the side door, and . . . well, I wouldn't." Morrison shrugged, looking disappointed that he didn't have more of a tale to tell. "I never even saw them. They kept to the shadows alongside the car."

"Oh, yeah? On which side of the train?"

"The left," Morrison said after a moment's thought. "Does it matter?"

Before my brother could answer—or, knowing him, *not* answer—the door to the platform opened, and Diana Caveo joined us inside.

She looked as fresh as if it were midmorning instead of midnight, having put up her dark hair and traded in her nightgown for a smartly tailored outfit of gray wool. She favored us with a smile as she walked up, and I gratefully replied in kind, relieved that she wasn't still mad at me for having Samuel stampede her from the baggage car earlier. She got no grin out of Wiltrout, though.

"Passengers should remain on the train," he huffed at her. "We'll be getting under way again shortly."

"Oh, I won't be long," Miss Caveo said, her smile undimmed. "I just need to send a telegram ahead to San Francisco. I'm sure news of the robbery is going to reach there long before we do, and I don't want my family worrying about me."

Wiltrout's eyelids fluttered, as if they were straining to keep the eyes beneath them from rolling heavenward. "We can't have the wire tied up with personal communiqués. We'll be in Reno come morning. You can send your message from there."

"Please, Captain," Miss Caveo persisted, stroking the man's pride with the rather overstuffed honorific railroaders use with conductors. "My parents will be beside themselves, and surely one little message won't—"

"If I let every passenger waste our time sending 'one little message,' we'd be here all night," Wiltrout interrupted in a tone of voice that added, *you silly woman.* "Now return to your berth *at once.*"

The conductor's pique seemed to pluck the pluck right out of the lady, and her cool, sardonic demeanor gave way to something weaker and weepier and more conventionally feminine.

"You don't understand. I had to leave the Exposition early because my father had a stroke and my poor mother's been under such a strain, and the smallest shock could . . . could . . ."

Her trembly words trailed off, and she brought up delicate fingers to wipe the pooling moisture from the corners of her eyes.

"Oh, now look what you went and did, you big bully," I said to Wiltrout. "I mean, really—DEAR MOM AND DAD STOP I AM FINE STOP. How long is that gonna take?"

"One message wouldn't be any trouble, Captain," Morrison added meekly. "And there aren't any other passengers around. Why not accommodate the young lady?"

Old Red chose not to weigh in. He simply watched with a detached air, as if observing the proceedings through a telescope.

"Oh . . . go talk to the stationmaster," Wiltrout grumbled. "If he has the time to send your message, fine. But *keep it brief.*"

"Thank you," Miss Caveo said, nodding first to Wiltrout, then to Morrison.

I got a nod, too—as well as a quick wink when she turned to go.

As she walked away, the door to the platform opened again. Wiltrout rumbled out a gruff growl of a sigh, apparently bracing himself for yet another passenger seeking special favors. But the man who sauntered in was hardly Pacific Express material—except perhaps as someone you might hire to scrub the dirt off between runs.

He was a chubby, chipmunk-cheeked fellow in clothes so wrinkled he appeared not only to have been sleeping in them but to have used them as his pajamas unironed for most of his adult life. When he saw me—and the badge on my chest—he broke into a grin so broad it bordered on unbalanced.

"Shoo-wee! Looks like you really took it on the nose, pussyfooter!"

The man guffawed at his own joke, the heaving of his belly shifting the folds of his creased coat to reveal something with a dull metal gleam pinned to his shirt.

He was wearing a star, too.

"Well, you are one lucky son of a bitch, whether you know it or not," he said to me, still chortling. "Last railroad dick Barson and Welsh got their hands on, we had to cut down from a telegraph pole."

The lawman turned his attention to Wiltrout, and his already maniacal glee took on a spiteful edge.

"But I reckon you're even luckier still, ain't you, Cap'n? An S.P. man livin' through one brush with the Give-'em-Hell Boys—that's fortunate. But two? That's downright miraculous. *Now*." He gave his flabby hands an earsplitting clap. "I was told you brought some stiffs with you this time."

"Let's get this over with," Wiltrout said sourly, brushing past the man on his way to the platform.

"So you would be Sheriff . . . ?" Gustav said as the rest of us set off after the conductor.

"*Constable* Leck Reeves, pride and joy of Carlin, Nevada."

"Riiiiight," my brother replied, clearly unconvinced that the constable was capable of inspiring either pride or joy in anyone.

Before we stepped outside, I stole a peek back at Miss Caveo, hoping to find her perhaps pilfering a peek at *me*. Alas, she was paying me no mind whatsoever—her full attention was on the stationmaster, who was jotting something down on a piece of paper as the lady hovered over him, whispering.

I looked ahead again just in time to find myself approaching the back of Morrison's head at an alarming speed. I stumbled to a stop, barely managing to keep my bloated nose out of the messenger's pomade-slicked hair.

"What the hell?" Wiltrout muttered.

I leaned around Morrison to see why everyone had stopped.

Up ahead, two men were grappling in the dark beside the train. And from the way they were punching and clawing and kicking, it looked like they meant to kill each another.

Eighteen

DISSIMULO

Or, I Introduce Myself—and Bid Farewell to Old Red

ooks like the little one's got the upper hand," Constable Reeves said with a chuckle, making no move to break up the fight. Quite the contrary, he seemed to be enjoying it so immensely I almost expected him to pull out his folding money and start quoting us odds—though which of the brawlers he would've backed was unclear, as they both leaned toward the puny side.

"Come on," Gustav said to me, and we waded in together and pulled the two apart.

I ended up grabbing Dr. Chan. Old Red got Kip.

"What's going on here?" Wiltrout demanded as we let them go stumbling from our grips. I'd expected him to roar like a bear with his butt in a steel-jaw trap, but he kept his voice to a mere growl. "Explain yourselves at once."

Kip snatched his cap off the ground and jammed it back atop his head. "It's a good thing I stayed out here to keep watch. I caught the Chinaman trying to sneak into the baggage car through the side door."

"I wasn't trying to 'sneak' in!" Chan protested.

"Keep your voice down," Wiltrout snapped. He jabbed a finger at the nearest Pullman. "There are *passengers* trying to sleep in there."

He said this as though Chan wasn't a passenger himself—and as far as the conductor was concerned, he probably wasn't. He was more like unwanted freight.

Chan nodded and took a moment to catch his breath and smooth out his suit, recovering the deferential manner a man in his position can't survive without.

"I'm sorry," he said, his tone low and even now. "I simply wanted to check my things. It's been an eventful evening, and I was worried that some of the baggage might have been damaged. I don't blame our young guard here for overreacting. It's my fault, really. I apologize for the disturbance."

Wiltrout nodded curtly, placated. "Alright, fine. Get back to your berth. We'll be leaving shortly."

"But he *was* sneakin'," Kip whined.

Wiltrout silenced the kid with a scowl like a funnel cloud on the horizon—a storm you wouldn't want blowing your way.

"Pardon me," Chan said warily, obviously not keen on drawing another squall down upon himself, "but where's Mr. Lockhart?"

"He thinks he can catch the Give-'em-Hell Boys single-handed," my brother told him. "I reckon he's headed to the nearest livery to hire himself a horse."

"Or the nearest saloon to empty himself a bottle," I added.

The mask of calm Chan had affixed to his face fell away, revealing a surprise bordering on panic.

"He can't do that. He can't leave the train."

"He can and he did," Wiltrout said. "Now if you'll excuse us, we have things to do here."

"But—"

"*If you will excuse us . . .*"

Chan was being dismissed, ordered from our sight. But he didn't scurry back to our Pullman—he hurried *away* from the train, toward the station building.

"I'll find him . . . bring him back. Don't leave without us. Please."

" 'Please' doesn't enter into it," Wiltrout said. "We leave when we leave."

Constable Reeves had been leaning against a post nearby, soaking in the scene with a smirk. He straightened up as Chan moved past him.

"I wouldn't tarry in Carlin, I was you. Your kind ain't too popular hereabouts."

The lawman was still smiling, but it was unclear if he was offering friendly advice or a veiled threat. Either way, it was enough to stop Chan—for a moment.

"I won't be long," he said, looking back at Wiltrout.

The conductor shrugged. "I don't care."

Chan started away again. If he'd so much as glanced at me as he walked past, I swear I would've marched right off with him. But he'd no doubt learned long ago not to look for help from the likes of me—unless, as with Lockhart, he was paying for it.

He kept his gaze straight ahead.

"Shouldn't we oughta—?" I said to Gustav.

"Probably," he cut in. "But right now we can't."

"You bet your ass you can't," Wiltrout snarled. "The only thing you 'oughta' is get those corpses off my train. Now."

I turned back to Old Red, crooking a thumb at the conductor. "We don't really hafta take orders off this big peacock, do we?"

"Nope," my brother said. "But it just so happens I was about to suggest we hand them bodies over to the constable, anyway. So we can move along to other matters, you understand."

"Well, now . . . that *does* sound sensible."

We stepped around a fuming Wiltrout and headed for the Express.

"The Chinaman wouldn't be lookin' for *Burl* Lockhart, would he?" Reeves asked.

"How'd you guess?" I said.

"Oh, I know Burl. I hear about a 'Lockhart' off to catch the Give-'em-Hell Boys alone—but stoppin' at a saloon first? Gotta be him. Used to be he knew every trick there was to robbin' trains, banks, and

women of their virtue. He really was somethin' back in the long-ago."
Reeves chuckled and clapped his hands over his prodigious belly. "But
then again so was I . . . and just look at me now."

While the constable was waxing nostalgic, Old Red and I were
climbing into the baggage car. We paused over El Numero Uno, who
was still tied to his chair, flat on his back and legs in the air like a dead
El Cucaracha.

"Ain't you gonna come up and have a look 'fore we unload this
poor feller?" my brother asked Reeves.

"Whatever for?"

"Well, it's the scene of the crime, ain't it?"

The lawman guffawed like Gustav had just told him the one about
the Irishman, the Mormon, and the thirsty cougar.

" 'The scene of the crime'? Friend, that ain't the scene of the
crime." Reeves waved a limp hand at the tracks behind the train. "*That*
was the scene of the crime. The Southern Pacific line. Elko County.
The Humboldt Range. Out *there*. I'm just here to collect them car-
casses. Whatever happened in the desert ain't none of my concern."

"Well, whose concern is it, then?" Old Red shot back.

"The county sheriff's, of course. But I'll let you in on a little secret:
He don't give a shit, neither."

Reeves busted out laughing again.

Wiltrout and Kip and Morrison all glared at him, and for a moment I actually felt a twinge of railroader-to-railroader kinship with
them. If the Give-'em-Hell Boys had strung up every last one of us, *this*
was what the law would have to say about it: *Ain't none of my concern.*
No wonder the S.P. hired its own police.

Reeves had ridden in on a wagon, and a minute later Old Red and
I were sliding the King of the Hoboes into the bed, throne and all.

"Don't bother cuttin' him loose . . . we'll just plant him that way,"
the constable had told us. "Ain't no way the good citizens of Carlin are
gonna spring for a coffin for a murdered tramp."

It took two trips to move Pezullo.

Despite the huffing and puffing required to tote around a couple corpses, Gustav kept up his end of things (the feet, to be specific) just fine. In fact, my brother was looking stronger with each passing minute—his second wind had blown in after all. He even had enough spare breath to pester Reeves with questions as we worked. The Pride of Carlin didn't mind, being the kind of flannelmouth who could jabber away about baseball, the weather, or whatever through anything and everything, with the (possible) exception of his own funeral.

Pezullo's body would go to the local undertaker's, he told us, where it would be boxed up to await word from the baggageman's family. El Numero Uno, on the other hand, would go straight into an unmarked grave as soon as the constable's deputy was awake to do the digging. And as for the Give-'em-Hell Boys—well, they were the Southern Pacific's problem.

"Mark my words: Railroad dicks or bounty hunters, that's who's gonna bed them fellers down in the end. Not a lawman, and sure as hell not a posse. Cuz no one's gonna stick their necks out for the S.P. unless they're gettin' paid to . . . and maybe not even then, right, boys?"

Reeves gave me and Old Red a wink like a secret handshake—a gesture meant to show we understood each other, were cut from the same cheap cloth. Somehow, I managed not to puke.

As the constable was hauling himself up into his wagon and saying his good-byes (and not getting any fond farewells in return), the stationmaster hustled outside with a piece of paper flapping in his hand.

"Finally heard back from Ogden, Captain!"

Miss Caveo followed him outside.

"Well, let's hear it," Wiltrout said.

"It's from Crowe." The stationmaster straightened his stooped back, as if he couldn't read the colonel's words without coming to attention. " 'Dispatching horse cars, S.P. agents to initiate pursuit. Do not, repeat, do not talk to newspapers about B and W statement, bounty. Pacific Express proceed to Oakland posthaste. Dissimulo orders same.' " The stationmaster's bony shoulders drooped again. "That's it."

"What's a Di-sim-u-lo?" Kip asked.

"It's Latin. Like, oh . . . *caveat emptor,* for instance," Miss Caveo explained, though I doubt our young news butch was familiar with the phrase (even if he did embrace its philosophy). "It means 'to keep secret.'"

Morrison turned toward Wiltrout, his silvery eyebrows shooting up so high they almost impaled themselves on his widow's peak. "Secret orders?"

"Don't look at me," the conductor snapped. "I have no idea what Crowe's talking about."

"I do," I said. "Dissimulo's the fake name the colonel had me and my brother travelin' under."

"So why have you been calling yourselves Holmes?" Wiltrout demanded.

I shrugged. "Just suits us better."

"I'd have to agree," Miss Caveo said. "It would be nice to know your real names, though."

I gave her my best stab at a courtly bow. "Otto and Gustav Amlingmeyer, at your service."

"Amlingmeyer?" Kip giggled. "Jeez, you two were better off with Di-sim-u-lo!"

"So," Old Red said to Miss Caveo, "if *dissimulo* means 'to keep secret,' how 'bout the handle Lockhart was usin'? *Custos?* That mean anything?"

"'To get stinkin' drunk'?" I suggested.

The lady shook her head. "'Guardian,'" she said.

"Well, all any of this means to me is 'waste of time,'" Wiltrout groused. "All aboard. We're going."

"Hold on," I said. "Chan ain't back with Lockhart yet. You can't just leave 'em here."

Wiltrout headed for the Pullmans. "I've left better men than them worse places than this."

"You haven't taken on water yet," the stationmaster pointed out. "Surely, there's still a few minutes to spare."

Wiltrout spun around and glowered at the man as if he'd just complimented the conductor on his cute little caboose.

"Of course, it's your decision, Captain," the stationmaster added meekly.

"And no one better forget it." Wiltrout yanked out a pocket watch and gave it a glare that should've melted its gears to slag. Then he shifted the glare to me. "You've got ten minutes."

"Thanks . . . Captain." I turned to the stationmaster. "Now if you could just point us to the nearest stables and saloons . . ."

There wasn't much pointing to be done—there were only two liveries and two drinking houses within walking distance.

"Hold up, Brother," Gustav said as I started to leave. "I can't go with, just yet. I still got things to do here."

"Things" meant snooping, I was certain, and it put a burr in my boot that Old Red would choose to look for clues rather than a man who needed our help.

"Fine," I said. "I'll just have to rustle up Chan and Lockhart by myself."

"No, you won't."

Miss Caveo walked over and linked arms with me like I was her escort to the debutantes' ball. There was nothing girlish or demure about her grip on me, though—that was solid steel. She looked up and smiled, and I saw that same steel aglint in her eyes.

"I'm going with you," she said.

Nineteen

THORNTON'S BOILER #2

Or, Things Heat Up When I Find Carlin's New "Coolie"

I wasted about a minute trying to change Miss Caveo's mind. I *know* it was about a minute, because Wiltrout shut me up with one word.

"Nine."

He was staring at his pocket watch like he was counting down the seconds to "Eight" . . . and zero.

"Go," Old Red told me.

Up till then, he'd stayed out of my debate with the lady—which hadn't been much of a "debate," really, since I'd been doing all the arguing. All she did was tug at my arm and tell me I was wasting time.

My brother shifted his gaze to her now. "But be careful."

I couldn't tell if he was warning her or warning me *about* her, and I didn't have time to get a better bead on his meaning. Miss Caveo was pulling at my arm like a team of horses in harness, and there was nothing to do but let loose the brake and go rolling off with her.

"So . . . which first?" I said as we hurried around the station toward the dusty streets of Carlin. "Stables or saloons?"

The lady simply looked up and cocked an eyebrow.

"Saloons it is," I said.

Miss Caveo finally let go of my arm, though she remained close at my side—we would've been walking shoulder to shoulder if she was a foot taller. As it was, we were (her) shoulder to (my) elbow. And she was still staring up at me.

"You might wanna look where you're headed," I suggested.

"I'm just wondering when you're going to ask me."

I turned my head and held her gaze, the two of us charging forward now with *neither* of us looking ahead.

"Ask what?"

A flicker of amusement passed over her pretty face without quite becoming a smile.

"Why I insisted on coming with you. When you were trying to talk me out of it, all you could say was it wasn't proper. You never addressed my reasons."

I shrugged—and looked away first. We were in the middle of the street, and I steered us left toward the only buildings in sight with light still aglow in the windows.

"I didn't think you *had* a good reason."

"Exactly. Because you didn't ask."

"Alright, then. Why are you so keen on helpin' Dr. Chan?"

"Why are *you?*"

I shook my head and chuckled and almost muttered something about the inscrutable ways of Woman. But it was plenty scrutable what a suffragette would make of such a comment, so I let it lie.

"Cuz he seems like a decent feller," I said.

"That's all? It has nothing to do with your job?"

"Miss, let me tell you something—I consider that a *much* better reason than my job."

"You don't like being a railroad detective?"

"I don't mind the 'detective' part so much. It's the 'railroad' I ain't fond of."

I glanced down and found her still watching me intently.

"You know, you sure are askin' a lot of questions. What is it that makes me so intriguin', exactly—my good looks or my way with words? Or is it just sheer animal magnetism?"

She broke off her stare. It was hard to tell in the gloom of night, but it looked like I finally got a blush out of her, too.

"Actually, it's your job," she said.

"Oh? You thinkin' of takin' Barson's advice and applyin' for it?"

This was intended as a funny, of course, and it even got a bark of laughter out of the lady—though the sound of it was far harsher than I'd have thought such a pretty throat could produce. A shout from up ahead cut her off.

"I said get me another drink, Chink!"

It didn't take any deducifying to know what that meant. We'd found Chan—and just in time.

The yelling was coming from a dilapidated saloon with all the elegance and charm of a sharecropper's shack. The peeling paint on the sign above the batwings said THORNTON'S BOILER #2. Assuming #2 was a step down from #1, #3 wouldn't have been much more than a bog hole with a jug in it.

"I hate to keep repeatin' myself, but this ain't no place for a lady. Wait here."

Miss Caveo didn't break her stride. "As a matter of fact, you *are* repeating yourself, Mr. Amlingmeyer. And I didn't appreciate hearing it the first time."

"Well, try hearin' it like this, then." I wrapped my arm around hers again and pulled her to a stop just outside the saloon. "I ain't just askin' you to stay out here cuz you're a lady—or even cuz you're an especially fine lady I'd hate to see hurt. I'm askin' cuz I'm the one wearin' this two-bit badge, so it's on me to keep Chan *and* you out of trouble. You're interested in my job? Fine. Stand back and let me do it. Please."

As I spoke, the peevish pucker to the lady's face faded away, and when I was through she was back to her old, sardonic self.

"That was positively inspirational, Otto. The Southern Pacific would be proud."

"Well, I still ain't proud of *it*." I turned my body toward Thornton's Boiler but kept my gaze on her. "You'll wait?"

She nodded. "You'd better hurry. Mr. Wiltrout's probably down to four by now."

I didn't point out that I'd been *trying* to hurry all along. When a man actually wins an argument with a woman, the last thing he needs to do is kick up a whole new one.

"What the hell is goin' on here?" I bellowed as I pushed through the batwings into the saloon. I was asking largely for effect, but it was actually a pretty good question.

Burl Lockhart lay flat on his back atop the nearest card table, the coins and greenbacks spread across his stomach and chest rising and falling with his every rafter-rattling snore. Three men—the dingy dive's only customers—sat around him. They had cards in their hands and frozen smiles on their dirty faces. Two of the men were oil-smeared railroaders, but the third had the grubby, dusty look of a prospector still hunting for his first big strike. Dr. Chan stood nearby, his spectacles askew, his fine suit clothes mussed, and an opened magazine draped over his head like a bonnet. A gray-bearded man in a sweat-yellowed shirt gaped at me from behind the bar.

"Well?" I demanded, coming to a stop legs spread, arms akimbo. I puffed out my chest, hoping the star pinned there would prove sufficient distraction from the emptiness at my hip where a six-gun should've been.

"A-ain't nothin' wrong," one of the railroad men stammered. "W-we're just h-havin' us a little fun is—"

"The Chinaman tried to take our lazy Susan," the prospector broke in. He was a big, grimy man—bigger and grimier than me even—and a pussyfooter's badge obviously didn't impress him. "I told him he could have the old sot if he played coolie for us for a spell."

"He said he'd help me move Mr. Lockhart if I bought a round for him and his friends," Chan said, equal parts angry and ashamed. He pulled the magazine off his head and let it drop to the floor. "Now he won't do it."

The big man grinned. "I'm still thirsty."

"Well, you can just go outside and find yourself a trough, then," I said. "Cuz these here gentlemen are passengers of the Southern Pacific Railroad, and they're gettin' back aboard their train—*now.*"

I took a step toward the table, meaning to haul Lockhart up and out of there. The railroaders weren't going to stop me. They were slouching low in their seats, completely cowed.

Their brawny pal, on the other hand, was all bull.

"God damn," he spat, pulling his chair around to face me fully— and put himself between me and Lockhart. "The Chink said he and the coot was from the Pacific Express, but I didn't believe it. Shit, what's next? They gonna start makin' folks share their seats with *niggers*? It ain't right. Someone oughta put a stop to it . . . huh, boys?"

"Th-that's right, Pat," one of the "boys" mumbled.

"I reckon so, Pat," the other added with a listless nod.

"It's settled, then." Pat pointed at Chan with a filthy finger the size of a sausage. "This here slant ain't gettin' back on that train."

I sighed and gave my head a slow, exasperated shake, as if I'd grown weary of the foolishness I had to beat out of such men on a daily basis.

"Let me ask y'all something," I said. "You ever hear of 'Big Red' Amlingmeyer?"

Lockhart cut loose with a raspy roar of a snore. The men gathered around him stayed silent.

"No? Well, that's alright. I appreciate every opportunity to spread my legend. Now . . . I can kick your asses one by one or two by two, but I'd prefer you didn't rush me in a bunch. You'd just get in each other's way, and it'd make things altogether too easy for me."

"Ha!" Pat scoffed. "You're so tough, pussyfooter, what the hell happened to your face?"

"Oh, this?" I waggled my fingers before my swollen nose. "Stand up, and I'll show you."

And he actually obliged me, hauling himself off his duff with a crack of his knuckles and a muttered curse. He was only half straightened up, not firm on his feet yet, when I stepped up quick and slammed a fist into his face.

It wasn't entirely fair, I'll grant you—but it was entirely satisfying. Pat toppled backward over his chair and ended up a moaning heap on the floor, blood spurting from his nose.

"So, boys—who's next?" I said to his drinking buddies.

But they weren't even looking at me. One was staring down at Pat, wide-eyed and white-faced. The other was gawping at something behind me, even wider-eyed and whiter-faced.

"*Papà! Papà,* what have they done to you?" Miss Caveo called out as she rushed into the room.

When I turned to look at her, my knee-jerk exasperation turned to ice-cold dread, for I also caught sight of the saloonkeeper—and the shotgun in his hands. The barrel of his scattergun hadn't quite cleared the bar, which was the only reason I still had a neck (and head) for the young lady to save.

"Is he alive? What happened?" Miss Caveo asked, swooping to Lockhart's side at the card table. "*Papà* . . . can you hear me? It's Lullabelle! Lullabelle's here!"

Lockhart snorked out another tremendous snore.

"Heavens, no! The vapors!" Miss Caveo swung around to face the bartender. "Please tell me you didn't serve this man alcohol!"

"I surely did. And why shouldn't I?"

"You don't understand—my father has toxophiliphalia of the liver!" Miss Caveo's brown eyes brimmed with tears, and she aimed an accusatory, trembly-lipped look at Chan. "What kind of servant are you? You know one sip could kill him!"

Despite all he'd been through, Chan managed some decent dramatics himself, hanging his head and mumbling an apology.

Miss Caveo began stroking Lockhart's thinning gray hair. "I'm taking him to San Francisco for a special cure, but he's been in such pain lately," she told the railroaders. "Perhaps . . . perhaps he wanted to end it all."

"It ain't my fault," the saloonkeeper whined, tucking his shotgun back under the bar. "The old geezer'd had a lot more than a sip before he even came in here."

"Shut up, Thornton," one of the railroad men snapped. He turned toward Miss Caveo but couldn't quite bring himself to look her in the eye. "I'm truly sorry about all this, miss."

"We didun mean nuh hahm," Pat added, struggling to sit up with a grubby paw pressed over his nose.

"I hope you can find it in your heart to forgive us, miss," the other railroader threw in. "Your pa came stumblin' in here hollerin' for whiskey, claimin' he was Burl Lockhart. Well . . . to be honest, we just pegged him for a crazy old boozehound."

"That's the toxophiliphalia," "Lullabelle" sobbed. "It's already affecting his brain!"

I stepped over and draped a comforting arm around her shoulders. "There, there, Miss Bernhardt. We'd best get your father back to the train pronto. I hear one of the passengers is a doctor. Maybe he knows something about . . . uhhh . . . the old gentleman's condition. We can have him take a look."

"Yes . . . it's worth a try," Miss Caveo whispered, fighting to choke back her tears. "I must hold on to hope. I must . . . strive to . . . stay strong."

She began weeping softly, and by the time Chan and I were dragging Lockhart toward the door, she wasn't the only one—I could've sworn I saw Pat wiping at his eyes.

"First you tell Wiltrout your daddy had a stroke," I said once we were outside. "Then it turns out he's got a fatal case of tacofaultyfamilia of the liver—and he's Burl Lockhart?" I shook my head, grinning with incredulous admiration. "Miss, you are without a doubt the most audacious liar I've ever seen . . . and I'm mighty grateful for it."

"As am I," Chan panted, straining alongside me like a farm horse in harness—with a limp Lockhart as the plow. "Thank you."

"You're welcome, gentlemen," Miss Caveo replied. "But, please— let's not call it lying. I'm merely . . . *persuasive*."

Footsteps echoed out of the darkness behind us, and I got set to drop Lockhart and bring up my fists. The gunbelt around Lockhart's waist—*my* gunbelt—would offer no help if Pat and his friends were having yet another change of heart. The holster was empty. My Colt was gone.

Fortunately, there was no need for either gunplay or fisticuffs: It was Kip dashing down the street toward us.

"Hurry!" the news butch called to us. "Wiltrout's tryin' to—" He skidded to a stop and pointed at Lockhart. "Is he dead?"

"Dead *drunk*," I said.

"Well, we better get him to the train quick." Kip circled around and grabbed Lockhart by the feet. "Your ten minutes was up five minutes ago."

We set off again at as quick a pace as the toting of a potted Pinkerton will allow.

"So did my brother just leave it to you to find us or is he actually out lookin', too?" I asked Kip.

"No, he ain't lookin' for you," the kid said. "In fact, he's been makin' it a point not to go nowhere."

We rounded a corner and came within sight of the station. Up ahead, a group of men were gathered by the engine, tugging at something stretched in front of the cowcatcher. For a moment, I thought we had yet another corpse to contend with. But then I saw that the body on the tracks was very much alive and kicking—kicking hard, too, for Bedford the fireman took a boot to the balls that dropped him to his knees.

"That's it!" Wiltrout roared. "Open up the throttle and flatten the bastard!"

"No need for that, Admiral!" I shouted. "We're back, Brother!"

Gustav sat up straight. "Alright—we can leave now, Wiltrout." He got to his feet and walked over to Bedford, who was still doubled up, gasping for breath. "Sorry 'bout crackin' your *huevos*. I swear I wasn't aimin' for 'em."

And off he went, heading around the engine to meet the rest of us at the steps into our sleeper. Wiltrout stalked after him, spluttering curses vile enough to strip the paint off a church. Old Red did his best to ignore the abuse, as if it was the buzzing of an angry bee he'd vowed for some reason not to swat. Yet the conductor didn't abandon his harangue, ranting and raving even as we hoisted Lockhart up into the Pullman.

"You're through, do you hear me?" he said, hopping in behind us and slamming the door shut. He stomped through the narrow vestibule toward my brother, jostling Kip, Chan, and even Miss Caveo out of his way as he went. "First chance I get, I'm sending another wire to Ogden and San Francisco. Mark my words: You're going to see some *real* Southern Pacific detectives on this train before long. If you're lucky, all they'll do is toss you and your imbecile brother off. Personally, I'm hoping you're not so lucky. Now get out of my way—and stay out of my way."

Wiltrout didn't wait for Old Red to step aside, shouldering him roughly into the wall as he marched off into the passenger compartment. And just as my brother was getting his footing back, he was stumbling again—as were we all.

The Pacific Express had heaved forward. We were leaving Carlin, hurtling back into the black desert night.

Twenty

NUTS

Or, We Get a Whiff of the Future—and It Doesn't Smell Good

It was quite the caravan that moved through our sleeper as the Express left Carlin behind. Chan, Miss Caveo, and Kip were in the lead, while my brother and I brought up the rear with Lockhart stretched between us like a whiskey-soaked hammock. We tried to keep our little cavalcade quiet, most of us practically walking on tippytoe, yet we needn't have bothered: Lockhart was snoring up such a ruckus one passenger after another popped out to shush us. Only one found anything funny about it all.

"Thank God he's snoring—it's the only way I know he's still breathing," said Mrs. Kier, leaning out of her berth as Gustav and I struggled to shove Lockhart up into his. "You know, he's lucky you two are so forgiving. After some of the things he said to you tonight, you'd be within your rights to chuck him right off the train."

With a final grunt, Old Red and I got Lockhart stretched out on his bed.

"We'll have our revenge yet, ma'am," I said. "When he wakes up, he's gonna have such a hangover he'll *wish* he was dead. Killin' him now would be sweet mercy."

Chester Q. Horner poked his head out into the hallway, his pompadour even more askew than the last time I'd seen it—it didn't seem to grow from his head so much as balance atop it like a puffy brown mortarboard.

"You wanna show some mercy, Otto?" the drummer said. "Hush up and let folks sleep."

When he saw Miss Caveo was with us, he grinned at her lecherously.

"Still out gallivanting with the boys at this hour?" He shook his head and gave her a teasing tsk-tsk. "Diana, Diana, Diana . . . if you'd wanted a reputation, you should've come to *me*."

He winked and slipped back into his berth before I could box his ears.

"Never mind him, dear," Mrs. Kier said. "You gallivant all you want. I would, if I were your age."

She winked at *me,* and then she was gone, too.

"Well, I don't know about 'gallivanting,'" Miss Caveo whispered, "but I certainly don't feel sleepy—not after what we just went through. Would anyone care to accompany me to the observation car?"

Of course, I would have gladly accompanied the young lady into the fiery pits of hell had she but asked. Yet I didn't wish to appear overeager.

"I guess that sounds alright—I ain't all that tired myself, now that you mention it," I said. "Only I think the dinin' car would suit me better. My brother and me ain't touched a crumb since breakfast."

"We haven't, have we?" Old Red muttered absentmindedly, rubbing a hand over his stomach.

"You can count me in, too," Kip said. "I'm so keyed up I don't think I'll *ever* sleep again."

So it was decided. Our rescue party would become a dinner party, with one abstention: Chan begged off, saying he needed rest and peace more than food. But before we went, he expressed his gratitude to us all, singling out yours truly for a particularly warm handshake.

"Thank you. You didn't have to come looking for me. If you hadn't . . . I'm afraid to think what would have happened."

"Don't mention it, Doc. As a great philosopher once said, 'It's every man's business to see justice done.'"

I probably don't have to tell you who that "great philosopher" was. I certainly didn't have to tell Gustav.

As we headed for the dining car behind Kip and Miss Caveo, my brother lagged behind, letting the distance between us and the others stretch out.

"So," he said, his voice just a quarter notch above a whisper, "Lockhart wasn't tryin' to hire hisself a horse when you found him, was he?"

"Not unless he was doin' it in his dreams."

Old Red grunted, looking pensive, and said no more.

"Did you finish whatever you was up to at the station while I was out roundin' up strays?" I asked.

He gave me a reluctant shrug. "I got me a few things done."

"Anything you'd care to tell me about?"

"Not now."

Gustav nodded at Kip and Miss Caveo up ahead, but I had the feeling they weren't the only reason he didn't want to talk. He looked haggard, pale, and his pace seemed to slow with every step. His sickness had been coming in waves all day, and it looked like high tide was rolling in again.

"Look," I said, "maybe you oughta head back to our bunk and—"

"Later. There's still detectin' to be done."

Old Red sped up and left me behind, though I could tell from his limping gait that he had to spur himself hard to do it. But I didn't try to slow him down. I figured the sooner he *detected* a plate of hot food, the better.

The train's electric lights had been turned down so low the aisles felt more like tunnels, and when we finally exited the vestibules connecting the third sleeper and the dining car, it was like stepping out of a coal mine into a sunny summer's day.

"Can I help you folks?" someone asked, and after a bit of blinking I managed to get him into focus.

It was Samuel. He was sitting at a table covered end to end with

146

shoes. In one hand he had a black half boot, in the other a brush. Two younger porters, each with shoe in hand themselves, sat at similarly laden tables, while Negroes dressed for kitchen work and table service were slumped on chairs nearby.

"Kitchen's closed," said a man wearing a grease-splattered apron. He sat up straighter as he talked, and all the other Negroes straightened up with him. Some of them had been wearing grins when we walked in, but their smiles melted quick as icicles in an oven. It reminded me of the way ranch hands' high spirits come crashing down to earth whenever the foreman barges into the bunkhouse.

"We don't mean to be no bother, Samuel," I said, "but we just had a hell of a time in town, and my brother and me ain't had a bite all day."

"No bother, folks," Samuel said (not entirely convincingly). He put down the shoe he was polishing and headed for the car's boxy little kitchen. "Pick yourselves out a place. I'll be right back."

We filed to the far end of the dining car and settled in around one of the tables. The porters and kitchen help watched us sullenly, but once we'd taken our seat, they relaxed, and before long they were chuckling and talking in low voices.

"Here you go," Samuel said, returning with a tray laden with sliced bread, plates, a butter knife, and a large, opened jar. "I'm sorry we can't do any cookin' for you, but hopefully this'll get you through till morning."

"Thank you, Samuel," Miss Caveo said.

"Yeah, thanks," I added. "There's nothin' better for settlin' a rumblin' stomach than—"

I leaned forward and peeked into the jar, expecting to see a colorful jam or preserve or marmalade. Instead, I found myself gazing into a pool of viscous brown oil.

"What in the Sam Hill is that?"

"*That* would be 'the wonder food of the future,' " Old Red said, his voice quiet and quivering.

He wasn't just queasy again. He'd ended up seated next to Miss

Caveo, as well, and the idea that his arm or leg might accidentally brush against those of a pretty young female had him positively petrified. If he was a tortoise, he would've drawn up into his shell.

"Nut butter," he wheezed miserably.

"'Professor Pertwee's Health Miracle Nut Butter,' to be exact," Samuel told us. "Mr. Horner gave us a case so passengers could sample it, if they wished."

"I don't think I wish," said Kip, eyeing the stuff skeptically.

"Seems to me the 'wonder' of a 'food' like that would be if anybody actually ate it," I threw in.

Gustav looked like he was about to throw *up*.

"You gotta mix it together some first," Samuel said. He picked up the knife and plunged it into the yellow-brown goo.

As he stirred, the aroma of peanuts that went up into the air was so overpowering I nearly swooned—and my brother actually did.

"For God's sake, take it away," he moaned. He clapped a hand on the table to steady himself. His other hand he clapped over his mouth.

"Yes, sir! Right away, sir! It's goin', sir!"

Samuel snatched up the jar and whisked it back to the kitchen lest something even uglier than nut butter put in an appearance on our table.

Gustav bent over and sucked in deep breaths while I slapped him on the back, Kip fetched him a glass of water, and Miss Caveo fanned him with a menu.

"I'm fine, I'm fine, I don't need no nursemaids," Old Red huffed after a moment, embarrassed by all the attention. "Somebody talk, dammit. *You*." He shot me a look that was both imperious and pleading. "Walk me through what happened back in town."

So I did. Everyone settled back into their seats, and the story of our escape from Thornton's Boiler proved to be just the distraction my brother needed to get his wind back and his gorge down. He listened intently as I served up the details, even tolerating the assorted asides and attempted witticisms with which I garnished the yarn. He only interrupted once, when I got to what I described as "Miss Caveo's fortu-itously timed debut as a thespian."

"That took some nerve, walkin' in there and makin' like you was something you ain't," he said to the lady.

"Well, it wasn't *really* my debut," she told him. "In high school, I played both Lady Macbeth and Juliet. It was the perfect training for tonight, actually. I just hope I didn't overplay the pathos."

"You were magnificent," I said. "Irene Adler herself couldn't have done any better."

Old Red looked downright renauseated by my fawning.

"So you know something of the stage, do you?" he asked Miss Caveo. "Playactin' and makeup and wigs and the like?"

"Oh, I've dabbled," she replied airily. "But we haven't heard the end of the story." She focused on me again, cutting off Gustav's line of questioning as cleanly as if she'd used shears. "You've left me in agonizing suspense, Otto. Did we escape?"

"You'll just have to listen and find out," I said, and I carried on with the tale. Old Red remained deep in dour thought through the end of my account, acknowledging its conclusion with only a muted "Interestin'."

" 'Interesting'? I think our adventure deserves better than that. At least an 'incredible,' if not an outright 'amazing,' " Miss Caveo teased. "So what were you doing while we were escaping from the bloodthirsty natives of Carlin, Nevada? It certainly looked like the situation at the station became rather . . . *interesting*."

The young lady was being playful, as was her way, but it had about as much effect on my brother as tickling a tombstone.

"Nothin' to tell," he mumbled at the tablecloth. "Wiltrout was anxious to leave, and . . . well . . . I ain't as good at persuadin' as some."

He was wrong about that. His immutable gruffness seemed to persuade Miss Caveo it was time to go. She noted the late hour, thanked Samuel (who'd lingered nearby after returning with a jar of plain, old-fashioned honey), and pushed back her seat. As good manners dictate,

Kip and I stood as she got up. The best Old Red could manage was a sort of crouching lean that took his butt cheeks all of an inch off his chair. He held the position only a few seconds, plopping back down, tearing off a chunk of bread, and chewing morosely as Miss Caveo walked away.

"What a peach," Kip sighed when she was out of earshot.

"She's somethin', alright," I said, trying to keep my gaze from growing too dreamy (or from lingering too long where it shouldn't) lest she glance back for a final wave.

"Yeah, you hit it on the head there, Brother," Gustav said. "That lady is *somethin'.*"

I wasn't sure what had kindled his doubts about Miss Caveo, but I could see them gleaming in his eyes plain enough, and I knew exactly what words he was leaving unspoken.

"That lady is somethin'," he'd said. *I just don't know what.*

Twenty-one

FOOD FOR THOUGHT

Or, Kip and Samuel Give Us Something New to Chew On

Whatever my brother's reasons, I knew better than to ask about them there at the table. Gustav plays his cards close to the vest when it's just him and me. Throw in Kip and Samuel and half a dozen other men in easy eavesdropping range, and he'd stuff those cards down in his boot.

So I just contented myself (for the moment) with a big bite of honey-slathered bread and a simple "So now what?" Which came out more like a "Sho noo wha'?" actually, but as my brother's long accustomed to hearing me talk with my mouth full, he had no trouble understanding.

"Now I'd like to ask the fellers here some questions."

He looked first at Samuel, then at Kip.

"Questions?" Samuel said. He'd been relaxing with his long, lean body propped up against a chair the next table over, but now he stood up straight and brought his feet in close together.

Kip froze with a hunk of bread just inches from his mouth. "Us?"

"Yup. You." Old Red started to take another bite of bread himself, but he changed his mind at the last second, dropping the half-eaten slice back on his plate and pushing it away. "You've been up and down this train more than anybody other than Wiltrout. If something queer was goin' on, you'd be the ones to spot it, most likely."

"What do you mean 'queer'?" Kip asked.

"Somebody actin' odd, lollygaggin' where they shouldn't—that kinda thing. I'm wonderin' about the vestibule up by the baggage car, in particular. Y'all didn't catch sight of anything up thataway, did you? Strange comin's and goin's?"

The porter and the news butch looked at each other. Kip shrugged, then Samuel shrugged, then they both turned toward my brother and shrugged together.

"Didn't see nothin' like that," Samuel said. "I was too busy."

"Sorry," Kip said. "Same for me."

Old Red screwed up his face like a man who's accidentally swallowed his tobacco juice.

"Well, how about that key of yours, Kip?" he asked. "It ever turn up?"

"Nah. I had to borrow one of Wiltrout's spares. And, boy, did he chew my ass for it."

"So you still ain't got no idea where yours got to?"

"None at all. I just went to fetch that *novelty*"—he winked—"that the drummer asked for, and when I got up to the baggage car . . . well, you saw. My passkey was gone."

"And you hadn't loaned it to nobody? Or left it lyin' around somewheres?"

"Nope."

"Wouldn't surprise me if someone swiped the kid's key without him noticin'," Samuel said. "We get passengers with nimble fingers from time to time. Some of them yeggs could snatch the gold from your fillin's between bites of bread."

I swallowed my latest mouthful and ran my tongue over my teeth. "Still there."

"This is a pretty high-class run to have pickpockets," my brother said.

"Better class of pockets to pick," Samuel pointed out. "You pussy-footers are supposed to keep tabs on the thieves and cardsharps, but we never even know if we got a company spotter aboard—cuz you're keepin' tabs on *us*, too."

I knew then why our fellow S.P. employees weren't fond of rail dicks. We weren't just guards. We were *spies*.

I would've tread lighter after learning that, but Old Red just brought his heel down harder.

"So neither of you saw a single thing out of the ordinary today?" he said, sour as vinegar taffy.

Kip and Samuel shook their heads.

"Not the way you mean," Samuel said.

"Well, how about the times we stopped for Pezullo and the Give-'em-Hell Boys? You can't tell me *that* was ordinary."

Samuel heaved an exasperated sigh. "Only thing I saw when Joe got throwed off the train was a faceful of sheet. I was in one of the closets diggin' out an extra pillow for Mrs. Foreman, that widow woman travelin' with her boys, and when the brakes clutched up, I was buried under a heap of linens. By the time I dug myself out, everybody had their noses pressed to the windows lookin' for long riders."

"So you were in there alone? Nobody saw you?"

"Of course, I was alone. You couldn't squeeze two people into that closet with a crowbar. So you'll just have to take my word on it."

A hint of a smirk tugged at one corner of the porter's mouth.

"When the Give-'em-Hell Boys hit us, though—that's a different story," he said. "I had a bad feelin' about that stop, what with the hour and where we were and all. It was too much like last time that bunch showed up—and you two know how fond they are of railroaders. So I ducked into the gents' washroom in Pullman one, thinkin' I'd lay low till it all blew over. But I wasn't the only one who got that idea. Wiltrout was in there already, and you should've heard the yelp he let out when I came bustin' in on him."

At the front end of the car, the other porters and kitchen workers exchanged sly glances and snickers. They'd obviously already heard Samuel's story and shared many a belly laugh at their "captain's" expense. To Kip, though, this was unexpected (and by no means unwelcome) news.

"Wiltrout was hidin' in the can the whole time?" The kid squealed out a peal of high-pitched laughter. "Oh, he's in for it now! By noon tomorrow, there won't be a man on the line who hasn't heard about it! They'll be waitin' for him at every station with a hot plate of humble pie!"

I chuckled along with Kip and the rest of them, but Old Red didn't join in. He just kept staring at Samuel—or more like *through* him—the wheels turning so furiously in his head I could practically hear them click-clacking like the rails beneath our feet.

"So, Kip," I said as the laughter trailed off into awkward silence, "what did *you* see?"

"Well, there ain't much to tell, really. When we stopped for Joe's body . . ." His own words sobered the kid fast as a slap, and the smile he'd been wearing disappeared. "—I was in the gents' in Pullman one," he went on grimly. "And, before you ask—yeah, I was alone. I was busy with something most folks prefer to do without an audience, if you know what I mean. Later on, when the Give-'em-Hell Boys stopped us, I was readin' a magazine in my berth."

Old Red blinked his way back from oblivion. "Where's that?"

"There are two empties in Pullman one, up at the front of the car. Wiltrout gets the bottom one. The top's mine. I rolled out to see what was up, and"—the kid looked down, his slender face flushing pink—"some bastard in a mask popped out and stuck a gun in my ear. You know the rest. Barson and Welsh showed up, they pulled Lockhart out of his berth, and—"

Gustav's index finger went up straight as a flagpole. "*Wait.* They grabbed Lockhart?"

"Yeeeessss," Kip said, dragging the word out like a schoolboy afraid he's giving the teacher the wrong answer.

"He didn't come out after 'em?"

"No. He was a little confused."

"A little *drunk*," I said.

"How is it Barson and Welsh knew where Lockhart was?" Old Red pushed on, ignoring me. "How is it they even knew he was on the train?"

"Oh. Huh. Beats the hell out of me." Kip offered my brother a small smile. "Say, you're really pretty good at this stuff, ain't you? You sure I shouldn't start callin' you Mr. Holmes again?"

"Old Red will do," Gustav replied—though he couldn't help looking a tad pleased despite himself. "I understand this ain't the first time the Give-'em-Hell Boys and the Pacific Express crossed paths. Was you fellers on the train last time, too?"

Kip swept his hand out at Samuel and the other porters and kitchen help. "We all were. The engine crew was different—we get a new engineer and fireman every eight hours or so. And it wasn't Morrison in the Wells Fargo car. But other than that, it was the same crew."

"So what happened, exactly?"

"I didn't see much," Kip said with a reluctant shrug. "To be honest . . . well . . ."

"Yeah?" Old Red prodded him.

"Last time, *I* was hidin' in the john," Kip admitted, shamefaced.

"Don't worry, kid," I told him with a wink. "It's only funny when it's Wiltrout."

"*I'll* tell you what was different last time," Samuel said. "The robbers actually did some robbin'. Dragged Wiltrout outside with a gun to his head and told the express messenger to open up *or else*. Made off with either a little or a lot, dependin' on who you believe."

My brother frowned and furrowed his brow. "Funny they didn't try that again. They had Kip. Why not use him to press Morrison?"

"Barson said they was makin' a 'social call,'" I reminded him. "Announcin' the bounties on Crowe and Powless and the S.P. board."

"Yeah," Kip chimed in. "Seems like they was just sendin' a message."

"But theirs ain't gettin' out," Old Red said. "We got orders not to talk to the papers."

"Word'll get out—and it won't take long," Samuel replied with the firm certainty of a sky pilot preaching the gospel. "Tryin' to keep a secret inside the S.P.'s like tryin' to keep water in your pockets."

Gustav nodded slowly and started digging around in his coat. "Alright. I got just two more questions. First off, either of you ever lay eyes on anything like this?"

He pulled out the little cup/bowl he'd found in the desert earlier that night. Samuel and Kip eyed it, then eyed each other, seeming to wonder if Augie Welsh hadn't just kicked my brother's ass but dropped him on his head, as well.

"No," they said in unison.

Old Red groaned in a resigned sort of way and put the cup away— then pulled out the golden yellow hunk of hair. He tossed it onto the table curls up.

"How 'bout this?"

Kip's jaw dropped so far, so fast, it almost ended up on the tabletop next to the toupee. Samuel, on the other hand, recognized it for what it was straight off. He grunted out a little one-note chuckle—"Huh"— and picked the wig up.

"I've seen plenty of these. Even had to help a few gentlemen get theirs fastened to their heads." He dropped the hairpiece back on the table. "This one don't look familiar, though. Maybe you oughta ask Mr. Horner about it. I bet he'd have a sharper eye for such things."

"Why would that be?" I asked.

"Oh, I'd never gossip about anything that might embarrass a passenger," the porter said—and he rubbed his hand over his own gray-tinged hair, as if smoothing down a cowlick.

I nodded, smiling, finally realizing why Horner's pompadour had gone so cockeyed after he'd climbed up into his bunk. He'd hung up his hair for the night the way most men hang up their hats. He'd have no mirror to go by in his berth, so whenever he wanted to poke his head out, all he could do was balance his little man-wig over his ears and hope for the best.

"How 'bout you, Kip?" Gustav croaked, his voice finally cracking under the weight of so many questions. "You notice this on anybody to-day?"

"Heck, no. If I had, I never would've stopped laughin'." The news butch reached out to stroke the toupee warily, like it was some exotic woodland creature Old Red had on a leash. "Jeez . . . I think I'd rather be bald. Where'd you find this thing, anyway? And why is it impor-tant?"

"Oh, it was just lyin' around. Might not mean a thing."

My brother swept the hairpiece off the table and stuffed it back in his pocket. Then he leaned back in his chair and sighed, suddenly seem-ing so weary the weight of his own skin looked like too much for him to bear.

"You done?" I asked him.

He nodded. "With these fellers, anyway."

"Well, then . . . seein' as you look like shit and sound like shit and have been generally actin' shitty, I'd say it's time for you to turn in."

Gustav pursed his lips and glared at me so long I started to think he'd fallen asleep with his eyes open.

"Alright, *Mutter*," he finally said. "I reckon you're right."

He put his palms on the table and slowly pushed himself to his feet. I stood, too, offering the good-nights and thank-yous my brother wasn't bothering with.

"Wait," Kip said as we started to leave. "Old Red . . . what's goin' on?"

"Yeah," Samuel said. "You're actin' like whoever killed Joe's still on the Express."

"Well, there's a reason for that."

The murmuring of the porters and cooks snuffed out, and for a moment all you could hear was the humming-rumbling-tapping of the little vibrations all around us—wood, metal, glass, porcelain, leather, all in motion, all rattling against each other, a million collisions a second all invisible to the eye.

"Whoever killed Joe *is* still on the Express," Gustav said.

And with that, he turned and headed for the Pullmans.

Every man there watched silently as he went, either wondering if he was crazy or *hoping* he was.

"Well," I said with a cheerful wave, "sweet dreams, fellers!" And I followed my brother back into the darkness.

Twenty-two

GUT FEELINGS

Or, Old Red Lays Out His Doubts, and I Lay Into Old Red

"So, Gustav," I began as we trudged through the dimly lit sleeping cars.

My brother was ahead of me a couple steps, and he glanced back just long enough to shoot me a frown. "Later."

"I'm just wonderin'—"

"Not now."

"But you ain't even heard—"

He looked back again, his frown now a full-blown scowl. *"Hush up."*

"So I ain't allowed to ask questions even when—?"

Old Red spun to face me, and I only barely managed to stop in front of him rather than on top of him. Yet he waved me in another step, and I pressed in so close we could've shared socks. He waved again, though, and I bent down and cocked my head, bringing my right ear in near enough to hear not just his whispers but the whistling of the wind through his nose hair.

"You got questions. Fair enough. I might just have an answer or two. But here's a question for *you* first: If the killer is still on this train, who's to say we ain't bein' listened to this very moment?"

"Oh," I whispered back, suddenly very aware of the black curtains all around us—and the possibility that a murderer was lurking behind them. "I get you. I can hold off a little longer . . . though there is one thing I oughta tell you now, long as we're huddled up like this."

"Yeah?"

"You *really* need to pop some of them peppermints Kip gave you—and not just to settle your stomach. Your breath's so bad you could send the killer to Boot Hill just by blowin' in his face."

Gustav replied with a grumpy snort and a turned back. We moved on again in silence, spotting nary another soul till we reached our own Pullman.

Toward the far end of the aisle, a small figure was hunched over by one of the lower berths. As we drew closer, headed for the gents' washroom at the front of the car, I saw that it was Dr. Chan—and he wasn't alone. He was speaking in hushed tones to Wiltrout, who wasn't so hushed in response.

"Why, you filthy little monkey," the conductor snarled. "How dare you?"

Just what it was he'd dared we weren't to learn. Upon noticing our approach, Chan murmured something else to Wiltrout, whose only response was to snap his berth curtains closed.

After that, Chan hustled back toward his berth—and us. The Chinaman had a quiet dignity about him that had weathered quite the gale that day, and he managed to maintain it even then, keeping his eyes down but his back unbent. He offered us a quiet "Gentlemen" as he scooted around us in the passageway.

"Night, Dr. Chan," Old Red said. "Oh . . . and I'm sorry for your loss."

"Yeah—my condolences, Doc," I threw in.

Chan's eyes bugged out so far it's a wonder they didn't pop the spectacles right off his face. "Excuse me?"

"We noticed that one of them coffins in the baggage car is yours," I explained. "Or . . . well . . . that it's got a tag with your name on it, I mean."

"Oh. Yes. Of course." Chan put a limp smile on his face, but he whipped it off quick, like it was a tie he'd decided didn't suit him. "A cousin of mine passed away suddenly in Chicago. He was helping me run the Chinese exhibit at the Exposition. Naturally, it's my duty to escort the body back to San Francisco personally."

Gustav nodded. "Naturally."

Yet there was nothing natural about the way Chan had answered: There was a rote quality to it, like he was a politician giving the same speech for the hundredth time.

"Well . . . good night again," he said, only slightly less stiff, and he ducked around us and fairly dove down into his bunk.

I offered my brother a *What was that all about?* shrug. He gave me his own shrug in reply, this one of the *Beats me* variety. Then he was shambling off toward the gents' again.

"Alright—you ain't got no excuses now," I said once we were in the privy. "Talk."

"Fine," Gustav sighed, opening the window just wide enough to let in a swirl of chilly night air. "But you need to be a mite more particular as to what you wanna hear."

"I would be, only I got so many questions it'd take all night just to get through all the askin'."

Old Red unbuckled his gunbelt and eased it down to the floorboards, then moved to the sink and brought a gush of water down over his head.

"But alright—start with Carlin, why don'tcha?" I plopped myself on the floor (the washroom being far too cramped for any seats other than the one it couldn't get away without). "What exactly were you up to back there . . . other than throwin' yourself in front of trains, I mean?"

"This and that," Gustav said as he toweled himself off. "Askin' my own questions, mostly."

He looked up at his reflection in the mirror over the sink and didn't seem to like what he saw—nor should he have. His pale skin was in such marked contrast to the bright red stripes of his mustache and

161

hair he looked like a candy cane from the collar up. The only pinkness to his face came courtesy of assorted scuffs and abrasions.

He splashed more water over his face, but he couldn't wash away the aching weariness we both saw there.

"Talked to the engineer and the fireman," he said, putting his back against the wall and sliding down slowly until he was on his keister between the sink and the crapper. "Found out what they saw of the 'robbery' up in the engine cab. Which wasn't much. They stopped cuz of the barricade on the tracks, and one of the gang hopped up and held a gun on 'em for the next however long. He was wearin' a mask—and he was dressed for ridin' and covered with trail dust."

"Well, what else would you expect a train robber to wear?" I pulled off a boot, then set to work on the other. "An evenin' gown and pearls?"

Old Red stared forlornly at the boots at the end of his own splayed-out legs, obviously wishing them gone but seemingly unsure if he had the strength for so monumental a task as taking them off.

"Think about it." With a pained grunt, he sat up straight and grabbed hold of his right boot like it was a greased pig that might slip squealing from his grip any second. He twisted at it irritably as he continued talking. "It sure don't sound like the feller who jumped the engine crew came out of any crate. Which means we still ain't found anybody who saw hide nor hair of that stowaway."

"Well, didn't Morrison say some of the gang was talkin' to him from outside his car? Maybe one of *them* was Jack in the Box."

"Why would Barson and Welsh squirrel a man away with a bunch of bricks just so he could jump out and gab at the express messenger?" Gustav had finally freed himself of his right boot and was now locked in mortal combat with the left. "They had all the men they needed if they was just 'sendin' a message'—especially if one of the crew or passengers was in it with 'em, the way it looks. So that feller from the crate . . . I can't fit him in with the Give-'em-Hell Boys any which way I look at it."

"But if he wasn't workin' for Barson and Welsh, then what was—?"

"I haven't the foggiest notion. I been tryin' to just follow the data, like Mr. Holmes'd do. But the damn data's twisted into such a pretzel I'll never get my brain unknotted."

Old Red had both his boots off now, and he sort of wilted back against the wall, spent. His eyes were bloodshot, with bags beneath them so puffy and dark he looked like a red-mustached raccoon. His eyelids fluttered, and I couldn't tell if he was fighting off mere sleep or a dead faint.

I had more questions—lots more—but the time for asking was past. It was time to do some telling.

"Brother, in case you haven't noticed, it ain't just your brain that's kinked up. Next time you get off this train, you need to *stay* off."

Gustav's droopy-lidded eyes went wide. "What?"

"You know what I'm talkin' about. You had a *hole* in you not two months ago, and now you're gonna go bouncin' over the Sierra Nevadas on a goddamn express train? Uh-uh. I'm tellin' you, Gustav—you can't take it."

As I spoke, my brother pulled his pipe from his coat pocket. Next came his tobacco pouch, and he got to loading the pipe with slow, meticulous movements that allowed him to keep looking down—away from me.

"We got work to do," he said when I was through. "Men are dead."

"Dammit, I know that. And I don't wanna see you end up the same."

Old Red put the pipe in his mouth and lit a lucifer—then changed his mind and tossed the match in the commode. He sighed, took the pipe out, flipped it over, and emptied the unsmoked tobacco right back in its pouch.

"I ain't anywhere near *that* sick, Otto. I'll be fine."

"Really? Cuz it seems to me the only reason you ain't pukin' right now is you ain't eaten nothin' but a slice of bread the last twelve hours."

Gustav tucked his pouch and pipe back in his pockets. Again, he moved with deliberate slowness, as if putting off some bigger chore he was anxious to avoid.

"I'll be fine."

"So you keep sayin', though I don't see what makes you so sure. Every time you get off the train, it don't take but a minute for you to start lookin' better. Then you get back on and you sick-up again—and you don't do nothin' about it."

"Ain't nothin' to do but ride it out." He finished with his pouch and patted his pocket.

"How do you know? Hell, you *still* ain't even dug out them peppermints Kip gave you. He said they cured the collywobbles, remember? Same goes for the Chinese tea Doc Chan gave you. Why don't you try 'em, for Christ's sake? See what happens."

Old Red shook his head, still looking down though he no longer had any excuse to do so. "Them things don't do squat for me."

And he winced. Not for long, mind you—the look lasted all of a second. Most folks wouldn't have even noticed it. But a brother would. I didn't know the what or why of it, but he thought he'd slipped up somehow.

"How do you know a couple of them candies wouldn't help? You try 'em sometime before?"

Gustav looked about as saggy as a man can, yet he managed to go even saggier. It was like my question turned his backbone to pudding.

"Yup," he said.

"On a *train?*"

I knew the answer even before he gave me his slow, mournful nod. I didn't set out to deduce it, but I suppose all the time I'd spent in Mr. Holmes's company helped me put the pieces together—even though I hadn't even realized I'd been looking at a puzzle at all.

"I can't believe it," I said, though I more than believed it—I felt the truth of it drive into my gut like a fist. "This ain't new to you, is it? All the years we been stickin' to the trails, goin' everywhere on horseback . . . it wasn't cuz you hate the railroads. It's cuz you hate *trains*."

Old Red just looked at me, and I could see him weighing his first inclination, the one he falls back on so often—telling me I'm full of crap. But I could see weariness in his eyes, too. He'd been carrying a secret, and the weight of it had worn him down.

"Jesus, Gustav," I said. "You lied to me."

"I never outright lied."

I gaped at my brother with such shock you might've thought he'd sprouted horns and poked me with a pitchfork.

"Oh, is that how you justify it? You never lied? You just let me make assumptions—theorize without all the data, as Mr. Hoity-Toity would say? So there I was, thinkin' you was stayin' true to your convictions, when all you was really stayin' true to was a flip-floppy stomach!" I shook my head, disgusted. "All them extra miles on the trail. All them days in the sun and nights in the cold. All them extra saddle sores on my ass! And you never told me the real reason why."

"You're right, Otto. It's just that . . . I . . . well . . ."

Gustav squeezed his eyes shut, and I could see he was groping around in the darkness inside, in that place where men carry the things they tuck away out of the light. For a moment, I thought he was going to dredge something out of there for me—a truth he'd buried down deep. But then he straightened his spine and puffed out his chest and opened his eyes, and I knew he'd stopped digging.

"We got things to talk over, sure. *Brother* things. But that can wait." He tapped the badge hanging like a shield over his heart. "This has gotta come first."

"Really?" I glanced down at my own star. It looked so dull and dusty—such a puny thing, yet it could make some men feel so big. "*Is* this what comes first for you?"

Old Red either failed to take my meaning or chose not to. "When there's a murderer on the loose? You bet, it is."

"Alright, then." I pushed myself to my feet and unpinned my badge. "These little trinkets mean so much to you, why don't you have two?" I tossed the star into Gustav's lap. "I'm through playin' lawman."

I snatched up my boots, turned my back to my brother, and started for the door—which slammed shut before I could reach it. Someone had joined us in the gents'.

Or some*thing,* I should say. Something dark and ugly and extremely pissed off.

It was a snake at least three feet long and black as a banker's soul save for a patch of white around its open mouth. It held its head high and swayed back and forth, licking at the air with a flick of its long, dark tongue.

"Sweet Jesus!" I cried out.

The snake didn't say anything. He just opened his mouth even wider and lunged at my legs.

Twenty-three

SNAKE EYES

Or, A Serpent Sets His Sights on Us, and I Throw in the Towel

The snake's teeth sank into my left boot. Fortunately, my left *foot* was elsewhere at the time.

I'd been carrying my boots out with me, and upon noticing that the line for the jakes had just grown longer by about forty inches of snake, I was so stunned I dropped the both of them. They landed directly in the snake's path, and the scaly SOB was on the left one in a black flash. It bit the boot again and again, thrashing and jerking its head in a squirming fury.

While the snake was doing its best to chew my boot like a plug of tobacco, I was Texas two-stepping on my tiptoes, trying not to land on it as it writhed underfoot.

"Oh, Christ! Oh, shit! Oh, Christ! Oh, shit!" I spluttered as I danced.

The tiny compartment didn't have much to offer in the way of high ground, but I found a spot and claimed it, sitting my ass down in the sink and swinging my legs up as high as I could get them. With a vigor I didn't think he still had in him, my brother shot to his feet and clambered atop the only other perch available: the commode. The lid had been left propped up, and Old Red certainly didn't take the time to put it down. So he ended up crouched upon the seat, his stockinged feet bowed out wide.

"How did that big bastard get in here?" I panted.

"How the hell do you think?" Gustav shot back. "He didn't shut that door himself."

Which meant we finally had our proof, much as we might dislike the shape it had taken (a slithering *S* at that particular moment). There was most definitely a killer still aboard the Pacific Express, and he hadn't had his fill of killing.

Once the snake abandoned its life-or-death struggle with my boot, it began wriggling this way and that around the room, its head lifted a good six inches off the ground as it slid from wall to wall. It looked a little like the rat snakes I'd seen around the farm a thousand times when I was a kid, though it was darker and sleeker, with more shimmer to the scales—and a *much* nastier disposition.

"He's as anxious to get outta here as we are," my brother said.

"Ain't nobody or nothin' could want outta here as bad as me."

"You recognize him?"

"Well, we ain't been properly introduced, but I assume he's the snake we saw crated up in the baggage car."

"Of course, he's the snake from the baggage car! I mean, do you know what kind of snake he is?"

"The black, ornery kind I don't care to get to know any better— that's all I know. You ain't seen its like before?"

"Never."

The snake had finally accepted that there was no way out—and it wasn't happy about it. Instead of circling the room again, it took to eyeing *us*. Blacker, more soulless eyes I've never seen on anything alive. It was like staring into the barrels of a shotgun.

For a moment, the snake curled up atop my brother's holstered Colt and shook the end of its tail rattlesnake-fashion, though it had nothing to rattle. Then it stuck its tongue out at me and moved in underneath my feet where I couldn't see it.

"Keep your legs up, Otto!" Gustav cried. "High as they'll go!"

I strained to keep my legs stretched out straight, but they were tiring fast and started to sag.

Something nudged my right calf from below.

"Oh, hell! He's nippin' at me, ain't he?"

"Nippin' and missin'," Old Red said, struggling to calm his voice—and not particularly succeeding. "Just hold on a little longer, and he'll—"

I felt another bump from below. There was a sharp edge to it this time, as if, for a split second, someone had clamped a clothespin onto my left heel.

The snake had gotten its mouth on me—just not quite enough to sink in its teeth. On its next try, it'd get me for sure.

"Well, *crap*," my brother spat, and he jumped off the john and grabbed for his gun.

But the snake was on him quick, before he could reach his iron. Old Red stutter-stepped backward across the room, ending up pressed against the door. He brought his left hand up behind his back and groped for the handle.

"If I can slip out without *him* slippin' out, I'll get help. But there's women and kids out there, so I can't—" His fingers found the door handle and gave it a jiggle . . . and nothing happened. "Oh, you are shittin' me! The goddamn door's been—"

The snake turned itself into a black arrow aimed at Gustav's shins. But my brother was already on the move, scurrying back toward his porcelain fortress, and the snake flew between his legs. It whirled on him fast, though, and by the time Old Red was climbing atop the toilet again it was right on his heels.

And it stayed on them. The snake started pushing itself up against the smooth white side of the commode, and before long its head lifted up over the rim.

"The bastard's actually comin' up after me!" Gustav gasped, wide-eyed. "Quick! Distract him!"

"How do you distract a snake?"

"I don't know! Whistle him a tune! Offer him a bowl of milk! *Something!*"

I hopped down from the sink and staggered on aching legs over to the towel rack beneath the washroom window.

"Here, snaky snaky snake-snake," I said.

The snake ignored me, flicking its tongue out toward Old Red's ankles like they were a couple of barbecued ribs it couldn't wait to taste.

I whipped down one of the towels and flapped it at the snake's head. The edge snapped just over his darting tongue.

"Olé," I said.

As if accepting a challenge for a duel, the snake curled around and slid toward me, its obsidian eyes locked on mine.

They weren't just cold as ice, those eyes. They turned all they touched to ice, too, and a shiver ran along my back like a fistful of snow stuffed down my shirt. I couldn't stand that death-cold gaze another second—so I tossed my towel at it.

The snake ended up covered almost head to tail, and it started rolling and thrashing beneath the rough cotton. I threw on another towel before it could fight its way free, then another and another till the rack was bare. Instead of having a slithering black serpent before me, I now had a fluffy white pile—albeit a pile that was undulating wildly.

I scooped up the whole heap in my hands.

The snake's wrigglings grew so frenzied it was like trying to keep a grip on a cracking bullwhip. One towel, then another, dropped to the floor. There was only one towel left when I reached the window, and I stuffed it—and the snake wrapped up in it—out into the black nothingness whipping past the train.

Something settled on my shoulder, and I only barely managed not to jump through the window myself.

"Good work, Brother," Gustav said. He took his hand from my shoulder as I turned around. "You alright?"

"Ask again in about five minutes . . . I ain't done with my heart attack yet."

I walked to the door and gave it a try. I didn't have any more luck than Old Red a couple minutes before.

"We're gonna have to bust this open," I said.

"Yup. But let's be careful about it." My brother gathered up his boots and sat on the john to start pulling them on. "For all we know, whoever sicced that snake on us is right outside."

"Oh, I hope he is." I started getting myself shod as fast as I could. "That'll be one snake I won't be afraid to stomp."

Gustav crouched down to get his gunbelt. While he was squatting there, he scooped something else up off the floor—a golden brown doodad only a little larger than a silver dollar.

"That mean you want this back?" He tossed me the S.P. badge.

"Not especially," I said . . . as I pinned it to my shirt. "But I'll wear it all the same. I'm warnin' you, though—the second we're done with this business, I'm doin' to this badge what I just did to that snake. And I just might do it to you, too, we don't clear up a thing or two. Now you'd best get that gun in your hand . . . cuz here I go."

I was mad enough to get the door open with one kick.

Twenty-four

KEY INFORMATION

Or, We Get Some Answers, but None Unlocks Our Mystery

There was no one waiting for us in the little nook outside the privy. Which isn't to say the nook was empty: A small crate done over with chicken wire on one side sat on the floor near the door.

I prodded the snake's box with a toe as Old Red holstered his gun and bent down to inspect the door handle I'd just busted with my boot.

"What's all that noise?" someone said.

Kip and Wiltrout poked out from behind the curtains of the nearest berths, their faces stacked atop one another like the heads on a totem pole.

"What are you doing over there?" Wiltrout asked gruffly (though quietly).

"We had us a tangle with one of our fellow passengers, Admiral." I held my hands about four feet apart. "A skinny black feller yay long."

"The snake?" Kip pointed his bulging eyes at the floor. "Jeez! Is he still loose?"

"I suppose so . . . about a mile back. I chucked him out the window."

Wiltrout rolled from his bunk and came charging at us, and Kip quickly dropped down to follow him. Both were fully (though wrinkly) dressed.

"What's all this about a snake?" the conductor demanded, somehow managing to sound like he was whispering and shouting at the same time. "And what the hell did you do to that door?"

"I *opened* it," I said.

Old Red finally turned away from the door handle. "Somebody locked it from the outside—with us and the snake on the inside."

Wiltrout's puffy face went so hot-iron red his bushy mustache should've burst into flame. "*What* snake, damn it?"

"An Indian swamp adder. It was boxed up in the baggage car," Kip answered for us. His voice went flat. "Joe showed it to me yesterday. Before we left Ogden."

"What sort of imbecile would bring an Indian swamp adder aboard my train?" Wiltrout fumed.

"The kind that sells peanut paste," Gustav said.

"And sports a he-wig," I added.

Wiltrout gave us a glare that said we were in no position to cast stones at imbeciles of any variety. "Who?"

"Mr. Horner, Captain—the drummer," Kip said. "I heard him braggin' about his snake to some of the other passengers. Said he bought it at the Exposition." The news butch gawked at me and my brother like he couldn't quite believe we were actually still alive. "One drop of its poison's enough to kill a dozen elephants."

There was a high-pitched gasp, and we turned to find a nightgown-clad woman watching us from the car's main passageway. She was pallid and gaunt, with hair that hung as straight and black as the curtains lining the aisle around her. I would've sworn I'd never laid eyes on the lady if not for the children she clutched to her nonexistent bosom: twin boys.

"A dozen elephants," either Harlan or Marlin murmured. He and his brother were in their nightshirts, grinning with that devilish glee peculiar to little boys.

"Gee whillikers," the other twin said, looking positively covetous. *What I couldn't do with a critter like that,* he seemed to be thinking.

"Boys, hush," their mother said, tugging them to her more tightly. She gave us a beseeching look that seemed to plead for comforting lies no matter what the truth might be. "Did I hear something about a poisonous snake being loose on the train?"

"Nothing of the kind, Mrs. Foreman," Wiltrout said soothingly. "It's all a simple misunderstanding. Here. Let me escort you back to your berths." The conductor reached down and ruffled the twins' thick gold locks. "Tell me, boys—do you want to be conductors or engineers when you grow up?"

"Neither," Harlan or Marlin replied as he and his brother and mother were hustled out of sight.

"We wanna be train robbers!" his twin chirped.

I didn't hear a yelp, so I could only assume Wiltrout resisted the urge to smack the backs of the boys' curl-covered heads.

"So . . . you said the door was locked, not jammed, right?" I said to Gustav.

He nodded grimly. "Ain't no question about it now: The killer's got a passkey. Otherwise, there'd no way to fetch that snake out of the baggage car or lock us in the jakes. Though it does make me wonder." He turned to Kip. "Why are there locks on the *outside* of the privies?"

"The porters have to lock 'em up when we're stopped at a station," Kip explained. "The crapper empties right down onto the tracks, so if you let people keep goin' in there—"

"It wouldn't be long 'fore every station on the line smelled like a shepherd's underdrawers," I finished for him.

"Or worse—like a *cowboy's* underdrawers," the kid cracked.

"Given what we just been through, it's a wonder mine don't smell a hell of a lot worse than they do," I said.

"Kip, would that key you lost work on the door to the jakes?" Old Red cut in with weary impatience. Our tussle with the snake had forced him to stoke up his boiler right quick, but now that it was over, he was losing his steam almost as fast.

"Passkeys work on *everything*," Kip told him. "I sure hope there's some other explanation, though. I'd feel awful bad if it was my key that—"

"Get back to your berth," Wiltrout snapped at the kid as he returned from getting the widow and her sons tucked in (or perhaps, in Harlan and Marlin's case, tied down).

"But I—"

"*Now*, Hickey!"

The news butch cringed like a scolded puppy and slinked away toward his bunk.

"The same goes for you two," Wiltrout said. "I don't know what *this* is all about." He glowered at the empty box and busted door in a way that said he would've found our story every bit as believable if we'd claimed to have been attacked by rabid fairies. "I just know wherever you go, there's trouble. So let's see if you can at least *sleep* without stirring up some kind of fuss."

I expected Old Red to retort that he had clues to pursue, so full speed ahead and damn the fuss. Instead, he gave a resigned nod and began shambling away.

"Oh. Just one question before we go," he said, stopping next to the conductor. "What was it Dr. Chan said that got you so riled up a ways back?"

At first, Wiltrout's face puckered with its usual scorn. When he heard the question through, though, his expression changed, and for once he seemed pensive rather than pissed.

"He wanted me to let him into the baggage car . . . alone. He even offered me a bribe. Of course, I turned him down."

"Of course." Old Red started toward our berth again. "Well . . . night, Wiltrout."

"Yeah, see ya in the mornin', Admiral."

Wiltrout was too lost in thought to give us more than a growl for a good-night.

As we passed by the first berths, I caught a glimpse of Kip peeping out at us.

"Sleep tight," he whispered. "Don't let the swamp adders bite."

"Pleasant screams," I replied.

When we reached our berth, Old Red stared up at it dolefully a moment, clearly wondering if he had the strength to get himself inside.

"Alright, step aside," I said. "*I'll* go first."

Once I was up in the bunk, I reached back down for Gustav. He wasn't much help, weak as he was, but I was able to haul him up and roll him over me toward the wall—which seemed to be all of five inches from the curtains. Being blessed as I am with more *me* than most (folks don't call me Big Red for my mouth . . . though I suppose they could), I would've found the berth a tight fit even without a brother to share it with. Nevertheless, after a lot of squirming and flailing, Old Red and I managed to get ourselves laid out side by side like a couple corpses squeezed into the same casket.

"Well . . . now what?"

"Now we sleep." Gustav dug out his gunbelt and plopped it atop my chest. "You nighthawk first."

"Oh, sure. I'll either wake you in an hour or when the killer slits my throat, whichever comes first."

"That'll work."

He seemed tempted to leave it at that. But he knew *I* wouldn't, so he kept on.

"Whoever set that swamp adder on us knows we'll be on our toes now. I don't think they'll try anything again tonight."

"But we ain't on our toes, are we? We're on our backs—where anyone could get at us."

"Which is why you've got that gun." Old Red turned his back to the aisle—and me—and pressed his face up against the berth's small window, which he cracked open to let in just a hint of brisk, gently whistling wind. "I admit it—I ain't in no shape to take first watch. But just let me get a little shut-eye, and I can take over."

"I don't give a shit about that, Gustav. I'll take watch all night. It's them other things I wanna talk about. Them *brother* things."

"Not now, Otto. I swear I'm too tired to talk."

"But—"

"In the morning."

"But—"

"In the morning."

"Alright. Fine." I rolled over on my side, Old Red's Peacemaker sliding off onto the bunk beside me. "Good goddamn night, then."

Gustav just snuggled in under his covers like a prairie dog burrowing out of reach of a coyote's snout. After that, we lay back-to-back, Old Red doing his thinking and me doing mine, the only thing between us a thick padding of silence.

Of course, quiet was nothing new to us. If he's not working out some deduction, my brother prefers not to open his mouth at all, except to take in air and food and expel the occasional sigh. He and I talked, sure, but there were long stretches where we didn't—and there was plenty we didn't talk *about*.

Five years before, I'd watched as our childhood—family, farm, and friends—was washed away by a river so swollen it seemed to swallow the whole wide world. And Gustav had never once asked me to speak of it. I'd been a burden to him in the days after that flood, a lame calf hitched to a maverick steer, yet *he'd* never spoken of *that*. Words weren't needed for certain things, because the mere fact that we kept on together said all that needed saying.

Or so I'd thought. Now it turned out there was something Gustav hadn't been saying for reasons all his own.

Trains made him sick. So what? Why hadn't he just told me?

I lay there waiting, hoping, desperate for Old Red to break his silence. Which, after a few minutes, he did.

He started snoring.

Twenty-five

NIGHTHAWKS

Or, My Mind Wanders—While Someone Else Wanders the Train

It was so late it was early, but there was little chance I'd fall asleep on my watch. I've done enough cattle-drive night-herding to know how to glue my eyelids open. And even if I didn't, it's easy to stay awake when you're bunked up with a murderer.

I could hear the wheezings of sleep from the berths around us, and the longer I lay there listening, the more all the log-sawing filled me with a jumpy dread.

That could be the killer, I'd think after a particularly loud snort.

Or, *Could a man sleep that sound with fresh blood on his hands?*

Or, *Maybe the killer's not asleep at all. Maybe he's waiting for* me *to start snoring.*

I distracted myself from these gloomy musings by aiming my ears at a particular berth—the one directly beneath us—making out a little muffled rasp that seemed then like the sweetest music I'd ever heard. Even so coarse a thing as a snore has its allure when it slips from betwixt the ruby lips of a pretty young lady.

Saddle tramps like me and Gustav don't stay any one place long enough to have sweethearts—not the kind you don't rent out by the quarter hour, anyway. But if I were to change that, settle in somewhere, Diana Caveo was exactly the sort of woman I'd set my sights on. She was good-looking, good-humored, sharp, and just sharp-*tongued* enough to cut through the bullshit I tend to lay on too thick.

Of course, she was also four or five years beyond me in age—not to mention four or five rungs above me on the social ladder. Yet such practical considerations are no match for a man's imagination, and my mind was soon busy concocting scenarios as unlikely as they would be embarrassing to relate.

Which is perhaps why I didn't notice the shush of parting curtains or the creaking of cautious footsteps in the aisle. What I did eventually notice—because it was practically puffing on the side of my face like a bellows—was the shallow, huffing pant of a man's breath.

Someone was lurking in the passageway, I realized with a jolt that jerked me from my moonings. He was lurking close, too—right beyond our berth curtain, mere inches from my head.

Now said head has been described as both hard and thick many times over the years, but not even Old Red would claim it was so dense as to repel lead. All it would take was one well-placed bullet to plug glugging holes in both my skull and my brother's. We had only one chance: put a hole in that other fellow's head first.

I yanked our curtain open and whipped up Gustav's .45.

I expected to find myself eyeball-to-eyeball with the killer, but all I was eyeball-to was skin. Before me was a scalp as white and smooth as a brand-new baseball. The man it belonged to was hunched over, staring at something beneath my berth. He straightened up quick, though, and the terrified eyes that met mine belonged to none other than Chester Q. Horner.

Even in the dim half-light that (barely) illuminated the car, I could see the color drain from his face. He recovered rapidly, however, plastering over his shock with a bright salesman's smile as he put up his hands in mock surrender.

"Sorry to disappoint you . . . I'm not Barson *or* Welsh."

He lowered his hands as I lowered the Colt.

"You scared the piss out of me, Otto," he went on, whisper-quiet. "Which is funny, cuz I was just draining the dragon down in the gents'. I've really gotta remember: no nightcaps on a train. All this swaying and rocking gets the liquor sloshing, and before you know it, your bladder's crowing like a rooster. You'd think a traveling man like me wouldn't forget."

He was moving as he talked, backing away toward his berth, directly across the aisle from mine.

"Anyway, see ya tomorrow."

And he threw himself up into his bunk and closed the curtains tight behind him.

It was over so fast it left me gaping, slack-jawed, thinking maybe I'd nodded off into a dream. But then I leaned out and looked down, wondering what Horner had been up to, and I saw proof that it had been plenty real.

The curtains of the berth below ours had been pulled open. Not all the way—just parted a foot or so. But that was enough to give anyone in the corridor a peep at the passenger inside.

Horner had been ogling Miss Caveo.

I stared down, disgusted by the liberty the drummer had taken . . . even as I took it myself without quite meaning to. I didn't have the right angle to see much, but what I saw made it hard to tear my gaze away.

Dark locks spilling across a pillow. A soft, slack hand, the delicate fingers curled ever so slightly. An upturned wrist as pure white as porcelain. A naked forearm disappearing into a lacy sleeve.

My heart got to thumping so tom-tom loud I was sure it would wake everyone on the train, and I leaned out farther to close the curtains, intending to avert my eyes while I was at it. My eyes refused to avert, however, and I got an even better look at Sleeping Beauty.

She wasn't the model of feminine perfection one finds in paintings and magazine illustrations. Her nose was a touch too bulbous, her face too freckled, her middle perhaps not wasp-waisted enough. But what some would label "imperfections" merely strengthened her hold on me, for they emphasized that this was a real woman. Not a goddess, not an image, not an ideal. She lived in the same world I did. She was something I could reach out and touch.

As was the book lying by her side. Having a nightie-clad female before me and all, it took me a moment to notice it.

It was *Rules and Regulations of the Operating Department,* published by the Southern Pacific Railroad.

My eyes widened.

Miss Caveo's fluttered.

"Feather," she moaned.

Or maybe it was "weather" or "heather" or "favor" or "father." I certainly didn't hang there upside down waiting for her to repeat herself. I closed her curtains quick and retreated back into my bunk.

For the next minute, I lay there, utterly still, listening for any hint that Miss Caveo had seen me. There was no gasp or squeak or scream, though, and finally I relaxed, convinced she'd slept through the whole thing. Without a doubt my brother had, for he honked out another mighty snore.

Most times, Gustav's the lighter sleeper of the two of us: He was working the cattle trails back when there was still a chance you could wake up with a Sioux brave's knife under your scalp, and it usually doesn't take anything more than a flea's fart to get him up grabbing for his gun. He had to be exhausted indeed to sleep through my encounter with Horner.

As pissed at him as I was, I didn't begrudge him a little extra shut-eye. So I stayed on watch as long as I could, passing the time as before with thoughts of Diana Caveo. They were different thoughts now, though.

I could tell Old Red didn't trust her, and he'd warned me more than once that I shouldn't trust *myself* when it comes to women. And she'd certainly proved herself to be an accomplished liar—or *persuader,* to use a term she'd probably prefer.

Yet I still couldn't bring myself to believe there was anything truly treacherous about her. She had peculiar taste in bedtime reading, sure, but I expected there was an innocent enough explanation. I'd wheedle it out of her the next day, along with whatever smiles and laughs I could get. Maybe I'd even feel her arm linked with mine again.

Maybe I'd even get a kiss.

This last thought was where the line between daydreaming and *dreaming*-dreaming had started to blur. Miss Caveo became Mrs. Kier, who became my sister Greta, who became the snake, who became (most horrifying of all) Wiltrout.

I gave Gustav a jab in the ribs. Without a word, we wriggled around till he was by the aisle cuddling the gun and I was by the window cuddling my pillow. At last, I could let my eyelids drop like the curtains on a theater stage.

The next morning, they'd open again on the final act.

Twenty-six

ALL THAT

Or, Gustav and I Try to Iron Things Out, and Up Pops a New Wrinkle

What seemed like mere moments after falling asleep, I was lured from my slumber by an enticement even my weary body couldn't resist: the aroma of fresh-brewed Arbuckle. I opened my eyes to find Samuel smiling at me, a cup of black coffee in his hands.

Gustav was gone.

"Good mornin', Mr. Amlingmeyer," Samuel said. He'd opened the berth curtains just enough to peek in and wave the joe beneath my nose. "I know you had a rough day yesterday, so I let you sleep long as I could. But I'm gonna have to ask you to come outta there soon. There's only two upper berths on the whole train that haven't been folded up yet, and you're in one of 'em."

Having long ago accustomed myself to the early-morning risings on cattle drives (which usually start before dawn with the cook banging a pan and kicking goldbrickers upside the head), I felt like quite the pampered prince awaking to coffee in bed.

"Thank you, Samuel," I said, propping myself on an elbow and reaching for the cup. I took a sip and smacked my lips. "Tough luck for my brother he ain't here to be coddled like this."

"Oh, he's been up for hours. Sendin' you the coffee was his idea."

"Oh."

The taste of the java took on a bitter bite.

"He's waitin' for you in the dinin' car," Samuel said.

The coffee was strong but it wasn't all that hot, and I swallowed the rest of it in two gulps. "I'll be cleared outta here in a minute. But you can tell my brother I won't be down to see him till I'm good and ready. I need a shave."

Samuel lingered, watching me, as I dug out a clean shirt. When I noticed he wasn't leaving, I grinned and stuck a hand in my pocket.

"For your trouble," I said, pulling out a nickel and handing it over.

"You're learnin', you're learnin'," the porter chortled, and he pulled the curtains closed.

After squirming out of my dirty old duds and into a fresh set, I hopped down into the aisle and made my way to the washroom. What I saw in the mirror was an improvement over the night before—though improving on hideous still won't get you handsome. The purple-balloon swelling of my nose had shrunk to a pink-tinged bulge. Rather than resembling a man with a plum stuck to his face, I now merely looked like a puffy-faced drunk.

Our Pullman was nearly deserted when I stepped out of the privy, and it wasn't hard to account for all the empty seats—the car had never been noisier. Mrs. Foreman's curly-topped hellions were re-creating one of Billy the Kid's train robberies (never mind that the Kid never robbed a train) with wild whoops and howling death throes. I was even obligated to die once myself, having been drafted into the role of an unlucky lawman. I guess the boys just assumed the part suited me.

As I made my escape toward the back of the train, I passed the last upper berth still down with curtains closed: Lockhart's. It was hunkered atop Chan's berth, so the Chinaman's bed hadn't been put up for the day, either. Given the mood Lockhart would be in (and the hangover he'd have to contend with) once he awoke, I could understand why Samuel hadn't hustled him from his cubbyhole. The longer the old Pinkerton slept, the better off we'd all be.

As I continued on through the next sleeper, I encountered our conductor coming the other way, and we had to do an uncomfortably cozy Tennessee reel to slide around each other.

"Your presumptuous, troublemaking, son-of-a-bitch brother's waiting for you in the dining car," Wiltrout growled. (He didn't actually *say* the "presumptuous, troublemaking, son-of-a-bitch" part, mind you—it was simply implied by the tone of his voice.)

A minute later, I had to do another passageway do-si-do, this time with Kip and his tray of nickel-and-dime diversions.

"Hey, Otto," the kid said as we maneuvered around each other, "your brother's waitin' for you—"

"I know, I know. In the dinin' car." I rolled my eyes. "Jesus."

A plump Presbyterian burgher seated nearby shot me a disapproving glare.

"Is Lord," I added.

The man wasn't fooled, but at least he directed his frown down at the *Saturday Evening Post* spread across his ample lap.

"Samuel and Wiltrout already told me the same thing," I said to Kip.

"I'm sure the captain just *loved* playin' messenger boy for Old Red. Your brother's got him mighty p-"—Kip caught himself before he offended any of his potential customers with the *-issed* that almost followed—"-erturbed again."

"What's he doin' now?"

"Just askin' folks a lot of crazy-soundin' questions. 'Have you seen a man with curly blond hair slinkin' around?' 'Did you see a bald feller creepin' out of the baggage car?' 'Have you lost a *teacup* recently?' "

The news butch shook his head, shaking off his usual air of cocky self-amusement in the process.

"You know, Otto—I appreciate your brother's stick-to-itiveness. Joe Pezullo was a friend of mine, after all. But Old Red's not exactly the smoothest talker in the world, is he? I mean, Wiltrout ain't the only person he's *perturbed* this morning. Maybe you better tell him to ease up if you don't want to get tossed off the train keister over teacup."

"Who says I *don't*?" I snorted.

Kip's expression turned quizzical, but I didn't feel like explaining myself. I wasn't sure I could even if I tried. I was mightily peeved at my brother, and the badge I was wearing still chafed against my chest. But just how mad was I—and what did I intend to do about it? That I hadn't thought through.

"Thanks for the tip, kid. I'll keep it in mind."

Kip nodded and got on his way, barking that he was offering "fresh newspapers, fresh spring water, fresh strawberries—with fresh talk added free of charge!"

A moment later, I was stepping into the crowded dining car. I spotted Old Red right off. He was hunched over at a table for two near the car's matchbox of a kitchen.

Whether he was being plagued by his conscience or the half-eaten serving of scrambled eggs on the plate before him, I couldn't say. Either way, he looked miserable.

When he saw me, he actually raised his hand and gave a timid wave, as if unsure I'd recognize him. I replied with a neutral nod and headed toward his table.

Drawing closer, I spotted something sitting next to his plate. Even halfway across the compartment, I could tell what it was—the printing on the cover hollered as loud as Kip at his most earsplitting.

The dime novel's title was *The Sons of Jesse James: The All-True Story of the Give-'em-Hell Boys.* Below that was a drawing of two gaudy-dressed gunslingers who resembled Mike Barson and Augie Welsh about as much as a unicorn resembles a pack mule.

So that's why he's been looking for me, I thought sourly. *He just wants me to read something for him.*

"Mornin'," I mumbled, my voice flapjack flat.

I slumped into the chair across from my brother.

"Mornin'," he replied quietly. "Nose looks better."

I shrugged. "That wouldn't be hard."

I could've added that he actually looked *worse.* His face was as pale as the bleached-white tablecloth, and hanging beneath his bloodshot eyes were bags so large Kip could have filled them with peanuts and peddled them to the passengers.

Yet I said nothing. Not to spare Old Red's feelings—I just wasn't in the mood to banter with him.

Gustav seemed to be waiting for me to say something, anything. I'm the talkative one, after all. For once I didn't know what to say, though, and I turned away and looked out the window.

In the night, the Pacific Express had escaped the Great Basin and its yellow-gray sea of alkali sand. Now we were in the Sierras, and everything was different. Whereas before all had been dingy sameness, our new view included a blanket of emerald pines, jutting towers of black rock capped with ivory-pure snow, shimmering blue water at the bottom of gaping gorges—such a variety of sights as to be almost dizzying.

And for Old Red, there was no "almost" about it. He followed my gaze, and one glance into the nearest ravine was enough to set his eyes spinning like paddle wheels.

He swiveled around to put his back to the window, muttering something I couldn't quite catch.

"Huh?" I grunted.

Gustav squirmed and toyed with his fork and looked at the floor.

"I said, 'I'm sorry, you know,'" he finally managed to croak out.

I gaped at him like he'd taken to spouting Latin. *I'm sorry* just wasn't a phrase I thought was in his vocabulary.

"Matter of fact, I *didn't* know," I said.

"Well, now you do."

"Alright . . . apology accepted. Now you wanna tell me exactly what you're sorry *for?*"

My brother fidgeted again, writhing in his seat like a worm on the hook. "Not particularly. But I reckon there's no gettin' around it, is there?"

"You reckon right."

Old Red pressed his fingertips to his head like it had come loose and needed straightening. "It's hard to talk out—cuz I don't entirely understand it." He shrugged. "Trains just make me sick. Queasylike. Always have, from the first time I rode one."

He shrugged again and went silent. I let him have a moment, then shook my head and gave him the palms-up, double curl of the fingers that usually means "pay up." This time, it meant "more." Gustav answered with a reluctant nod.

"Maybe it's cuz it's something I can't control," he said. "A horse, a buggy, a wagon—you got reins. But these damned things?" He gave the car around us a limp little wave. "All you can do is sit here and hope there's someone workin' the gears who knows what the hell he's doin'. And even if there is, what if a trestle washes out? Or bandits mess with the rails? Or another train ends up on the wrong track—*your* track, comin' straight at you? Why, you wouldn't even know it till . . ."

My brother's voice had grown louder with each word, and he cut himself off when he noticed the stares he was drawing from the tables around us.

"Look, I can understand all that," I told him. "What I can't understand is why you didn't just tell me you felt that way."

Old Red sighed. "I guess maybe it was pride. Partly. But there was more to it than that. Do you remember . . . after . . . you know? The flood and all that. I had you come down to meet me in Dodge City?"

I nodded. *The flood and all that* was what had set me and my brother adrift together—the destruction of our family farm and our family with it.

"I couldn't even bring myself to ride a train up to get you, see that our people was buried proper." Gustav's voice was growing hoarse, his eyes red and moist. "That left me feelin' . . . pretty low."

His gaze drifted down toward the floor again. But then he cleared his throat and forced himself to look me in the eye.

"And then there you was in Dodge—my baby brother, lookin' at me like I was *Vater* and *Mutter* and Buffalo Bill Cody rolled up in one. You was just a scared kid tryin' to feel safe . . . needin' something to believe in, I guess. A hero. I couldn't admit *I* was just as scared as you. So when we took to the trails, I let you assume what you would."

He gave his head a woeful shake of the kind he usually directs at me with a roll of the eyes. But it was himself he was disappointed in now.

"Later, I was afraid how you'd take the truth. And not just cuz I'd misled you. There was all them extra days in the saddle, too. I wasn't sure you'd put up with it anymore if it was just cuz I was yellow about something. I wasn't sure you'd still put up with *me*. You see, I'd got used to havin' you around, Otto. And . . . well, dammit, I reckon that's all there is to say."

My brother wilted back in his seat looking winded—and for good reason. He'd just been digging hard, dredging down as deep as he'd ever gone with me before. For him it was toil, hard labor, talking like this.

But he'd done the job right.

"You were wrong back in Dodge," I said.

Old Red's face shifted, tightened, as if he was expecting the worst. "I know, I know. I shouldn't have—"

I shook my head. "I ain't talkin' about what you done. I'm talkin' about why you done it. I didn't need a hero, Gustav. I just needed my *brother*—and there you were. As for ridin' trails 'stead of trains all these years . . . well, if I was willin' to go to all that extra trouble for principle, don't you think I'd do the same and more if I knew it was for *you*?"

For a moment, Gustav didn't seem to know how to react. Then he *tried* to react—tried to smile, actually—but the best he could manage was a sort of trembly-lipped grimace.

"I suppose you would."

"You bet I would . . . and I will." I pointed a finger at him and gave it a shake. "Now, that don't mean I'm any happier about workin' for the S.P. But I can see how much it really means to you. Your gettin' on the Express shows that. If you could get over your feelin's about trains, I suppose I can get over a thing or two myself. So I'll see this through with you—to Oakland and wherever else, to the end of the line."

Gustav gave up trying to smile and settled for a simple nod. "Thank you, Otto."

"Don't mention it," I said, and that's not just an expression for me and my brother. Most likely, we'd never speak of this conversation again.

Perhaps a minute passed in silence while we let it all sink in—the look I'd been given into Old Red's heart and whatever change this might bring about between us.

It was my stomach that spoke first, unleashing a roar that commanded *Feed me!* in no uncertain terms. Man cannot survive on bread alone, the old saying goes, and I'd add that bread and java *still* isn't enough to get by on. So I waved the steward over and put in an order for kippered herring, griddle cakes, eggs, sausage, bacon, biscuits, potatoes, and, if available, a horse, since I was hungry enough to eat one.

"Alright, then," I said as the steward staggered away under the weight of my prodigious order, "how goes our investigation? Anybody see Wiltrout sneakin' around with a snake? Or a stranger in a curly blond too-pay lightin' up a stogie with the manifest?"

My brother sat up straighter, looking profoundly grateful for the change of topic. "Nobody saw nothin'. But I ain't through askin' around just yet. And there's other ways to get at the data we need."

He spun the dime novel around and slid it across the table.

"The Sons of Jesse James" stared up at me from the cover. They were Westerners as only an Easterner or a schoolboy could imagine them: neatly groomed, dandified, with a silver six-gun in each hand and eyes alight with the will to fight for what's right. They were the ideal— Old Red and I, the grimy reality.

"Where'd you get this thing, anyway?" I asked, rapping a knuckle on the magazine. It looked as ragged as my brother's Holmes tales, with dog-eared pages and creases in the cover.

"Kip. He didn't have anything new he could sell me on the Give-'em-Hell Boys—folks bought out everything he had, 'cept for that. It's his personal copy."

"And he just gave it to you?"

Gustav took to dusting imaginary crumbs from the table. "Sold it to me . . . for a buck."

"That little pirate," I chuckled.

I flipped the magazine open and started skimming through the story. The bellowing blast of the first sentences was all it took to turn my snickers into a groan.

Reading Doc Watson's tales has often left me uncertain as to my own skills with pen and paper. The man weaves quite a tapestry, whereas it sometimes seems like my own fumbling fingers produce nothing but knots. That was part of the reason the book I'd written was tucked away in my war bag rather than sitting on some New York editor's desk.

The dime novel before me had the opposite effect, however: Reading it, I couldn't help but feel like Mark Twain by comparison.

"What do you think you can learn from this?" I asked Old Red.

"That 'robbery' yesterday's still sittin' about as well with me as that is." He scowled at the uneaten eggs on his plate as if he'd been served a generous helping of hot scrambled pig shit. "I figure the more I know about the Give-'em-Hell Boys, the more what they done might start to make some kind of sense."

"They rob trains, and Barson and Welsh are the brains. That's all you need to know . . . and it's more than you'll get out of this." I gave each of the Sons of Jesse James a little flick of the finger.

"You don't know that for a fact. There could be some important data buried in there somewheres."

"Oh, yeah? Alright, then. Let me know when we get to the 'important data.' "

I assumed the chin-up, chest-out bearing of a Shakespeare-reciting ham.

" 'Ka-pow! Ka-pow!' " I intoned with lugubrious solemnity. " 'The shots ring out! The Give-'em-Hell Boys have robbed another Southern Pacific train! The railroad men curse! The ladies swoon! And some—yes!—some cheer! Who are these daring desperadoes? What turned them from peaceful farmers into the most feared bandits in the West? Read on! Read on! Read on!' "

I looked up at my brother. "Shall I read on?"

But Old Red didn't answer. He'd been struck dumb by something behind my back, near the door to the Pullmans. When I twisted around to see what it was, I, too, found myself tongue-tied—and scared stiff.

Burl Lockhart was striding toward us. In his hand was the gleaming steel of a gun.

That's when everything went dark.

Twenty-seven

A BIG OL' HEAP OF QUESTIONS

Or, I Tie Up Loose Ends While Lockhart Continues to Unravel

hat the hell?" I blurted out.

Light returned almost immediately, but it was different now—the weak glow of electric lights, not blinding-bright sunshine. Outside the window, it remained black as night.

"Snowshed," Gustav explained tersely, clearly unnerved. "Third today."

"Oh," I said.

I'd read about the sheds—wooden tunnels, miles long, built to keep mountain tracks free of snow. I would've paused to marvel at the sight of one (or lack of same, since there wasn't anything to see but dark), but there were more pressing matters to attend to.

The man moving up behind me with a drawn gun, for instance.

"Mornin', Mr. Lockhart," Old Red said, sliding a hand down toward his Colt. "What can we do for you?"

The Pinkerton brought his gun up fast—and slammed it onto the table before me.

"There," he said. "I owe you that."

Then he marched off without another word.

For a moment, he was the only thing in the dining car in motion. Everyone else had frozen—waiters clearing plates and passengers holding cups of coffee halfway to their lips and Old Red and me with our jaws hanging as loose on their hinges as a couple of porch swings.

No one moved until Lockhart sat at an empty table and hid himself behind an upraised menu. Once he was out of sight, it was as if he'd never been there at all, and within seconds the chatter of conversation and the clink-clatter of silver on porcelain was louder than ever.

I finally looked down at the hogleg on the table.

"Hey, that ain't mine."

The gun Lockhart had taken from me the night before had been a beat-up rubber-gripped .45—a no-frills affair made for slinging lead and nothing more. But the frilled-up iron before me now was something else entirely.

It was a pearl-handled, silver-plated Smith & Wesson .44 engraved with ornate scrollwork and the letters *B.L.* in fancy, flowing script. And it was notched: Seven stubby little nicks were lined up along the outside curve of the grip.

"Holy shit . . . it's one of Lockhart's own six-shooters," I said reverently, as if whispering a prayer. I'd seen too much of Lockhart the man to hold him in any awe, but the gun—that was a link to Lockhart the *legend.* "Looks like a match for the gun the Give-'em-Hell Boys took off him last night. 'Aunt Virgie.'"

"You oughta go talk to him about it," Gustav said, nodding at Lockhart's table. "We need to ask him some questions, anyway—and you're the one to do the askin'."

"Me?"

"Sure. I couldn't ask the man the time of day without him takin' offense."

"Or you givin' it."

Old Red shrugged. "He and me don't see eye to eye. But you . . . you could see eye to eye with an ant or an elephant, either one. Or at least talk like you do. If there's one of us who could get some answers outta Lockhart without gettin' his teeth knocked out for his trouble, it'd be you."

I drummed my fingers on the table, weighing the chance to lose a few teeth against reading more of *The Sons of Jesse James*.

"What kinda answers you lookin' for?"

Gustav didn't smile, but a gleam came to his eyes I hadn't seen for quite some time. "Where he got that gun, first off—he didn't have it in the Pullman last night. And was he up to anything in Carlin other than gettin' fall-down drunk? And how did he know to send us to Colonel Crowe back in Ogden? And why's Chan so keen on gettin' into the baggage car?"

"Anything else?" I asked. "His boot size, maybe? Mother's maiden name? Favorite color?"

"No," my brother sighed. "That's it."

"Alright, then." I scooped up Lockhart's fancy .44 as I got to my feet. "Wish me luck."

"Good luck. And . . . thanks, Brother."

"Just doin' my duty," I said, giving my badge a tap—though it wasn't my duty to the Southern Pacific I was thinking of.

As I turned and started toward Lockhart's table, the craggy old Pinkerton was putting in an order with the steward, pointing at something on the menu even as his sunken eyes locked on me. If he'd looked like death warmed over the day before, now he was death served cold—gray, dried out, stiff. He watched me drawing closer with a stillness icy enough to freeze the balls off Jack Frost himself.

I approached him holding the hogleg cradled sideways in both hands, the way you'd hold an offering, not a gun you aimed to use. When I reached his table, I placed the .44 gingerly before him. The steward scurried off toward the kitchen—and cover.

"Thank you, Mr. Lockhart, but I can't take this," I said. "That beat-up Peacemaker I loaned you last night wasn't worth a tenth what this is."

Lockhart lifted his bony shoulders in a listless shrug. "I owe you a gun." He nodded toward the Smith & Wesson without looking at it. "That's a gun."

"It sure is. One hell of a gun. If I might ask . . . how'd you come to have it with you? Sure don't look like a toy you bought off Kip."

Lockhart's gaze bored into me. Not in an angry way, though—more like he was afraid to let his eyes slip somewhere else. Down, say, to the six-shooter that lay gleaming between us as shiny as King Arthur's armor.

"That's Aunt Pauline, one of the two best guns I ever had—and I've had plenty. She was packed away in my trunk last night or I guess she wouldn't be here now. I had to twist that son-of-a-bitch conductor's arm till it nearly snapped to get into the baggage car and dig her out. So you just go on and take her . . . and be grateful you got her."

I made no move toward the .44.

"Seems to me she's mighty special to you, Mr. Lockhart."

The Pinkerton chuffed out a bitter snort. "I'll tell you how special she is to me. Do you know what I did with your Colt?"

He knew I didn't, of course, so I just gave him the head shake he was looking for.

"I was in such a fired-up hurry to set after the Give-'em-Hell Boys last night, I didn't even stop to get Aunt Pauline there. No time. I was gonna track down Barson and Welsh and gut 'em like catfish. After what they done, what they *said*, I had to. They were practically darin' me to come after 'em. But you know what I also had to do? Get me one little drink first. To steady my nerves, I told myself. Well, one drink didn't do it. Two didn't do it. *Three* didn't do it. And before you know it, I was tradin' your gun for booze. I can even remember thinkin', 'A half-empty bottle of rotgut—that's all they'll give me for this piece-of-shit Colt? If I had Aunt Pauline here, they'd give me every damn bottle in the place.' Yeah, I would've traded her. Like *that*."

Lockhart snapped his fingers, his thin lips bowing into the most colossal frown I've ever seen—a curving pucker the shape of a horse-shoe.

"Well, you saw what happened," he went on, still scowling. "And the next morning I roll out of bed not knowin' how I got there, and that mouthy news butch tells me a Chinaman, a woman, and a dumb lummox with a third-rate badge dragged my sorry carcass back to the train."

He jabbed a finger at the gun, still unable to bring himself to look at it. "So I mean it—you take Aunt Pauline. I already let them Give-'em-Hell bastards have Aunt Virgie. I reckon I ain't worthy of either of 'em anymore."

Despite all that Lockhart had just said, I knew better than to pick up that .44. It wasn't just his gun lying there—it was an old man's notion of everything that had once been noble about himself. Take that away, whether he told you to or not, and he'd hate you for it.

"If Burl Lockhart ain't worthy of that gun, I don't see how a 'dumb lummox with a third-rate badge' is," I said. "You wanna give away Aunt Pauline, that's your business. But I'd just ask you to wait till a better man than me or you comes along. My guess is, you'll end up holdin' ol' Pauline a long, long time—cuz you're still Burl Lockhart, after all."

Lockhart's jaw worked up and down beneath his frown, as if he was trying to chew some little bit of gristle he couldn't quite catch between his teeth. Then the chair across from him slid out from the table—pushed by his foot—and the corners of his lips made the long journey upward, curling into a smile.

"Have a seat," he said.

Lockhart paused to take a sip of water as I thanked him and sat down. When the glass left his mouth, his smile was gone.

"What's your handle again?"

"Otto Amlingmeyer, Mr. Lockhart. But my friends call me Big Red."

The Pinkerton snorted at the obviousness of it. When you're a strapping six-foot-one redhead like me, folks don't call you "Little Blue."

"Well, I reckon 'stead of gripin' about you gettin' me back aboard the Express, I really oughta be thankin' you. So . . . thanks, Big Red. And I apologize for that 'dumb lummox' remark."

"I've been called worse—by my own kin, even." I shrugged. "And no need for thanks for last night. It just seemed like the thing to do. Anyway, it was Dr. Chan who went after you first."

"Course it was." Lockhart waved the thought away irritably, like cigar smoke puffed in his face. "Don't think he did that out of the kindness of his heart. Them crafty little buggers always have a scheme cookin', and I know his. He was just scared, is all."

"Scared? Of what? That he'd have to ride on to Oakland with no nanny holdin' his hand?"

I bugged out my eyes, as if I hadn't intended my question to have quite so sharp a point to it. But I had—and the needling worked, too.

"Get this straight," the Pinkerton snapped, his long face flushing. "Burl Lockhart don't play nanny to goddamn Chinks!"

As dining cars are packed so tight you could accidentally slice up your neighbor's steak without realizing it wasn't on your own plate, the folks at the nearest tables heard every word. Most of them miraculously finished their breakfasts at that exact moment, hopping to their feet and leaving coins they didn't bother to count.

"I apologize, Mr. Lockhart," I said as the tables around us cleared. "I didn't mean nothing by it."

"Oh, don't apologize," Lockhart sighed. Though anyone who could've eavesdropped was dashing for the nearest exit, he dropped his voice anyway. "I know how it looks. The Pinks have been tryin' to put me out to pasture, but still . . . they wouldn't do me like that. I ain't here to protect *Chan*."

"I *knew* they wouldn't have you here just to nursemaid some nobody. You're Burl Lockhart! It had to be something big."

I was lathering up the soft soap so thick it's a wonder Lockhart could see me through the suds, yet he showed no sign of catching on.

"You nailed it, Big Red," he said. "Chan ain't diddly. It's what he's takin' back to San Francisco that's big."

"You're aboard the train to bodyguard . . . a *body*?"

The Pinkerton smiled again, though he only managed it with his mouth this time, not his eyes. "You noticed Chan's name on that casket, did you? Well, you just remember what I said about Chinks bein' sneaky. That ain't no coffin—it's a treasure chest."

Lockhart hunched over the table and gestured for me to do the same. When I'd bent in close enough to suit him, he went on in a just-between-you-and-me whisper.

"Here's the thing. Chan helped put together the Chinese exhibit at the Exposition. It's got Chink art, music, dancers, food. And Chink treasure. Or it did, anyway. I don't know what it all is, exactly—rubies and jewelry and crowns and such, I guess. I've never even seen it. It was all boxed up back in Chicago."

"I get it," I said. "In the coffin."

"Bull's-eye. Chan got most of the stuff on loan from a big-time collector back West. Put down a hunk of his own cash as collateral. Then last week, that collector feller's bank went under in a run, and the SOB called in every debt he could—includin' them trinkets. If Chan don't deliver, he won't get a penny of his money back."

"Which is why Chan ain't takin' any chances gettin' everything back to San Francisco."

"There's that. Plus, he told me he's got him a 'sacred duty to his ancestors' to look after the stuff." Lockhart shook his head. "Crazy yellow bastard."

"Does Colonel Crowe know all this?" I asked, trying to sound pouty, as if hurt that my new boss wouldn't share such secrets with me.

"He knows. I went through him to get the tickets—didn't want any trouble about a Chinaman on an S.P. special. It was Crowe who picked out that fake name for me: Custos. Now what the hell kinda name is that?" Lockhart's expression soured. "The fake mustache was my idea. I suppose I was tryin' to be more of a 'modern' dee-tective, like that English nelly your brother's keen on."

I forced out a laugh, thankful Gustav was too far away to hear me let the poke at Holmes pass.

"Them dime-novel dicks wouldn't stop with just a mustache, Mr. Lockhart. They'd have done themselves up with a peg leg, an eye patch—"

I was about to say "and a stuffed parrot," but a sudden inspiration struck me, and I veered off on a new trail.

"—and a curly blond wig."

I watched Lockhart for a flush or a blink or a twitch—any sign he knew what I was talking about. But all he did was snort again.

"You're probably right. Crowe told me not to bother with the mustache. Said it wasn't in keepin' with my 'moodus opera randy.' I'll be damned if I know what that meant . . . but I guess I shoulda listened."

"So Crowe's an old pal of yours?"

Lockhart waggled a lanky hand like scales tipping this way and that. "Sorta. I've known him and Jeff Powless a lotta years, anyway. Used to be, all them railroad big shots was just linin' up to work with ol' Burl Lockhart. . . ."

The Pinkerton looked thoughtful for a moment, his eyes shifting to something else, something beyond me. Then with a *snap* you could almost hear, his gaze shot back to me.

"You sure came packin' a big ol' heap of questions."

I applied a shit-eating grin and shrugged shyly. "I just can't help myself. It's kinda embarrassing, but . . . well . . . my brother's got Sherlock Holmes, and I've got . . ." I cut loose with a jittery laugh. "I've always had you."

Lockhart beamed with such prideful delight I actually felt guilty. "Awww, a little hero worship ain't nothin' to be ashamed of, Big Red. When I was a nipper, all us boys wanted to be Kit Carson. I reckon we all need someone bigger than us to look up to. The only mistake's tryin' to *be* that person. Cuz it ain't a person you're tryin' to be. It's a dream."

His smile went wistful, and his rheumy eyes lost their focus again.

"Just look at me. Here I am still tryin' to be Burl Lockhart . . . and I just ain't up to it anymore. Hell, maybe I never was."

"Well, now," I said, intending to offer up something soothing. But the flapdoodle just wouldn't flow for once. Lockhart may have been an old fool, but what was *I* to keep fooling him further?

Uncomfortable silence settled over us like a wet quilt. After a moment, Lockhart threw it off with a raspy chuckle.

"Would you listen to me? Talkin' that way to a freshly minted Southern Pacific railroad dee-tective. You still got yourself a lotta excitin' days ahead."

"Thanks to you. That was mighty good of you, steerin' us to Colonel Crowe the way you done."

"Oh, I was just playin' the big man for a couple young punchers who reminded me of myself, once upon a time. And it was a chance to do a favor for Crowe. He's so desperate for agents he can trust, he'd pin a badge on his own mother, if she'd let him. Hell, he might even take *me* on when the Pinks finally cut me loose."

He reached into a coat pocket, pulled out a flask, and unscrewed it with one well-practiced twist of the wrist.

"Anyways, ol' Burl Lockhart's the past. Here's to the future."

He saluted me with the flask, threw back his head, and took a long swallow.

"Well, thank you for your time, sir," I said, coming to my feet before Lockhart could ask me to join him. "I best be gettin' along. My brother's got us askin' folks all kinda questions. For our official report, you know. We ain't done so good as railroad police so far, but maybe we can paint a prettier picture on paper."

Lockhart toasted me again.

"Smart boy," he said, somehow seeming sincere and smirky and melancholy all at once. "I do believe you're gonna go far."

Then the old man took on a golden glow—literally. The Pacific Express had finally emerged from the darkness of the long snowshed, and sunlight once again streamed into the car. I turned and headed for my brother's table, anxious to tell him what I'd learned.

I had plenty to tell—but no one to tell it to. Old Red was gone.

Twenty-eight

ARCHIE

Or, We Learn Who Tried to Kill Us the Night Before—Sort Of

Your brother left a few minutes ago, Big Red."

I turned to find Lockhart grinning at me.

"He stuck around a while to keep an eye on us—though he tried to look like he wasn't. He didn't leave till he knew *I* was watching *him*. He's in the observation car now."

"Thanks, Mr. Lockhart. Gustav does tend to hover like a mother hen."

I kept my voice as chipper as I could, trying not to let on how much the old man's wiles threw me. I'd been pretty proud of the job I'd done buttering him up, yet now I had to wonder if I had some oleo on me myself.

After pausing just long enough to shovel down the skillet-fried feast the steward had left for me at our table, I set off after Old Red.

The observation car was packed, with passengers standing in prattling clumps, lining the seats along the windows, and clustering around the plush, circular couch in the middle of the car. Gustav was squeezed into a corner, his body angled so as not to put him in line of sight of the snow-crowned peaks and rocky bluffs passing by outside. Instead, a more mundane scene absorbed all his attention: a woman and a man at a small table playing cards while another woman sat nearby pretending to read.

I say "pretending" because it's well known that reading a book is next to impossible if you never look at the pages. And Diana Caveo's eyes rarely left the card players—Mrs. Kier and Chester Q. Horner. Miss Caveo was behind and to the left of Mrs. Kier, and Old Red was behind and to the right of *her,* so it was quite the cat's cradle of spying going on when I spotted my brother.

"What's goin' on?" I asked once I'd worked my way through the herd to reach his side.

"Keep your voice down. Your head, too. I wanna see how this plays out." Gustav spared just the briefest glance over and up at me. "You are one conspicuous SOB, did you know that?"

"Hey, you're an S o' that B yourself—and she weren't no B."

My brother winced. "You're right. My apologies to you and *Mutter* both. I should've said you're one conspicuous *horse's ass.* Now would you for God's sake do something about it?"

Old Red had *The Sons of Jesse James* in his hands, so I snatched it away and threw myself into the nearest seat, the magazine held up over my face—upside down.

"That better?" I whispered.

"It'll do."

Despite his griping, Gustav almost seemed to be enjoying himself. If we could needle each other, maybe that meant things were getting back to normal between us.

"So," he said, "what'd you and Lockhart talk about?"

I filled him in while we watched Miss Caveo watch Mrs. Kier and Horner. The drummer was keeping score, and as the game went on, it seemed to take him longer and longer to do the tallies. The numbers were adding up.

Gustav listened to my report silently, only nodding occasionally or leaning this way or that to peer around a roving passenger's rump. Seeing Horner and Miss Caveo so close together reminded me of all I'd witnessed on night watch, and I passed that along, too: Horner's peeping, the bald spot on his head, and the S.P. manual in Miss Caveo's bed.

Old Red didn't bat an eye at news of Horner's perverse prowlings. Yet when he heard about the lady's curious preferences in reading matter, he didn't just bat his eyes—he practically popped them out of his skull.

"Is that the manual there?" he asked, nodding at the book Miss Caveo was (not) reading now.

"Nope. Too thick. Cover's a different color, too."

My brother's face scrunched into a look of all-consuming concentration. Whatever smoldering suspicions he'd had about the lady seemed to have been fanned up into an outright flame.

"Don't go gettin' foolish notions," I told him. "Respectable gals like that don't get mixed up in messes like this."

Gustav tore his gaze away from Miss Caveo to look me in the eye. "You know better than that."

"Well," I said, and I said no more.

It hadn't been a woman who'd put a bullet through Old Red a few months before, but it may as well have been. That mess didn't just have a "respectable gal" mixed up in it—she'd done most of the mixing herself.

I'd been fooled then. What did I really know about Diana Caveo now? Strip away her sweet exterior, and maybe she'd make Lizzie Borden look like the Virgin Mary.

Still, what a sweet exterior to strip . . .

"Hel-lo," Gustav mumbled.

As if to prove my brother's point about what you can expect from a supposedly respectable lady—which is just about anything—Miss Caveo put down her book, walked over to Horner, and whispered something in his ear, grinning lasciviously. The drummer winked up at her and dropped his cards on the table.

There was some hurried chitchat with Mrs. Kier—obviously pardons for an interrupted game and promises to pick it up again soon—and then Horner and Miss Caveo were weaving their way through the crowd together. When they reached the far end of the compartment, they stepped outside, onto the observation platform. Even all the way at the front of the car, we could feel the gust of cool wind that blew in before they shut the door behind them.

"Pretty nippy out there," Old Red said.

I grunted.

"Funny that those two should feel the need for privacy all of a sudden."

I grunted.

"Makes you wonder what they've got to talk about."

I grunted. *Loudly.*

"Oh, Jesus, Otto—you ain't jealous, are you?"

"No, I ain't jealous," I said. "I just wanna rip that degenerate asshole's big, bald head off."

Gustav ran a hand over his mustache and mouth, weighing options—and not seeming to like how they balanced out. "Think you can hold off on that for a few minutes?"

I copied his gesture, rubbing my fingers against my clean-shaven chin. "Ohhh . . . I suppose. Why?"

"Cuz I'd like to join 'em out there."

"Really? You think you're up for that?"

I jerked my head at the nearest window. The train was spiraling upward along a narrow, curved overhang, the ground dropping away so quick it almost looked like we were flying.

"Well," Gustav said weakly, "all I can do is promise you this: If I have to keck again, I'll make sure none of it lands on *you.*"

"Fair enough." I stuffed *The Sons of Jesse James* into my coat pocket and stretched a palm out toward the back of the car. "Lead on, Brother."

As we shuffle-stepped sideways around the card table, we got a smile and a nod from Mrs. Kier, who'd already convinced a prim middle-aged couple to join her in some pinochle.

"My friends back home play for a halfpenny a point," she was saying as we squeezed by. "Otherwise, what's the point of points, they say! But I don't know . . . I'm not much for gaming, myself."

When we reached the door to the observation platform, Old Red took hold of the handle—and stopped dead in his tracks.

"Otto, I might need you do something for me," he said.

"What's that?"

"Push."

He opened the door.

He didn't need any help getting outside, though—he practically threw himself through the door. I was right on his heels, anxious to get a look at Miss Caveo and Horner before they could stop anything that needed stopping.

All they'd started, apparently, was a conversation. They were side by side at the railing, talking earnestly as a ribbon of track wound down the mountain behind them.

As I closed the door, Gustav pressed himself backward into it, staying as far from the railing as possible.

"Hello," he said.

Horner and Miss Caveo turned toward us looking both cold (as in not overglad to see us) and cold (as in chilled). The mountain air was as crisp as a cracker, despite the time of year, and I stuffed my hands in my pockets to keep them warm—and from Horner's throat.

"I do hope we're not interruptin' anything," I lied.

"Not in the least," Horner said amiably. "We were just appreciating the view."

A sudden rough gust of wind ruffled Miss Caveo's skirts and set my hair waving practically on end. I eyed Horner's fluffy lump of fake hair, hoping it might take off like a kite, but unfortunately it was so securely anchored to his skull it barely gave a flutter.

"Anyway, I've done enough sightseeing for today," Horner said. "Next time I want to take in the grandeur of the Sierras, I'll just buy some stereopticon slides. You don't get frostbite looking at those!"

He moved toward the door.

Old Red didn't step aside.

"I'd like us to have a little chat, Mr. Horner."

Horner came a step closer. He wasn't a large man, but he was bigger than Gustav, and I didn't like the way he was crowding my brother. So I did some crowding of my own, moving in so close my chest was practically polishing the shiny buttons on the drummer's jacket.

"My, I feel so lonely all of a sudden," Miss Caveo joked, shooting for flip nonchalance—and missing. "Really, gentlemen, there's plenty of room out here. No need to—"

"I'm cold," Horner said. His usual backslapping heartiness was gone, snuffed out as quick as a candle flame squeezed betwixt your fingers. "I'm going inside."

"*After* we talk," Old Red grated out. He was staring at Horner with a fierce, squinty-eyed intensity that would've seemed almost demented had I not known the real reason for it: He had to focus all his attention on something, *anything*, to keep his eyes (and mind) off the train's rattling, rumbling climb up the mountainside.

It worked in more ways than one. Gustav managed not to faint, and Horner backed off.

"Alright, Sherlock—ask away," the drummer said, his voice full of phony cheer again. He rejoined Miss Caveo by the railing. "My goodness. You ride ten thousand miles on a railroad, and this is how they treat you. No wonder some people don't like the Southern Pacific."

"We had us a little trouble with your snake," Old Red said.

Horner's freshly reapplied smirk vanished. "What? Trouble? With Archie?"

I cocked an eyebrow at my brother.

My brother cocked an eyebrow at me.

" 'Archie'?" we said together.

"That's his name," Horner shot back. "What happened?"

"Somebody tried to kill us is what happened," I said. "Locked us in the WC with 'Archie' last night."

"My God," Miss Caveo gasped.

Horner had a very different reaction: He barked out an incredulous laugh. "You're joking."

"No, sir," Old Red said. "It's a miracle we didn't get bit."

Horner laughed again, the sound of it even harsher and more

207

mirthless. "Do you know what would've happened if Archie *had* bitten you?"

My brother shrugged. "You tell us."

"Nothing," Horner said. "Archie's not poisonous."

"Not poisonous?" I said. "The Indian swamp adder?"

"Oh." Horner's eyes went wide. "Shit." He glanced over at Miss Caveo. "Begging your pardon."

"Never mind that," the lady said, shooing away propriety with an irritated wave of the hand. "Just explain what's going on."

Horner nodded, looking abashed. "Right, well, here's the thing. Archie's not an Indian swamp adder. As far as I know, there's no such thing. That's just what they were calling him in Chicago, at the Exposition. He was on sale in the East India Bazaar. I bought him as a gag—something to show off to the boys back home."

Gustav frowned skeptically. "How'd you *know* he wasn't a swamp adder?"

"Because I used to see snakes like him every day all summer long. In *Ohio,* where I grew up. He's a black racer. They're nasty when they're cornered, but I know for a fact they're not poisonous. If they were, I would've been dead three times over by the time I was twelve."

Old Red and I exchanged another look. My brother was looking pretty abashed himself just then, and I could understand why. It's a tad humiliating to learn you were chased onto a toilet by a critter no more dangerous than an angry squirrel.

"So how'd you get Archie back in his cage without getting bit?" Horner asked us. "You didn't hurt him, did you?"

"I'm afraid we had to . . . put Archie off the train," I said. "Through a window."

"You *what?*"

"Why'd you tell folks he was a swamp adder?" my brother jumped in before the drummer could kick up a fuss about his lost pet.

Horner heaved a defeated sigh. "I'm a salesman. Saying I just bought the most poisonous snake in the world . . . it makes me memorable, keeps the talk going. A lot of the people on this train are merchants, grocers, potential clients. They might be on holiday, but I'm not. I never am."

"Alright," Gustav said. "I suppose that makes a certain kinda sense."

"Oh, I'm *so happy* to hear that," Horner snipped. "Can I go now?"

My brother slipped a hand into his coat pocket. "I got just two more questions for you."

The train was now moving through a gently sloping woodland thick with tall firs and pines, and perhaps because we no longer seemed to be dangling over a bottomless pit, Old Red felt steady enough to step away from the door, toward Horner.

"This mean anything to you?" He brought out the little cup he'd found in the desert.

"Why, yes, it does," Horner said. "It either means it's time for tea or you're a complete crackpot. Which is it?"

Gustav put the cup away and reached into another pocket. "How 'bout this?"

The toupee's golden rings of hair writhed in the wind like something alive.

"What about it?" Horner growled, his face turning a shade of purple I'd seen only on certain grapes up till then.

"You don't know what it is?" I asked innocently.

That's when Miss Caveo got it. I saw her gaze flick from the hairpiece to Horner's head then back to the hairpiece again, her eyes crinkling with amusement.

"What does that have to do with me?" Horner snapped at my brother.

"We been lookin' for the man it belongs to, and we hear you might be able to help."

Horner muttered something under his breath, then snatched the hairpiece from Gustav's hand.

"Fine—let me see it," he said gruffly. He rubbed his thumbs over the top of the toupee. "It's well made. Small, though—not as large as the ones *some men* wear."

I glanced at the mud-brown hair bun atop Horner's head and real-

209

ized what he was saying: His bald spot was surely too large to be covered by the puny little wiglet he was holding now.

"This is for someone who's only begun to bald," Horner went on. "Someone in his twenties or early thirties, maybe. Obviously, the hair he has left must be curly. This"—Horner gave the toupee a little wave—"would look pretty ludicrous on a man whose hair is *straight.*"

Horner turned his head sharply to the right to face Miss Caveo, then to the left to face me, showing off what was left of his natural hair—which was as straight as straw.

"But if you really want to find out who this belongs to . . ."

Horner turned the toupee over and ran his fingers over the rough interior. He nodded, gave a self-satisfied grunt, and picked at a spot along the edge, where the outermost ring of tresses was woven into the leatherish material that held the hairpiece together.

A tiny, pink tag had been tucked inside. Horner slid it out and squinted at it.

". . . you should talk to 'Msr. Philippe of San Jose.'"

"This 'Miz-year Phil-leap' . . . he a wigmaker?" I asked.

"No." Horner tossed the toupee back to Old Red. "He's probably a blacksmith. Sticking his name in men's hairpieces.is just a hobby."

The drummer turned to Miss Caveo. "Thank you," he said.

Then he headed for the door again. This time Gustav stepped out of his way—which was a good thing. Horner was moving with such fuming determination a brick wall might not have stopped him.

"Before you ask, let me assure you," Miss Caveo said after Horner slammed the door behind him, "that hairpiece wouldn't fit *me,* either."

"Thank you, miss," Old Red said gravely, stuffing the toupee back in his coat.

"Saves us the trouble of havin' you try it on," I added.

A sudden shriek snapped my spine straight, while Gustav gave such a start his knees almost buckled. Miss Caveo, on the other hand, was more startled by our reactions than the blast of the engine whistle, and she watched in a way that seemed both tickled and sympathetic as we caught our breath.

The engineer gave the whistle another long, ear-piercing toot, and the train began to slow. The woods on either side of us thinned, then disappeared, and soon we were rolling into a small town. Most of the houses and storefronts and whatnot were squat and ramshackle, but a large, freshly whitewashed structure rose up from among them like a glacier from the mud.

"What the heck is that?" I asked.

"Summit House," Miss Caveo replied. "A hotel. We've reached the highest point on the line—Summit, California." She smiled. "It's all downhill from here."

The train was barely moving now, and a long wooden platform slowly slid up beside us. We were stopping at the station.

"Miss Caveo," Gustav said as we finally lurched to a halt, "I hope you don't mind, but I've got a question or two for—"

"You'll have to excuse me," Miss Caveo blurted out. Something behind my brother had caught her eye, and her smile dimmed like a lantern running out of oil. "I just remembered something I have to attend to. If I don't hurry I'll—"

Whatever else she said, we couldn't hear it. She was on the other side of the door, bustling through the observation car.

"Now what was that all about?" I mused.

"Them, I reckon," Old Red said, glancing over his shoulder.

Standing outside the station house not thirty yards away were two men so absorbed in conversation they didn't even notice us gawking at them. One was a young fellow with a bowler hat set upon his head at such a rakish angle it seemed to be dangling from one of his ears. He was scribbling frantically in a notebook with a stubby pencil.

The other man was a barrel-chested, fortyish fellow who was dressed for the city and the range in equal measure: suit jacket, necktie, and straw boater up top, boots, jodhpurs, and gunbelt below.

He was also wearing a badge.

Twenty-nine

SUMMIT

Or, A Top Dog Sends Us to Chase a Wild Goose

He's an S.P. man," my brother declared.

It was hard to be certain from where we stood, but the shape and color of the man's badge did seem familiar. And even if it hadn't, Old Red's got eyes so sharp he can sex a mosquito from a hundred paces, so I was willing to take his word for it.

"Why, sure," I said. "He must be here to pin our medals on us."

"Come on," Gustav grumbled, opening the gate on the platform side of the railing. "He'll have questions for us . . . and I got questions for him."

As we headed toward the railroad detective, a flurry of activity at the front of the train caught my eye. A second locomotive had been hitched there—to help haul us up the mountainside, no doubt—and a crew of yardmen was moving in to get it uncoupled. Our fellow passengers were taking advantage of the delay, escaping the cars for some fresh air and a stretch of the legs while they could get them.

A burly figure burst from their midst.

"Mr. Powless!" Wiltrout called out, barreling the same direction as us—toward the S.P dick. "Mr. Powless! A word, please!"

The man with the badge turned to look at him.

Gustav and I turned to look at each other.

Apparently, we were about to meet our boss: Jefferson Powless, chief detective of the Southern Pacific Railroad Police.

Wiltrout reached him before us, and the first thing the conductor did was turn and point our way, talking fast and low. Yet despite whatever poison Wiltrout poured in his ear, Powless offered us his hand when we stepped up a moment later. There was a quick round of introductions, and we learned who Powless's companion was: a *San Francisco Examiner* reporter named Johnny Schramm.

"So . . . you're the boys Colonel Crowe hired yesterday," Powless said coolly. "Quite a first day on the job you had."

It was hard to tell if he was being critical or comical or ironical. He had a puffy face that seemed to mask his feelings, as if he could hide behind the extra blubber padding his cheeks and chin.

"Yeah," Schramm jumped in. "You look a little worse for wear. The Give-'em-Hell Boys lived up to their names, huh?"

The newspaperman pressed pencil to paper, ready to get scribbling.

Powless gave his head a shake so quick you could miss it in a blink.

"They tried to," I said with a shrug, and I stopped there.

Old Red never got started—he didn't say a word.

"How about Burl Lockhart?" Schramm pressed us. "Is it true he was on the train? What kind of fight did he put up?"

"Johnny, Johnny, Johnny." Powless laid a meaty hand on Schramm's shoulder in a way that seemed both fatherly and vaguely menacing. "Can't you see the boys are exhausted? Let them rest a minute before you start pelting them with questions."

Schramm didn't look convinced. "Well . . ."

"I'll tell you who you really ought to talk to," Wiltrout said. He pointed at the express car. "Milford Morrison, the Wells Fargo messenger. The whole gang was outside his door throwing down threats. But would he open up? No, sir. Now *there's* a hero for you."

"Yeah?"

Schramm jotted something in his notebook, thanked Wiltrout, and scurried off toward the express car.

"He won't get anything," the conductor told Powless. "It's not just robbers Morrison won't open up for—it's reporters. There were two of them waiting for us in Reno, and the only quote they got was 'Go away.'"

Powless gave a curt nod. "Good man."

"If you don't mind my askin'," Old Red said, "why bring along a reporter if you don't want anyone talkin' to him?"

"I *didn't* bring Schramm," Powless said. "Word got out about the robbery—and that 'bounty' on our board of directors—and he came up here to meet the Express on his own. I assume he'll be on the next train to Carlin, just like me."

"Mr. Morrison? You in there?" Schramm rapped on the express car's side door. "Johnny Schramm from the *Examiner* here! I'd like to ask you a few questions!"

"Go away!" Morrison called back from inside the car. "I've got nothing to say!"

Powless grunted out a gruff chuckle. "Well, that won't hold Schramm long. Wiltrout, you and I better find someplace private to talk. You two"—he turned to me and my brother—"there's another S.P. agent who might be in town, at Summit House. Dan Woodgate. Run up and see if he's there. If he is, get him down here."

When Gustav and I were a safe distance away, trudging up the sloping street toward the fortresslike hotel overlooking town, I crooked a thumb back at Powless.

"Whadaya make of him?"

"Awww, he's just gettin' us out of the way so he can hear Wiltrout's side of things," Old Red replied glumly. "By the time we get back, he'll probably want our badges."

"Why that ungrateful bastard." I kicked at a rock. "And after all we've done for the Southern Pacific. . . ."

My brother picked up his pace.

It took us five minutes to reach the hotel; five minutes to establish that there was no Dan Woodgate inside, outside, or anywhere nearby;

and another four minutes to come back down the hill to the station—where we found Powless waiting for us alone.

"Well, thanks for looking, boys," the S.P. man said. "Dan probably cleared out as soon as he got the wire this morning. The directors are in a real lather about that bounty: Every man we've got's either babysitting a board member or on his way to Nevada to get after Barson and Welsh. By tonight, you two'll be the only S.P. agents west of the Sierras who aren't sitting around some mansion on guard duty."

Not only was Powless making no move to snatch off our badges, he was acting as chummy as a lodge brother. I looked around for Wiltrout, thinking maybe we'd misjudged the man. Instead of bad-mouthing us, it seemed more like he'd put in a good word.

I spotted him off near the train, talking to Schramm, who was jotting down notes and nodding and grinning. The reporter had apparently given up on Morrison, settling instead for an interview with the heroic conductor who'd so bravely faced down the infamous Give-'em-Hell Boys at dire risk to life and limb. At least, that's how I assumed it would play out in the *Examiner*.

Wiltrout caught me looking at him, and the scowl he gave me in return was so blistering hot I could've branded a steer with it. He stepped away from Schramm and hollererd, "All aboard!" almost as if he'd been waiting just for us.

"Off you go, boys," Powless said. "Better stay on your toes. If anything happens between here and Oakland, you're more or less on your own."

We said our good-byes and headed for the Express.

"It don't make no sense," Gustav mumbled, racing for the train with all the eager, hard-charging speed of a Kentucky-bred colt. With a broken leg. Who knows he's being led to the glue factory. "He didn't even ask us for a report. No questions. Nothin'."

"All aboard!" Wiltrout barked again entirely for our benefit. All *were* aboard except for him and us.

Old Red shuffled to the stairs into our Pullman and got a foot planted on the first step.

And there he stopped, half-on, half-off the train. I could practically hear his stomach squirming in his belly as he considered what lay ahead: a long ride down the mountainside with only the Express's new-fangled air brakes between us and a quick plunge into the nearest gorge.

I clapped a hand on his back.

"Just remember, Brother . . . I'm right here behind you," I said. "For God's sake, don't fall on me."

Gustav sighed and shook his head—and hauled himself up the steps.

Wiltrout climbed up after us into the vestibule at the front of the Pullman, and soon the train was rolling again. Almost immediately, the car took on a downward tilt that grew steeper with each second, and my brother grabbed for the handrail.

"Better hold tight, Amlingmeyer," Wiltrout jeered. "We might hit fifty, sixty miles an hour on this stretch . . . assuming we stay on the tracks."

"Oh, ain't you got something to conduct somewhere?" I said.

"It just so happens I do," Wiltrout snapped back. "I have an express train to conduct. And just because you've got friends in high places, don't think I'll put up with—"

"'Friends in high places'?" Old Red cut in. "What are you—?"

The door to the passenger compartment flew open, and Burl Lockhart leaned in.

"There you are!" he said to Wiltrout. "Did you see the Chinaman get back aboard?"

"I never saw him get *off*," the conductor said.

"How 'bout you, Big Red?" Lockhart turned to Gustav. "Or you?"

"I ain't seen Dr. Chan since last night," my brother said.

I shrugged. "Same for me."

"We gotta get back to Summit, then," Lockhart declared. He jerked his head at Kip, who'd stepped up behind him to peer into the passageway at us. "Cuz he ain't seen him, neither."

"That's right," the news butch confirmed with a wide-eyed nod. "The Chinaman's just plain gone."

Thirty

MOMENTUM

Or, Old Red and I Discover There's No Turning Back

Chan ain't on the train?"

My brother's spine snapped so straight so fast it's a wonder the whiplash didn't pop his head right off his neck.

Wiltrout had the exact opposite reaction, slouching and shaking his head.

"Nonsense," the conductor said.

"I tell ya, he's gone!" Lockhart insisted, his whiskey breath so strong a blind man might've thought we were passing a distillery. "I've been from one end of this train to another, and there ain't a sign of the little bugger."

"You missed him, that's all." Wiltrout sounded like he couldn't quite decide whether to be irritated or bored. "It happens all the time. People go into hysterics, and then it turns out junior or grandpa or whoever was just taking extra long in the john." He threw a sharp-edged glare at Kip. "I would've thought *you'd* know that by now."

"I looked in the damn crappers," Lockhart said.

Wiltrout shrugged blithely. "So the Chinaman came down the aisle while you were in one. You passed each other. *It happens all the time.*"

"Not to Burl Lockhart, it don't."

The wiry Pinkerton stepped up close to Wiltrout, a strip of beef jerky going toe-to-toe with a Christmas ham.

"You stop this train—*now*—or I'm gonna pull the bell cord and stop it for you."

"Pull it, then!" Wiltrout roared with sudden fury—or fear masquerading as fury. "Then you can *walk* back up to town! Because not only is this train not going back to Summit, it *can't* go back. We're down to one engine again, and we're already a mile down the mountainside. We don't have the boiler power to get up that grade again. So just get ahold of yourself. I'll find your little friend for you."

The more the conductor spoke, the more Lockhart seemed to shrivel, as if his outrage had been the only thing pumping him up to man size. Another minute of it, and I would've expected the old lawman to wither into something impossibly tiny and wrinkled and shapeless—a prune, perhaps.

"He ain't my friend," Lockhart said hoarsely. He backed off, eyes down, and nodded at the door with a sideways snap of his head. "Alright. Let's go."

Wiltrout took the lead, followed by Lockhart and Kip. Old Red joined the parade, so I did, too. We all filed down the aisle wordlessly, passing the widow Foreman and her twin tornadoes and, a little farther on, Miss Caveo, who peeked up from her book just long enough to give us a quizzical look.

The moment we'd stepped past the young lady, Old Red stopped and whirled to face me, his finger to his lips. For the next few seconds, we just stood there, silent, as Wiltrout, Lockhart, and Kip trooped into the passageway to the next car. Before the door had quite closed behind them, Kip turned and slipped back through.

"You ain't gonna help look for Chan?" he asked us.

"Not Wiltrout's way." Gustav got down on his knees and peeked beneath the nearest seat—which just happened to be Chan's. "Hel-lo."

"Now I know Doc Chan ain't exactly tall," I said, "but there is no way you just found him stuffed under his seat."

"It ain't Chan I'm lookin' at."

My brother stood up wearing that empty-eyed expression he gets on his face when his brain goes galloping off and leaves his body behind.

"Well, what *did* you see?" Kip asked.

"Nothing," Old Red replied dreamily.

"For 'nothing' it sure made an impression," I said.

Gustav nodded slowly. "Sometimes nothing tells you something when something would've told you nothing at all."

Several of the passengers were staring at us now—including Miss Caveo, who'd swiveled around and put her book down.

"My brother, the philosopher," I said to her.

She smiled. "He sounds like a nihilist."

"If that means he's talkin' like a lunatic, I'd have to agree."

The lady's expression turned serious. "Did I hear you say you're looking for—?"

Old Red stepped between us. "Sorry, miss—no time for chitchat." He pointed at the front end of the car. "The widow," he said to me. "She's our best bet."

I offered an apologetic shrug as my brother herded me away, but Miss Caveo didn't seem inclined to accept just then. She wasn't simply staring daggers at Gustav's back—she was staring swords, bullets, and cannonballs.

"Must you be so damned rude?" I said to Old Red.

"Must *you* be so damned dense?" He waited a moment—till we were well past the lady—before saying more. "That nothing under Chan's seat . . . it ain't hard to Holmes out what it means." He glanced back at Kip, who was tagging along behind us. "I bet you got it figured."

"Well," the news butch began, sounding uncertain, "I guess you should've seen his valise or carpetbag—whatever he's usin' to tote around his clothes and toiletries and all. Samuel would've stowed it down there when he folded up the Chinaman's bed for the day."

"So if Chan's bag is gone . . . ?" my brother coaxed.

"Yeah, alright," I said. "It took me a little time, but I got there. You're thinkin' Chan slipped off the Express last night."

"Could be. And I figure I know how to find out for sure if he did. But first . . . pardon me, ma'am."

Old Red brought us to a stop facing Mrs. Foreman and her matching set of curl-topped terrors. The widow was slumped against a window, her veil over her face. It was impossible to say if she was awake or asleep—or alive or dead.

Harlan and Marlin, on the other hand, couldn't have been more lively. They were up on the seat across from their mother, bouncing so high off the cushions it was only a matter of time before one or the other flattened his head against the ceiling.

There was a rustling like the wind through a pile of dried-out leaves—the crepe and crinoline of Mrs. Foreman's mourning dress crinkling as she pushed herself upright. She turned toward us, and I could make out the barest outline of an embarrassed smile lurking behind the dark gauze of her veil.

"I'm sorry. Are the boys bothering you?"

"Not at all, ma'am," Gustav assured her with as much cordiality as he could muster—which wasn't much. He placed a hand on the back of the boys' seat (doing his best not to let on that he was leaning against it for support) and kept his gaze on the widow in a way that might have seemed piercing if you didn't know he was trying to block out the craggy peaks and ravines whipping past the window behind her. "Actually, I need to talk with you in my official capacity."

The twins stopped their hopping.

"How could *I* help you?" Mrs. Foreman asked, an extra quaver in her already timorous voice.

It's funny the power a badge has over some folks. Pin a star to even as unimpressive a physical specimen as my brother, and they'll break out in a sweat if he so much as tips his hat.

Of course, a badge has the opposite effect on certain other people—six-year-old boys, for instance.

"Did you ever find that snake?" either Harlan or Marlin asked.

"Or are you here to ask us about the robbery?" his brother threw in.

"We didn't see much—Mother wouldn't let us get out of our berth."

"We could hear what happened to *you,* though."

"The Give-'em-Hell Boys really gave you a whupping!"

"Harlan, Marlin—don't be impolite," Mrs. Foreman chided them weakly. "And remember what I said about that name."

"Yes, Mother," the boys sang in unison.

One of them turned to the other and cupped a hand against his brother's ear.

"The Give-'em-*Heck* Boys," he "whispered" loudly.

Kip chuckled, which was all the encouragement the twins needed. They doubled up laughing, then went back to jumping on the seat shouting, "Heck! Heck! Heck!"

"Boys," Mrs. Foreman said in that hopeless tone mothers use when they know they're going to be ignored.

"It's not actually the robbery I need to ask about," Old Red said to her. "It's Dr. Chan—the Chinese gent."

Harlan and Marlin settled down again, eager to listen in.

"What about him?" The widow sounded puzzled and discomfited, as if she couldn't understand why such a disagreeable subject as a China-man would be brought up in the presence of a lady like herself.

"I happened to notice our conductor havin' words with Dr. Chan last night," my brother said. "Forceful words. Seein' as your berths are so near Mr. Wiltrout's, I was hopin' you heard what it was that agitated him so."

"Why don't you just ask Mr. Wiltrout or Dr. Chan?" Mrs. Fore-man asked—thus giving Gustav part of the answer he was looking for. If she hadn't heard anything, she would've simply said so.

"We're havin' trouble findin' Dr. Chan at the moment," Old Red tried to explain. "And Mr. Wiltrout . . . well . . ."

There was no mannerly way to say he already *had* asked Wiltrout—and was now testing the truthfulness of the man's reply. So I jumped in with a lie. In polite circles, I've found, it's often the best way to go.

"We did ask him, ma'am. But he says he was so sleepylike, he don't remember the conversation at all." I shook my head gravely. "The poor man's been under such a strain, you understand."

"Well." The widow considered her audience—two bruised, contused, rather scruffy-looking men and a gangly, overeager kid in a news agent's uniform. Badges or no, we couldn't have inspired much confidence, and Mrs. Foreman seemed reluctant to admit to eavesdropping just for our benefit.

Fortunately, her sons had no such scruples to overcome.

"We heard it!" one of them proclaimed, hopping higher than ever.

"We heard it *all*!" added the other, bounding into the air beside his brother.

"Boys—," Mrs. Foreman began. But their little mouths were already racing too fast to be reined in.

"The China-man said he wanted to check on his luggage!"

"And the conductor said no!"

"So the China-man said, 'I'll give you *twenty dollars* if you let me into the baggage car!'"

"And the conductor said—"

The twins looked at each other, identical expressions of crazed glee on their cherubic faces as they matched each other bounce for bounce.

"'You filthy little monkey!'" they shrieked.

"And then later—," Harlan or Marlin went on.

"A lot later!"

"—after the snake tried to bite you—"

"Whoa! The snake!"

"—we heard the China-man come back!"

"And this time all he said was—"

"'Puh-leaze!'" they called out together.

They came crashing down on their butts side by side, snickering.

"That's all you heard the second time?" Gustav asked. He'd been following the boys' story so intently I almost expected him to start jumping up and down with them. "'Please'?"

"That's all he *said*."

"But we heard someone moving around."

"Like he was getting out of bed."

"We peeked when we didn't hear anymore."

"But the China-man was already gone."

Old Red drifted off into one of his stupors again, staring over the twins' heads as the rest of us stared at *him*. Since no more questions—in fact, no words of any kind—seemed to be coming from my brother, I thanked his little spies for him.

"Nice job, you two," I said, bending down to further tousle either Harlan or Marlin's already mussed-up hair. "You've got yourselves some mighty fine ears under all them curls."

Usually, Gustav sort of eases himself down from the clouds after he goes floating off. But for once he came crashing back to earth with a *thud*.

"Hel-lo! Yes! Good Lord!"

He turned on the widow with such quickness she cringed.

"Ma'am!" he said, stuffing a hand into one of his pockets. Then he seemed to trip over his own excitement, and he muttered, "Oh my," looking embarrassed. He drew his hand out again and rubbed it absently over his chin.

"Yes?" Mrs. Foreman prompted him, though she didn't seem eager to hear what he might say.

"Ma'am," Old Red began again. "Please. I hope you'll forgive my askin', but . . . your husband. He was a young man when he passed?"

"My husband?" the widow gasped, the thin crepe of her veil fluttering slightly. Obviously, a question about her dearly departed was the last thing she'd expected. "Why, yes. He was only thirty."

"He had a heart attack," one of her sons reported solemnly.

"In Chicago," the other added, equally somber.

"Boys," Mrs. Foreman said, the word coming out harder than before—almost like a threat.

"At the Exposition."

"On the Midway."

"Boys," the widow said again.

"In the Street in Cairo exhibit."

"Watching girls dance the hootchy-kootchy."

"*Boys!*"

Harlan and Marlin took to staring at their shoes, silent and still, for once.

"My condolences, ma'am," Gustav coughed out. He couldn't have looked more mortified if the widow had jumped up on her seat and had a go at the hootchy-kootchy herself. "I hope you won't mind just one more question. Your sons . . . they take after their father? Looks-wise, I mean."

"Yes."

Mrs. Foreman seemed to be on the verge of saying more, but she held back, as if waiting for something. Too late, I realized what it was— a handkerchief from one of the "gentlemen" nearby. When none of us leapt to do the chivalrous thing, she reached into her handbag and produced a delicate hankie of her own. She maneuvered it under her veil and dabbed at her eyes even though no actual tears seemed to appear.

"I've seen pictures of Christopher—my husband—when he was a child." She turned a bittersweet gaze on Harlan and Marlin. "The resemblance is remarkable." When she looked back at Old Red again, her voice turned so cold any tears she might've shed would've turned to icicles on her pinched cheeks. "Why do you ask?"

"Oh, they're just such fine-lookin' lads," Gustav said, making a half-assed stab at nonchalance that quickly collapsed into stammers. "N-not that you're not fine-lookin' yourself, I mean. For a widow. Y-you know. In a p-proper, ladylike, widowy sorta way." He cut himself off with a mighty sigh. "Ma'am, as you've no doubt noticed, I am an utter simpleton—and a very tired one who's feelin' more than a bit poorly. So let me just apologize for intrudin' and wish you and your sons a very pleasant journey back to San Jose."

Mrs. Foreman acknowledged the apology with a slight tilt of her head, though she didn't bother responding to (or contradicting) anything my brother had said.

Kip and I added our own good-byes, which were received with

equal iciness by the widow but not her twins. Marlin and Harlan smiled and waved as we left, then leaned out into the aisle to watch us follow Old Red toward the front of the car. When I turned to wave a last farewell, I saw that someone else was watching, too: Miss Caveo was peering at us over the top of her book.

I waved to *her,* as well. And she waved back.

"What was that all about with the widow lady?" Kip asked as we gathered near the door to the forward vestibule.

"I can show you . . . if you'll help us," Gustav said. He sounded both grave and eager, like a man in a hurry to get to his own funeral. "But I gotta warn you—there might be some danger."

"Danger?" Kip's face flushed red behind his freckles. "Does this have anything to do with the Give-'em-Hell Boys . . . or Joe Pezullo's murder?"

"It has *everything* to do with *both.*"

The news butch looked terror-stricken. "Jeez . . . in that case . . . if you think it might be dangerous"—he let a cocksure grin bust through his mask of fear—"you'd darned well *better* let me help. What do I gotta do?"

My brother gave the boy a slap on the back. "Just whip out your passkey, kid . . . and then be ready."

"Ready for what?" I asked.

"Answers," Old Red said, and he turned and headed for the baggage car.

Thirty-one

ANSWERS

Or, We Find Solutions to Our Mysteries, but Not Our Problems

Gustav led us into the baggage car, his hand hovering over his holstered .45. When we were all inside, he skulked off to scout things out—and ordered me and Kip to "fort up" the door.

"You want us to *what* now?" I said.

"Fix it so no one can get in here 'less we want 'em to," Old Red called back, disappearing into the stacks of baggage. "Push Pezullo's desk in front of the door, maybe. Or gum up the handle somehow. Whatever you can do. We don't want anyone bargin' in here till we've seen what we've come to see."

"Which is?" Kip asked as he strolled over to the car's only chair (its mate having been buried in the Nevada desert tethered to a dead hobo). He dragged the chair to the door and jammed it under the handle.

When Gustav reappeared, he gave the makeshift barricade his approval with a single downward jerk of his head. Then he picked Pezullo's crowbar up off the desk, walked across the compartment, and dropped it atop the plain pinewood casket Chan was hauling back to San Francisco.

"Aww, jeez!" Kip moaned, looking horrified. "You can't be serious!"

I stepped up to the coffin and knelt down beside it. "No need to fret, kid. There ain't no body in here." I looked over my shoulder at Old Red. "Right?"

My brother's response did little to bolster my confidence: He shrugged, then backed off a couple paces to give me room to work—or to get out of smelling range should Lockhart's tale of a casket packed with "treasure" prove untrue. There was a crunch underfoot as he moved, and he crouched down to peer at whatever he'd just ground into the floorboards.

"Sliver of glass." He looked up and scanned the car. "Either of you see that empty whiskey bottle that was in here yesterday?"

Kip and I shook our heads.

"Must've broke," Kip said, still looking rattled by our would-be grave-robbing. "We've sure had enough sudden stops to do it."

"I suppose. But then the question is, who swept it up?" Gustav stood slowly, wobbling with the car's gentle swaying as he strained to straighten his legs. "Anyway, we got us other questions to attend to first."

"Shall I begin attendin' then?" I asked.

Old Red nodded, and I dug in the crowbar's claw.

"Wait!" Kip yelped. He appeared to have lost his appetite for adventure—and looked like he was about to lose his breakfast, as well. "This ain't a good idea, fellers. It's a miracle Wiltrout ain't got you fired already. Bust open a coffin on his train, and he'll see to it you never *ride* the S.P. again, let alone work for it."

"I could live with that." I turned to my brother. "You?"

"Yup." Old Red gave me another nod.

I worked cautiously at first, prying the lid up just a fraction of an inch. When no cloud of rot gas came billowing out, I grew bolder, tugging one side of the lid up high enough to get a peek inside.

"It's stuffed with straw," I was relieved to report. Both Kip and Gustav suddenly found the nerve to crowd in closer.

With a few more quick jerks, I got the lid off entirely. I prepared to shield my eyes lest I be blinded by the sparkling of rubies, sapphires, and carbuncles. But black velvet doesn't put up any kind of gleam whatsoever, and that's what we saw packed in the straw.

There were maybe a dozen wads of velvet visible, with plenty of room for more to be buried beneath them. They ranged in size from apple-ish to pumpkin-ish, with most leaning to the smaller side.

I picked up one of the little bundles and gingerly unwrapped it, Kip and Old Red pressing in on either side to watch. Beneath the velvet was newspaper, and beneath that cotton.

What I found under that last layer did indeed glisten, in a cold, hard, flat kind of way. But it was no precious gem.

It was porcelain—and it was very familiar.

I was holding a small, handleless cup exactly like the one Old Red had found in the desert after the robbery. As if there could be any doubt, my brother produced the cup's twin, and we held them up side by side.

They were as much a match as Harlan and Marlin. The size, the dark blue pattern running around the rim, the leaves painted on the side—everything was identical.

While I rewrapped the cup I'd taken out, Old Red gently settled his back in the straw like an egg he was returning to its nest. Then he fished out the biggest bundle in the box and unswaddled it just enough to give us a glimpse of a large, ornate teapot.

"I don't get it," Kip said. "What is all this crap?"

"Well, they was supposed to have 'priceless treasures of the Orient' in the Chinese exhibit at the Exposition." I waved a hand at the casket packed with tea party fandangles. "I guess that's it. Or some of it, anyway."

Kip gave me a skeptical frown. "A dumb old teapot's a 'priceless treasure'?"

"Why not? For all we know, that teapot's as old as Adam. Put some years on anything, and it gets to be valuable. Why, a hundred years from now, even them dime novels you peddle might be worth something."

The kid shook his head. "Still seems like crap to me."

"Dr. Chan didn't think so," Gustav said. He spoke haltingly, almost reluctantly, as if his thoughts were leading him someplace he didn't want to go. "That's why he kept tryin' to get in here—to make sure this stuff was alright. He wouldn't just up and leave it."

"But his bag—?" I began.

"Tossed off the train to make it look like Chan skedaddled," Old Red cut in. "It'd be easy enough to get the bag from his berth once Chan was out of the way."

"Whoa!" Kip hooted. " 'Out of the way'?"

"Chan's dead, most likely," Gustav announced glumly. "Brought in here and walloped with a whiskey bottle." He looked over at me. "I admit that's pure theorizin' of the sort Mr. Holmes wouldn't have tolerated, but it fits the facts snug enough."

"Just this once, I'm gonna hope you're wrong," I said.

Old Red nodded. "Just this once, I will, too."

"Hold *on*!" Kip protested, standing up and waving his hands. "Why would anyone kill the Chinaman?"

"Probably cuz he kept sniffin' around the baggage car," I told him. "There's something in here our killer's been tryin' to hide."

"Like what?"

"Like . . . well, that's a good question." I turned to my brother. "Care to attend to it?"

"As it so happens, I was just about to." Gustav reached into the coffin, snaking his hands through the straw to grope at the bottom of the box. "Joe Pezzulo found the first hidin' place, so there was a change of . . . hel-lo! Here we are."

He grunted and drew his hands out of the casket. They emerged wrapped around a thick, bricklike blob that shone like gold—for good reason. There were words and numbers stamped into the top, and I read them out loud.

U.S. MINT

$21^{7}\!/_{16}$ *KARAT*

400 OZ.

"Shit," Kip whispered.

"Now, now—no need to be goddamn vulgar," I muttered. I turned to my brother. "So that's how that teacup ended up in the desert, huh? Some of Chan's tableware got tossed out to make room for this?"

"Yup. There's probably fifteen, twenty more under all that straw."

Old Red set the bar on the floorboards with a *clunk* and dusted off his hands. Like the gold, his fingers were now flecked with sand.

"So where'd the toupee come from then?" I asked. "You can't tell me *that's* an ancient Chinese treasure."

Old Red stood and moved to the second casket—the fancy one Mrs. Foreman was lugging back to California.

"'It is of the highest importance in the art of detection,'" he said, "'to be able to recognize, out of a number of facts, which are incidental and which . . .'"

He pulled the toupee from his pocket and dropped it on the coffin.

"'. . . *vital*,'" I said with a chagrined nod.

"You know," Kip said, "I have no earthly idea what you two are talkin' about."

"Don't worry, kid," I told him. "You'll catch up."

I had. Finally.

I'd seen the curly blond hair on that little man-wig, and I'd seen the curly blond hair atop the Foreman boys' heads. I'd seen the tag in the toupee that said it came from San Jose, and I'd seen the tag on the coffin that said it was *bound* for San Jose.

I'd seen clue, clue, clue, and clue. Yet I hadn't seen how they lined up like the very rails we were riding upon, tracks that could have but one destination: the casket I was about to open.

Gustav had seen it, though. And I was reminded with the power of a swift kick in the pants that there was another reason I tagged along after him as he chased his dream of detecting. By God, he was actually *good* at this deducifying stuff.

I dug the crowbar claw in under the lip of the coffin lid and pushed down. Almost immediately, the stench of decay seeped out into the car.

"Oh, jeez . . . you gotta stop!" Kip groaned. "That sure don't smell like gold!"

"Could smell a lot worse," Old Red said, and I took his point and kept on prying.

Given that it was summer and the late Mr. Foreman had been dead at least four days (since it would have taken two just to get the body from Chicago to Ogden), the odor should have been retch-worthy when it was, in point of fact, worthy of a mere pinch of the nose.

It didn't take long to see why the stink of death wasn't stronger. Mrs. Foreman had sprung for fine mahogany with hinges along one side, so after just a little more jimmying I was able to pop the lid up and get us a look inside . . . at perhaps thirty more gold bars.

The exact number I didn't have time to determine, for Gustav told me to close the casket quick.

"We've seen what there is to see," he said. "Foreman's gone, but he was lyin' in there long enough to leave some skunk behind."

I put down the lid, then swiveled around and sat on it, my elbows on my knees and my chin in my hands. Something hazy and blotched was swirling before my eyes—an explanation—and if I could just give it the right squint, it might come into focus.

"Would one or the other of you be kind enough to tell me *what the heck is goin' on*?" Kip demanded.

Old Red could see I was straining my brain to deduce it through, and he gave me a little bow and held out his hands, palms up.

He was offering me first crack at it. And I took it.

"Well . . . I think the gist of it is the Give-'em-Hell Boys wasn't stickin' us up yesterday," I said, talking slow so my mouth wouldn't outpace my mind. "They was loadin' us up. I'm sittin' on the same gold they stole off the Pacific Express two months ago."

Gustav nodded, so I forged ahead a little quicker.

"When they hit the train back in May, findin' that gold in the ex-press car must've been a surprise . . . cuz it looks like they didn't know what to do with it. There was no way they could tote off all them heavy bars on their horses—long riders gotta move quick. So they buried it right there on the spot, outside Carlin. They'd go back later and lug it

231

away. But how? Everyone in the country knows Barson and Welsh by sight, thanks to the papers. If they tried haulin' freight around in the back of a buckboard, they'd be spotted before they got a mile. So they came up with another way to move the gold. They filled a crate with bricks . . . for the weight?"

My brother nodded again.

"Then they got it put on the Express," I went on, "probably with help from an S.P. man or a passenger who had it loaded in as luggage. When the train got to where they had the gold stashed, they planned to stop it, throw out the bricks, load in the gold and then . . . *damn,* Brother. You really think they'd try it? They'd need balls the size of tumbleweeds."

Gustav nodded yet again, clearly pleased that I'd followed it all through myself, even if I did find the final step hard to take.

"They'd need balls to try *what?*" Kip asked, growing impatient with my start-stop storytelling.

"Well, the crate—it had airholes," I explained. "We figured that meant somebody got himself snuck on back in Ogden. But that wasn't the plan at all. Someone was aimin' to hitch a ride *after* the robbery. Barson and Welsh were gonna put their own guard in with the gold!"

"Only Pezullo spotted them airholes and opened the crate—which is why he had to die," Gustav finally jumped in. "Then *we* found it, and the box was still pried open when the Give-'em-Hell Boys stopped the train. So they knew they couldn't sneak anyone on the Express, and they needed a new place to stash their gold."

"Right here," I said, patting my coffin bench.

"They dumped Foreman in the desert," Old Red continued.

"His wig fallin' off when they moved the body," I snuck in.

"And they threw out some of Chan's 'treasure.' "

"Though somebody dropped a cup."

"Course, they couldn't have nobody seein' what they were up to. Which is why they had someone talkin' to Milford Morrison on the *left* side of the train while they got to unloadin' and loadin' on the *right* side."

"But poor El Numero Uno was stuck out here, wasn't he?" I said. "He must've seen it all."

"So he ended up a notch on someone's shootin' iron," Gustav finished for me.

Kip had been watching our back-and-forth with a pop-eyed look of wonder upon his face, and now he shook his head and chuckled. "You know, you two are really something when you stop your bickerin'."

Old Red and I traded sheepish glances.

"But you slicked right over a mighty big question," the kid went on, his tone turning serious. "Who killed Joe?"

"Well, you tell me," Gustav said. "Who's the first person Pezullo would've told about that crate? Who had a key that let him get in and out of the baggage car as he pleased? Who knew Chan was tryin' to snoop around near the booty? And whose berth is next to both the gents' washroom and the passageway to the baggage car—givin' him the chance to sneak out that snake and set it on us?"

Kip blinked at my brother a moment, his face slack, before the name came to him. When it did, he didn't seem to know whether to scoff or cheer.

"Why, sure . . . it all fits, don't it?" the news butch marveled. "*Wiltrout.* It . . . all . . . fits."

"Just about—though there's something you'll have to explain to *me*," I said, turning to my brother. "Who stole Kip's passkey? Wiltrout had his own already, and extras to spare. Why take Kip's? And how'd he do it?"

"I ain't got that part figured yet," Old Red admitted. "It might've been to throw us off the scent, get us lookin' at passengers 'stead of em-plo-yees. Or maybe someone's helpin' him. Or it might've just been a coincidence."

Gustav spat out that last word like a bite of rotten meat, and the foul taste of it lingered on his tongue afterward to judge by the scowl on his face.

"You know, we ain't got much in the way of actual proof, either," I pointed out. "And there's a lot we still don't know about what the Give-'em-Hell Boys had planned. Why take the gold west? How are they gonna collect it if they ain't got men travelin' with it?" I shrugged. "Seems to me we ain't out of the woods yet."

My brother shambled over and slumped next to me, the excitement that had been buoying him sinking out of sight.

"You're right . . . but at least we got a trail to follow." He tapped the casket beneath us with the back of his left heel. "The gold. Wiltrout's gotta hand it over sooner or later—he'd get his throat slit if he don't. So we confront him with it. He ain't as tough as he acts. Could be he'd sell out the gang to save his neck."

"Or maybe we wire S.P. H.Q.," I suggested. "They could have someone keep an eye on the coffins after we get to Oakland. When the Give-'em-Hell Boys show up to collect—*bang*. We bag 'em." I rubbed the tips of my fingers gently over my now not-quite-so-swollen nose. "We might even get another crack at Barson and Welsh themselves."

"I'd like that," Old Red said with a slow, brooding nod. "I'd like that a lot."

While my brother and I blathered, Kip walked around us and squatted down next to the Chinaman's coffin.

"Claimin' some of the gold for yourself?" I asked him. "Or is it that tea set you're partial to?"

"Actually, there's something you two overlooked," Kip replied. "Something that would explain *everything*."

The kid stretched a skinny arm across the casket lid—and yanked my brother's .45 from its holster.

"Sorry, fellers," he said cheerfully, hopping back a few steps. "I can't have you messin' with that gold. I was hopin' I wouldn't have to do this, but . . . well . . ."

He pointed the hogleg at Gustav and thumbed back the hammer.

Thirty-two

THE KID

Or, Kip Has the Time of His Life—While Fixing to End Ours

"**T**hat ain't funny, kid," I said, trying to sound like a stern father stepping in when some childish prank's gone awry. "Put the gun down before you hurt somebody."

"I think hurtin' somebody's the general idea," Gustav said. He pounded the coffin we were sitting on with both fists. "Shit! I can't believe I didn't see it sooner!"

"Don't be so hard on yourself, Old Red," Kip told him, as genial as ever. "You've been sick as dog and you still got closer than anybody else. Hell, Burl Lockhart himself didn't figure it out."

"Mr. Holmes would've," my brother muttered.

"Could be," Kip conceded. "You know, I like them Sherlock Holmes yarns myself. That sure was one clever bastard. Woo! Imagine *him* goin' up against the Give-'em-Hell gang!"

The kid's eyes took on the evil gleam boys get when they're dropping two tomcats into a barrel just to see what'll happen.

"So that's who *we're* still up against?" Gustav asked.

"Well, at the moment you're just up against *me*," Kip told him. "And I'd like *you* up against that door."

He waved the gun at the baggage car's side door.

Old Red didn't move. So I didn't move.

Kip shook his head.

"I've already killed two men the last day. Don't make me take it to four." The kid pursed his lips and cocked his head. "Though you know what? I might actually like that. I mean, what's the most you think Jesse James killed in a day? Or Billy the Kid? Not four, I betcha. I'd probably top 'em both!"

"Stop playin' games," Old Red said. "You ain't about to shoot off a gun in here."

"And why not?" Kip asked. "We're in the noisiest car on the train with two doors and a vestibule between us and the nearest passenger. What's a little *pop-pop* mixed in with all the racket a train kicks up? And anyway—so what if someone *does* hear? You had me jam the door shut, remember? Ain't nobody gettin' in here till I want 'em to. So don't make the mistake of thinkin' I'm afraid of this." His finger caressed the trigger with light, almost lewd strokes. "Cuz I ain't."

I wasn't sure if I believed the kid or not, but I knew one thing for sure: We didn't stand a chance sitting on our asses with a couple coffins between us and him. At least standing we could try to rush him when the time came . . . assuming a time *would* come.

I nudged my brother and got to my feet. After staring up at me sourly a moment, Gustav slowly pushed himself upright. The Colt in Kip's hand followed us as we moved across the car.

"Thank you, gents," the kid said once we had our backs against the side door. He eased himself down where we'd been squatting—on top of Foreman's casket. "Now, Otto, if you wouldn't mind . . . open it."

"You know, I rather think I *do* mind."

"Well, then let me put it another way." Kip shifted his wrist ever so slightly, giving the .45 a tilt up and to the right. "Open that door or I'll decorate it with your brother's big ol' brain."

I turned and reached for the latch. "My God, kid," I said as I jerked the bolt, "how'd you turn out so rotten?"

"Oh, I ain't rotten. I'm 'daring.'"

I slid the door open maybe three feet—enough to fill the room with a roar as loud as any tornado. What little light came in with the howling of wind was broken into yellow-white lines that flashed and blinked in spurts. Otherwise, all outside was black.

We'd been so busy playing bandit-and-lawmen, we hadn't noticed the baggage car's small windows going dark. The Pacific Express was passing through another snowshed.

"Close it!" Kip hollered.

I was happy to oblige. If the kid had forced us to jump out into the wooden tunnel, my brother and I would've bounced off the walls and ricocheted straight back into (and under) the train, and it would've been sheer guesswork which mangled pool of goo belonged in which grave.

Kip had the same concern, I was guessing. Not about reducing Gustav and me to *menudo*—he'd enjoy that. But he wouldn't want anyone in the Pullmans noticing the splash of blood on a window or the thumping of our bodies disintegrating beneath the train. Better to be rid of us when the Express was out in the open.

And surely, making us jump wouldn't be enough. "Men with broken legs tell no tales" is *not* how the old saying goes. Before we went through that door, Kip would see to it that we'd already passed through the pearly gates.

All this streaked through my mind in the two seconds it took to slide the door shut. While that wasn't nearly enough time to think up a plan, it did let me plant the seed of a chance: When I worked the bolt again, I merely fiddled it around in the latch. The door remained unlocked.

I turned to find Kip gnawing on his thoughts every bit as furiously as I just had. His head was tilted to one side, his eyes narrowed—and his finger was stroking the trigger again.

Why wait? I could see him thinking. *Two little twitches of the finger, and I'll top Jesse James himself.*

"So all along it was you who killed your buddy Pezullo," my brother said.

The kid's lips curled into a little smile that slowly slid sidewise into a smirk.

"He found the airholes and the bricks," Gustav continued, "and before he went to fetch Wiltrout, he showed 'em to his little pal—who brained him with the first thing he could grab."

Kip gave Gustav's Peacemaker a little roll in the air. "Go on. Tell me what else I did, Mr. 'Holmes.'"

"Alright. Let's see . . ."

My brother furrowed his brow and rubbed a hand over his mustache, looking less like a prisoner facing a firing squad than a man in a general store who can't remember what brand of talcum the little woman told him to buy. Even with the Grim Reaper set to take a swipe at us, he couldn't resist an opportunity to deducify.

"That business with your passkey bein' stolen," he said. "That was bullshit. A distraction. Something to get us settin' our sights on the passengers instead of the crew."

Kip nodded and gave the Colt another twirl.

"Later, when the Give-'em-Hell Boys took you 'hostage,' that was your chance to tell 'em where Lockhart and me and my brother was," Gustav went on. "And you told 'em about Pezullo and the crate, too. So that's when the plan got switched around."

The kid nodded again, his gaze locked on my brother. I searched for the nerve to make a run at him—and found I didn't have it. It would have taken five or six strides to reach him, while his finger needed to move less than an inch to put a bullet in my belly.

Old Red went on theorizing.

"Chan you had to get rid of cuz he was so fixed on checkin' his old Chinese thingamabobs. If he saw someone had monkeyed with the coffins, it'd cause trouble. So you . . . lured him back here somehow?"

My brother sent a hand smacking into his own forehead. "Oh, hell! I would've seen it if this damn train hadn't been rattlin' my brain. Your berth's right above Wiltrout's! When Chan came back and said, 'Please,' he was talkin' to *you*!"

Kip's smirk broadened into a sneering grin. He was actually enjoying himself, entranced by the chance to hear his own crimes repeated back to him, spun out like a tale from a detective magazine.

"He asked me to come up to the vestibule for a private chat," he explained. "Offered me ten bucks to let him into the baggage car. I can't believe he offered Wiltrout twenty! Guess he figured he could get a news butch for half price. If I'd said no, he probably would've offered Samuel five."

He waggled his eyebrows and chuckled at his own joke like we were customers he could still jolly into buying a bag of lemon drops.

"You were right about what happened once we were in here—I pasted him with the whiskey bottle. It didn't outright kill him, but then again it didn't have to. I was able to roll him out over a trestle in the middle of nowhere. He's food for river fish now."

The kid laughed. "It's funny, ain't it? The Chink brings along a coffin with no body, and now he's a body with no coffin!"

He was so tickled by his own cleverness—not just with joke-telling, but killing—I think he actually believed we'd laugh, too. And I almost couldn't blame him, the way my brother had been chitchatting with him, the two of them nattering away like old women comparing recipes for rhubarb pie.

For Gustav, it had been a matter of nailing down the how of it all. But it was an entirely different question that was eating at me.

"Christ, Kip," I said, "why? All this death . . . for what? Do you hate the railroad that much? Or are you just in it for the money?"

"*You're* askin' me why?" Instead of wilting, the grin on Kip's narrow face grew even wider. "I would've thought you two would understand more than anybody. I'm livin' what I used to just read about. I mean, I come from a little town so boring it's big news if the damn sun comes up in the morning! And now here I am, part of something big, something wild. And I am havin' the time of my life!"

The train jostled and took on a markedly steeper pitch—so much so that I feared the door would slide open on its own. My brother and I stumbled into each other, and even when I managed to get my feet planted, Gustav kept leaning into me, his knees wobbling.

"When the Give-'em-Hell Boys robbed the Express back in May, I wasn't scared. I was thrilled!" the kid went on, too wrapped up in his tale—A Kip Hickey Adventure—to let our stumblings slow him down. His skinny arm must have been growing as tired as Old Red's legs, for he propped his elbows on his knees and took to gripping the gun in both hands. "I slipped outside when they were leavin'—nearly got myself shot! And I got down on my knees and I *begged* Augie and Mike to take me with 'em. But they were smart. They came up with a plan. And now, I'm a bona fide Give-'em-Hell Boy!"

"And killer," I said.

"Hey, I don't give two shits about the Chinaman, but I wasn't happy about doin' in Joe. And when I set that snake on you two, I actually felt pretty guilty . . . for a couple minutes. Then I was just pissed it didn't work." His shoulders twitched ever so slightly—a wee little shrug from arms that were growing weary under the weight of four pounds of shooting iron. "Oh, well. Better late than never."

The Colt's barrel had begun to sag, but now the kid brought it up again and pointed it at me.

"You can't get rid of us that easy, Kip," Old Red said, straightening up and taking a step to his left—putting himself between me and the gun. "We're bein' watched. You come outta here without us, it's gonna be seen."

Kip snorted. "Oh, I already know about her. Saw her whisperin' with Jefferson Powless when you two got sent off to pick daisies or whatever."

" 'Her'?" I asked.

"Miss Caveo," Gustav said.

"Cutest damn spotter *I* ever spotted!" Kip crowed. "Makes sense, I guess. A sweetie like that . . . men drop their guard, go all tenderhearted." He leered at me. "And softheaded. Yeah, I reckon she'll come in right handy when the time comes."

I almost made a run at the little rat right then and there. *"What are you talkin' about?"*

Kip sighed and rolled his eyes. "Shit—what do you expect me to do? Talk you through the whole damn thing? Maybe playact all the different parts for you?"

"Why not?" Old Red asked, sounding like this was a perfectly reasonable request to make of a fellow who should've shot you five minutes before.

Light flickered behind Kip, off to his right, and I glanced at it just as the news butch was distracted by something to our left.

There was light in the car's little windows again. We were out of the snowshed.

"I'm sorry, boys," Kip said, and I heard a genuine regret in his voice that told me with a cold certainty that our extra five minutes were over. "I ain't got time for more talk. And neither do—"

I twisted to my left and threw the side door open, creating a wall of blinding-bright light behind us. Kip squeezed his eyes shut and looked away just long enough for me to grab Gustav's coat and drag him with me as I leapt from the train.

I heard the sharp crack of a gunshot, but I was too discombobulated to fret about whether Old Red or I might be hit. A blur of brown and gray and green—otherwise known as *the ground*—was rushing at me at God knows what speed.

Who had time to worry about bullets? The fall would probably kill us.

Thirty-three

DIE

Or, Gustav and I Take a Tumble and Nearly Crap Out

I fell just long enough to think, *Lord, if you're gonna kill me, could you do me a favor and make it quick?* Then I hit—hard.

My left side slammed into grass and gravel and clods of dirt. Then it was my right side smacking into the sod. Then my back. Then my left side came down again. And so on.

I was tumbling like dice, and there was nothing I could do but ride the roll through. As I spun along, it was my head I worried about, mostly: While I might have brains to spare compared to some folks, I don't have so much that I could leave half dashed out against a rock without it slowing me down a mite.

Fortunately, when I finally came to a stop, my brains (as well as my bones and other vital innards) remained where I prefer them—inside my body. I was lying on my side on a gently sloping embankment, my face pointed at the tracks winding down the mountain. For all of two seconds, I could see the Pacific Express hurtling away. Then it dipped out of sight, and soon even the sound of it was gone.

"Otto? Otto!"

"Hey, Brother," I croaked. "You alright?"

"Nope . . . but I'm breathin'."

I gave myself one more roll, wincing as pebbles and turf mashed into my tenderized flesh. Gustav was stretched out about twenty yards away, his head pointed down the slope, his boots toward the tracks.

"How *you* doin'?" he asked.

"Remarkably well for a dead man. I am dead, ain't I?"

Old Red grunted. "You're alive."

"Oh . . . that's a relief."

I heaved out a big sigh—and quickly resolved not to do it again anytime soon. My ribs were so sore I would've avoided breathing altogether if I could've gotten away with it. The thing to do was just lie there till I felt well enough to get up. A week or two would probably suffice.

But then suddenly I was sitting bolt upright, and as much as the movement pained me, it was blotted out by an entirely different kind of hurt.

"Diana!"

"I know, Otto."

"That crazy kid . . . Sweet Jesus, who knows what he'll do?"

"I know, Otto."

"And here we are stranded in the middle of nowhere!"

"Otto!" My brother was still lying flat, but he craned his head up so I could see into his eyes. *"I . . . know."*

He wasn't just telling me to stop my squawking. He was making me a promise: *We ain't gonna take this lying down.*

And to show he meant it, he started to hoist himself off his back. By the time he took his first step up the slope, I was heading up, too, having somehow convinced my body that it was capable of the climb no matter what those whiny, goldbricking legs might be saying about turned ankles and busted kneecaps and such.

Old Red and I joined up at the top of the hill and made a survey of our surroundings. What we saw was a whole lot of big, beautiful nothing. On the other side of the tracks was a short stretch of plateau ending in a drop-off so sudden you could go from walking on rock to plummeting through cloud with a single step. Beyond that was emptiness and, in the distance, pine-studded peaks identical to the one we were stranded on. In between must have been a mighty deep gorge, but we weren't close enough to the edge to see it.

Up the tracks, back toward Summit, were craggy bluffs and trees. Down the tracks, toward the Sacramento Valley, were more craggy bluffs and more trees—and, snaking through them somewhere, the Pacific Express.

"We got two choices," Gustav said. "Climb up to Summit, send a telegraph ahead of the Express, and hope we ain't too late. Or make our way down to God knows where and do God knows what."

I turned to get another look up the mountainside. The incline was so steep the tracks almost looked like a ladder into the sky. The way the train had come charging down from Summit, we must have covered at least twenty miles by the time Old Red and I made our unofficial whistle-stop. I tried calculating how long it would take my aching legs to get the rest of me back up to town, but gave up when the answer pushed over from hours into days.

"No," I said. "We ain't got no choice at all."

And down we went.

We stuck close to the tracks so as to be within easy hailing range of any other trains that might pass by. But the only things we had the opportunity to hail were rocks, pine trees, and the occasional slow-circling hawk. Other than that, it was just us.

"I can't stop thinkin' about Miss Caveo," I said as I limped along like a ranch hand fresh-tossed from a bronco's back.

"Me, too," Old Red replied. But it wasn't concern I saw on his face so much as confusion.

"You're just tryin' to figure how you missed it for so long," I said, the words coming out with more edge than I'd intended. "Her bein' on the S.P. payroll like us."

"It's . . . disappointin', I don't deny it. I had a hunch she was an S.P. agent after Summit, but I should've put it together sooner." Gustav turned his face toward me, and looking into his eyes straight on I could see a weight dragging on him I hadn't noticed before. "But don't think it's just wounded pride that's on my mind. I'm worried for her, same as you. Only consolation is the lady's got smarts and backbone both."

"I'd feel better if it was a *gun* she had."

"Yeah. But don't forget how she hauled your ass outta the fire back in Carlin. That wasn't gunplay—just quick thinkin'."

"I guess she was tippin' her hand a tad there, wasn't she?" A little smile almost flickered to life on my face, but I snuffed it out fast. There'd be no smiling till I knew Miss Caveo was safe. "So what other clues were there?"

Old Red looked away and shook his head, clearly wondering how his brother Helen Keller could fail to see so many clues. But he managed to swallow his usual vinegar and just spit out the facts.

"When we saw her watchin' Horner and Mrs. Kier playin' rummy in the observation car, you noticed the old lady stackin' the deck, right? Dealin' seconds and all that cardsharp stuff?"

Actually, I hadn't, but I was in no mood to admit it.

"It was plain as day," I said.

"Well, once the 'points' started turnin' into big dollars, Miss Caveo stepped in with a wink and a grin and whisked that chucklehead Horner away. When we came bargin' in, I'm sure she was tellin' him, 'Mister, you're gettin' yourself rooked.'"

I felt that little tickle of a grin again, though my expression remained grim. It was gratifying to learn that Miss Caveo and Horner's powwowing had been business, not pleasure, but now was hardly the time to jump up and click my heels.

"Then not ten minutes later we pull into Summit," Old Red went on, "and there's Jeff Powless at the station—and the lady bolts on us. Obviously, the man knew her, and she didn't want him lettin' it slip. She'd been keepin' an eye on us, I'll wager, and she was supposed to keep at it a bit longer."

"Keepin' an eye on *us?*"

"Sure. We're new fellers, hired out of the blue. First train we step on gets stuck up? Of course, the S.P.'s gonna be suspicious. Back in

Carlin, Miss Caveo said she was sending a wire to her family, remember? I reckon that message went to Crowe and Powless. They probably told her to ride herd on us, quietlike. Only, I figure Miss Caveo don't think we're crooked herself. When we left Summit, Powless seemed to almost trust us, and Wiltrout griped about our 'friends in high places.'"

"Yeah, I see it now. Miss Caveo must've talked to Powless after we got shuffled off on that fool's errand. She put in a good word for us."

Gustav nodded. "There was other clues, too. Colonel Crowe made the arrangements for Lockhart and Chan's berths as well as ours, and she was right in between us . . . in the perfect spot to keep tabs on all of us. And then there's that S.P. manual you—"

My brother staggered to a stop like he had brakes and someone had just yanked the bell cord.

"Look," he said, pointing at a large, blocky, gray rock at the bottom of a butte about a quarter mile down the track.

"Yeah?" I said.

Old Red sighed. "*Look,* dammit. You know—with your eyes?"

I looked again—and realized that the boulder wasn't just blocky but perfectly square. And it wasn't the steel gray of stone but the drab, dusty gray of sun-bleached boards.

It was, in other words, not a boulder at all. It was a shack.

"Come on!" I shouted, and off I went, pounding down the hillside despite my knees' pleas for mercy.

It didn't take long for the clomping footfalls behind me to fade away, and I knew I'd pulled ahead of my brother a good distance. I didn't slow down or look back, though. Something told me that shack was our only hope, and I had to know *now* if it offered deliverance or our final defeat.

"Hey! Hey, anyone there?" I hollered. "We got us an emergency! *Hey!*"

But no one answered, and as I came huffing and puffing up to the shack, it was easy to see why: There was a bolt and padlock on the door. No one was there.

I gave the door such a kick the thin, rotted-out wood splintered around my foot.

"Goddamn it!"

"Tool shed . . . for linemen . . . I reckon," Gustav panted as he hop-skipped his last few steps down the hill.

I gave the door another taste of boot leather.

"God*damn*!"

The Lord rewarded my blasphemy by steering my toe to a stronger board in the door, and this time the wood held firm while it was my foot that seemed to shatter.

"Goddamn son-of-a-bitch piece-of-shit bastard!"

"Yeah," Gustav said, "that just about sums it up." And he spat out a curse of his own and started around toward the back of the shack.

"We should finish bustin' through that door," I said as I hobbled after him.

"Awww, you're just mad at it."

"*No.* There might be something in that shed that could help us."

"Like what? A spare train?"

For the second time within the span of five minutes, Old Red slammed to a halt as sudden as the one you'd get walking smack into the side of a barn. Only this time I was hustling along behind him, so I walked smack into *him*. After some stumbling and (on my part) grumbling, I noticed what had my brother so frozen up—only it had the opposite effect on me.

"Well, would you look at that?" I cried, whooping and jumping straight up in the air. "A spare train!"

Thirty-four

THE AMLINGMEYER
EXPRESS

Or, Things Truly Start to Go Downhill Fast

O f course, there was no mighty locomotive awaiting us amidst
the scrubby knots of grass and loose shale behind the shack.
What we actually found looked more like a stable door on wheels with
a couple bent-up shovels stuck on top.

A handcar, the railroad men call it. To judge by the rust on the
wheels, gears, and arms, this one hadn't seen service since around the
time Noah started loading his ark.

I hurried over and got a grip underneath it, and after some grunting
and sweating, I managed to heft the wheels on one side a good half foot
off the ground. The thing was heavy, but not immovable.

"Probably easiest to push it over to the tracks," I said. "We don't
want to lift it till we have to."

I hunkered down, ready to start shoving, and waited for Old Red to
join me.

And waited.

And waited.

Finally, I looked back at my brother. He was standing where I'd left him, staring, stiff and still. In my excitement, I'd forgotten what rail travel did to him.

He looked like *he* wanted to forget, too . . . only he couldn't.

"Gustav—"

"No." Old Red closed his eyes tight, as though there was something behind them he was trying to keep from clawing out. *"No."*

Then his eyes popped open and he stomped over to join me.

It hadn't been me he'd been speaking to at all—it was the fear he was carrying around inside him. He was telling it to go to hell.

It took us less than two minutes to get the handcar over to the tracks—and five times as long and ten times the effort to place it upon the rails. But at last there it sat, and though we'd thoroughly herniated ourselves, we didn't waste any time on rest. We just climbed aboard—me in front, Old Red in the rear—and grabbed hold of the pump handles that powered the car.

I looked across the seesaw arms at my brother, and he locked eyes on me. He was bruised, scratched, perspiring, pale, and trembling so hard I could practically hear his bones shaking like maracas.

"You ready to do this?" I asked him.

"Hell, no," he growled back.

And he pushed down on the pump.

The section of track that arced by the linemen's shack was on a fairly level stretch of ground, so it took a lot of pumping to get us going. The rust-choked wheels squealed like pigs at first, but the squeaking died down as we picked up speed. It became easier to push down the pump, too, and once the car was back on a decent incline it was no effort at all.

When we were moving downhill fast enough to let gravity do all the work, I belted out a huzzah.

"The Amlingmeyer Express is under way! *Yeeehaa!*"

My brother didn't join in, of course.

"Just hang on, Gustav! I bet it won't be thirty minutes before we hit a station!"

I was trying to sound comforting, but it's hard to comfort with a bellow. I had to shout to be heard above the rattling of the car and the metal-on-metal drone of the wheels and the wind whipping past our ears.

"Us movin' along so easy's got me wonderin'!" Old Red yelled back, his knuckles white on the handles of his pump arm. "What's wrong with this thing?"

"What do you mean?"

"Linemen wouldn't throw it out for no good reason! There's gotta be *something* on it that don't work right!"

A huge pillar of rock loomed up before us. The track coiled around it so tight the whole handcar tilted, the wheels on one side lifting off the rails for several nerve-fraying seconds. There was nothing to keep us atop the car's spare wooden platform but our grips on the pump and the grace of God, and I didn't have much faith in either. So I stretched out a foot toward the brake—a T-shaped metal pedal on the right-hand side of the car—and pushed down.

Nothing happened.

I tried again, with the same result. The pedal went up and down in its slot, yet if anything we were moving *faster*. Which answered my brother's question about the handcar, albeit a little late: The brake was broke.

I looked up at Gustav, about to suggest that we hurl ourselves from the car before it hurled itself over a cliff. Yet Old Red wasn't looking at me or the brake. He was staring past me, gaping openmouthed at something I *knew* I didn't want to see, whatever it might be. All the same, I forced myself to swivel around and peek over my shoulder. By the time I got turned, there was nothing there but a yawning black mouth that quickly swallowed us whole.

We'd entered yet another snowshed. Heavy timber planks streaked past on both sides, so close it would take but a hop, skip, and a jump (or, in our case, a bump, bounce, and a splat) to reach them.

Seconds before, it had merely been a possibility that a leap from the handcar would snap our spines. Now it was a certainty. We had no choice but to ride through to the end.

Looking my brother square in the eye, I offered my assessment of the situation: "Aaaaaaaaaaaaaaa!"

To which he replied, "Eeeeeeeeeeeeee!"

And then even the car itself seemed to be shrieking, its whirring hum jumping up an octave. The tracks had arced into a sudden, tilting curve, and glancing down I saw in a serendipitous burst of light from a loose side board that one set of wheels had again lifted off the rails—and was staying lifted.

"Lean left! Lean left!" I screeched.

Fortunately, Old Red had noticed, too, and he leaned to his *right* while I leaned to *my* left. (I'd lacked the presence of mind to switch the directions for his benefit.)

The car settled back down with a clank, and when the track straightened itself a few seconds later, Gustav and I straightened up, as well. The ground around us grew flatter, and we finally coasted onto a more-or-less level stretch of rail.

I sucked in a breath—my first in quite some time, it seemed like—while my brother went up on his toes, trying to peer over me at whatever lay ahead.

"We're slowin' already," I said, relieved. "Won't be long before we can just step off and—"

"Lean right!" Gustav hollered.

"*My* right?" I asked uselessly.

Old Red was already leaning to his left, so I had my answer. I put all my weight to my right just as the handcar jerked into a turn so sharp it felt more like we were going in a circle than rounding a bend. Once again, I heard the drone of the car kick higher, and the platform tilted like a drawbridge going up.

"Lean! Lean! Lean!" my brother screamed.

I just screamed.

But the tipping point never came, and when the tracks uncurled, the car righted itself. The wheels slammed back into place with such force Gustav and I were almost bucked off the car, and both of us ended up on our knees inches from the side.

As we hunched there, panting, a glow was quickly growing all around us: the literal light at the end of the tunnel. Only when I turned to face it, I saw something else there, too—a dark, hazy hole in its center, large and growing larger.

By the time I realized it was a train, it was almost too late to jump.

Thirty-five

COMINGS AND GOINGS

Or, We Run into Some Friends . . . at Forty Miles an Hour

You might think the word *fortunately* has little place in any retelling of a collision with a train. In fact, it's hard to believe a collision with a train could be retold at all, except perhaps by the horrified onlookers.

Fortunately, the train in question wasn't moving at the time, which was what gave me and my brother the extra second we needed to hurl ourselves from the handcar before it smashed into the back of the Pacific Express.

Unfortunately, though I bounced my way to a stop with only new bruises atop old to show for it, Gustav let out a sharp cry that told me he hadn't been so lucky.

As soon as I stopped rolling, I hopped up and started running, fearful that I'd reach my brother's side only to find a broken rib or a railroad spike poking from it. So I was almost relieved when he sat up, face twisted with pain, and clutched his right ankle.

"Broken?" I asked, kneeling next to him.

"I don't think so."

He put his foot down and tried some test pressure on it—and collapsed on his back again, his foot in the air and a curse on his lips.

"What in God's name . . . ?" a deep voice rumbled behind us.

I turned to see Wiltrout standing about twenty feet away, gaping at the back of the Express. Our handcar was wedged under the observation platform, its pump arms smashed.

"How the hell did you end up *behind* us?" the conductor asked, more bewildered than angry—for the moment.

"Ain't no time to explain," Old Red said, forcing himself back into a sitting position while straining to keep his injured foot up off the ground. "Have you seen Kip the last few minutes?"

"Or Miss Caveo?" I added.

"No time to explain *this*?" Wiltrout shook a finger at our handiwork, his voice growing louder as rage shouldered surprise from the forefront of his mind. "No time to explain destruction of Southern Pacific property and the endangerment of—?"

I jumped up and stalked toward him. "Listen, you big dumb son of a—!"

"*Otto,*" Gustav said sharply. "There ain't time for that, neither."

I stopped. He was right, of course. Damn him.

"Look . . . you," I growled at Wiltrout. "At this very moment, a female agent of the Southern Pacific Railroad Police is in mortal danger—from *your* news butch, who has already killed two men on *your* train. If the slightest lick of harm befalls her, *Captain,* you can rest assured I'll tell Jefferson Powless and Colonel Crowe and the *San Francisco Examiner* and anyone else I can get to listen that you didn't do a damn thing to stop it. Now . . . have you seen Kip or Miss Caveo?"

Wiltrout glowered at me as I speechified, his jaw clenched so tight I could almost hear his teeth cracking like walnuts. But when I was done, he let up the pressure and opened up his mouth.

"No. I haven't seen them."

"I have," Samuel said from the back of the observation car.

Gawkers had crowded out onto the deck—Horner and Mrs. Kier among them—and the porter had to squirm his way through the throng to reach the mangled railing.

"Maybe five minutes ago," he said. "Kip was talkin' to the lady, all serious and whispery. Then the two of 'em headed up to the baggage car. I thought it was peculiar, but—"

Samuel gave me a gloomy *How could I have known?* shrug.

"Alright," Old Red said, "I ain't got time to pussyfoot around it: Samuel, you gotta find us some guns—quick."

The passengers packed around the porter gasped and murmured, while it seemed to require every bit of willpower Wiltrout could muster not to explode like a bottle of nitro whacked with a hammer.

"Ask around," Gustav went on, giving no heed to the fuss he was stirring up. "I bet somebody's got an iron we don't know about."

Samuel nodded grimly and turned to go, but a plump hand on his shoulder stopped him.

"Is Miss Caveo really in danger?" Mrs. Kier asked Old Red.

"We think so, ma'am."

"From *Kip*? The news butcher?"

"Mrs. Kier, just look at me and my brother," I said. I brought up my hands and stood there a moment, showing off my newest contusions and ripped, mud-splattered clothes. "This is what Kip did to a couple of full-grown men within the last hour. And what he's done in the last twenty-four is a whole lot worse. Yeah, he's just a kid. But trust us. He's a *bad* one."

"Well, then." The lady—and I still thought of her as such, even though I now knew her to be a sharper—reached into her handbag and drew out a shiny derringer, which she offered to Samuel. "Miss Caveo may be a spotter . . . but I like her."

"Thank you, ma'am." I had no hat to tip, so I offered her a little bow. She gave me a little curtsy in reply.

"Bring any other guns you can round up to the baggage car's side door," Gustav said to Samuel. "We'll meet you there."

"Oh, and while you're it," I jumped in. "Fetch Mr. Lockhart—and tell him to bring Aunt Pauline."

I turned back toward Old Red, expecting some snip from him for inviting Lockhart to the party. But he'd apparently decided there was no time for *that,* either. All he said was "Help me up."

He couldn't so much as set toe to earth without swooning, so he tried hopping to the baggage car, one arm slung over my shoulder. It made for slow going—what with my extra height and his boogered-up foot, we were hobbling like a three-legged mule.

"What's more important?" I asked after we'd taken a few staggering steps toward the train. "Miss Caveo's safety or your dignity?"

"The lady, of course. What kinda question is that?"

I answered by swinging my left arm down behind his knees and scooping him up off the ground.

"Oh, Lord," Gustav moaned. He didn't tell me to put him down, though.

I started toward the baggage car again, my pace much improved despite the big, mustachioed baby cradled in my arms. (He wasn't much of a load to bear, really—Gustav's got about as much fat on him as a licorice whip.) As we passed the observation platform, I noticed Chester Q. Horner eyeing us anxiously.

"Hey, Horner—you gonna help us?" I asked, thinking it'd be nice to have him around to step behind should bullets start flying.

"Well, I . . . I . . . I think I should leave it to the professionals," he said, his smooth talk coming out lumpy for once.

"Good thinkin'," I called back as we hustled away. "Let me know when they get here."

Wiltrout drew up beside us, striding fast with firm, manly purpose—all the better to impress the passengers watching us through the windows.

"Why'd the train stop?" Old Red asked him.

"I have no idea." The conductor didn't look over at us as he answered—I think conversing with a man wrapped in another man's arms made him a touch uncomfortable, for some reason. "I haven't had a chance to talk to the engineer. I assume someone pulled the damn bell cord again."

When we got to the baggage car, I settled Gustav on the ground, leaving him balanced precariously on one foot like some long-legged bird. A moment later, Samuel dropped from the nearest Pullman carrying three guns: Mrs. Kier's derringer, a snub-nosed Colt pocket .41, and a dinky, ring-triggered .22 so squat and rusty brown it could've passed for a dog dropping. I took the Colt, brought the derringer to my brother, and offered the .22 to Wiltrout—who refused it with a shake of his head. There was no audience for him now, and he was keeping a discreet distance from the side door.

"Mind if I hold on to that gun?" Samuel asked.

"Mind? I'd appreciate it."

I gave the .22 back to him.

"Joe Pezullo—he was alright," the porter grumbled. "But I never did like that damned kid."

"Where's Lockhart?" Old Red asked him.

"He had to . . . ready himself."

"Sober up, you mean," Lockhart said, stepping stiffly from the passenger car. Aunt Pauline was holstered at his right hip. "No time for java, though, so you'll just have to take me as I am. Now—what's the trouble?"

I filled him in quick as I could, noticing as he moved from the train's shadow into sunlight that his face was glistening wet. Either he'd just splashed himself with water or he was sweating up a river.

"Quite a tale . . . almost good enough for a dime novel," he said when I was finished. "So you wanna try the side door first, huh? Good. Best to keep things out of doors—we got women and children about. Still, somebody's gotta cover the door in from the vestibule." He clapped Samuel on the shoulder. "Keep an eye on it, would you? You, too, pork chop." He glanced at Wiltrout just long enough to jerk his head at the steps into the Pullman.

Samuel paused a moment before leaving, looking like he didn't want to miss whatever was to come next.

Wiltrout scurried away with no hesitation whatsoever.

"I do so hate it when bystanders go and get themselves shot—even the ones who deserve it," Lockhart said, staring at the conductor's back. He drew Aunt Pauline and cocked her hammer. "Alright, boys . . . shall we?"

I helped Old Red hobble closer to the baggage car as Lockhart gave the side door a rap with his gnarled knuckles.

"We need to talk, son," the Pinkerton said, pressing back flat against the train and pointing Aunt Pauline up at the door. It was obvious just what kind of "talking" he was fixing to do. "Kip? You in there?"

No one answered.

"We gotta try the door," Gustav said, sounding unhappy about the idea—and I wasn't exactly in love with it, either. If the door was unlocked, whoever poked his head through first might very well get it shot off.

Nevertheless, I was about to step up and volunteer when Lockhart holstered Aunt Pauline and flattened his palms against the door.

"I'm comin' in, Kip," he said. "Don't lose your head, now. I just wanna chat."

He pushed, and the side door slid open, leaving him totally exposed—a thin, wizened target, but an easy target all the same. Yet no on tried to hit it.

Lockhart started hauling himself inside, but he could barely get a foot up into the car. After he'd dangled there a few awkward seconds, I crammed my Colt under my belt and climbed in myself, doing some extra grunting and puffing so as not to bruise the old Pinkerton's pride any further.

"Let me scout it out, chief," I whispered once I was crouched inside.

"Well . . . alright," Lockhart replied as if he just might argue me on it. He dropped back down to the ground. "But be careful."

"Yeah," Gustav added, bringing up Mrs. Kier's derringer and pointing it at the shadows ahead of me. "*Very* careful."

I nodded and pulled out my borrowed Colt.

"Hey, Kip . . . it's Otto," I said as I crept farther into the car. "I ain't mad about what happened—Gustav and me made out alright. So why don't you just let Miss Caveo go, and we'll settle this thing peaceful-like. What do you say?"

He said nothing—because he wasn't there.

"Empty," I announced once I'd checked the whole car. I opened the door to the vestibule—slowly, so as not to startle anyone on the other side with their finger on a trigger—and waved Samuel and Wiltrout through.

"Check the gold," Old Red said.

I walked over and pushed back the lids on the Give-'em-Hell Boys' coffin-shaped piggy banks.

"Looks like it's all here."

Wiltrout gaped at the caskets' contents, clearly stupefied to finally see proof my brother and I weren't raving lunatics.

"If you can't believe your eyes, you could always try touchin' it," I told him.

Samuel peeked over my shoulder. "Personally, I'd be afraid to touch that much gold. I might never wanna stop."

"They can't have gone far," Lockhart announced, turning to survey the terrain. A thick tree line set in not far from the tracks, rising to rocky bluffs high enough to serve as perches for harp-strumming angels. "There's nowhere to go."

"Maybe Morrison spotted 'em," Old Red suggested. "Unscheduled stops don't exactly sit easy with the man. I'm surprised he ain't poppin' off with his Winchester already."

"Good thinkin'," Lockhart said with only the slightest hint of resentment, and he turned and headed for the express car.

I jumped down from the baggage car and threw my arm around Gustav's shoulders again. Samuel and Wiltrout followed us as we stagger-hopped after Lockhart.

"I still haven't seen any proof that Kip's mixed up in anything," the conductor said.

"You better pray you *don't* see any proof the next few minutes," I shot back. "Cuz till we find the lady—"

"Take cover," Lockhart snapped. He pressed himself against the baggage car and waved for us to do the same.

After a few seconds of fumbling, we got ourselves lined up one-two-three-four-five along the train.

"What's wrong?" I asked Lockhart.

"The express car door," he said. "It's open."

I leaned out around him and took a look. The door couldn't have been ajar more than a crack: You couldn't see the opening from where we were at all. What you *could* see was a thin, dark line running from the door down to the ground—a trickle of crimson liquid.

It was like taking a pair of spurs to the side. I bolted without even thinking about it.

"Otto, wait!" my brother shouted, but there was no pulling the reins on me. Seconds later I was pushing the express car side door wide, ready to blast Kip to hell as he stood giggling over Miss Caveo's lifeless body.

Yet all I found was poor Milford Morrison, loyal Wells Fargo man, facedown in a puddle of his own blood. He'd been gagged with his vest, his hands tied behind his back with twine knotted so tight his fingers had turned purple. His head was a gore-splattered tureen, the back open bowl-style to offer a full serving of shattered bone and pulpy meat.

"It's Morrison," I told Old Red, who was limping after me with Samuel serving as his new crutch. "Got his brains beat out."

I leaned into the car (careful to avoid smearing myself with blood) and saw a desk, slots for sorting letters and packages, a safe, and an unmade cot in the corner. What I didn't see—and Morrison could have used, apparently—was a broom: The floor was covered with a layer of dust so thick the messenger had left tracks all around the car like footprints in the snow.

"No sign of Kip," I reported. "Other than the body, I mean."

"Still fresh," Lockhart said coolly as he stepped up beside me. "Ain't been dead more than fifteen minutes."

"Morrison . . . dead?" Wiltrout muttered hoarsely. He stayed rooted in place even as the rest of us gathered by the express car, and I knew for sure then that all his bullying was just paint slapped over the yellow streak down his back.

"It don't make sense," Samuel said. "Why would the kid kill Morrison?"

"I sure would like to ask the little bastard," I said, turning away from the car. "He's gotta be around . . ."

My words trailed off as I caught sight of my brother. His eyes were as big and round as a couple fried eggs—and not because he was looking at Morrison's cracked-eggshell skull.

Gustav was staring at the man's *hands*.

"Goddamn my stupidity," he whispered.

He leaned forward for a peep inside the car, and some terrible realization drained what little remained of the color in his face. His next words were shouts directed at no one in particular.

"The engineer! *Why ain't we seen the engineer?*"

Lockhart took a few quick steps away from the express car, angling for a better look at the locomotive.

"You don't think the kid's crazy enough to try—?" he started to say.

"Stop!" a voice cried out.

Up ahead, a dark shape dropped from the engine cab. It was a husky man in overalls, covered in soot—the train's replacement fireman. The second he hit the ground, he started jogging toward us, his hands in the air.

"Stay back!" he said, his voice quivery with fear. "Stay back or I'm dead!"

Beyond him, another figure appeared, leaning out of the cab. He had a gun in his hand and a grin on his face.

"And he ain't the only one!" Kip called to us, and he leveled his iron and pulled the trigger.

Whether he was aiming at the fireman's back or our fronts, I don't know. But it was Samuel he hit, sending the porter spinning into my

261

brother with an ugly splotch of red on his snow-white jacket. They fell together, landing side by side on the rocky sod.

The rest of us hit the dirt, too, diving for cover just as the engine grunted and heaved forward.

The Pacific Express was leaving without us.

Thirty-six

BURL LOCKHART'S DAY

Or, The Train Falls Apart As the Last Pieces of the Puzzle Come Together

Everyone was bellowing something—curses, questions, commands, screams—and then it was all drowned out by another blast of gunfire.

"—stealing the express car and the baggage car!" Wiltrout was yelling when I could hear something as puny as words again. "They're leaving the sleepers!"

I looked back at the Pullmans and saw that Wiltrout was right— they weren't going anywhere. The locomotive was pulling away with just the tender and the express and baggage cars in tow.

"Goddammit!" Lockhart roared. "While we were playin' hide-and-seek, that sneaky little shit was uncouplin' the passenger cars!"

"*Vaya con Dios,* assholes!" Kip called from his perch on the engine cab, and he punctuated his farewell with yet another potshot at us.

We all buried our faces in the grass again. I peeked up just as the baggage car rolled past me.

I jumped up and set after it.

"Otto, wait," I heard my brother say. "It ain't—!" And then his words were blotted out by the ear-pounding clatter of the car I was chasing.

There was no time to turn back and ask him to repeat himself. The kid's wild lead slinging had actually given me a chance—but it wouldn't last long. Shooting off a gun kicks up a considerable cloud of scorched powder, and that (combined with the black puffs blowing back from the smokestack) would hide me as I made my dash for the train. Maybe.

By the time I drew up next to the door, the smoke was already starting to clear. I had to jump—*quick*—or I'd soon run headlong into a bullet.

And then a hand was there, reaching down from above like it belonged to God Himself. It was bony and brittle looking, yet surprisingly steely when I grabbed hold and made my leap. I felt a jerk on my arm, and then my knees were settling on wood and the hand let go.

"Thanks . . . Mr. Lockhart," I wheezed, gasping for breath on all fours like a winded dog. "I didn't . . . even know you'd . . . made it."

"I might be stewed half the time and old *all* the time, but I ain't forgotten how to run just yet," the Pinkerton said. He clapped his hands together and rubbed them the way some fellows do before they sit down to a steak dinner. "Now—two grown men oughta be more than a match for one runty pup. The kid'll be distracted, what with the engineer and the lady to keep an eye on. So our only problem's gonna be gettin' up there to him."

"And makin' sure the hostages don't get hurt," I added.

"Yeah, that, too," Lockhart said dismissively, as if hostages were a niggling detail he expected to take care of itself. "So . . . you wanna see how a bandit stopped a train back in ol' Burl Lockhart's day?"

I was dimly aware of some reason to pause, to ponder. But with my heart pounding and the car rocking and the wind ruffling my hair with its ghostly cold fingers—and, most of all, with Miss Caveo still in jeopardy, so far as I knew—I wasn't going to slow down and deduce it through. Momentum isn't just for trains: People get carried along by it, too.

"Mr. Lockhart, seems to me this *is* your day," I said. "What's the plan?"

Plan, it turned out, would be a charitable description for the course of action Lockhart proposed. *Suicidal stunt* hits closer to the mark. Lockhart had his own phrase for it: *the blind-baggage hop.*

An old long-rider trick, he said, was to hitch a ride in the blind baggage—the space between the tender and the express car—then climb over the coal and pull a gun on the engine crew. Of course, I pointed out that we weren't *in* the blind baggage, but Lockhart thought that was easy enough to fix. We'd just climb atop the baggage car, jump to the express car, and drop down into the tender from there.

It was crazy, but there was a strong argument in its favor: It was our only choice.

The best way to get onto the roof was to squeeze out one of the small windows toward the back of the car, then use the sill as a stepladder to clamber up. I went first, being the taller of the two of us and hence the more likely to reach the roof.

Just as I came to the most dangerous part of my climb—the moment when I had to draw a foot up and actually try to stand in the windowsill—I felt a sudden, unexpected pressure on my legs.

Lockhart had grabbed hold of me by the shins.

The old man could tip me over as easy as shaking out a sheet, and my mind raced back to Gustav's shout as I'd sprinted after the train. "It ain't—!" were the last words I'd heard. Was this what he'd been trying to warn me about?

It ain't a good idea to let Lockhart talk you into squirmin' through a window—cuz he'll shove you out and splatter what little brains you got!

I'd like to say it was coolheaded, Holmes-style logic that got me through. It was really just panic. In a frenzy of fear, I kicked away Lockhart's hands, got my heels on the sill, and shoved myself upward. A stovepipe was sticking through the roof nearby, and I grabbed hold of it and swung myself up with all my might.

I made it. I lay there a moment, facedown, letting myself breath a deep sigh of relief. I almost laughed, thinking how I'd spooked. Lockhart had been trying to steady me, that's all. Why would he help me onto the train only to turn around and hurl me off?

I couldn't let go of my unease, though. My brother *had* been trying to warn me about something, I could feel it. But I couldn't *think* it—not lying there spread-eagled on top of a speeding train.

Lockhart was surprisingly easy to haul up: The lean old man was so light it felt like he'd blow away in the wind if he didn't have Aunt Pauline to anchor him. Once he was up top, we crept forward with slow, cautious steps, our guns drawn. The whole train had taken on a tilt again, the angle growing steadily steeper as the tracks edged closer to a sheer drop-off to our left. Before long, the incline was so sharp it seemed like we could slide all the way to the cowcatcher like kids sledding down a snow-covered hill.

But there were still jumps to make—from the baggage car to the express car, then from there to the tender. Lockhart went first, soaring over to the express car as graceful as an eagle in flight . . . before landing with all the grace of a moose dropped from a hot-air balloon. He tripped, stumbled, and went rolling toward the edge of the roof. Before I knew it, my hold on his gunbelt was the only thing keeping him from spinning over the side—I'd made the jump without even thinking about it.

"Thanks, Big Red," Lockhart said as I helped him from a sprawl back into a crouch. "It would have been mighty disappointin' to go and get myself killed before I could go and get myself killed."

He turned toward the front of the train. Up ahead, the smokestack spewed out clouds of black that blew back fast into our faces. Through the smoke, I could just barely make out the tracks as they curved into a long spiral that clung to the mountainside like the stripe running down a barber's pole.

"Well, this is it," Lockhart said. "Can't dawdle now—not with a snowshed comin' along any minute to scrape us offa here. So let's move Indian-style, single file. Most likely Kip won't be lookin' for us, but just in case, we don't want both our heads poked up like a couple tin cans on a fence."

I nodded and turned to go, taking point, but Lockhart reached out and grabbed my arm. When I looked back at him, he brought up Aunt Pauline and gave her a little shake.

"Ladies first."

"You sure?"

The old Pinkerton grinned, flashing me gap-spaced rows of crooked teeth as gray as headstones.

"Son . . . ol' Burl Lockhart was *born* sure."

He crept away in a bent-backed stoop. As I waddled after him, I tried to picture what he'd see when he reached the end of the express car. Aside from a little smoke in his eyes, he should have a good view down into the tender and engine cab.

Where would the kid be? How would he have his hostages lined up? Could he keep an eye on them while watching out for the likes of us?

I figured I knew the answer to that last question: He sure as hell could. After all, he'd managed to kill Morrison, uncouple the passenger cars, and get a gun on the engine crew, all while dragging Miss Caveo around as his prisoner. Anyone who could do all that by himself could do just about anything.

Or could he?

I'd spent the last few minutes ducking, running, jumping, climbing, *reacting*. Everything but thinking. And now that I paused to let a thought linger, I reacted again—by stopping cold, dread running down my spine like a trickle of ice water.

"Mr. Lockhart, *wait*," I whispered.

I don't even know if he heard me. He'd already reached the edge of the car and was poking his head up for a look at Kip . . . who was free to just stand there waiting for him, because he didn't have to keep watch on his prisoners at all.

"Shit! There he is! Up there!" I heard Kip screech, and I knew the rest of it now—the warning my brother had given me one second too late.

It ain't just Kip.

He's got help.

Thirty-seven

HELL ON WHEELS

Or, The Situation Takes a Sharp Turn for the Worse

The thought that Kip's partner might be Diana Caveo tied my already kinked-up stomach in a knot. Yet the alternative didn't loosen the cinch much. If Miss Caveo wasn't in it with the kid, that meant she'd be in the engine cab as his prisoner—or somewhere else entirely as a corpse.

So when Kip's compadre hollered up at Lockhart with a gravelly voice that was both decidedly male and disturbingly familiar, there was actually a splash of relief mixed in with my shock.

"Don't move!" Augie Welsh barked. "Not unless you think the lady'd look prettier with a hole between her eyes!"

"You pull that trigger, you're dead," Lockhart said. He'd gone perfectly still except for his right arm, which snaked around behind his back, the hand curling up to wave Aunt Pauline at me as I huddled out of sight behind him.

I knew what he was asking me to do, though I couldn't see the sense of it. I stretched out a hand and took his gun.

"You ain't in no position to make threats, old man!"

Lockhart waggled his fingers, but I was at a loss this time. What did he want me to do? Give him a tickle?

"You better throw down your iron, Mr. Lockhart!" another man called out, and though his voice was soothingly calm, it did anything but soothe or calm me.

Mike Barson was down there, too.

"Augie's a bit on edge," he said, "and enough innocent blood's been spilled already, don't you think?"

Lockhart's finger-wiggling grew frantic, and I finally understood what he had in mind. I took the snub-nosed Colt Samuel had given me and pressed it into his hand.

"Alright," Lockhart said. "You win."

He eased the Colt around, then lifted it up over his head and held it there a moment before tossing it over the side of the train.

"Thank you, sir," Barson said amiably. "Now why don't you come down here and join us? It's a trifle crowded, but we'd be happy to make room for Mr. Burl Lockhart."

I was about to lose my cover, so I scooched back a ways, spreading out flat as Lockhart reluctantly rose to his feet. He took a step forward, paused, then jumped. There was a clatter and a grunt from below—Lockhart landing in the coal tender.

The talk started up again then, but it was quieter now, no shouting necessary, and I had to slither up perilously close to the edge to hear it. I didn't dare try for a peek—not yet.

". . . saw you jump on. Said you look pretty spry for a gent your age," I could hear Barson saying down in the cab. Even now, after all that had happened, he had a friendly, relaxed way of talking, as if he and Lockhart had just bumped into each other at an ice-cream social. "I'm glad to see Augie didn't hurt you too bad with that beating last night. It was nothing personal. We just wanted to get you mad, that's all. So you and those railroad dicks would leave the train and try to track us. We didn't intend any disrespect by it. In fact, you've always been a hero of mine. When I was a boy—"

"Ain't nobody else up there, is there?" Welsh cut in, his gruff voice like a bucket of mud and twigs when set next to Barson's honeyed tones.

"Oh, sure. I brought Sherlock Holmes himself with me. Come on down, Sherlie! They're onto you!"

Naturally, I didn't take this as a serious invitation, and I just lay there, barely daring to breathe.

"Well, hell—I just remembered," Lockhart said. "Ol' Sherl's dead, ain't he? Guess I'm alone after all."

"Har har," Kip jeered.

"I wish you *had* brought help, old man—like them redheaded sons of bitches," Welsh said. "We owe them something real special after all the trouble they put us to."

"Be careful what you wish for," Lockhart shot back. "Those two might be green, but they've got grit. You never know when one of 'em might just get the drop on you."

"They're gonna have a long damn way to drop, right, fellers?" Kip said. "Like a thousand miles!"

"Shut up, kid," Welsh snapped.

Lockhart whistled. "A thousand miles? Don't tell me you're sneakin' to California just to catch the next boat to Panama or Peru or some such. And here I figured 'the Robin Hoods of the Rails' was goin' after the S.P. on its home turf."

"Actually, that's exactly what the gang thinks we're doing," Barson said lightly, gliding back into the conversation smooth as soft butter across hot bread. "They're up in the Humboldt Mountains at this very moment leading Colonel Crowe and Jefferson Powless on a merry little chase while we slip out to San Francisco unseen. You see, Augie and I needed special travel accommodations on account of our legions of admirers. You know how it is, Mr. Lockhart. Fame does have its drawbacks."

A new voice joined the conversation—though it wasn't new to me.

"You say the gang *thinks* you're going after the Southern Pacific," Miss Caveo said. "So what is it you're really doing?"

Her words rang out strong and clear: She didn't sound like a woman who'd been brutalized or injured. Yet I allowed myself only a small measure of satisfaction from that. Anything more would have been presumptuous, as there were still opportunities aplenty for brutalizing, injury, and worse.

"You know what, miss? I'm going to tell you," Barson said. "Because once you see how harmless it is, you won't mind helping us."

"Helping you?" Miss Caveo scoffed.

"By serving as our escorts," Barson explained. "We might need to take on more coal and water before we find a good spot to ditch the train. If we run across a stationmaster who's not inclined to be accommodating, you'll provide a little additional persuasion."

"By standing there with guns to our heads."

"Exactly! That's all it'll take!" Barson enthused, glossing over the scorn in Miss Caveo's tone. "And then we'll slip out of the country, and the Southern Pacific will be rid of its two greatest enemies. Why, you'll be heroes, really."

Barson kept going, speaking faster, his manner so slick it finally crossed over into outright oily.

"You see, miss, lucking into that gold shipment changed everything for Augie and me. The prospect of living rich . . . it can lighten a fellow's outlook. We don't feel the need to carry on this feud with the railroad any longer. Unfortunately, the rest of the Give-'em-Hell Boys aren't inclined to be so practical. They think we're taking a share of the gold back to California so we can wage war on the S.P.—pay off assassins, buy dynamite . . . blow up the Oakland terminal!"

I couldn't hear Barson's sigh or see the rueful shake of his head, but I sensed them even from my hiding place.

"Insanity. They're good men—but at heart they're still just angry farmers. They're bitter, and it's going to get them killed. Augie and I aren't like that anymore. We've changed."

"Into what?" Lockhart sneered.

"Professionals," Barson said. "Speaking of which, it's time we—"

"I have something to say," Miss Caveo announced.

"Sit back down," Welsh growled at her.

"Don't rile the man, miss," said a panicky-sounding fellow I hadn't heard yet—most likely the engineer.

"No. I won't sit down. Not until I've had a chance to speak my mind. I know what's in store for us, and—"

"Shut your damn mouth!"

"Or what, Mr. Welsh? You'll shoot me? That's not much of a threat, considering it's what you're going to do eventually anyway."

"Jesus, lady . . . do like he says!"

"You can't leave witnesses behind who know your plan," Miss Caveo went on, ignoring the engineer's pleas. "But tell me this: Will killing us really keep you safe? Anytime *your backs are turned,* you're in danger. You'll be *looking at your next victim,* and the law will *sneak right up behind you.* You might be in control *now.* But *now* can end awfully fast."

If I'd waited much longer, she probably would've just come right out and said, "For God's sake, Otto—do something!" Fortunately, I realized what she was up to before she had to be quite so blunt. Lockhart's crack about Sherlock Holmes had tipped her off that either my brother or I was with him, and she'd done her part by whipping up a distraction. Now, it was my turn.

I got up on my knees and pointed Aunt Pauline down into the engine cab.

And there they were. As Miss Caveo had hinted, Barson, Welsh, and Kip all had their backs to me. And a glance at those backs was all it took to solve the final mystery: how Barson and Welsh could be there at all. The bandits' clothes were powdered white with dust, just as El Numero Uno's had been the day before. So after killing the King of the Hoboes, they'd made like hoboes themselves, hitching a ride underneath the Express. They got into the Wells Fargo car sometime later—probably in Carlin, when Kip was "guarding" the train while we were in the ticket office.

All Old Red needed to put it together was one Morrison's purple hands (which must have been bound for hours, I could see now) and the dust covering the express-car floor. All *I'd* needed was to have the facts shoved in my face like a fist.

This was no time to fret about my shortcomings as a deducifier, though. I had something much more important to stew on: how to get through the next couple minutes alive.

Barson, Welsh, and Kip were lined up in the center of the cab, facing the controls—and Miss Caveo. Her hair was mussed, and there were smudges on her dress and a bruise just to the left of her jaw that someone was going to regret. But her back was so straight and her gaze so steady you'd have thought riding in hijacked locomotives was her hobby, something she squeezed in between suffragette rallies, choir practice, and bicycle rides in the country.

In contrast, a terror-stricken man in engineer's dirty overalls cowered at the controls, his eyes bulging from his soot-blackened face like a couple baseballs floating in a bucket of tar. Lockhart was sprawled atop the coal in the tender, and though Barson and Kip were looking at the lady, their .45s pinned him in place. Welsh had Aunt Pauline's sister, Virgie, pointed at Miss Caveo. The gun's shine was gone, replaced by a darker, wetter sheen—Milford Morrison's blood.

There was no way I could shoot Barson, Welsh, *and* Kip without at least one of them squeezing off a shot, as well. So I could sacrifice Miss Caveo or I could sacrifice Lockhart. Or I could try to do things the hard way, lawman style . . . and maybe just sacrifice myself.

"Hold it right there, boys!" I called out. "I got the drop on you!"

"Well, it's about damn time," Lockhart grumbled.

"Really, Mr. Amlingmeyer—I was beginning to think I'd have to send up a flare," Miss Caveo added.

For once, I was in no mood for joshing with the lady.

"No tricks," I said, squinting at Barson, Welsh, and Kip in a way that I hoped was intimidating. (I had to hope so, for the squinting wasn't voluntary—the wind and smoke blowing into my face had my eyes watering as bad as peeling an onion.) "Y'all just ease your guns down and let 'em go."

Kip looked at Barson. Barson looked at me. Welsh kept his eyes on Miss Caveo. And not a one of them lowered their guns.

"No. I think you're the one who'd better disarm himself," Barson said, genial and composed, and even from my perch more than twenty feet away, I could see his piercing blue-gray eyes crinkle with what looked like amusement. "I hate to tell you this, but if you don't, Augie here is going to blow your lady friend's brains out. And I know you don't want to see that."

"You're right. I don't," I told him. I swiveled my wrist just a bit, pointing my gun squarely at Barson's oh-so-pleasant face. "Which is why I'm going to kill you—you, Barson, *you*—in three seconds if he doesn't lower his gun. One, two—"

I counted fast. I didn't want to give Barson—or myself—time to think. He didn't know if I'd shoot, and *I* didn't know if I'd shoot, but ultimately he was the one taking the bigger risk if I reached three.

"Alright, alright!" Barson blurted out, finally losing his air of unflappable cool. "Do as the man says, Augie."

Welsh cursed bitterly, but pointed Aunt Virgie downward all the same. He finally looked over his broad shoulder at me, hate etched into his feral, stubble-covered face as plain as the name above a mausoleum door.

"That's a start," I said. "Now I wanna see all them hands empty."

"Sure, sure," Barson said, and he and Kip and Welsh began to bend slowly at the knee, lowering their six-guns toward the floorboards.

"Miss," I said, "why don't you move over to—?"

Just a flick of the eye toward Miss Caveo—that was all the opportunity Barson needed. He spun around, bringing his Peacemaker up while simultaneously stepping back and pulling the engineer in tight to his chest. He got off a wild shot that thudded into the side of the express car beneath me, and either from the kick of his hogleg or the struggles of his would-be shield, he jerked back hard into the train's controls, pressing down on a red bar that protruded from amongst the various gauges and valves.

I flattened myself, more bullets blasting up at me from the cab below. As I lay there, the shimmying of the express car grew into a bucking as fierce as any bronc's. The whistling of the wind grew stronger, too, building to such a gale I feared it would peel me right off the roof.

When I dared a peep up, I saw distant bluffs to my left and an all-too-close bluff to my right. We were running along the edge of a gorge, and doing it faster than would've been safe on the Kansas flats.

The lever Barson had stumbled into was the throttle.

The train hit a curve that put such a slant to the car I nearly slid off the roof like a johnnycake off a greased griddle. There was a sudden metallic clang and a piercing scream, followed by an awful thumping and ripping and cracking. Someone had been knocked over the side—and been snagged and chewed by the chugging gears.

The time for ducking was over. As soon as the track and train straightened up again, I did the same, popping up with Aunt Pauline at the ready.

Not only wasn't I immediately shot, I wasn't even noticed. The engineer was beyond noticing anything—most of him was crumpled on the floor, though a bullet had spread various bits from the neck up hither-thither around the cab. Lockhart and Welsh were grappling nearby, both of them clawing at Aunt Virgie, while Miss Caveo was trying to keep Kip at bay with the fireman's shovel, the kid panting curses and waving his apparently emptied Colt at her like a hammer.

Barson was gone.

I didn't have a shot at either Welsh or Kip that didn't have a chance of hitting Lockhart or Miss Caveo, so it wouldn't be Aunt Pauline to the rescue—it would have to be me. But as I got ready to jump in and join the fray, I saw something that nearly had me jumping right out of my skin instead.

Perhaps a quarter mile ahead of us, the rails wound around another rocky bend, this one so sharp it almost looked like the tracks weren't turning but simply stopping. It was the kind of curve any sane engineer would take with the brakes on, the throttle back, and his fingers crossed. And we were about to head into at full speed.

Even if I could've reached the brake (assuming I could figure out where it was in the next thirty seconds), it was too late. The Pacific Express may have been built for the rails, but it was about to take its maiden voyage as an airship.

"We're gonna crash! Jump! Everybody!" I shouted. Then I took my own advice—only I wasn't heaving myself over the side of the train, but down into the tender.

It was like leaping onto a haystack . . . with a pile of bricks buried inside it. Despite the pain that slammed into my backside as I landed, I managed to slide quickly down the black mound of coal and get Aunt Pauline pointed at Welsh's head—just as he twisted Virgie into Lockhart's side and pulled the trigger.

My shot caught Welsh just above the right eye.

Lockhart and Welsh fell together, crumpling into one heap, as if they were two parts of the same, suddenly lifeless body.

"Augie!" Kip cried, dropping his gun and throwing himself onto the floor at Welsh's side.

I knelt down next to him, hoping to find Lockhart still breathing. But there was no dime-novel miracle. The old Pinkerton's flask hadn't stopped the bullet. And there weren't any whispered words about carrying on and getting the lady to safety, either—no jaunty wink as the death rattle set in. Ol' Burl Lockhart was just plain dead.

"We gotta get outta here, kid!" I shouted at Kip as I got to my feet. "We gotta jump! Now!"

But Kip wasn't listening. He was too busy trying to peel Aunt Virgie from Welsh's hand. Tears were streaming down his face as he clawed uselessly at fingers wound as tight as the grip of Death itself.

Something slipped around my left hand, and I turned to find Miss Caveo by my side.

"Which way?" she said.

On the right side of the track was a sheer rock wall speeding by no more than six feet from the train. On the left side was nothing—not even ground, so far as we could see.

One side was instant death, the other . . . not so instant. So I picked the latter. Don't we always?

"Trust me," I said as we stepped to the edge of the cab hand in hand. "I think I'm gettin' the hang of this."

We jumped together and we fell together. And the last thing I knew when the impact came, bringing the darkness with it, was that her fingers were still entwined with mine.

Thirty-eight

MISS CORVUS

Or, I Meet a Dear Friend Again for the Very First Time

When I started to come to, the first thing I became aware of was pain. Someone had been using my skull as an anvil, it seemed, and my whole body was still quivering from the pounding of the hammer.

The second thing I noticed was my brother. He was there with me, wherever "there" was. Maybe I heard his breathing or smelled the scent of pipe smoke and sweat on his clothes—something Holmes-y like that. But I don't think so. His presence wasn't something I deduced. It was something I felt.

"Gustav," I said.

"Hey, Brother. How you feelin'?"

"Been better. Often. In fact, I don't think I've ever been worse."

"You took quite a blow to the head, Otto," said someone else—a someone else I was most relieved to hear. "We were worried about you."

I opened my eyes, hoping the first sight they'd alight upon would be Miss Caveo's pretty face. And I did indeed find myself dazzled, though not by the lady's beauty: I was stretched out on my back, my face pointed up at a blinding-bright afternoon sun.

I winced and shut my eyes again.

"Landed on my head, huh?" I said. "Well, that's a stroke of luck. I can get by without that ol' thing—right, Gustav?"

"Been doin' it for years."

I turned toward the sound of my brother's voice and dared a little eyelid crack. There he was sitting next to me, looking as bad as I felt: haggard and hurting, held together by little more than the last unripped stitches in filthy, frayed clothes. He wasn't beaming down at me—he couldn't even bring himself to smile. But I could see that he wanted to, and that was enough.

Miss Caveo was next to him, pressed up much closer than I would've thought my brother could withstand without melting like butter left too close to the stove. Her dark hair was tangled and frizzed, her face a patchwork of bruises and scratches, her dress torn and smeared with dirt.

She was a lovely sight.

As I lay there mooning up at her, my vision unfuzzed further, and I realized that the swirling shapes behind my brother and Miss Caveo were rocky outcroppings and overhangs—and that they were moving. Or seemed to be, anyway. Actually, *we* were moving.

The three of us were squeezed onto the battered remnants of the hand car, coasting down the mountainside with all the roaring speed of an arthritic snail.

"You came after me," I said to Old Red.

"As best I could. Obviously, I was too late to be any help."

"Don't be modest, Gustav—you know that's not true," Miss Caveo said.

A flush as red as strawberry preserves smeared itself across my brother's face.

The lady turned toward me. "After you and I jumped from the engine, we rolled down an incline into some boulders, and you were knocked unconscious. I could barely get myself back to the roadbed, let alone carry *you*. Fortunately, your brother soon came along, and we were able to improvise a rope of sorts and haul you up."

"'Improvise a rope'?"

Old Red's blush went from red to purple.

Miss Caveo smiled coyly. "Let's just say I've finally discovered an advantage to the ridiculous overexcess of modesty imposed on my gender by respectable society."

I couldn't help it—my eyes darted down for a peek at her skirts. It was hard to tell from the way she was sitting, but it did seem like they weren't as fully rounded as one would expect.

Of course, a lady's frilly underthings aren't called unmentionables for nothing, and I thought it best to move the conversation along lest poor Gustav survive a run-in with the Give-'em-Hell Boys only to die of embarrassment less than an hour later.

"What happened to the engine?"

"It went off the rails, just as you feared it would," Miss Caveo said. "The train's at the bottom of a canyon in a million pieces."

"Most of 'em still on fire," Old Red added. "I was probably half a mile away when the boiler blew, and it still like to pop my eardrums."

I nodded, silent, thinking of everything that had quite literally gone up in smoke.

Lockhart, Kip, Barson and Welsh, Morrison, the nameless engineer, Chan's "treasure." Even the Give-'em-Hell Boys' stolen gold had probably melted in the blaze, slithering away into crevices and under rocks like snakes escaping the midday sun.

And I'd lost a treasure of my own, I realized with a queasy jolt. My war bag had been in the baggage car—and my book had been in my bag.

For weeks, I'd been trying to pretend that bundle of tattered, ink-splattered pages didn't exist. And now that it truly didn't, I tried to push it from my thoughts again. It seemed wrong to mourn a thing when so many people had just died, even if it wasn't just a book that had been destroyed but a hope I'd been too cowardly to let myself feel.

"So," I said, almost choking on the word, "how'd Samuel make out?"

He was fine, Gustav told me. Kip just winged him. In fact, the porter bounced back so quick, even with his arm in a sling he tried to come after us with Old Red. Wiltrout had put a stop to that.

My brother related all this reluctantly. Not so much like he didn't want to tell me—more like there was something else he wanted to tell me first, something he wouldn't or couldn't say just yet.

"Miss?" he said shyly. "You're gonna have to excuse my askin' like this, but . . . now that we know Otto's alright . . . well . . . ain't it about time you told us who the heck you really are?"

The lady laughed. "I suppose proper introductions *are* past due, aren't they?" She held out a hand to my brother. "I'm Diana Corvus."

Old Red took the ends of her fingers and gave them a loose, gingerly shake, as if her hand might shatter should he wrap his around hers.

"Miss Corvus," he mumbled.

Even flat on my back feeling like I'd just been fired out of a cannon into a brick wall, I managed a more enthusiastic handshake.

"So you're what they call a spotter?" I asked.

She nodded. "An extremely inexperienced one, I'm afraid. This was only my third trip as a Southern Pacific agent. I'm supposed to be watching for confidence men, cardsharps, thieves—"

"And crooked railroad detectives," Old Red said.

"Yes . . . and crooked railroad detectives," Miss Corvus admitted. (I felt a little wistful thinking of her as "Miss Corvus" now. It was almost as though "Diana Caveo" was a sweetheart I'd never see again.) "Colonel Crowe wanted me to keep an eye on you. If I noticed anything suspicious, Jefferson Powless would have paid you for your time and sent you on your way."

"Let's see," I said. "Murders, the Give-'em-Hell Boys, a wreck . . . nope, nothing suspicious about any of that."

Miss Corvus fixed a quizzical gaze on Gustav. "Actually, I did see something . . . well, I wouldn't call it suspicious, exactly, but it was definitely peculiar. That package you gave to the stationmaster in Carlin. What was in it?"

I turned a stare on Old Red, too. "Package? In Carlin?"

My brother squirmed and cleared his throat. "This ain't how I wanted to tell you, Otto . . . I'm through keepin' secrets from you."

He glanced at Miss Corvus, clearly flustered by her presence but hardly able to ask her to step outside and give us a moment alone.

"After all our arguin' yesterday, I wanted to do something for you. You were helpin' me do what I wanted to do even though you didn't wanna do it yourself. So I figured the least I could do was do for you what you wanted to do—whether you knew you wanted to do it or not."

As there weren't enough specifics in what Old Red had said from which to even forge a decent question, I had to make do with "Huh?"

"When I sent you outta the baggage car? As we were pullin' into Carlin?" Gustav said sheepishly. "I dug your book out of our bags. And when you set off lookin' for Lockhart, I took it to the stationmaster and asked him to mail it to *Harper's Weekly*."

"You *what*?"

"Book?" Miss Corvus asked.

"Yes, book," I said. "*My* book. Which *I* wrote. For me to do with—or not do with—as I please." I pointed a finger at Old Red and shook it like a switch I was itching to cane him with. "You sneaky, presumptuous, high-handed jackass." I flattened out my hand and slapped my brother on the knee (careful not to hit the leg he'd boogered up earlier). "God bless you!"

"So . . . you ain't really mad at me?"

"Of course, I am! But that don't mean I ain't grateful, too!"

Gustav looked relieved, Miss Corvus looked confused, and me—I just had to laugh.

My brother hadn't just given me my dream back. Without meaning to, he'd showed me how to dream it better. A man doesn't need to be fearless to get what he wants. He just needs to look his fears in the face . . . so he can thumb his nose at them.

If Old Red could drag himself onto the Pacific Express, I could weather a discouraging letter from *Harper's Weekly*—and from *Collier's, Scribner's,* and every other magazine and publisher on through to *The Ladies Home Journal,* if that's what it took. I had a story to tell. Hell, now I had *two*.

After another hour on our beat-up barn door of a train, Gustav, Miss Corvus, and I came gliding into a little jerkwater town called Cisco. A rescue engine was quickly dispatched to fetch what was left of the Express, and not long after that we were back amongst our fellow passengers—few of whom seemed particularly forgiving when told that their luggage was now cinders at the bottom of a ravine. *Refund* was a word I heard bandied about quite a bit. *Lawsuit* was almost as common.

While everyone around us grumbled, Miss Corvus and I chattered away cheerfully (if, in my case, rather woozily) about my book, my adventures with Old Red, and anything else I could think of to keep the conversation going. My brother even joined in from time to time when his stomach allowed it, bashfully but tenaciously debating the lady on the Lizzie Borden trial, which both she and he (through me) had followed in the papers the month before.

It was the lengthiest discussion I'd seen him have with a woman since our days on the farm in Kansas, when he and my sisters, Ilse and Greta, would spar over such weighty questions as the proper way to husk corn and who'd cut a fart in the kitchen. I was pleased to see him overcome his other great fear—females—so long as he didn't get crazy ideas about courting this one. Those crazy ideas were reserved for *me*.

When we reached Oakland that evening, a dozen S.P. officials swooped down on the passengers with ticket vouchers, meal tickets, promises, sympathy, and lips ready, pursed for the smooching of butts. None of which was directed at me, my brother, or Miss Corvus. News of the crash had reached town hours in advance of the train, and before any reporters could get to us, we were hustled from the station (if it's possible to be "hustled" when, like Old Red and me, you can barely walk).

Gustav and I were told to await instructions in a nearby boarding-house. The lady was rushed off elsewhere—and I haven't seen her since.

If I'd had any inkling our parting was to be so permanent, who knows what I might have said? Something painfully sincere and utterly mortifying, most likely: "It's been a treat gettin' to know you—and I'd sure like the chance to know you better." Or "Let's not let this be good-bye." Or even "Diana Corvus, I think I love you." I had taken a blow to the head, remember.

But all she got from me was "Good night, miss. I hope we'll be seein' you round H.Q. real regular."

"I hope so, too," she said. Her high spirits had taken a curious dip after the S.P. men had scooped us up, and she sounded dead serious—almost dour—now. "You're exceptional men . . . and that's what I'm going to tell Colonel Crowe and Jefferson Powless."

"Did you hear that?" I said as a jittery Southern Pacific functionary ushered her away. " 'Exceptional men,' she called us."

"She's just sayin' she'll do what she can to help us."

"Help us? We're heroes, ain't we?"

Gustav made a noise halfway between a growl and a grunted chuckle. He knew what was coming—and late the next afternoon, it came.

Thirty-nine

THE END OF THE LINE

Or, The Amlingmeyer Express Runs off the Rails

We were on the front porch of the boardinghouse, letting a cool breeze from the bay blow over our various lumps and scrapes, when we spotted a beefy fellow striding up fast. Even a block away, we could tell it was Jefferson Powless—and that he hadn't come for a friendly chat in the sunshine. When the railroad dick reached the front steps, we were already on our feet, waiting to lead him upstairs to the privacy of our little room.

"You saw the newspapers this morning?" he asked as soon as we had the door shut behind us.

"Sure did," I said. "They're runnin' the headlines so big they can't squeeze in much more than a letter a page. 'Butch Turns Butcher on S.P. Special'—that was a catchy one. 'Lockhart's Last Stand' was pretty good, too."

" 'Fisherman Lands Chinaman,' " Old Red threw in, limping over to our bed and seating himself with his sore leg stretched out stiff.

"Yeah, that was our favorite," I said.

It had been a pleasant shock to learn that Dr. Chan had actually survived his run-in with Kip: A man out for some early-morning angling had found him on the bank of the Truckee River, still out cold. By the time Chan came to and could convince someone his story about a killer news butch wasn't sheer delirium, we were already beyond Summit and beyond help.

"To tell the truth, that was the only story this morning I could stomach," I told Powless. Our room had a single chair, in the corner, but I didn't sit down—or offer the S.P. man a seat. "I mean, how is it we don't rate so much as a mention in a single article? You know, seeing as we tangled with the most famous gang in the country and came out on top?"

"And funny that all them stories make out like Barson and Welsh are still on the loose in Nevada," Old Red added, not sounding like he found it funny in the slightest.

"We've been telling the newspapers the truth as we know it," Powless said, his tone flat, his gaze cold. "I've heard what you two claim happened. But any proof went up in flames with that engine."

I crossed my arms to hide my hands—which I couldn't help but clench into fists.

"You think we're lyin'?" I spat. "Well, what about Miss Corvus? Surely she backs us up."

"Keep the lady out of it," Powless rumbled. "Frankly, none of this reflects very well on her, either."

"Now hold on," Gustav said. "If you don't believe us and you don't believe her, why'd you come all the way back to Oakland? Barson and Welsh ain't dead? Alright. Shouldn't you be up in the Humboldt Range on their trail?"

"I had other business to attend to here."

"Oh, I know you did, Mr. Powless," Old Red said. "Like us and Miss Corvus and makin' sure the papers printed the right tall tales."

Unlike me, Powless didn't bother hiding the clenching of his fists—his hands were curled into big red bricks he obviously wanted to slam down over my brother's head.

"Barson and Welsh really ran rings around you, didn't they?" Gustav pressed on, almost daring the man to act on his anger. "It was only dumb luck that Otto and me was where we was when we was to stop 'em. I can't believe you'd want the S.P. board knowin' that—especially when you got the poor bastards scared out of their wits with that bogus 'bounty' Barson put on their heads."

Powless just scowled at my brother, conceding nothing. So Old Red gave him a heap more to concede.

"And another thing—Mike Barson claimed his gang made off with a hundred bars of U.S. Treasury gold the first time they hit the Express. But all Wells Fargo and the S.P. admitted to was four or five thousand dollars cash. Well, Barson may have been a killer and a thief, but I know he was closer to the mark than y'all . . . cuz Otto and me seen a bunch of them bars with our own eyes. So as I figure it, you don't want the truth out, cuz you got enough trouble with long riders as it is. If you fess up to losin' a regular mint, every farmboy with a horse and an old flintlock's gonna try to rob himself a train."

As much as my brother was goading him, Powless remained motionless, and if it hadn't been for the deepening ruddiness of his broad face, it would have been easy to mistake the man for one of the life-sized waxwork dolls they dress up with fancy duds in department store windows.

"*And,*" Old Red said, "there's the reward. If you admitted Barson and Welsh died yesterday like we say they did, then the Southern Pacific would owe Miss Corvus and Otto here something on the order of twenty thousand dollars. That ain't really much for the likes of the S.P., I know, but why pay it if you don't have to?"

Gustav finally stopped talking, and silence settled over the room. Powless still just stood there, looking like he was willing to keep on standing there forever if that's what it took to prove his skin was infinitely thicker than any of my brother's little pinpricks.

"Well?" I prodded him.

"Are you done?" he asked Old Red.

Gustav shrugged. "That depends on what you've got to say."

Powless moved at last, swinging up his right hand, the index finger pointing at the ceiling. "A wrecked train." He uncurled another finger.

"A dead engineer." He continued the count. "A dead messenger. A dead news butch. A dead baggageman. In baseball, you get three strikes and you're out. You've already got at least five."

"But," Old Red said—and stopped there. He knew there was more coming or we would've been fired already.

"But," the railroad man said with a nod, "we can get past all that. It could be forgotten, with time. You're smart. The young lady told us as much, and I can see she was right . . . though you sure gab a hell of a lot more than she led me to expect. So the question becomes, can you be trusted? Will you do right by the Southern Pacific? If so, you can report to the Oakland yards tomorrow as guards. When you've proved you're reliable, we'll talk about other assignments."

Powless stepped toward Gustav and brought up his right hand again—to offer my brother a shake.

"Do we understand each other?"

I understood—and I fumed.

Keep your precious badge, Powless was saying. *Call yourselves detectives. And then go to the yards tomorrow and beat the crap out of tramps and collect your ten dollars a week for it. And maybe,* maybe *I'll let you actually detect one of these days. But in the meantime, you best shut up and stay out of the big boys' way.*

Gustav reached up and took Powless's hand. It looked for all the world like my brother was striking a deal with the devil. Yet I had absolute faith it wasn't so.

That morning, after we'd had our first look at the papers, I'd seen Old Red unpin his badge and place it *just so* on the dresser near the door. And before we'd hobbled downstairs to stretch out on the porch, I'd placed my badge *just so* beside it. They were lined up together like railroad ties or hoofprints, depending on your preference. Either way, the important thing was they were pointed in the same direction.

"I understand you, Mr. Powless," Gustav said as he shook the railroad man's hand, "but I can't accept your terms."

Powless threw my brother's hand away like it had scorched him.

"Nothing personal," Old Red went on, unruffled. "You're just tryin' to keep your ass outta the fire. I can appreciate that. But Otto and me, we ain't gonna lie or crack skulls for the Southern Pacific Railroad. Am I right, Brother?"

"You are undeniably, very, *extremely* right, Brother."

Gustav pointed toward the dresser—and the door.

"Our badges are over there. You can take 'em on your way out."

"Oh, I'll take them alright," Powless snapped. "And understand *this:* You two didn't quit. You were fired. You're just saddle trash that couldn't hack it as railroad police. If you go telling fairy stories to the newspapers, that's the story *I'm* going to tell. And trust me—my story's a lot more believable than yours."

He turned and walked away with calm, measured steps, pausing by the dresser to scoop up our badges. He replaced them with two five-dollar bills—our due for three days on the Southern Pacific payroll. Then he left, pulling the door closed behind him with a gentle click that seemed to echo through the house like a clap of thunder.

Old Red stared at the door glumly. "We just burned ourselves a bridge, Otto."

"Kind of a rickety-ass bridge, you ask me," I said. "There's better ones."

"Yup." My brother shifted his gaze to me. "I reckon there are."

It's been almost three weeks since then, and we've just about mended up. Old Red's ankle still pains him, but he's been getting out and about as best he can while I've been scribbling away on this new book of mine. Every few days, we take the ferry over to San Francisco and drop in on the offices of the Southern Pacific Railroad—Gustav told the stationmaster in Carlin to make that the return address on the package he sent to *Harper's*. Going there doesn't exactly conjure up happy memories, but I don't mind: One of these days, we'll bump into a certain S.P. employee I'd like to see again, and that'll make it all worthwhile.

Old Red's been looking for the Pinkerton office over in San Francisco, too, although he says he's not ready to go in even when he finds it—not with him still looking like something the cat hacked up. Yet even as the bruises on his face fade, another, deeper one remains unhealed.

"Two days late and ten bucks short, that was me on that damn train—and just look what happened," Gustav grumbled only yesterday. "Ol' Holmes would've had the whole thing deducted before we reached the first station."

I know he'll snap out of it sooner or later, though—because if he doesn't, I'll do the snapping myself.

Last night, I looked up the Pinkertons' address: 600 Market Street. One day soon, after this is in the mail to New York, I'm going to take him there.

ACKNOWLEDGMENTS

The author wishes to thank:

Agatha Christie and William Goldman—for inspiration.

Ben Sevier, Wonder Editor—for patience, perception, and a free hand with the St. Martin's bar tab.

Elyse Cheney, Wonder Agent—for not pulling any punches.

Annabelle Mortensen and Mike Wiltrout—for answering the Bat Phone on the first ring.

Kyle Wyatt of the California State Railroad Museum, Charlie Vlk of Railroad Model Resources, and various and sundry railrans (especially Larry Hochhalter, Bob Pecotich, Brian Jennison, Jim Betz, Jim Hill, and Randal O'Toole)—for everything I got right about trains. (For everything I got wrong, there's no one to "thank" but me.)

Fisher L. Forrest—for everything I got right about guns. (For everything I got wrong, see above.)

David Baldeosingh Rotstein, Tim Cox, Anita Karl, Cecily Hunt, and Steve "Eagle Eye" Boldt—for making me look good.

ACKNOWLEDGMENTS

John Harrington, Dan Kelley, Billie Bloebaum, Matt and Laura Nigro, Mark and Alyssa Nickell, Mom and Dad, and everyone who showed up—for making Hockapalooza '06 *rock*!

All the fabulous St. Martin's and bookstore folks who've helped spread the word about Big Red and Old Red—for getting me started on the *right* track.

Kate and Mojo—for keeping me grounded in the real world.

Mar—for the whole schmeer.